PAPER
BOATS

PAPER BOATS

A NOVEL BY
ERNDELL SCOTT

Erich Scott Group
2016

PAPER BOATS

A novel by Erndell Scott

Cover design: Fiona
Book Design: Desert Isle Design

Edited by: Tracey Coutts and Nicky Fournier

Copyright © 2016 by Erndell Scott

For book review opportunities, press information, speaking and signing engagements and book reproduction information, please contact Erndell Scott's PR representatives at:

Erich Scott Group
PO Box 13293
Tallahassee, FL 32317
850.421.9007
nclick@mayfieldpr.com

Printed in the United States of America

First Edition

ISBN
978-0-9972339-0-2

"Tolerance over time breeds resentment.
Only through understanding, that comes from
the acceptance of one another's differences,
shall we find true peace."

– ERNDELL SCOTT

Chapter 1

Dust fills the eerie morning sky, choking any glimmer of sun as bricks—centuries old, released from their bonds—fall without course, finding their resting place upon a ravaged ground. Artillery and heavy weapons fire breathe new life into the sounds of the day while taking life as they speak. War awakens. Its foul stench is grotesque and twisted. Its air ripe with the burning of oil washed with the putrid metallic taste of blood. What is human and what is beast becomes a mystery that no one wishes to spend any time investigating. The rotting flesh of both lay silent, unable to tell their story.

War has come to the once invincible Third Reich. Its crooked philosophies, outlandish mysticism, and promises of superior existence are vanishing. Berlin, the heart of its war machine, is in shambles. Its people are lost, disturbed, and without purpose. Its armies are tattered and wasted. The Russians pursue unchallenged from the east and are hellbent on its conquer and acquisition. Racing from the west are the British and Americans, just as tenacious in their quest to reap the spoils of war. The atrocities against humanity witnessed in Stalingrad, Malmedy, and Dunkirk are fresh in the minds of the Allied armies. It is a bad time to be German.

Young Otto Kaufmann wipes his eyes from years of horror and pain, offering a clearer view of the streets as smoke billows and swirls freely around the skeletons of buildings struggling to stand before him.

"Well, I should think, Private Vogler, this hiding place in the cellar made for quite a splendid little fort for us last night. I think sleep came to me rather quickly."

"Ha, my dear courier to the High Court, it seems the innocence of your youth leaves you without alarm. It should do you well to remember we must cross this street safely if we are to reach General Heinrici and then return to the Führerbunker on time. I'm surprised I found you. I should think Herr Bormann would not be at all amused by your delay."

Otto nodded, a frightened glare reshaping his face. "That is a name I wish not to hear."

Private Vogler peeked from their hiding. "If my memory serves me well, this was once a prominent Jewish neighborhood. We are not far from your home, are we, Otto?"

Otto offered a hardened frown and a deflated breath. "Yes, Private Vogler, my home is not far from here. These streets were once a place of solace, but it was not to last. My people were herded and marched by force down this very street by the dreaded SS. I find little joy staring upon this place now."

Private Volger reached out and put his hand on Otto's shoulder. "Do not despair, Otto. I would have you smile again as a young boy should. Let's see to your mission and then get you back safely. Quickly, lad, gather your things. We leave now. Follow closely."

Otto stuffed his wool blanket back into his musette bag, and together with his leather satchel, hoisted them around his shoulder, both bags coming to rest on top of his back. He planted his hands to the ground and prepared his run as his heart quickened its pace. Otto watched the private stare into the streets, planning their moves. He could see his nerves swimming in terrified doubt. His eyes were twitching and straining to make reality of the world, looking for clues of sanctuary. He clenched his rifle. The blood in his fingers abandoned its veins, and they turned ghostly white. He hastened his move and dashed across the torn and rubble-strewn street, but the eyes of hell are seldom closed. They lay gaze to his movement, and with a single shot that echoed with death, he fell limp to his knees. Lifeless, he collapsed to the ground.

Otto's eyes widened, and his lips trembled. His knees weakened, and his arms struggled to keep him upright. "No. Please no," he gasped.

Otto slowly sat down, and without moving his head, he used his eyes to canvass the area. "Damn, a Russian sniper. I am sure of it from the sound of his rifle's report. Oh, will those incessant Russians ever rest? His shot rang from above, but I am unable to see much from my hiding. Hmm, he'll need to fire again if I am to determine his whereabouts. Just not at me."

Otto fixated on the dead private's body, a twisted wreck spread out in the street. His glistening blood slowly oozed its way through the cobblestones, damming in some places and flowing freely in others, yet always finding the path of least resistance. Otto wiped the tears from his eyes and tightened his belongings for action. "It's time to find a new exit from this fort. No use moving forward from this position. I'll slip out the back and approach the street from a new angle. I trust that Russian death dealer will not follow."

Artillery fire ceased for now, but small arms fire could be heard cackling through the streets. Using these sounds to drown his movements, Otto quietly scurried from shadow to shadow, dodging the open daylight and the undiscriminating travel of a well-placed bullet.

"These missions of mine are getting more and more dangerous. How am I ever to reach General Heinrici under these conditions? I can barely recognize the streets anymore. The repetitious pounding from land and air has erased any signs of human existence. I have no way to tell direction. The ravages of war are all around me, the sounds of which are deafening, maddening to my ears and relentless in their terror."

Otto hurried his steps, forcing his sickened emotions back into the darkness of his soul. "How I wish to be with Annie again, down near the River Spree making dams and sailing paper boats. I welcome such visions. It sure helps me pass the time when war is not bleeding on my heels."

He came upon a small side street and stopped half way down. Its gloomy and desolate appearance of disfigured concrete and metal loomed overhead. "It seems the reaper is not idle," Otto observed as he quickly burst back to reality. "Something is not quite right in the air. The street in front seems particularly odd."

Otto stood motionless, looking down ever so slowly, his hands frozen, the sounds of the world around him becoming silent. "Damn. I'm in the middle of a minefield." He turned his head slightly backward, looking for traces of his steps and more importantly looking for clues of deadly mines.

"These damn Germans are very meticulous in their laying of mines and brilliant at hiding them. There are sure to be Teller mine 43's scattered about. Those plate-shaped little trolls are easily concealed under anything of little weight, and such debris has littered the ground here in tons. Yet the S-mines worry me the most, as they will have been buried and hidden from sight. Come to think of it, I think I've quite forgotten what that German engineer taught me on how to prevent them from detonating should I step on one. I don't fancy the little bugger popping up from under the earth and releasing a barrage of burning hot scraps of metal tearing into me. Well, at least a quick death would be assured."

Otto continued surveying the ground around him. The street looked too perfect. Small piles of rubble, broken wood fragments of furniture, an errant leather shoe, twisted pieces of metal where there should be none, and torn remnants of clothing were all out of place, as if strategically set at equal distances apart. The relationship between all these objects was obvious, not to the Russians, but to Otto. They hid mines. Otto turned and slowly placed his first step. One good thing, he thought to himself, at least I now know there is an army group nearby, probably watching me and wagering on my outcome. Otto's steps were delicate and precise. He retraced his movements until he assured himself he was in safer territory where the ground looked naturally foul with the exploits of battle.

"Two days I have been gone from the Führerbunker and still I am nowhere near my objective. I'm exhausted, and my mind is numb. I should think a bit of rest to gain my wits after that relatively mild entanglement with the minefield could not hurt to replenish my spirit."

Finding a chair of Rococo design with a leg missing, Otto propped it up using a pile of bricks for the fourth leg. Here, shadowed by the towering, ghostly figure of a building, he coiled up in a fetal position, put his head down, and closed his eyes.

Chapter 2

The worn, muted coloring of the sun was passing noon and still struggled to shine, hidden by the acrid, vomiting smell of sulphur and the spoiled gaseous air. At times Otto would shudder and emit a slight cough as the wicked environment irritated his body. No sooner had he faded into a troubled sleep when he was suddenly jostled awake by a shaking of his shoulder. He reacted slowly, turning his weary head up into the eyes of a German soldier. He was surrounded by a poorly armed patrol of ten men, probably sent to scout the front lines and advances of the Russian infantry.

"Have you seen the Ivans?" asked the soldier, a corporal in rank. Forget 'are you lost or are you hurt?' Nothing mattered in regards to Otto personally. There was nothing strange these days in seeing a young boy out on the streets alone.

Otto answered quickly as he searched the grounds for an escape. "No. I have not seen the Russians. Only have I heard their Katyusha rockets screaming through the air."

"Run then, boy. Be lucky you are not woman nor swine. Run and leave here," the corporal shouted.

Otto got up off his chair and, standing tall, pulled the military orders from his leather satchel, handing them to the corporal. "I am the official courier of the Führer, his High Court, and personal adjutant of Reichsleiter Bormann. I am on a military mission to see General Heinrici. He awaits my presence."

The German soldiers in the patrol raised their heads and looked up, aroused and in full consciousness. It had been a long time since there had been any word from their Führer, who had vanished into hiding a little after mid-January.

The corporal's eyes grew wide. The skin between the folds of his brow where the dirt had not penetrated now shown white with alarm as fear overtook him. Two of the soldiers in the patrol began harassing Otto, pushing him to the ground and rummaging through his musette bag and satchel. The corporal noticed his sergeant walking towards him and motioned for his attention.

The sergeant gritted his teeth and swung his rifle to his shoulder. He did not appear to be at all amused. "What is going on here? Why have we stopped!?"

"It's a boy, Sergeant. His dress is of a strange mix, and he carries these documents." The corporal handed the papers to the sergeant, and immediately, the sergeant's eyes swelled with rage.

"You fool of a Hun! Do you not see the initials 'A.H.' on this document?"

"Yes, Sergeant, but it is my counsel we be cautious. His story seems suspicious to me."

"I didn't ask you for your counsel, Corporal. We have little choice but to believe his story. There is word among the ranks that the German High Court is sending SS death squads out to execute any soldier who disobeys orders, surrenders, or speaks of false hope against the Fatherland. The boy will come with us. Let our superiors deal with his story." The sergeant turned and barked at the two soldiers. "Quickly. Dust that boy off and give him back his things. Hurry now."

The sergeant approached Otto, his tone friendly and reassuring. "My dear boy, you will be safe with us. Come, we mustn't delay. You are far from where General Heinrici is supposed to be. Communication among army groups is poor. There is much confusion and chaos, but mostly we do not know where any of us stand. The Russians have broken through the General's 3rd Panzer Division defenses with retreat in full. Berlin has been breached, and we are surrounded."

Otto was not sure what to make of the sergeant's frantic words. Was the end really so near, he wondered? Am I nearly free?

The patrol came into a small park, a square unfamiliar to Otto. It now looked like a makeshift staging area and command center for an army group. The sergeant walked off as the patrol made rest under a tree by a destroyed fountain in the center of the park. He approached what looked to Otto like a higher ranking officer.

Otto glanced away from the two officers and began examining his surroundings, planning an escape route, if indeed he needed one. He noticed how disheveled, tattered, and completely undisciplined the soldiers in this group looked in contrast to the soldiers of not so long ago. These soldiers were unshaven, dirty, and worn, wearing ripped and torn uniforms. He thought they looked more like ghosts than humans, wallowing in the never-ending shallows between earth and hell. Gone were the hearty battle songs, the victory parades, and the swilling of beer. Gone were the plentitude of weapons, the ammunition, and the liters upon liters of gasoline reserves. Gone was the great mechanized force, the inventors of tank warfare. What armor Otto did observe were few in number. He counted one half-track; a scattering of personnel vehicles, mostly motorcycles; and one tank, a late model Panther, which, from the frustrating looks and foul language of the mechanics deep in the engine compartment, was not operational. Horses seemed to remain plentiful and roamed about the square searching for what little grass remained. Otto chuckled with the thought that such a modern army still continually relied upon horses to move their war machine.

Otto glanced back at the officer he had seen with the sergeant now walking towards him. The officer had a gentle, warm presence despite the roughness of his appearance. He had a hard, lean

15

figure and was somewhat tall for a German, with ruffled dark hair. He looked exhausted and walked with slumped shoulders and vacant eyes. Otto observed a peculiar, inquisitive look on his face as he approached ever so intently but with little speed. Perhaps he was practicing his interrogation in his mind before his greetings, which made Otto terribly uneasy. He knew very well that officers were quite untrustworthy, had little patience, and were very unpredictable in their moods. The officer stepped next to Otto and sat down beside him, letting out a big sigh, an exhale of breath seeming to release years and years of struggle. He then fumbled in his pocket for a moment and pulled out some chocolate, offering a piece to Otto.

Always the chocolate angle with these German officers, Otto thought. I should have many cavities by now from all this chocolate. Dr. Richtman won't be happy with me. These officers should know by now that a Luger put to the head is a much more persuasive interrogation tool than sweets. Perhaps that's why the Germans aren't winning the war.

He took the chocolate from the officer and, without inspection, put it into his mouth. "Thank you. Mmm, Belgian, my favorite."

"Yes, very good indeed. Well, I suppose a proper introduction is called for, seeing who your papers say you are. I am Major Erich von Hans, son of Gerthard von Hans of Rosenthaler Strasse. Around you is my command, the hard-fighting 25th Panzergrenadier Division. Well, what's left of it for the most part. Nevertheless," he continued, his voice becoming inflamed, "we are to defend Berlin at all costs for the Reich, for the Fatherland." The major sighed and put another piece of chocolate into his mouth. His eyes softened, and his body calmed. "So tell me, my young boy, adjutant to the Führer, messenger of the High Court, who might you be?"

Otto became suspicious of the major's drastic change in manner, his eyes looking for that possible escape route. Off to his left over the major's shoulder he noticed a small hole in a fence leading to another courtyard, which would be easily reachable with a quick sprint. Otto hastily swallowed his chocolate so as not to be rude and, in a reserved manner, offered little information. "My name is Otto Kaufmann, son of Solomon Kaufmann. I live on Nord Strasse."

"Nord Strasse? Yes. Yes. I know it well. It's in an old Jewish neighborhood. There was a delicious bakery there that baked the best apple strudel east of Berlin."

Otto's eyes lit up for a moment, breaking his focus from his fence escape. "You, you know of Neumann's Bakery?"

"Know it? My son, I practically lived there. I have more gold in my mouth filling cavities than in the whole of the Reichstag."

Otto did not know what to make of the major's excited remarks. He had seen such trickery before, but for this moment, he thought of Annie. Perhaps someone who knew of her father's bakery could not be such a bad person. Slowly, Otto felt himself becoming more relaxed, and he asked for another piece of chocolate. The major, without reaction, reached back in his pocket and handed Otto another piece, a broken corner that was dented and mutilated and unrecognizable as candy. Otto took the crumbled chocolate and thanked the major politely, putting a small piece in his mouth and saving the rest for later.

"Yes, well, I was a school teacher," the major shared, as if he were distracted by his memories. "I taught world history before all this started. This war is old. It grows on me now. My heart and bones are tired, encrusted with horrid memories not thought possible in this world. I can think of no way to remove them." The major turned his head to Otto and offered a hopeful smile. "Perhaps you, my little friend, are the start of a new beginning."

Otto was too busy gnawing on his chocolate, but still he felt the good-natured presence of the major. Again, not to be rude and not wanting to cause another outburst, Otto glanced over acknowledging him, relaxed but on guard nevertheless. The major noticed Otto enjoying his chocolate and knew he had earned a bit of his trust, drawing him closer to his intended objective. He wanted answers.

17

Otto and the major sat resting under the sprawling oak tree, its health seemingly vibrant despite the hell surrounding it. They both looked into the sky, enjoying their sweets and the visions of a shared life they once knew happily dancing in their heads.

The spoiled light of the day worked to find its way to darkness. Artillery and small arms fire had drifted off, leaving its effects of smoke to freely loft in the wind, the fires that gave its birth creating microclimates of weather unpredictable to those on the ground. Unsettling, this quiet. War, even without a voice, still was ever present. It was still killing.

The major knew the possible fate of Otto's family and his people. He had known many comrades who presided over such matters. He had not the heart to tell Otto. As a civilian, he felt pity for the boy. As a soldier, he cared for and gave hope to his men. His mind was filled with many questions. He wanted more answers about the war, his country, and his leader. In his mind if all was lost, then he wanted to save his men by retreating and surrendering to the west. However, if the war was truly being won, he wished to fight on to victory.

Breaking their moment of silence, the major removed his gaze of the heavens and faced Otto. "My dear Otto, so how did you come to this place? How did you escape the concentration camps, steering away from that hell to find this hell? How in almighty God did you become a courier for the Führer's High Court?

The calmness in the major's voice was reassuring to Otto. He was beginning to enjoy the major's companionship, although his questions were peculiar to him. There was caution in Otto's eyes.

"I do not know of these, how did you say it, concentration camps? However, I do remember when your soldiers came and took us all away. I will not forget it.

"Annie and I were down at our favorite creek playing with the paper boats we had made. She had the idea to build a dam to create a big pool because the water in the creek was too fast and it would take our boats way downstream into the River Spree, only to be lost. This idea was very welcomed by me because Poppa always got mad when he learned I was at the River. Good idea or not, I was still worried because Momma warned me not to get wet. I always did. Many times Annie would splash me when putting rocks in the water for the dam. I always thought she was starting a splash fight, so I would splash her back. It wasn't long before we were both thoroughly soaked.

"My paper boats never stayed afloat for very long. They would take in water, become saturated, and the folds would come apart. There in the middle of our little pond would be a flat, soaked piece of paper with hints of the fold marks still present. Annie would laugh at me, remarking how much better they were now than when I first set them adrift. I must say, that made me mad. She would say I was not folding the paper correctly because I didn't line up my paper edges properly, which created gaps that the water could seep into. I don't know. When she wasn't watching, I would look over her shoulder to copy how she was doing it. She wasn't doing anything that I wasn't. Poppa owned a market, which was next door to Annie's poppa's bakery, Neumann's Bakery, where you ate apple strudel. Poppa always gave us paper to make our boats with, but I suspect somehow she wasn't using it. She was using something else. That's probably it. She was cheating.

"Then, all of a sudden, we heard screams coming from town. I could hear yelling and crying and all this terrifying noise. Annie thought maybe there was a fire, but I didn't see any smoke and heard no alarms. We both looked at each other not knowing what to do. Annie looked frightened, as if she had seen a ghost. The noise continued, so we started running home. My shoes were soaked through to my feet, and I could hear the water inside squishing at each step.

"We got to town and decided to take short cuts through the alleyways to save time. Even with wet shoes, I was faster than Annie. I could even beat my older brothers in running races. I stopped for a moment to wait for Annie. We were behind our houses now, in the alleys connecting the main street to the backyards. It was wash day, and everyone's clothes were hanging on the lines drying. It looked like a million flags flying and waving in the wind. My brothers used to run through them all the time with their arms spread out into the air. They would get caught up in all the sheets, pulling everything off the lines. That used to get Frau Finkelstein so mad. My brother, Samuel, came home one day, and he had her big, ugly brassiere on his head. It got wrapped around, and he couldn't get it off. That sure got Poppa angry, more so than my being down at the river.

"As Annie was catching up to me, she was pointing at the window on the second floor of our neighbor's home. I turned to look and could see Herr Rauschenburg waving to us frantically, but he wasn't saying anything. I could see his mouth moving. I don't know why he wasn't talking. Annie was getting really scared, which didn't make me feel very good. We were walking slowly now. Annie was too tired to run anymore. I tried holding her hand, but it was slippery with sweat and shaking. So I held onto her arm instead.

"As we walked closer to the front of the street, I started thinking about times past. I remember the first day your soldiers came. They nailed a list of rules on all the doors. They painted a Star of David in yellow and black on Poppa's store and Neumann's Bakery. Poppa said they did this to anyone Jewish who owned a business. On some of the windows, they painted a man with a big nose. I thought they were funny and would laugh when I saw them, but Poppa, upon hearing my giggles, would scold me. I never knew why. I didn't know who these soldiers were. I never knew they existed.

"I would lay awake at night pretending to be asleep and would try to listen in on Momma and Poppa's conversations. Herr and Frau Neumann would visit sometimes for coffee, and they would all talk softly around the dining room table. Every so often, Momma's voice would crack slightly when speaking, and I could sense her troubles, her doubts. The soldiers kept coming back, forcing new rules on us that we had to follow. We could not go out at night after certain hours. We even had to wear the Star of David on our clothes. I asked

Poppa once about the soldiers, but he said never to speak of them. He said to never mind. 'Keep your mouth quiet,' he would say. 'They will not hurt us.' So I pretended they were never there even though I really wanted to talk to one. I was curious, which, as Poppa would say, always got me in trouble."

Otto noticed the major gazing ahead, perhaps listening, perhaps not. He seemed to be calm, so Otto continued his story guessing that the major was in a fair mood.

"As Annie and I came to our street, the noises became louder and my heartbeat quickened. We turned off the alley and were greeted with the most frightful sight. Annie swung her arm free of my hold and brought her hands to her mouth trying to hold in her scream. Tears filled her eyes as she took an awkward step forward, stumbling. I stood frozen. Shocked. There before my eyes I could see piles upon piles of furniture, clothing, and every other conceivable household object strewn across the street creating distorted shapes. Around them there were people, hundreds upon hundreds of people, crying, vacant in mind. Some were yelling, resisting, which only led to a quick rifle butt to the head followed by being dragged by their hair. Others stood quiet, focused, heads down as if counting ants on the ground. Two men were on their knees, hands tied behind their backs. Not a moment of time passed, and they were face down in a sea of glistening red, silenced. The soldiers were back.

"My head was spinning. I whispered to myself over and over, 'Poppa, they will not hurt us. Poppa, they will not hurt us.' But now they were hurting us."

Otto looked up at the major, his voice finding little remorse, as if numb to his own words. "This was the first time I had ever seen a dead person. I am used to it now. Sometimes I think death is a good thing. It silences the pain. While you and I, Major, live with it." Otto turned his head from the major, who sat silently with no response. His mind remained in a trance.

"Without thinking, I turned to find that Annie was gone. Looking up, I caught a glimpse of her long, tasseled black hair running through the bewildered crowd. I followed chase without hesitating. I knew she would go to the bakery to find her parents. Strange, at that point I don't remember thinking of my family. I was just worried about Annie. I ran as fast as my legs would allow through the crowd, a horrid sight of lifeless apparitions. These were my neighbors. My friends. My people.

"I caught up to Annie and found her in her mother's arms in front of the bakery as expected. Knowing she was safe, I turned to our corner store to see Poppa and Momma with suitcases. Momma was crying but making no sound. Poppa stood utterly expressionless. I ran over to Momma, and upon her seeing me, she dropped to her knees with open arms. I began crying because my feet were wet again, and I begged her forgiveness over and over. Sound now followed her tears as she squeezed me like a giant snake. Over Momma's shoulder through my teary eye, I could see my brothers, Yoram and Samuel. They were cowering behind Poppa holding suitcases close to their sides.

"Momma released her hold, and Poppa put his hand on my shoulder. He knelt down next to me, his voice gentle yet firm. 'My dearest Otto, please listen to me very, very carefully. The time has come. Now more than ever, I need you to listen with both ears and look at me with both eyes. You must obey every word I say to you. Days of frivolous questions or idle chatter are far away from us now. We are to leave our neighborhood as ordered by the soldiers and follow their direction. Where to, I do not know. Momma has prepared your suitcase. You must carry it on your own. There can be no words of struggle, crying, or whining about it. I must not hear so much as a peep. Do you understand me?' I nodded my understanding, and he gave me a big hug.

"I had so many questions, but Poppa just told me not to ask him anything, so I had to keep quiet. That was hard. I picked up my suitcase, which was smaller than my brothers'. Yoram and Samuel were both older than I. Yoram was twelve, and Samuel was four-teen. Older meant they were stronger to carry bigger and heavier suitcases, for which I was thankful. I walked over to Annie, who was standing next to her mother. She carried a small suitcase like I did. 'I don't think we'll be going to the creek anymore.' She looked up but said nothing. She took my hand and held it tight.

"The soldiers were busy barking orders and scurrying about pushing people into a long, packed line, all walking with their suit-cases. The screaming, yelling, and crying carried on, polluting the air with its torments. My family and the Neumanns got into line as well. I walked with Annie, still holding hands. Poppa and Momma walked with Annie's parents next to us. My brothers were in front of them. I never looked back at my neighborhood again. I just kept walking forward with Annie, our heads down. Nobody talked. Nobody said a word. It seemed we walked for hours. Every so often, a gunshot would go off, sometimes a whole bunch in a row, but we just kept walking.

"It was early October, and the Linden trees were beginning their journey from green to yellow. The days were still quite warm, the nights surrendering to cold. Some leaves had already fallen and lay brown and torn on the ground. I started to kick piles as I walked, which was fun, and it brought another smile to Annie. Poppa saw no humor in it and scolded me. 'Be quiet, Otto,' he uttered, his voice stern yet somewhat muffled, spoken through gritted teeth. Even with-out seeing Poppa, I could see him. Soldier trucks filled with people were speeding past us. I wondered why they got to go in trucks and we had to walk. I turned my head while walking to ask Poppa. Upon opening my mouth, I realized my question would be met with anger, remembering that Poppa had said 'No questions.' I turned back and let my thoughts find somewhere else to go in my head.

"I was getting tired of walking to wherever we were going and just wished we could run. It would have been faster. Annie was not holding my hand anymore. She needed it for holding her suitcase.

23

I tried to help her, but Poppa told me not to. He said it would show that she was frail. Poppa was always very smart. He had great foresight and intuition. I later found out from another officer that my Poppa was right. This was how they removed the weak. The soldiers would surely have killed Annie right then and there if they had seen her struggling with her suitcase.

"We walked into an unfamiliar part of the city. I noticed the street sign indicated 'Levetzow Strasse,' and we soon came to a synagogue. Thousands of people like us, wearing the Star of David on their coats, were being formed into huge lines. I couldn't see the beginning of the line. There were too many people. Poppa and Herr Neumann were in front of us. Momma and Frau Neumann were in back, and Annie, my brothers, and I were sandwiched in the middle. The lines were moving slowly, giving us enough time so we could put our suitcases down to rest.

"Poppa wasn't going to tell me anything about the soldiers, so I began to watch them with great curiosity. None of them smiled, and it seemed as if you could see through them. A warped transparency of the soul. I wondered if they all thought the same thing. They all looked and dressed the same. Their dark, wool coats and trousers were appointed with glistening metal and deep, dark, leather accoutrements. Their boots, belts, and weapons were polished and poised. Their helmets were set low over their brows, creating sinister shadows upon their faces, veils of terror. They were ordered by men without helmets who were always yelling. They were officers like you, Major. The soldiers never moved or did anything unless these men told them to. When they did move, they did so with such peculiar grace. Their movements were abrupt, stern, and direct, with purpose.

"We got to the front of the line after waiting many hours. There were officers sitting behind large desks, rows and rows of desks with guards standing at their sides, ready with their rifles positioned as if wanting to shoot. Farther back were hundreds of trucks with more soldiers forcing people onto them. I wondered where they were going.

"Poppa and Herr Neumann were ordered to approach the desk by the officer. I was about three meters behind, so I could hear their conversation. The officer told my Poppa he would have to declare and surrender all property and admit he was an enemy of the Reich. I did not hear Poppa answer, but he must have done so, for I could see the officer faintly smile and put his head back down to continue his work. Poppa then began filling out many, many papers in what seemed like a whole drawing pad's worth. After a long period of time, Poppa turned and walked towards us. He handed us each a small booklet with stamped papers. He told us not to lose these documents or there would be grave consequences. He said we were being deported, to where he did not know. I put my papers in my front pocket as instructed. Poppa was getting very serious now. His voice remained firm, and his words held great strength. I had never seen him like this.

"At that moment, without alarm, soldiers came over and forced us forward, pushing my brothers and the Neumanns. They guided us with much persistence to the trucks. They grabbed our suitcases and tossed them aside. I was fine with that because I couldn't carry it anymore. Poppa and Herr Neumann climbed up into the truck first and then helped the rest of us. Annie and I were together at the front of the truck, our families surrounding us. A woman, I don't know who she was, tried to sit, but a soldier quickly jumped aboard and grabbed her by the hair, forcing her to her feet. Her screams could have awakened the dead. Annie and I turned our heads, burying them in my Poppa's coat, trying not to hear. They packed us in very tightly. There was no room to sit. We had to stand. I could not see what was happening but could hear the tailgate of the truck slam and the soldier's orders to move out. The truck roared to life, and we were off to an unknown place. It was that unknown that frightened us the most.

"It was late in the day, and the sun was giving up its warmth. There was no cover over the back of the truck, and the wind coming over it was uncomfortably cold. Time seemed to be moving very fast. My thoughts were reeling, and I became very dizzy to all that had passed. Annie had gone to huddle next to her father. Poppa had his coat around me as I stood nestled up against him, facing forward. Over the front of our truck, I could see faintly the other vehicles, like ours, full of people moving forward with speed. I sure had many questions, but I knew Poppa would have none of it. I tried to see to my sides, see where we were, but it was difficult because we were so tightly packed together. When I did get a glimpse, the landscape was a blur and nothing was recognizable to me. I had a feeling I was far away to another side of the city, far from my neighborhood. I must have been squirming all over to see, because I could feel Poppa's hands tighten around my shoulders, his fingers following the contours of my shape, pressing into my body. I stopped moving immediately.

"We came to a stop after about an hour. It could have been longer. I do not know. I could hear the soldiers getting out of the trucks, their hobnail boots click-clacking in staccato as they moved with urgency. The tailgate to our truck was unchained and dropped without guidance, left to crash against the bottom bumper of the truck. The soldiers yelled in perfect unison, 'Jeder raus jetzt!' over and over with great intensity.

"I turned slowly around in order to be ready to get out of the truck and was standing in back of Poppa now. I could hear people in front of us groan as they knelt down to slip off the back of the truck. I was stiff, too, from the cold and from having to stand in one place for so long. As I began moving, I noticed Poppa side-step to the left and then continue his move forward. I was looking at him and wasn't watching where I was going and tripped over something. I recognized it as the body of the woman who had tried to sit down when we first got on the truck. She was face down, crushed, her limbs twisted and grotesque, her hair entangled and snarled among the splintered wooden floor of the truck. Her fingers, bent in odd ways, were compressed and flattened but spread apart as if trying to find a stance at which to lift her struggling body. I was horrified and looked up just to get a glimpse of Poppa's eyes as he glanced back. He brought his index finger to his lips. I side-stepped left, following Poppa's movements without uttering a word. Yet as I passed her, I couldn't help but look down again out of curiosity. Her eyes were open, as was her mouth, still yelling but without sound. I never heard a word of her screams for help. She must have tried to sit down again but was soon overcome as the soldiers continued packing us on the truck. No one had helped her back to her feet. No one had wanted to be associated with her. Life was becoming grimmer. It was showing its cruel side."

Suddenly, the major turned to Otto, his mouth opening as if to say something, something that was weighing on his mind and could not wait. Otto stopped his story. He leaned towards the major ever so slightly, his eyes fixated on the major's, anticipating his speech.

"Please, Otto, please. You must be kind and tell me of the Führer? Where do we stand? What has become of our country? I ask you not for myself, but for the brave souls surrounding you, once all innocent boys, missing their homes and a soft bed, missing mothers and fathers and a gentle embrace, missing quiet days of laughing under trees and the coming of warm summer breezes. I ask you for them. This is not their war. I have not the heart to continue this fight or to send them to their deaths."

Otto sat silently, his eyes observing the beaten and defaced soldiers milling around him. They coughed and lamented, their foul voices echoing into the air. A dark, glazed look came from one, spellbound, perhaps praying for an end. Otto hated these men. He hated their very existence. There was trickery in the major's words, Otto thought. How dare he know of my street, my bakery, my life. How dare he contaminate my memories with his filthy bearing. Otto put his head down between his knees, trying not to listen to his thoughts. Perhaps the major was with just cause. With his head still bent over, Otto asked the major, "What will become of me after I have told you all?"

"You will have two of my best men escort you safely back to the Führerbunker."

"There is no safety for me. A failed mission means I go hungry, or if the mood serves them, I will be killed."

"Please, Otto, do not despair. I will get word to General Heinrici myself and will write a letter to Herr Bormann explaining our situation and reasons why your documents could not be delivered. I will make it clear on your part of no wrong doing against the Fatherland or the Führer."

Otto lifted his head from his knees and looked to his escape route. Darkness was closing in, and it would be easy to evade such saddened soldiers. But to where? At this point, his options were few. Returning to the Führerbunker with a failed mission was not wise during such an unstable time, especially without just cause. Being alone in a burning city with Russians scurrying about was even less inviting. He looked up at the major with discerning eyes staring into the heart of him.

"Fine. I will tell you all I know."

Otto sighed, took a deep breath and exhaled; his shoulders slumped forward to a rested position.

"Well, the lights go out often in the Führerbunker and it gets very dark, so dark that I can't see my own hand in front of my nose. I like to play games when that happens. I try to see my hand in front of my face before it touches. I can't do it, but Helga Goebbels can. She's very good at it."

"You mean Reichsminister Goebbels is there?"

"Yes, Major, he is there. He's been there for many weeks. I don't see him often, just his children. I really only play with Helga, but she's not as much fun as Annie. I can't get her to do any jokes with me. She seems very sad most days, and I see pain and suffering in her eyes. It's almost as if she knows something but won't tell."

"Yes, yes. All very good, but what of Herr Goebbels? What of him? What of the Führer?"

Catching his anxiousness, the major dropped his head, sighing in frustration. Raising it slowly, he turned to look at Otto, his eyes peering off and then back. "I am sorry, my boy. Please excuse my behavior. Please, please continue."

Otto looked at the major with great reservation. The years of war had washed the life from him, he thought. His mind was fragmented and broken. Otto's wariness for the major was growing. He did not know what to say to him, as he did not know what words would provoke his outbursts. He tried to think of things related to the soldiers he observed or knew in the Führerbunker that would interest the major. The chocolate had dried his mouth, and his throat felt raw and beaten. He wanted to ask the major for water but thought better of it. No need to press an already sensitive situation. Swallowing hard and trying to coat his throat with spit and mucus, Otto started again, keeping one eye focused on his escape route.

"Herr Goebbels doesn't come out much from his room. When he does, he looks sullen and dazed but is always well-dressed, his hair perfectly parted. He always proceeds with direct intent on where he is going. He never says anything to me, only pats my head offering a ghoulish smile and continues down the hallway through the dining hall into darkness, towards the other side of the bunker. He never stays long wherever he is going, and his mood never changes upon his return. As the days have gone by, he seems to move from his quarters less often.

"There are many bunkers within the complex of the government buildings. My main residence, when not called upon for a mission, is in the bunker of the Party Chancellery where Herr Bormann resides with his staff, service officers, and SS guards. Herr Goebbels also has his own shelter in the cellars of the Propaganda Ministry. As of late, it seems they have all but abandoned these posts for the Führerbunker because the Führer calls on them incessantly at all hours of the day and night.

"I am forbidden to go to certain parts of the bunker, especially near the Führer, so I don't know what to tell you of it. It's creepy and scary in the bunker. Cold, dismal. It feels like we are living corpses lost within a huge narrow-chambered coffin. Even the slightest of noise echoes throughout. I sometimes hear loud discussions, maddening rages and rants that quiver and shake throughout the cold concrete walls, but from whom they come, I do not know. It is from someone I have never seen, as I know for the most part everyone in residence there. I suspect it is the Führer himself reprimanding his generals.

"When called upon for a mission, I must await either in the telephone switchboard room or in the machine room in the lower part of the bunker. It is here where Herr Bormann comes to give me my orders. I prefer to sleep in the machine room where it's warmer and thus not have to walk all the way to the cellars of the Party Chancellery. I only get away with this when Herr Bormann is absent. Hannes Hentschel, 'Onkel Hannes,' as he lets me call him, is the chief technician of the bunker and resides in this room. He's pleasant to be with and shows me all the tools and materials that keep the bunker operating. He's not a soldier. At least I think he's not. He doesn't wear the uniform of the elite SS or that of a regular infantryman. He wears these big brown overalls that have years of dirt and grime imbedded in them. I wish I had a pair of those when building dams with Annie. I think I would not get as wet with those monster things on.

"Next door is the telephone switchboard room. During the day when I am not out on a mission, I sometimes like to go in there. It's fun to watch and listen to all the calls going in and out. There are a few telephone operators with different shifts. Sergeant Misch is one, and Corporal Huber is another. Corporal Huber is always very good to me and sneaks extra treats for me when he can. I can sense the goodness in his heart more than any other soldier I have ever met. He says one day he and his newlywed will have a son. One like me. Well, he'll be in for trouble then, I should think.

"Corporal Huber is often present, and I feel safe knowing his two sharp eyes are near. I usually see him operating the telegraph lines. He is always scurrying about receiving, sending, or delivering messages. I sometimes sit next to him and listen to the messages and his conversations. He lets me plug in wires here and wires there. I don't know what they do and how the voices come through the wires, but it's fun. Mostly these talks are with generals from all over the country relating what is happening."

"What do they say, Otto? Please, please do tell."

"It's hard to tell you exactly what they say because I never understand them. I am not well-versed in the comings and goings of generals. Corporal Huber would know, Major, but he hides his worries very well, yet even I can see he is sad and unhappy. He works day and night and always has a bead of sweat running down his face, causing a stream that flows in and out of the wrinkles near his eyes. I catch him at certain moments where he looks off from the switchboard, slowly raising a hand to softly touch the photo of his beloved wife on the desk.

"After a long and hard bombing from the airplanes, Sergeant Misch, Corporal Huber, and Onkel Hannes hurry about fixing the lights and checking the outside of the bunker for exposure of the roof. I've gone with them a few times to fix things, but only when they force me. I hate to disappoint Corporal Huber as he's very good to me. So I go. Everybody is frantic and hysterical after a bombing, and it puts them in a terrible mood. I feel better staying in the servants' quarters in the upper bunker and hiding under the bed. I pull the blankets over the side and make a little fort. I bring a candle, and I have a drawing pad. I wish I had chalks, but the pencils Corporal Huber gives me work fine. Mostly, I draw pictures of Annie with her long, midnight-colored hair; her small, pudgy nose; and her perfectly placed dimples at the top of both her cheeks. Annie said dimples are where the devil has kissed her, which sounds silly to me. I mean, why would the devil kiss you? Sounds like parent mischief to me.

"One time I heard Frau Goebbels crying and screaming out loud. Well, I think it was her. There are so many girls coming in and out of the bunker, it's hard to know. I think it was her. Helga won't tell me, but looking into her eyes gives it all away. Herr Goebbels was yelling too. He's easy to recognize because of his strong, vicious, and maddening voice. In the Party Chancellery bunker, the girls have been coming and going less often as of late. Herr Bormann is always with them, as well as the rest of the High Court. They stay up all night laughing, dropping bottles, and sometimes I hear these strange moans. I have never heard such noises before, though I think I heard my Poppa and Momma make the same noises one night when I got up to go to the bathroom. I prefer listening to people laugh."

"Bormann! Bormann is there as well? What of that scoundrel? I have only met him once, but I never fancied his ill-demeanor."

"Yes, Major. Herr Bormann is there, but he seldom finds kind words for me. When he smells of liquor, I get scared and that's often. He gave me a mission late one night during one of his parties. He summoned me to the dining hall where many officers were sitting around the table. Bottles were strewn about the room, and they were smoking and playing cards. Their tunics were unbuttoned from the neck to about midway down their chests. Their cheeks were red and patchy, like a marble floor, and their hair was disheveled. A ragged bunch, I thought. They certainly didn't look like the army that came and took my family away, not the stoic, dignified, volatile group that taunted and herded us like swine.

"There were no girls around the table as is usual, though I could hear them giggling in the next room. Herr Bormann directed me to go to his office in the Reich's Chancellery and get some more bottles of cognac. As you know, Major, the Reich's Chancellery at one point in its history was a magnificent palace appointed with high ceilings, marble, gold, and wall-to-wall mosaics. I was permitted access through its grand halls to the Führerbunker, which was how most people entered. There was another entrance to the bunker as well, an emergency entrance from the gardens, but I was not permitted to use it. It was only for the Führer and his High Court.

"Now, however, the Reich Chancellery is very dangerous and not many people venture into it. It is mostly rubble at this point, and the walls, floors, and ceilings are very unstable, another victim of the Allied bombing efforts. In the basement, there is a makeshift hospital where Colonel Schenks treats the soldiers who have been wounded in their last vain efforts to defend the city. I have never been down there, but its unfathomable stench finds its way to the upper corridors of the building, only to disturb the questionable living. That in itself is enough to prevent any investigation.

"For me, deciding to go on missions is simple, really. I go, or I am shot. They always have a sentry with me when I am summoned for my missions, just to remind me. My trip to Herr Bormann's office was uneventful. The night was still, and the moon was a sinister pale blue. I picked up the bottles of cognac where Herr Bormann had said they would be, but upon my return, the stairs gave way under me and I crashed through to the floor below. I knocked myself unconscious for quite some time. When I awoke, I tried to get up and was struck with excruciating pain. I realized I had dislocated my shoulder and was covered with deep cuts and scrapes. With my other arm, I picked up the case of cognac and slowly made my way back to the Party Chancellery bunker. The sentry met me at the entrance and taking the case of liquor away from me, firmly grasped my good arm.

"Herr Bormann became extremely enraged upon my return. I was ready for my punishment. I always rationalize to myself during these times that if I think of myself as already dead, then there's no need to worry about dying. This leaves me free to act, to focus, and to perform my missions. Herr Bormann walked over to me briskly, and the table of officers became dreadfully silent. The pain was shooting up my arm into my neck, and I felt weak again. Herr Bormann stopped within inches of me and noticed the case of cognac. In a stern and aggravated voice he asked why I was delayed. I told him

I had fallen through the stairs to the floor and had hurt my arm. He looked at the case of cognac again and reached down to inspect the bottles. He stood up, whipped his head back, and let out with a wicked, roaring laugh. His shriek filled the room and echoed with darkness, outdoing the lonely corridors of the bunker. My mind was foggy and I gritted my teeth, my lips trembling as my eyes gazed forward trying to quell the pain. As he calmed, he turned his head and faced the rest of the officers. 'Well, my good friends, it seems our little adjutant has completed his mission despite being terribly late.' Turning back and squatting down, he looked me dead in the eyes, his foul, liquored breath clouding the air around me. 'And for that, because no bottles were damaged, you shall live.' He let out one last despicable snort and patted my head, tossing my hair into my eyes. The sentry let go of his grip, and I immediately fell to the hard, damp concrete floor, missing the soft, padded rug by a centimeter.

"I don't remember much after this, but when I awoke again, I was in the infirmary of the Führerbunker. Corporal Huber was next to me holding a cold wet towel to my forehead. My shoulder had been snapped back into place, and my arm was in a sling. I could feel it throbbing, pulsing my temple on the side of my head in a rhythmic beat. 'You are quite resilient, little one,' Corporal Huber offered. 'The German army should have fifty divisions of men with your stamina. Perhaps at one time they did, many years ago. Now don't move, young Otto. Be still and find rest. Your missions are over for now. I have asked Sergeant Misch to let Herr Bormann know of your condition. He will not be bothering you for a while. Besides, he is busy patronizing the rest of the High Court, as he always does. The Russians are pressing the inner territory of the city, and he will have too much on his mind to worry about you.' I smiled faintly at him, turned my head away, and drifted back to sleep."

"Those Bastards!" yelled the major as he swiftly threw his arms up in disgrace to the sky, his eyes widening, his lips agitated and shaking. Reaching down, he grabbed a hand full of dirt and threw

it to the wind. "Liars and crooks they are. Scoundrels. Disgusting
filthy swine. These are our leaders? This is our High Court? We
suffer and die with terrible ends while they lay hidden in cowardly
safety, drinking and engaging in debauchery. I have lost good
friends, old friends and comrades. I have seen sons die who could
have been my own. Women raped and beaten beyond humanity.
Young boys frozen solid in miserable winter cold without boots or
blankets. For what?"

Two soldiers off to Otto's right looked up and slowly grasped
their rifles after hearing the commotion. They looked at each
other, not knowing what to think of the major's sudden outburst.
Their rifles became better poised for action, the bolts sliding ever
so carefully to locked positions, safeties ever so delicately moving
to the fire position. Other soldiers milling about looked over but
paid him no mind.

The major became calm and quiet found his face. He sat next
to Otto not moving, staring straight ahead. "All I have believed in
is lost." He gave a heavy sigh and dropped his head down towards
the ground.

Otto became nervous. He had lingered here much too long. He
looked over the major's back, finding his escape route again. His
attention was suddenly disrupted as he noticed a single tear hit the
soft, ruffled dirt without the hint of a splatter, only to be soaked up
by the dry, thirsty ground. Otto said nothing. It became apparent
to him that this war had brought both pain and suffering to enemy
and friend alike. Otto's thoughts soon drifted to his family, as it
often did when he felt vulnerable to actually caring for these people.
However, this was pain brought upon by themselves. The choice was
theirs and theirs alone. He pitied them more than he felt sorry for
them. Enough of this. My mind is erratic with too many emotions.
All this caring will get me killed. I feel nothing for these people.

Out of the looming darkness, faint shrieks could be heard in
the distance, their terror becoming louder and louder as they

approached. A loud cry followed with the acknowledgement of the beast coming to bear, "Incoming mortars! Take cover!"

Otto started to dash towards his escape route, only to be swallowed by the major's arms and thrust to the ground, pinned by the weight of the major's body. All at once, explosions ripped throughout the courtyard, mangling bodies and throwing them effortlessly through the air. In an instant, dirt, metal, and flesh became one, mixed until unrecognizable. Limbs from the innocent oak tree came crashing down and splintered atop the major and Otto. As quickly as it had started, it stopped. Echoes of the shrill moved off into the night, their screams waning in the moonlit air. Otto could see nothing but smoke, dust, and darkness. He heard nothing but torture and agony. His eyes squinted to make out any forms of life, but nothing moved. Death was circling about.

Otto struggled to release himself from the confines of the major's grasp, wondering why he wasn't letting him up. Around him, fires began where the mortar shells had hit, igniting anything that would carry a flame. Otto felt a slight wetness on his face and hesitantly touched his skin. He looked at his trembling fingers, and with the light of the fires, he could see that it was blood. Feeling no pain of his own, he knew it was the major's. He squirmed and contorted his body to force himself from under the major, pushing away the smaller tree limbs that half buried them. Standing free, Otto looked around him. All was still except for the crackling of flame, creating menacing shadows on the pockmarked walls of the buildings. Soldiers lay strewn about in awkward positions. Dead. War machinery that once wielded such punishment became nothing but twisted scraps, burning and oozing black smoke. Horses were no longer standing on four legs, now lying on their sides, puddles of their entrails marking their existence.

Otto looked down at the major, and bending closer to him, he could see that the major was dead. Shrapnel from the mortar fire had torn away half his body, the rest crushed and distorted from the heavier tree limbs. He stepped away from the major, stumbling and nearly falling over a tree branch while still looking at the major in horror and disbelief. He turned to his escape route and slowly moved towards it. Otto quickly noticed that the hole in the fence was gone. The entire fence was blown out of existence from the shelling. He knew that if the major had not prevented him from running to his escape, he would have been killed. The thought baffled Otto. It disturbed him. Perhaps in the end of the major's life, while searching his thoughts, he realized all his wartime feats had been for ill-will. Maybe he had found in this final act one good deed, one good act of humanity.

Otto gathered himself and slowly moved off the square. As he was creeping through the clutter, he heard off to his left a very troubled gasping for breath. Otto walked around the Panther tank the mechanics had been working on and came to a young soldier lying on his back with his head propped upon a dented petrol can. The soldier was shaking profusely with his hands up in a clenched manner in pain. His chest was torn apart. Tears washed away the blood on his face while running down its side. Otto knelt down next to the soldier eyeing him top to bottom. He's a mess, Otto thought. Mistaking his shivering for cold, Otto began looking around for a blanket and found a window curtain. He folded it in two and covered the soldier from his feet to his neck. Otto reached into his pocket and took out the piece of chocolate the major had given him, the one he was saving. He paused for a time, looking at the distorted shape of the chocolate with intense thought and wonder.

"Hmm, I do not feel like parting with it. It would be wasted on this sorry figure before me. He will be dead in a matter of time. It probably even came from Neumann's Bakery. A shame really. Such a waste."

Otto stared back down at the shaking soldier and put the chocolate into the soldier's mouth. The soldier began chewing slowly, and a slight smile came to his face, changing the falling course of his tears. Otto stood up, suddenly startled, his eyes becoming

alert and paranoid. Off in the distance, he could hear the scurrying of boots and the metal sound of rifle slings swinging back
and forth. He could always recognize the distinctive movements
of German troops by the sounds of their hobnailed boots clicking
on the ground. These were not those sounds. These were Russians.
Otto made haste and ran quickly through the dark, bypassing good
hiding places for the better choice of distancing himself from the
threat. As he ran, he heard a lone pistol shot come from the square
and could only imagine the Russians had come across the wounded
young German soldier. At least he died with a smile on his face,
Otto thought. Chocolate will do that.

Chapter 3

Otto looked back as he hurried through rubble choked streets, searching the deepest shadows in the dark to stay hidden. No one had followed him, and he heard nothing. He ducked into a building to hide, one that hadn't seen too much bombing and where its facade was still somewhat solid.

Back to the blackness of the cellar I go. Not even the bravest of soldiers would venture to follow me down here. Besides, grenades work better when clearing out a building. He hopped down the stairway and found a corner in which he sat to catch his breath and decide what he should do next. The death of the major troubles me. How could a school teacher who obviously liked children be part of such a destructive army killing good people for evil leaders and then all of a sudden sit down, share chocolate, and protect me from bombs? For the first time in this war, I am thoroughly confused.

As I see it, I have two choices. I can go back to the bunker with a failed mission and be shot, or perhaps just be beaten until I wake up in the infirmary again. Or, I can try to escape from a city surrounded by ill-tempered Russians. Sergeant Misch warned me about the Russians. He told me that if I were caught, I would be sent to the coldest parts of Russia to work in labor camps and dig in mines. I would be given frozen potato soup and sewer water as food and drink.

I would be imprisoned until I wasted away into oblivion. Hmm. Poppa always gave me three choices when I was being punished. The wooden spoon, the hand, or the belt. My life is filled with poor choices. At least Poppa always gave me a hug afterwards and some sweets.

The floor was becoming cold as Otto sat and pondered his options, making the thought of frozen potato soup less appealing as a choice. It was damp, and water was dripping from the ceiling, splattering him when hitting the floor, launching droplets like mortar fire on his lap. Well, it would be best to go back to the bunker and take my chances. Perhaps Corporal Huber can alleviate any tensions and find in such twisted men a heart to spare me. Perhaps after all these years of malicious exploits, there's a little piece of the major in these men too.

Otto stood up from the wet floor and slowly maneuvered his way out of the building, first peeking out of a cellar window for any signs of enemies. "These snipers are gnats by day and cats by night. They see everything in the dark."

Convinced the night was still, Otto moved from the building and into the street. Finding his way back to the bunker would not be easy as war continued to disfigure the landscape. Most street signs had been destroyed by bombing or removed by the Germans to confuse and disrupt enemy movements. As he moved silently for a few hours, things became more familiar: a bent light post, a window with certain panes of glass broken, a woman's long, blonde wig hanging from a tree branch. Convinced that he was on the correct route to the bunker, he decided to hide for the remainder of the night. He came across a bombed-out auto that had been pushed into a side street and climbed through the smashed front windshield into the back seat. Parts of the seat were torn and burned, with springs sticking through the leather into the air. Otto laid his jacket over the springs, and paying no mind to his discomfort, he slipped into a deep sleep.

Morning sunlight clipped the edge of the eaves on the building high above, dappling light and shadow upon the ground below. The sky began its day, turning its blackened face into radiant and stunning reds, yellows, and oranges. Otto opened his eyes and stared up at the roof of the auto. A quick blink and he looked out the front window through which he had crawled. Another blink to the right window, and another to the left and back. The world looked very different in the light, he thought. Funny how objects at night play on the fears of our inner minds, fooling us to create creatures that do not exist, a monstrous troll, an evil spell-casting witch, or a five-headed giant lizard. Then at light, we giggle to ourselves when such an object is revealed to be just an ordinary bush, tree, or combination of both configured in such a way as to alter reality.

Otto sat up to further get his bearings. As always, he checked for movement and signs of life. Looking back at himself, he realized he had stripped out of his clothes as if getting ready for a normal night's sleep, tucked gently into bed by his momma, kissed on the forehead, and wished a blessed goodnight. He smiled to himself at this thought as he furled his woolen blanket into a tight roll and gathered the clothes he had strewn across the back of the auto.

Otto, for the most part, wore the uniform of the Hitler Youth combined with pieces of the regular German infantry soldier. His light-brown, woolen shirt had chest pockets on both sides and was the standard shirt of the Hitler Youth. He favored the standard German soldier's dark grey field trousers, which were made of wool and offered warmth, protection and, most importantly, hung loosely on him, enabling him to move and run freely. His woolen jacket was the Hitler Youth winter blouse in dark blue that buttoned all the way down. His trousers fell to his ankles and were tucked into high-top, dark brown field boots. These boots were a prized possession of all members of the Hitler Youth who were wealthy enough to afford them or lucky enough to be given a pair. Otto had taken his from an unfortunate dead member. He had also been given a field cap but had discarded it when the siege upon Berlin had begun. It made him look too much like a soldier. It made him a target.

Otto's uniform was terribly disheveled now. Where there should be wool, there was none, just bare skin scraped raw with scars and callouses. His boots, once polished and sound, were rough and discolored by water and dried mud stains. He carried two bags on his person. One was a German soldier's musette bag made of heavy, dark green canvas that Otto had filled with everything possible to survive from a blanket, food, and canteen to pliers, tape, and string. The other bag was his leather-bound satchel in which he kept the documents he was to deliver. He never carried weapons of any kind. His only protection was a Hitler Youth knife given to him by Artur Axmann, the Commander of the Hitler Youth. Otto also carried a small pocket knife he used mostly for opening his iron rations or cutting bread, if given any.

Otto put on his jacket and noticed the major's blood on his left sleeve, a still fresh and vibrant red hue, waiting for time to turn it brown and ugly. "Hmm. I am a mess. When I return home to Momma, she will not recognize me in the least, except that I do look like I fell into the stream again. Oh, I think she'll remember me."

Otto finished dressing and put his musette bag and satchel around his back using the straps. He slowly crawled out of the auto, staying in the shadows. He decided to approach the bunker during the day when the occupants would be milling about and would not see anything out of the ordinary, as opposed to the night when the guards would be easily startled and their senses more heightened. He would head straight to Corporal Huber, tell him everything that had happened, and look to him for council and guidance. He would look to him for safety.

Otto moved quickly with little mind to past events. His focus was on a safe arrival to the bunker. He came to Wilhelmstrasse, a major avenue that ran north and south through the city. Normally, it would be an easy walk down this street to the bunker, but he did not trust the major streets and avenues. They now allowed greater access for tanks, artillery, and infantry, which were strategic routes the Russians were sure to use. He favored smaller, less discreet side streets. While taking longer, they offered better safety.

"This day seems unusually calm. Too calm for a war. I had better scout the area," Otto whispered. Looking to the sky, he entered a building and climbed the creaking stairs to the highest floor. He found a blown out door providing access to the roof, obviously created by a sniper. Crawling to the edge of the building, Otto wiped the dust and sweat from his eyes and peered below. At one time, he carried binoculars for such a situation, but they often broke during his missions, the cost of which was a hand across the face. Otto's eyes widened, and he could sense there was great evil stirring below.

Looking to the north, he could make out signs of the beginning of gun emplacements, an indication the Russians were building momentum and setting strategic offenses. To the south, he could see the Germans scrambling with no clear objectives, frantic as they made haste to gather their defense. Sporadic small arms fire began ripping back and forth, bullets ricocheting to new targets, perhaps victims, and changing sound as they moved through the air in a new direction.

All of sudden, Otto heard the shrills and screams that sounded like a thousand dying cats echoing through the ghostly corridor of the street. Looking across from his perch to the building on the other side of the street, he saw a woman running along the top of the roof. Terrified, stumbling, and bloodied, she was naked except for the tattered remains of a sock on one foot. Behind followed her conquerors in pride and salute to their motherland. Otto could feel his heart quicken as it sank to his stomach. The hairs on his arms stood on end, piercing the wool of his jacket. The woman fell at the corner's edge of the building, gasping for breath, pleading for life, her escape route at an end, her screams only at their beginning. The group of Russian soldiers was not quite done with its favored pastime. They reached down and grabbed her, one of the soldiers hoisting her over his shoulder. Satisfied, they began walking back from where they had come. The woman continued her cries, kicking her feet and pulling on the soldier's hair. The soldier turned and faced his comrades, as if asking for advice. One of his comrades hunched his shoulders and threw his hands to the air, as though he had no answer for him. Without hesitation, the soldier carrying the woman faced the building's edge, took a step, and effortlessly dropped her over the side.

Otto gasped in horror and turned with the speed of light away from the edge, drawing his legs to his chest into a fetal position. He began crying to himself without sound, convulsing without breath. The woman's screams as she plummeted were not of this world. Otto clasped his hands over his ears, which were begging for mercy. Then all was quiet.

Otto lay silent but was shaking loudly. He turned his head slowly and looked just centimeters over the edge, just enough to see what he did not want to see, but what he was compelled to see. There was nothing. Looking off beyond the other rooftop across the street, he saw nothing. No soldiers. Nothing. It was as if the event hadn't even happened. It was now just another gruesome memory embedded in his mind, able to be replayed upon the thought. His brain was further marked.

Otto pulled his eyes from the other rooftop and changed their course to the sky while turning over onto his back. Smoke, dust, and the errant, vile smells of war passed by with ease, and the brilliance of blue faded in and out of focus. Otto reached into his pocket, thumbing around for the piece of chocolate he had saved, then realized he had given it to the dying German soldier a day ago. His shaking slowly stopped, and he began breathing calmly. He turned back onto his stomach and looked off the edge of the building again to decide his next move, burying the memory of the woman's death deeper into the inner realms of his soul.

The streets were taking on more activity as machine gun and artillery fire erupted. Otto knew this was a sure sign of troop movements, and the streets would soon be swarming with enemies. He decided it was too dangerous to continue down Wilhelmstrasse. He would have to find an alternate route. From his musette bag, he pulled a map he had drawn many years ago and unraveled its torn and wrinkled paper. Examining the map, he weighed the many courses he could take. All but one would require more time, resulting in his arriving at the bunker well after dark, a choice he decided against. The best choice was still risky. He could cross Weidendammer Bridge spanning the River Spree to the Friedrichstrasse Subway Station. The subway cars had all but been destroyed, their calendar of operation stilled. He could then follow the tube that ran down Friedrichstrasse to Stadtmitte Station. From there, he would head west to Kaiserhof Station and exit to Voss Strasse. A hurried run through Wilhelmplatz and he could be at the back emergency entrance to the bunker.

"Great." Otto kidded to himself. "Just great. I hate the subway tunnels. I hear tales of mischief and wickedness happening down there. However, the Ivans won't be thinking of them yet. Their eyes are fixated above ground where there's plenty of Germans to be killed."

The dark, shady underworld of the Berlin train tunnels during these days were not much safer, Otto feared. This was where the new ghettos of the city were hidden in squalor. Its homeless beggars and thieves lay in wait, stealing from passersby and those vulnerable to crime, making the air naturally foul, making it dangerous.

"It seems again I am plagued by the lesser of two evils." Otto stuffed the map back into his musette bag, crawled from the edge of the roof, and, at a safe distance so as not to be seen, got up on his feet. He went back down the stairs to the ground level, being careful to make as little creaking noise as possible. He peeked from the building and without incident made his way around the corner towards the bridge.

"Damn." I forgot I had to cross Wilhelmstrasse to get to the station.

Otto moved up the side street to the corner of Wilhelmstrasse staying in shadows. He crawled to where he could get a better view of the actions at street level. The Russians are to my left and the Germans to my right. Both would shoot me if in sight, since both would not know who I was. Truth be told, they would shoot me anyway. Heavy weapons fire was still sporadic, perhaps each side testing the other's numbers. Remembering Private Volger's death, he found it rather ironic that he was now in the same predicament.

"I suppose Private Volger thought he had no choice. Either die waiting, still without cover, or die trying to find it."

Otto took off his jacket and stuffed it into his musette bag as he prepared for a forty-meter sprint across the street. "Ah, that's better. I should be much faster without the confines of that jacket. Well, this goes against my rules of staying hidden in shadows, blinding others to my movements, but here I go." With the speed of a tornado's rage, he darted across the street, jumping over rubble and sidestepping scraps of metal and other ungodly waste. Otto could hear the hollow, spooky sounds of bullets buzzing by his head. He could feel their vacuous wind circling in motion en route to put something down, to put something to death. Luckily, the shots were high, which brought Otto relief because he knew he was not seen—yet. Otto held his breath until he came to the other side of the street where, in his last efforts, he sighted a ditch covered by debris. He dove underneath into its darkness and inhaled for much needed air.

"My word, what is that ghastly stench? A sewer main must have been destroyed by an aerial attack." Otto followed the rays of light shining on the ground of his little fort, which revealed decaying rats scattered about, complete with an endless cloud of flies buzzing with excitement over their prizes.

"Nice fort. Just when I find a little piece of fun, the horror of reality finds me. I am tiring of this." He climbed to the top of the bomb crater, pushing the dead carcasses of its inhabitants aside. Peeking out from the debris that provided his cover, he could make out no human forms. Otto felt his person for all his belongings, and convincing his mind all was there, he slowly pushed aside his cover to make further movement. It's not wise, Otto thought, to linger in such a place, an obviously good one soldiers will surely seek in their advances. Best to keep on moving.

Otto rose from his hole and followed a hedge row between the sidewalk and the apartment buildings, which hugged both sides of the street. The neighborhood was vacant of life. Windows once open to a summer's heat and draped with free blowing curtains lay still, hollow, and blackened, portraying the gaze like a ghostly skull. The buildings' vibrant facades of sculpted brick and mortar, all but slagging off into the streets, hindered Otto's path.

He reached the end of the street and found himself needing to cross another. He got on his stomach and crawled to the corner of the street using his feet, knees, elbows, and hands, remaining hidden beneath a hedge. Looking south, he could see the River Spree with the subway station on the other side. Damn. Another street to cross. This grows old for me.

Otto lay hidden at the corner and took inventory of his surroundings. Street crossings were not taken lightly. Otto thought of following this street to the river and then following the river to the Weidendammer Bridge. However, moving along the river was unwise. He would be far too open for a sniper or a well-positioned machine gun emplacement. Across the street, Otto could see a small alleyway leading behind the buildings. According to his map, there was a small garden which would allow enough cover to reach the bridge.

"One worry after another. First there are road crossings, then gardens, possibly full of machine gun nests. To top it off, I need to cross a bridge over the river in open daylight. My options for a safe return grow thin."

Otto decided to make haste for the gardens and take his chances there. He came to his knees slowly and with a higher viewpoint took in his surroundings again. He then rose to his feet, following the same procedure. War looked very different from different levels. What was once obscure suddenly becomes clear, which was how a sniper thought. As the reality of his decision set in, Otto's heartbeat quickened. Blood ran hot and moved with speed, tingling the very ends of his fingers, which twitched as his arms raised to begin his move. And then calm. Otto quieted his whole being as he moved across the street, limping, dragging his leg to fake a wound. He had seen this trick used before. While alerting a marksman, it usually proved non-threatening. He would not be considered a target, just an unfortunate passerby lost in a barren land. It was better to use a bullet on a real threat.

Otto found the other side without incident and slipped from the street into the alleyway. Its darkness offered him solace. He sighed in relief and moved on without pause. Coming to the edge of the back of the building, he peered from its safety. The garden lay before him as depicted by the smeared ink on his map. He moved into the garden, which, as he advanced, resembled a graveyard. There were German dead scattered over the ground, bloated and laying in warped positions, wanting burial from the world.

Kneeling down to lay low from sight, Otto noticed a German musette bag that seemed to be full. His curiosity piqued heavy interest as he crawled to the sack. "Hmm. Could this be what I am hoping?" He opened the bag, and seeing its contents caused his stomach to rumble with hunger as he pulled from the bag four cans of German iron rations.

"Sorry, Mr. Stomach, but there is no time to linger and have a feast." Otto quickly extracted his new found treasures and put them in his musette bag while his eyes kept watch of his surroundings. The garden was in shambles, as expected. The grass was unkempt, tall and growing without care. Tree branches and limbs were torn from their majestic homes and lay at rest with no hope of the flowers beneath to find sun.

"This patrol looked to be shot from behind," Otto observed as he remained low, mimicking a cat on its final prowl before springing on its prey. He noticed the grass trampled to his left. A large army group had moved through here, but there are no signs of hobnailed boots scarring the bare earth. These are Russians, he concluded.

"This is not good. This is not good at all. The Russians are closer to the Führerbunker than I had suspected."

Otto turned from the Russians' path and quickly made his way, hopping from tree to tree, bush to bush, until he came upon the edge of the garden between two buildings that faced the Weidendammer Bridge. The sun strained to hold its place in the sky but slowly started its path to shadow. Otto remained hidden at the edge to think of his next move. "Well, I have a street to cross and then a bridge. If I am correct, the Russians have probably built quite a stronghold in front of the bridge." Looking up and to his left verified his suspicions. "Yes. There they are."

Otto's movement to stand mimicked the movement to sit back down. He decided he would not enter the open and make for the bridge in broad daylight. He would travel again at night.

The Russians were on a tenacious path. They would not be stationed in silence for long. Their numbers would soon be greater, and by morning, Otto surmised, they would lay siege of the bridge. Across the river he could faintly detect German counter movements. Both armies worried him. Both were at heightened emotions for different reasons. The Russians wanted Berlin and the Führer. The Germans wanted not to be caught and pushed into forced labor or, worse yet, just plain shot for being German. Otto slipped back off the edge of the street to find a more secure place to hide. The Russians would surely use this position as a sound angle for cross-fire and advancement.

Otto backtracked to the garden, remembering a large, recently fallen tree branch that lay in contorted shapes. Tall grass intertwined through the dead limbs, further adding to its advantage as a well-concealed hiding place. Yes, this shall do rather nicely. He quietly slid under the tree branch, finding a comfortable position which he could endure until darkness but which also provided a sightline in multiple directions, preferably towards the bridge. However, that idea proved fruitless because once under the limbs, the world seemed to grow dark. Only a few streams of light insisted on reaching the ground, dappling their gaze across Otto's face like the twinkling light of a pale moon's glow upon a shivering lake.

"I have got my fort," Otto chuckled. "And without the smell of rotting rats."

Staring up at the sky, Otto focused on one lone star, only losing its brilliance when a torrid of dark smoke would delay its light. Lovely, he fantasized, for all this ugliness, there is still beauty. Perhaps if Annie and I had never left the stream. Never left our paper boats. Never ran back home. Perhaps if we had built a fort under a huge tree, we could have watched the war pass us by in a glimpse. Perhaps.

With the waning of the sun, cold found its way to life, its last few months of existence still clinging to winter's grasp, still breathing its fate upon the weak and ill-prepared. Otto shivered with the coming of night and sought his jacket from his musette bag. Putting it on proved difficult in his position without causing a stir. Wrestling his arms and contorting his body, he managed with enough fidgeting to get it somewhat on. At that moment, Otto heard a noise, a shuffling sound like leather touching leather as it moved. Someone was coming.

Otto froze, closing his eyes so as not to let the white of his eye draw attention to his position. The noise got louder, and he could hear the voices of the oncoming threat. He was confident he was well hidden, but nothing is safe when overzealous and alert patrols with their hawk-eyed senses were snooping around. Otto could hear them clearly now as they approached his downed tree limb hiding place. His fear grew steadily. They were Russian. Otto knew their personalities were fierce and unwavering but knew little else about them. The soldiers stopped next to Otto.

Otto slowly opened one eye. He could see the silhouettes of five soldiers. Hardly a combat patrol, he thought. While he could not understand their words, it seemed to Otto that the soldiers were relaxed and off their guard. They spoke as if there was no war going on, just a bunch of comrades trading bits of quiet laughter and humor. Well, they're certainly not after me, Otto thought. With this realization, he became more at ease. He was even enjoying their banter and found himself smiling, almost wanting to laugh with them. Four of the soldiers pulled out cigarettes while the other one moved off to relieve himself at a bush. Thank you, God, for not letting that soldier go on me. I smell too much like a sewer as it is.

The Russians continued their conversation, talking in whispers and smoking. The smell of the smoke was recognizable to Otto as it drifted aimlessly to his nose and beyond, swirling and rolling to the effects of the breeze. It was obvious they were German cigarettes, probably raped from their quarry as they lay dead, never again to enjoy such delights. Otto lay still. He kept his one eye open to keep tabs on the soldiers. While he was rather enjoying their company, he started thinking of his exit should he need one, quickly realizing, however, that he was trapped. If detected, it would be his end. Worry shaped his face. They have lingered here far too long. Look over there. That's the war. Go get it. Schnell! Schnell! Get out of here, you rotten Ivan rats. Go destroy Germans!

Suddenly the soldiers reacted to something walking towards them to the north. Otto tilted his head left to observe the abrupt change in the Russians' behavior. The soldiers quickly pulled their rifles from their sides to be at the ready. Another soldier came upon them, obviously of higher rank, and in a quieter yet stern voice commanded the soldiers to fall in. Ah, caught, are we? They're lucky they weren't shot, leaving their posts for a leisurely smoke. The Russian officer pointed at the five soldiers and was not amused by their disappearance. The scolding was easy to understand despite not knowing what was said. He watched the Russian officer turn and walk away.

The five soldiers mumbled to themselves their distaste for the officer as they gathered themselves to leave. The soldier closest to

Otto took one last deep inhale of his half-smoked cigarette and then flicked it into the air towards Otto. It bounced off the tree limbs as it fell, finding its way onto his bare stomach, which became exposed when he had tried to put on his jacket. He flinched at the landed cigarette, still burning red, still burning hot. He grimaced, held in his breath, and clenched his teeth tightly as the burning cigarette carried on its duty. The heat turned to a tingle which then turned to agonizing pain in the matter of seconds. Otto could smell his flesh burning. He tilted his head to the left again to shockingly see the Russian soldiers still present.

Otto closed his eyes tighter until he could hear the muscles of his eyelashes straining. He clenched his hands, grasping the grass and earth below him, digging holes like a mole, ripping at his fingernails. Tears found his eyes and ran down his cheeks in steady beads. His hands were trapped, unable to swipe the cigarette off of him. There were too many branches in the way to do so. He had to bear it. Another test for survival, he thought. Burn here quietly or be found and shot by the Russians. An easy decision.

Otto took one last glance from his fort and found the soldiers had finally left. He quickly wormed his way out from under the grasp of the lifeless branch, freeing himself into the openness of the garden. He immediately brushed the cigarette off and ran to the edge of the garden to a building located in the opposite direction from where the Russian soldiers had come. He sank down with his back against the wall and tore off his jacket and shirt. The wound was terribly grotesque. A button-sized, red cavernous hole oozed a putrid and unknown fluid surrounded by blood. The smell of burnt flesh was nauseating.

Otto quickly pulled an American airman's medic kit from his musette bag. It had been a welcome surprise he had found a few years ago in a B-29 Bomber that had been shot down. He ripped open the package of sulfa powder and, without wincing, sprinkled it on his wound. Gasping for air, Otto tensed his whole body, the pain causing his eyes to twitch and spasm. He reached back into the medic's kit and pulled a bandage roll, quickly unraveling it and wrapping it around his body while still gripped by the pain. He held his breath to stop himself from making any sound, every few seconds or so exhaling in rhythmic grunts to ease his agony. In the darkness, he felt the damp ground searching for his shirt and jacket. The cold was upon him again. He put on his shirt and tucked it deep into his trousers. He slipped into his jacket, which he pulled down as far as it would stretch. And then he stretched it even more. He tilted his head back against the wall and exhaled a breath, his wound throbbing.

Darkness was upon him, and he would stay no longer. Otto slowly sat up and carefully made his way back to the edge of the street in front of the bridge. He moved slowly, readjusting his bandages as he moved. He reached the edge of the building where he had been hours ago. He could see nothing. Maybe the Russians moved beyond the bridge farther into town, he thought, but I would have heard them. Surely, I would have heard them. There would have been a battle, a fight for the bridge. There's always a fight for a bridge. That's what armies do, fight over bridges. The dark was thick and ink in color. Every few seconds, a glimmer from a flame would expose wisps of smoke trailing off its burning origin.

Otto secured his musette bag and satchel and gave his jacket one last stretch. With his first step, he was out into the open, into the night. There were no escape routes and no hiding places or shadows to find solace. He was exposed, which made him terribly uncomfortable. It was uncharacteristically light on the street, and the features and shapes of certain objects became visible. Otto could see and feel the decay and destruction strewn about in random fashion. Bricks, tree limbs, cobblestones, wires, wood, fabric, and a baby's toy doll missing a head lay still and created a barrier to movement. Otto ran directly across the street, not looking back, only forward. He came to the river's edge and without pause followed it towards the north end of the bridge. He used the railing as his guide and for balance.

He could smell the mist off the river, which unleashed wonderful thoughts of his Annie. A smile came to him as he stumbled along awkwardly amidst the rubble, a smile which forced his ever-present agony and painful wound to bury itself somewhere else in his mind.

Otto came to the edge of the bridge and slowly knelt down to scope out his immediate surroundings before making his way to the other side. The quiet was still bothering him. This area, he thought, should be swarming heavily with both armies. The only evidence of war was lazy small arms fire and sporadic cannon reports coming from another front on the other side of the city. Looking south, he could see a number of things burning, wheeled vehicles, either tanks or other armor, but he was unsure. He could not discern from whose army they belonged.

Otto rose from his kneeling position and slowly rounded the corner of the bridge. He was immediately startled, his eyes widened and frozen. His breath exhaling suddenly, but softly, in short bursts of disbelief. There in front of him he found a barrier had been built. Piles and piles of sandbags laying across the bridge entrance, supported by huge steel gates, now blocked his path.

"Curse them. Surely this little entanglement will have guards. Hmm. I don't see any human forms, either standing, sitting, or laying prone in firing position."

Otto crept closer and closer until he came upon the barricade. My word, he thought, not another one of these grotesque steel behemoths. Must they really spend so much time building such contraptions? I must admit that without the correct explosives or heavy equipment, they are quite handy in suppressing the advancement of an army group.

Otto looked through and past the gate quickly while contorting his small, thin frame to breach its web. Such body shapes he had wanted to avoid as they aggravated his continuously throbbing wound. It was a fruitless effort but one with good intent. He squinted his eyes tightly and locked his jaw, anticipating the shot to end his life. None came. Reaching the other side of the barricade, he righted himself and scrambled with hurried pace, keeping to the west side of the bridge. Debris still marred the ground and clumsily altered his movements. He turned his head north, then south, then back, always focused on changes in the landscape as he moved. Anything that seemed different would alert him. Otto turned south and moved quickly across the rest of the bridge. If there were guards present anywhere, he did not care to find their whereabouts any time soon.

Otto came to the end of the bridge and knelt down to scout the immediate surroundings. The crumbled armor in the street that he had noticed from across the river became clear. They were German and in poor condition. Further observation led Otto to recognize German dead littering the ground. The dead were easily dismissed and became one with the earth quickly. No use worrying about them, Otto thought. They can't hurt me now.

The German dead surrounding ruined German armor meant one thing, Otto thought. The Russians had now breached the inner city. But why leave a bridge barricaded and unguarded if they had already passed this way? Why not keep it open to troop movements and heavily guard it? No army liked giving up ground once fought for, unless the Germans had pulled back to defend a more strategic front. As always, Otto was confused and frustrated when trying to decipher military strategies. He looked closer at the dead. They were indeed all German. There were no Russians among them. These men had died from artillery.

Otto whispered softly to himself, deadpanned and distant, his mind in a gaze, thinking, putting the puzzle pieces together. "But that would mean I am in the eye of the storm. I'm in the middle of the initial assault."

The answer soon came in the sudden shrieking of Katyusha rockets with their evil screams terrorizing the skies, pounding the streets and buildings surrounding Otto. Machine gun, tank, and cannon fire arose all at once from a menacing sleep and in harmony similar to the beginning of a Wagnerian overture. Battle cries sounding through the night began their eerie drone, setting the course for the gruesome events to follow. Otto rose from his position. He could feel the glaring eyes of the enemy upon him, knowing at the diminished beats of the artillery assault that this place would be crawling with battle-ready Russians. This was no place to be.

"I think it's time to run."

It was a mere eighty meters to the subway station and the relative safety of the dark passages of the tunnels. Otto secured his belongings and started running down Friedrichstrasse, jumping over the contorted dead and rubble with care not to twist an ankle or turn a knee. He ran like only he knew, deep extended breaths that expanded and contracted his belly and ribs. Otto could feel his wound open and close, the torn skin around it stretching and cracking with each breath, with each painful step enlarging its presence. The showers of artillery shells came to the ground unabated, unchallenged, with the intent of leveling anything human or human made. A new landscape would appear here, one without the laughter and bustle of a once vibrant city street.

Without warning, Otto's run became even more dangerous as the defenders themselves opened their call in answer to the Russian barrage. German infantry seemingly grew from hidden nooks and crannies in the scarred landscape to return with their own allotment of evil and menace. Their MG-42 machine gun fire ripped past Otto from his front, hurling down the middle of the street towards the barricade, the pinging vibrations of the ricochets off the iron gates finding new paths, hopefully fulfilling their purpose to cause death. There would be many. Otto knew the MG-42 machine gun very well, having witnessed its devastation in many battles. Even the bravest of soldiers would cower at its presence. It liked to harvest the living.

Tank and cannon fire soon joined the fray, hoping to sustain an advancement. The German's return call was not as demonic or plentiful, for they had little munitions left at their disposal and even less means for making them, thanks to constant bombing from the Allies. Their fanaticism and superior-minded philosophies would be of little help to them here and now. It would not save them. It was steel, lead, and flesh that were needed most.

Otto continued running. His pace quickening with each landing of a shell burst, with every snap of a bullet across his face. The subway station was in sight just a few breaths away. Otto reached the stairs to the station and skipped every other step as he frantically charged hard to the entrance. Cresting the top of the stairs, he immediately looked for the entrance to Stadtmitte Station, his intended route south under Friedrichstrasse. Catching a glimpse of the sign for Stadtmitte off to his left, Otto suddenly changed his course of direction. He had gathered so much speed that stopping his run to set a new course caused him to skid across the dust and rubble-strewn floor. His arms and hands flailed as he turned his body to the new direction, and without delay, he found his balance and continued his pace. The tunnel down the stairs to the subway platform was blackened, emitting no light and, as of yet, no life. Otto hopped down the stairs, again skipping steps intermittently until he landed on the platform. He stopped, turned around, and saw nothing.

Chapter 4

The odors in the deep darkness of the tunnel were wet and dank. Combined with the unpleasant whiffs of urine and feces, the smell hit Otto with the power of an oncoming train. The continued throbbing from his abdomen shut off all worries, the least being rotten air. While still at a quickened pace, he looked up and down the tunnel for movement, and seeing none, he jumped off the platform onto the soft gravel of the tracks.

Otto's newest threat was the third, electrified rail in the middle of the two tracks upon which the train cars rode. From pure sight, there was no telling if the tracks were taking current. Running down the tunnel in the dark without knowing would be unwise, he thought. He would need to know. Looking around the track area, he searched for anything he could use to test the track for an electrical current. It was too dark to recognize anything without light. He started walking south away from the platform and down the tunnel, and to his good fortune, he happened upon a small bit of wire encased in its plastic cover. Quickly, he knelt to the ground while slinging the musette bag from his back. He pulled out a pair of small pliers and began stripping the casing from the wire. Sweat caught up to him as droplets began their decent down the sides of his face, taking dirt and grime with them and creating lines of whiter skin. The tickle on his cheek caused by the drips alerted Otto to their presence. Without pausing his work, he wiped the beads of sweat from existence, smearing dirt across his face. A whiff of air from the tunnel found him, and the coolness meeting his damp skin caused a welcome chill.

His work completed, Otto gathered his things, stood up, and carefully placed the right end of the wire on the outside of the first rail next to the platform. By placing the left end of the wire on the middle rail, he would cause a short, a few electrical sparks, and he would know. He dropped the left end of the wire onto the middle rail while taking a step back and shielding his eyes with his arm from any glare. Nothing. All was silent and still. Darkness prevailed. Otto moved his arm from his eyes and, with a smile, dropped his tense shoulders and took a step farther south. Suddenly, Otto froze. He realized the noise from his step was not of his making. The sound happened before his foot hit the ground. Again, another sound of pieces of gravel grinding against each other. Then a light flashed into Otto's eyes, blinding him.

"Stoi! Stoi!" Otto knew this Russian word well. It was the only word he needed to understand. The pace behind the flashlight's owner quickened. Otto could see the light move up and down, blurring with streaks like a shooting star as the enemy approached.

"No, I won't be stopping," Otto murmured. Without hesitation he sprang to life and bolted down the subway tunnel following in cadence with the railroad ties that lay just inches above the gravel, giving him firmer ground upon which to run. In front of him, he could see the flashlight's glow wandering about him, trying to rein him in. Shots rang out and echoed through the dark as their misses ricocheted down the tunnel. Otto moved with agility, running left to right within the confines of the middle and right rail, which gave him enough wiggle room to help him avoid a bullet's path. He could hear that ever present, hollow crack the bullets made as they passed by him.

Otto turned to look behind him, and in that instant, arms lifted him from out of the darkness, pulling him to the ground and dragging him into the walls of the tunnel. He could feel the locked grip around his wrists as he tried to regain his stance to no avail. He could not resist. He was exhausted from all his running. Whatever it was, it had him. Otto could hear a breath and disturbed grunts and determined it was a man. The man pulled him into a small room, let him go, and crouched beside him, putting his hand over Otto's mouth.

"Shush, my boy. Be still," the man whispered.

Echoing through the corridor from which they had come, Otto could hear the Russians run by without stopping. He was relieved, but now felt he was confronted with greater danger.

The man slowly removed his firm grip from Otto's mouth. "You are a squirmy little devil with great speed. I nearly lost my footing as I grabbed you amidst your run. I wasn't sure if I had been hit by a train or not."

Otto wiped the saliva from his mouth that had gathered from being held quiet. Breathing from his mouth moved to his nose, his breaths slowing from short bursts to calmer rhythms. He said nothing.

The man stood up and walked away from Otto to the other side of the room. He lit a small candle and sat down facing Otto without so much as a glance at him. "Running from the Ivans? Yes? Seems odd a small boy would create so much interest. Stolen something, have you? Hmm, but then, this is war. Anything moving is a target during such unsettling times, I suppose."

The man lifted his head and smiled at Otto. "Do not be frightened, my young boy. You are quite safe in here. I should know. I'm a train conductor. Well, I was at one time. Nobody knows these tunnels better than I, I should think. But, please excuse me. With all this excitement, I think I forgot to close the outer door to our little hiding place."

The man rose to his feet, slipped past Otto, and vanished down a long, narrow corridor. Otto's eyes followed the man until he left the room. The light from the candle flickered and formed strange shadows in all directions upon the walls. The room, he noticed, was small, about fifteen meters long and three meters wide, and of solid concrete with no windows. Like the main subway tunnels, it was damp and reeked of muddy water. Otto chuckled, as the room reminded him of the Führerbunker. Is there nothing beautiful underground? In the corner there looked to be blankets and other personal belongings of the man. It was obvious to Otto he had not frequented this place long and was always on the move, like himself.

Otto's stomach growled and offered other strange noises. He pulled his musette bag to his lap and took out a tin of the German iron rations he had found in the garden. "These are the army's infamous 'Iron Rations.' For once, I hope it's either pork, turkey, or beef, and please let it be the hard bread instead of the biscuit they sometimes put in here, which is always stale and soggy. Let me see. What have we here?" He carefully tried to focus his eyes to read the tin's label in the candlelight. "Hmm, horse meat. Oh, the bad luck of it all. What are the odds?" Otto began prying open the top of the tin with his pocket knife, peeling back the top. "Well, they may say it looks like pork, but it doesn't taste very much like pork."

No sooner had the stranger left when he suddenly returned, closing the thick, wooden door to the room behind him. He took up the same spot against the wall in front of Otto. "All secure," he confidently announced. "Now where were we? Ah, yes. Your running, or was it our hiding place I was explaining? No mind. Perhaps we can start at the beginning as we have not been properly introduced. Good then. My name is Ekkehard Bauer, son of Dietrich Bauer of the South End. Now, I beg you, don't go calling me Herr Bauer, my new friend. Be gone with formalities. There's little room for them in the deep, dark places of this world. I insist you address me as 'Ekkehard.' I come from a family of good, strong, ancient Germanic names I am told. Ekkehard means 'brave and hardy,' which I suppose is very fitting for the life I have led for the past few years. So tell me, my young friend, who might you be?"

Otto put the tin of horse meat he was eating down and worked to swallow so he could return Ekkehard's question in kind. His wound was stinging him, and he thought it would be better to see to its status first. Otto tilted his head down, unbuttoned his jacket, and pulled his shirt from his trousers. The wound had become reddened and swollen from movement and neglect. "I mean not to be rude, Herr Bauer, I mean Ekkehard, but this small wound nags at me and needs attention."

Otto felt at ease with his new friend despite his unknown situation. Ekkehard's eccentricities and bumbling manner were a far cry from and a welcome behavior compared to what he had experienced from the German High Court. He placed his right hand on the small dressing caked with dried, grotesque fluid and blood, while his left hand kept his clothing away. He took a brief breath and winced in pain as he pulled the dressing from his skin, the sticky fluid creating web-like strands as he pulled the bandage away. "My word. Unbelievable how in such a short period of time a wound can become such a mess."

Otto looked up at Ekkehard with half a smile as he pulled a new dressing from his musette bag and began attending his wound. "Don't fret, my friend. I, too, have seen harder times than this. I see in your face a gloomy sadness and pity for me, a young boy not yet of a man's age. Well, I tell you, I have seen men four times my age break, crying as a baby embraced to its mother's own bosom, when tormented with such wounds. No, don't look to me with pity. What we don't share in age, we share in mind," Otto offered with strength.

Ekkehard's face was sullen as he realized he was caught staring at Otto. A false, forced smile cracked his pursed lips with pity and forgiveness. "I am sorry my eyes became fixed and gave to pity," he said with a soft voice. "While we are at war and nothing is normal, I often live as though it is, with some sense of dignity and respect. No. I do not pity you, my young friend. No. Sorry. I do not know you as my own. I pity the idea that a young boy must live in such a world at all, that you should see such times. Where are the dreams of children? That is the travesty of humankind."

"True," Otto smiled and nodded his head. "But," he continued with his philosophy, "no matter boy or girl, man or woman, the real question before us is, shall we choose life or death? There is but one choice."

"Yes, my young boy. There is only one choice. It is with life we must put our hopes. In choosing life, all in the world will return to peace and show us its grace."

"Yes," Otto whispered. And Annie will be with me again.

"So my dear boy, I still do not know your name. If we are to keep conversing about such deep, important matters, it would seem fitting. Don't you think?"

"Yes. With all my apologies, Ekkehard, I was somewhere else in mind, and this nasty wound doesn't help. Forgive me." Otto finished attending his wound and moved to tucking in his shirt and buttoning his jacket. He caught Ekkehard again staring, but this time at the tin of unfinished horse meat next to Otto. "Are you hungry? Here. Have a tin." Otto removed another tin from his musette bag, read the label out of curiosity, and handed it to Ekkehard. "Hmm. Seems that luck is with you today. It's turkey."

Ekkehard smiled in receiving Otto's gift, reviewing the label. "But does it taste like turkey?"

"No. Not really." They looked at each other silently for a moment and then began laughing, their echoes warming the damp, barren room.

Otto picked up his own tin from the dank concrete floor where he had set it. He stared into it to guide his finger as a makeshift fork. "My name is Otto Kaufmann, son of Solomon Kaufmann. I live on Nord Strasse on the west side off of the River Spree. I have two brothers, Yoram and Samuel, but I have not seen them in years. I haven't seen or heard from anybody in years. Poppa was a merchant and operated a large store filled with many wonderful things." He paused and licked his finger, no longer caring that he was eating horse meat. "Until war took us away, far away."

Ekkehard's face turned solemn. Immediately, he knew Otto was Jewish. His name told him much. He had heard the rumors about some of the atrocities but did not know of their truth. Ekkehard stared at Otto, surveying him as they both sat and returned to their food. "You wear the uniform of the Hitler Youth. You carry their bags and eat their food. There is something strange at work here, my boy. There is more to you than the simple son of a merchant."

Otto quickened his swallow, looked up at Ekkehard, and smiled, if but for a minute. "There is truth to your observations. Seems we who run all share the same traits, quick observations being the most important."

"Ah, yes. And running being the next."

"Yes, that's how I came to all of this, by running very, very fast."

"A messenger of the German Army, are you? Indeed, that would explain your swift speed in the subway tunnel." Ekkehard looked at Otto with suspicion but was kind and respectful. "Well now, my young Otto, a Jewish boy running the errands of the German Army? That is a great feat."

"I am not sure what being Jewish has to do with it, but yes, I am the personal messenger of the Führer and his High Court. I am of the allegiance and honored service of Reichsleiter Bormann. I am returning from an important affair and must get back to the Führerbunker to report of my mission, failed as it is."

Ekkehard was astonished and overwhelmed by Otto's words and became silent. His half-chewed bite of turkey fell to the floor in crumbles as he changed focus, his lips becoming still, unable to hold his food. He trembled noticeably as he whispered, "The Führer?" His face quickly became angered and hard. "Tell me of the Führer.

Where is he? Does he live? This is all of his making. He is a wretched being, foul and twisted is he. He is lost in beliefs of ancient farcical mythologies and heretic magic, a mind gone mad with the blood of us all. I wish he comes to a million hells upon his death."

Otto watched as Ekkehard's enraged face contorted to many shapes in projection of his anger. It did not startle Otto. He'd seen this before.

"I never am allowed to see the Führer, my dear friend Ekkehard. Only am I to run his tasks. I do not know of him. I only hear his outbursts and demonic screams and protestations echoing through the halls into the depths of the Führerbunker. For me, that's close enough."

"Ah, yes. A broken man then is he, cowering in the wells deep in the earth. Then hell is surely upon him."

Ekkehard paused, his head dropping down, his neck straining to keep it poised. After a moment, he brought his head to bear, a tear running down his right eye following the lines of age, the candlelight announcing its travel. Gaining his composure, he spoke softly, hurt following his words as they found Otto's ears. "Father was a prominent banker. He was a good man. Came from nothing. Worked hard and built his world around him with his bare hands, never letting age or time slow his course. He fathered three handsome sons. Now don't laugh, Otto." He pointed and shook his finger in jest. "I count myself a handsome lad."

Otto chuckled openly for a moment before he could hide it.

"And I received very good marks in school. A math wizard I was."

Ekkehard took a shallow breath and slowly exhaled to ease the passing of emotion. Otto sat quietly, clinging to Ekkehard's every word. He could feel Ekkehard's breath reach him in the cool damp confinement of the room. There was no escaping such a release, nor did Otto want to.

Ekkehard reached into his tin, scraping the sides, withdrawing a small fork's full. "Father schooled us well, and we took to fine universities. I married. Herta was her name. A wonderful, stoic, and beautiful wife was she. I fathered two of my own. Sons, they were. Gentlemen with a passion for sport and the hunt. Father had a chalet near a lake, high in the Bavarian Alps. We would visit often. Summer days were spent enjoying fog-choked mornings fishing off the dock, only to retire in the afternoons to the splendors of warm alpine breezes. Mother baked her very best apple cakes and pastries, which everyone in the valley miles away could smell. Even amidst Germany's uncertain years, life was good.

"The one thing you can always count on, my dear Otto, is life changing. War came to my family too. Father was forced to exploit his bank for the malicious wares of the Third Reich. They destroyed his world, extorting, stealing, and cheating for a government built upon lies and deceit. Germany and her people became their puppet for the deeds of a warped few. Father died, saddened from misery borne from such darkness. My boys, also taken. Stripped from me. Forced off from life's path. Forced by the German war machine to the Russian front, never to come home. With them, their mother vanished as well. Her heart could not bear it. I am alone, Otto."

Otto continued his silence and gaze upon Ekkehard. He had nothing to offer. His own tear found his cheek as his reflections returned to his neighborhood, to Neumann's Bakery and his little Annie. I hope her heart can bear it, he prayed. Otto's attention returned to Ekkehard. "No, Ekkehard. You are not alone. You have me."

Ekkehard smiled softly at Otto, pausing with a slight chuckle, realizing the realities of life. "Ah yes. I do for now, my son, but you must be off in time. Your mission, it is of concern to you. It shows through your eyes. Indeed, you wear it thin. Tell me of these missions, Otto. What does the High Court of Herr Bormann thrust upon you?"

Otto wiped his tear and began his story, a small sniffle turning to words. "As I was saying, Ekkehard, I run fast. My family and I were deported from our home to a wretched and miserable place far,

far away. Poppa said we were in Poland. I remember studying about this country in world geography class, but I didn't like my teacher so I never paid him much mind. So, my knowledge of this country is thin. My teacher smelled like my grandmother. Funny I think about that, but I always knew when grandma was visiting because I could smell her. It was a weird, nasty odor, like she was rotting." Otto began giggling, his stomach caving in and out to find breath for his laughter. Ekkehard shared his smile which made his eyes squint and look shut.

"I would peek out from my room, look down the hall in our house, and see where she was. Grandma would always come to me, scrunch down, her bones squeaking, and move to pinch my cheeks, squealing out loud, 'Shayna Punim!' I had to bear it as her 'pretty face' and smile politely, but always I made a sour glare when her back turned. Momma would take notice and scowl at me, pointing her finger frantically. She knew I was up to no good. Poppa would always walk in at that moment and see Momma's face. Then he would quickly look at me in one graceful move. He'd scold me when Momma was looking, and as soon as she turned away, shaking her head in disgust, Poppa would hunch down and laugh with me. Poppa would pinch his nose in jest, making light of Grandma's odor. Always at that moment, Momma would abruptly turn back around and Poppa and I quickly sprang to attention like innocent kittens that have just tipped over their milk bowls. Momma would give us that scowl again and furiously shake her finger once more, moving it from me to Poppa and then back to me, doing this many times at the speed of a gazelle running from its pursuer. Momma was very smart. She knew."

Otto's smile and laugh quickly folded, his thoughts returning to a darker place. "I don't know what became of grandma. She never made the march from our home to the trucks. Never made it to the train. Poppa never said why. I have not seen her since this all began. Funny, I miss her smell now. It would be a welcome bed of roses on a warm summer morning compared to the filth I've been suffering."

Otto continued his story without missing the place from where he had stopped. "It was called a ghetto, Ekkehard. Yes, that was it. Well, at least that's what we were told by the German officers. Yes, I can play the events in my mind and see it clearly. It was called the Lodz Ghetto, after the town in Poland. Poppa never spoke of the ghetto, but I was curious about this barbed wire trap we were placed in so I kept my ears open during my time there. They say women are chatty, never keeping secrets, but I've found men in small groups do an amazing amount of chatter themselves. I learned many things from the streets, some of which I don't quite understand, but you may, Ekkehard. One thing I did learn was that it had been decided by the Germans that the Jews would cause a problem politically for the new German State. Under orders by someone, I'm not sure who, they conceived a temporary plan, which declared all Jews would be removed from Germany until a permanent solution could be found. Methodically, and I might add swiftly, Jews were moved into these ghettos in the German occupied territories. Poland was the biggest and most convenient location for the ghettos because it shared a border with Germany, making transportation and setup of camps easier. There were other rumors swirling about, talk of permanent camps of terrible evil. I have never seen or been to one, so I am not sure of their existence. What really escapes me is why they have so much hate towards my people."

Otto cleared his throat, swallowing a rough piece of meat from his iron ration, helping it down with a gulp of water from his beaten canteen. He offered a drink to Ekkehard, who smiled and took it graciously from Otto. "Be careful, Ekkehard. This canteen has seen many battles and leaks from the seams on the top."

Otto leaned back against the cold, dusty concrete wall and continued his story. "After we got off the truck that they stuffed us into like herded swine, we were led to a train car. It looked like we were being stuffed again. I had never seen this train station. It was far from our neighborhood. There were lots of people like us there.

Young and old alike. All you could ever hear were the soldiers yelling at people. No one spoke back. Those that did were shot and left to be trampled by the lines of people getting onto the train cars. It was Annie's and my turn to get onto the car. Annie is like your Herta, Ekkehard, but probably younger than her. Poppa picked us both up one at a time and handed us to Herr Neumann, who was already in the car. It was dark and smelled like horses inside.

"Annie and I shuffled farther into the car and found my brothers and Annie's momma propped against the wall in the back corner. We learned very quickly it's best to have a wall at one side so you can lean on it to rest and not fall down. Falling down is dangerous. You won't be able to get back up, and no one will help you, that I can tell you, Ekkehard. Poppa helped Momma in, and when she stepped aboard, her long dress caught on a splintered piece of wood on the outside of the train car and tore it almost off her. She leaned over expressionless, seemingly without a care, and tore the dress, further continuing the same travel route of the rip. She had a short dress now. Poppa hopped on and came to us. We were a family again. The train car was stuffed once more, and we were forced to stand again. No one disobeyed that order from the guards. Like I said, falling down is dangerous. You get squished like a toad.

"The door of the car started to move, rolling rusted steel wheels that squeaked and squawked as they gained momentum, concluding with a terrible crash. This was followed by further vicious noises of the latches grinding, forcing painful metallic sounds to our ears as they were swiftly brought to a locked and fixed position. There were small half-inch cracks between the wooden wall boards on the side of the train cars that let a little fissure of light through. This was the only piece of life to the outside world we would see for a few days. After waiting about an hour, the train began to huff and puff. The iron behemoth roared to life with its imprisoned guests, lurching forward with winter's chill teasing us. There was much cold yet to come.

"Annie, my brothers, and I were against the wall of the train car with our parents surrounding us, cocooning us from the other passengers. There was little talking but much to talk about. I kept remembering that my Poppa had told me 'not to make a sound.' Annie and I would play with the light coming through the cracks in the wall boards. It was a hide-and-go-seek sort of game. We were always good with making up the silliest of games out of nothing. I would rise up, my head coming into the light. She would have her eyes closed and then open them all of a sudden to try and catch sight of my eyes. I was slow in that regard, and she would catch me without much effort. I was still a faster runner than she, though. Well, Annie would snicker every time she caught me, which in turn caused a strong grasp of Poppa's hand on my shoulder. It was reassuring to know he was there, still standing, but I wished for once I could have fun. I never was on a train before. It should be fun. Perhaps one day it will be different."

Otto quieted for a moment before remembering that Ekkehard had mentioned he was a train conductor. "Tell me of the trains, Ekkehard. What are they like?"

"My dear son, I was a subway conductor. I have never operated a train such as the one you were on, but yes, I know of them. Large steam locomotives, they were. However, the tunnels and subway cars I do know about. It was quite exhilarating dashing along in the dark, passing other trains, hearing the whipping sounds as they passed, waving to my fellow conductors. I always felt a sense of power, a kind of responsibility to my passengers to ensure they arrived safely and on time. It was great joy greeting the same folks day in and day out, sharing stories of lives lived. I got to know some passengers quite well. Frau Beck would bring me treats often, and not to offend her, you know, I had to eat them because she would always ask how they tasted. I fancied them well, indeed. However, Herta started to notice my waistline enlarging, and well, that got me into a bit of trouble."

Otto laughed along with Ekkehard as he shared his stories, for it interrupted the painful ones of his own.

"Well then, Herta quickly monitored my food portions, but to frustrating results. I kept eating Frau Beck's pastries and cakes. Sometimes, my dear Otto, it is difficult having a kind heart. Just remember, somewhere, somehow, someone is always going to feel hurt. You certainly cannot please everybody, but I had a plan. I eventually had to tell Frau Beck I could not receive her treats anymore. She asked me why, and I said for her to look at my tummy. She looked down and gasped, astonished with embarrassment, blushing as red as a turnip. 'My, oh my. Herr Bauer, you do fancy my sweets. Yes, perhaps I need to show a bit more restraint.' With that, I was off the hook. I watched her walk away, and when I was convinced she was out of sight, I reached under my shirt and pulled out a pillow from my stomach. I hadn't realized I had an audience of passengers and colleagues, and an uproar of laughter was enjoyed by all. I frowned and walked away, but I couldn't help but chuckle to myself."

Otto began laughing at Ekkehard's story. He enjoyed his little visit with him, a much welcome stop. "I should thank you for saving me back there on the tracks, Ekkehard. I apologize for not offering my appreciation sooner."

"There are no apologies needed, young Otto. In all honesty, it happened quite unintended. I was merely having a look before I was to journey forth. It's very dangerous down here these days. The Russians are losing their fear of the tunnels, moving in larger groups and shaking us trolls of the underworld out. Although, I now wonder who the trolls really are. So tell me, Otto, what happened beyond your train ride?"

"Yes, Ekkehard. I will finish my story. Forgive me. Sometimes it's hard to share the memories." Otto took a breath and continued.

"The trains moved very slowly, which was a welcome event. The crisp, October air was just cold enough to be a nuisance. We huddled to stay warm, Poppa always embracing me close under his overcoat.

Momma did the same with my brothers. The soldiers stopped the train a few times during our trip to let us out for a bathroom break. I don't know why they did this because we just relieved ourselves in the trains. There were cracks between the floor boards, and we just went through them. However, it's not easy to do when standing and moving in a train. It didn't all hit its mark. The smell was nauseating at best, but the stench kept you awake; it kept you breathing and fighting for life.

"During one of our stops, we witnessed a few soldiers taking some of the elderly out into the field. They stood them up a hundred meters or so from the train. They fiddled with their rifles for a moment, smiling and chuckling back and forth to each other, mumbling in a cavalier manner. They raised their rifles, took aim, and fired. The people fell lifeless to the ground, dust whisking off their clothes as the bullets found their mark. I saw a bullet pass clear through one of them, a smallish, frail old man not five feet tall. A puff of dirt shot into the air from behind him farther down the field. They did this event a few times with different people, but mostly they were the elderly. Whispering to Poppa, I asked what they were doing. He said they were sighting in their rifles so that their aim was always deadly. I swallowed hard when hearing this. A warped thought immediately came to my mind. If they really wanted a smaller target to practice their aim, a child would work rather splendidly. The thought forced me deeper into the warmth of Poppa's body, and I pulled his overcoat tighter over me.

"From here, we came to a small train station somewhere. I didn't know if we were in Germany anymore. We disembarked and were immediately scuttled into a make-shift camp with crude shelters made of nothing more than wood logs strewn together to form one large room with bunks four high built into both sides of the left and right walls. There was no fireplace, fire pit, or anything of the sort to give warmth. The shelter had no door and only a poorly constructed roof to keep in whatever warmth there might have been.

The ground was barren, a combination of worn dirt and mud, frozen into eerie, contorted shapes, like thousands of people, their arms raised, screaming desperately for aid. As it turned out, this was to be our home for the next few months. Poppa had overheard we were in a temporary camp until our final home could be finished. To me, this didn't seem as pleasant as it sounded. I was thoroughly convinced wherever we were to go, it wouldn't be better.

"Food was scarce. We were given water, and if we were lucky, we would perhaps see a few barley beans floating up to the surface. We were allotted some bread, but it was always stale and moldy in places so I gave it away to another person I did not know near our bunk. Poppa scolded me for doing this. I was shocked by his behavior. Poppa was always a very gentle and giving man. There was a time he would give our neighbors, people who had less then we, free supplies from our store without so much as a thought. His heart was turning. I was frightened for him. You know, Ekkehard, I came to the understanding that Poppa was learning, like I have all these years, to survive and he was teaching us to live. All this time, he understood that the less I knew, the better I would be in handling situations. That is why he asked me to be quiet from the moment this all began. He taught me to learn through observation, to observe the soldiers instead of asking them questions that would get me killed. Poppa was very intelligent. I am alive now because of him."

Ekkehard sat listening to Otto's story with great intensity, his eyes opening large to some of Otto's words, closing to others that he wished he hadn't heard. He raised Otto's canteen high in the air as if saluting. "Here's to honorable men and great fathers. May they be in peace wherever they may be." Ekkehard took a sip from the canteen and passed it back to Otto.

"Here, here!" Otto added as he sipped in salutation, pausing to swallow. "Yes, and may they be somewhere warmer than we are." They both had a laugh together, each deep in their own minds, yet seemingly thinking as one.

Otto continued his thoughts, turning them to spoken words. "Well, it wasn't too long before we were on a train again. However, this train was of a different type. It did not have a roof. It was early February and blistering cold. I had never felt such cold. Luckily for us, the trip did not last long. After a short day's journey, we were there. Our final place. The Lodz Ghetto. I was correct in my assumption, Ekkehard.

"Yes? And what was that my dear friend?"

"This place was no better than what we had just left. We were forced off the trains and moved into the street. I'll never forget the sounds of the thumping feet on the wood planks as we left the station, thousands of rhythmic beats getting increasingly louder, as if our own hearts were resonating their fears and doubts. All around us, ghostly eyes stared into our souls through high, barbed wire fences that cut them off from the streets. We were new here. Welcome was thin as we made our way. Voices in command echoed, followed by shrills and shrieks. A quick look left and a man was being beaten and tormented. A look right and a group of police were pinning another man to a wall. The buildings overhead were dark and in shadow, as if they had never seen the warming light of a summer's day. There was great suffering here, and it was imbedding itself into my bones.

"We walked for a number of blocks, how many I cannot guess, until we were moved into a large building that was once a school. There was little learning and nurturing going on here now. We were put into a classroom with many other families, and there we waited, huddled together on the floor with no wall behind us like on the train. It was cold and damp in this room with a little light on the ceiling that flickered on and off. It bothered me terribly seeing that light do that. It made me think that some of us would not survive, the light going off, but some would, the light coming on. The light staying off for too long frightened me. I wished it to stay on. I sometimes hated how my mind played tricks on me, creating worlds where there couldn't quite possibly be one. Annie sat next to me, and we would whisper to each other often, playing in those worlds. I told her about the light, and she giggled, calling me a silly boy. Then the tight hand of Poppa on my shoulder came to bear, and again we would be quiet.

"All of a sudden, the door came crashing open and four men in uniforms came in and started randomly grabbing people from the room. These were not soldiers but were, I later learned, our own people. They were Jews formed into police groups armed with rubber batons to keep peace and order in the ghetto. Behind them were other uniformed men, the German police called Schupo, armed and ready to oppose any rioting. The people that these Jewish police took were mostly the elderly and a few children that I noticed seemed to be without parents. Poppa huddled us closer, covering us under his overcoat, and it looked as if he were a big, fat man. The Jewish police walked through us briskly, choosing an older woman sitting next to us. Those chosen were all hurried out of the room. We never saw them again.

"I was terribly hungry, and I could hear my stomach grumbling again. I was getting used to being hungry, so I let my mind wander elsewhere. The outside world was quiet, but inside echoes from people coughing and fidgeting careened off the walls surrounding us. Hours later, two Schupo officers entered the room. One of them asked for the fathers of all the families to come forward. Poppa and Herr Neumann looked at each other in a dead stare, alarmed at the possibilities. Poppa put his index finger over his mouth and puckered his lips as his head found us all in obedience. He slowly got up with confidence and authority, fixed his overcoat, and sidestepping us, made his way to the men at the door. Herr Neumann followed in kind. Neither looked back at us. Momma kept her straight gaze with no emotion as she slowly pulled my brothers and I closer now to her. Annie found the security of her momma's embrace as well. Poppa and Herr Neumann left the room with the men, and all was quiet again, except for the coughing. Cold crept over me, and I missed Poppa's overcoat. Momma tried her best to shield her bare legs but without success. She shivered inside, and I could sense her agony through her eyes. Momma was strong. She hid her pain from us well.

"Night came upon us, and a pale moon began its show in the sky, offering glimmers of light through the dust-caked windows. The ceiling light had since gone out. It too could not face the cold and succumbed to silence. It would flicker no more. It was eerie sitting in quiet, looking through and across the room at the other people imprisoned here with us. The moon's glow defined the saddened shapes of human figures hunched over and highlighted a captured frown in despair. I moved off from Momma to see where Annie was and found her still with her momma. I whispered in her ear to see if she could play. She looked at me like I was out of my mind. 'Otto Kaufmann, I am freezing. How are we to play in this dark and dreary, cold and nasty place? Sometimes I just don't know about you silly boys.'

"I told her, 'Well, if we play, then perhaps we'll ward off this cold and create some heat.' When I looked around the room, however, it seemed play would not be a very welcome guest. I scurried back to Momma with Annie scowling at me as I made my way. Fine, I thought to myself. What troubled me more was that I thought Annie was becoming hardened like Poppa. At that realization, I was determined not to be. Although, as I look at myself now, Ekkehard, it appears I have failed. Hardened are my mind, heart, and soul."

Ekkehard nodded as he scraped the bottom of his iron ration with his fork, finding the last remnants of food. "There are many things in this world, young Otto, that you can control. As well, there are many things of which you have not the power to control. Take control of the things you can."

Ekkehard smiled softly and looked back into his can, searching for one last bite. There was none. He sighed in disappointment and set the can to the ground next to him. "Hardened? Or set to survive?

These are choices you have made. I am sure after the world has righted itself, 'Otto the Playmaker' will certainly choose once again to return." Ekkehard paused to put his fork back into his own musette bag and gave Otto a reassuring wink. "Trust in my words, Otto."

Suddenly, there came a disturbance from down the corridor by way of the subway tunnel. Otto's head turned with alarm, and then he froze, leaving his ears to discern the cause of the sound. Otto whispered to Ekkehard as he slowly rose from his seated position. "Boots."

"Gather your things, my son," Ekkehard commanded as he came to his feet. "We have lingered here far too long. Your story, as interesting as it is, will have to be delayed. We must move off from this place. It is not safe. Soon the Russians will have overrun us, if indeed they have not already."

Otto gained his stand and secured his belongings. His thoughts soon turned back to his mission. "I must make my way to Stadtmitte Station then off to Kaiserhof. My end is the Führerbunker. I must bid you goodbye, dear Ekkehard. This cannot be your path. I am sorry."

Ekkehard turned to Otto, concealing a thought of disappointment he did not want to share. "Then until we meet again, my dear boy. Now, quickly, follow me into the tunnel and turn right for the Stadtmitte station. Once you arrive, do not go up to the main station. Pass the Stadtmitte platform and stay right. This will bring you to the tunnel heading towards Kaiserhof station."

Otto nodded to Ekkehard's directions without speaking. Ekkehard loaded his small bag and made for their exit. Slowly, he turned the cold iron-cast handle and tugged open the thick, wooden door a slight crack. The corridor was empty from this view, and the sounds they had heard dissipated with distance. Ekkehard gently waved to Otto as if he were petting a kitten to move behind him. Otto took a step clumsily, kicking over the tin from which he had been eating. The can tipped to its side and rolled across the room until a distortion in the floor ended its path. The shrill-laden, tinny sounds echoed from the room, spilling into the corridor.

Ekkehard sighed and took in a deep breath, slowly letting it out as he closed and opened his eyes. "Quietly, my boy."

Otto shook his head with anger. I have let down my guard, he thought to himself. Foolish. This will get me killed, all this resting and storytelling. As if anybody cares for me. No more, Otto promised himself. No more.

Otto stepped next to Ekkehard, and both moved from the room. They made their way down the corridor and passed the second door to the tunnel, Otto watching intently each placement of his step, each step a reminder of his wound, still an ever-present burden. Ekkehard came to the meeting of the corridor and the tunnel and paused for a moment. He slowly reached his head beyond the raw, concrete wall just enough to glimpse down the tunnel to his left, then right. All was clear. Quiet was in his ears, except for the echo of the rhythmic plops of dripping water disturbing the calm and making their way to the puddles they had created. Ekkehard turned to Otto with a reassuring grin as he took a step into the tunnel.

"Stoi!" yelled aloud from the dark as bright beams flashed, announcing the presence of their owners one at a time, both high and low, surrounding Ekkehard. Arms lurched forward from the dark, emitting tense-clenched fingers that grasped Ekkehard. He lost his footing and fell backwards as the stomping of boots, tearing of fabric, and crashing of wooden and metal weapons all came to a crescendo as the struggle grew large.

"Run!" Ekkehard yelled into the dark as he was being pulled to the ground against his will. "Run, my boy!"

Otto stepped into the tunnel, and turning around to look for Ekkehard, he paused and lost his ground, tripping as he moved backwards. Shots rang out into the tunnel, but their hollow snaps did not pass him. The shots were not directed at him. The struggle had deterred the soldiers from noticing him. With the cry of the shots, he screamed, "Ekkehard!" There was no reply. The Russian soldiers quickly changed attention and flashed their lights down the tunnel, offering a glimpse of Otto's bright, opened, and paralyzed eyes.

"Stoi! Stoi!" the soldiers demanded, regaining their presence and starting to chase Otto. Their speed was no match. Otto quickly righted his heading, and without delay, he gained his stride in full as he tore down the tracks again, using the rail as his guide. A number of shots were called upon to find their mark but innocently passed over Otto's head. The rifle fire hardly startled Otto. It was but a firecracker to his mind.

Otto ran straight without letup for what seemed hours. Farther down the track to his right, he could see a somewhat brighter area. This must be the Stadtmitte stop, he thought. Still running, he slowed his pace to help keep his eyes more focused on his nearing objective. As he approached, he forced himself to control his heavy breathing and quiet his arrival. His lungs obeyed, but the gnawing, throbbing of his wound did not.

Otto stopped and knelt on one knee. He quickly looked behind him, but nothing gave chase. He looked back towards the brighter area to allow for more observation. He noticed a strange shadow in the dim light of the station stop on the platform. It was coming from the stairway that led to the station entrance above. This shadow was moving, he thought as he scrunched down a bit further to the ground listening.

"Soldiers," Otto whispered to himself. Friend or foe, I will not wait to learn. Ekkehard was correct in his judgment. It's much safer not to rise above to the main station.

Otto's head dropped in pity as he remembered Ekkehard. Poor Ekkehard. What will become of him? He is dead, I fear. Those first shots were not for me. I rather fancied that silly old man. Otto lifted his head, regained his composure, and fixed his eyes upon the platform. The shadows had moved again. They grew larger, growing to the point of suddenly revealing two soldiers. Russian sentries, Otto thought to himself, men left behind to guard the rear of a larger patrol. They must have come from the main station above. Perhaps they heard the shots? No matter. That's too bad for me. I can't delay here.

Otto slowly began to move as he lifted himself to his feet but kept low, which forced him to move like a duck as he waddled beneath the platform that passed in front of the guards. Oh, this is just the silliest thing I have ever done to elude my enemy, he thought. Annie would be laughing hysterically if she were to see me now. He could hear the soldiers mumbling to each other quietly but could not hear what they were saying. He paid no mind to it as he couldn't understand Russian anyway. He could hear their breaths, inhales and exhales. The smell of their cigarette smoke found Otto's nose, and he determined the cigarettes were of German make. The spoils of war were being enjoyed, he thought. When do such spoils come my way? I should think not for quite some time, if ever.

Otto quickly came to the end of the platform and rose to his normal height. He took one last glance behind him and continued his pace, quickening his breathing to support another swift run. Just a few more meters to the Kaiserhof station and I will be but a few minutes from the Führerbunker. His run in full, Otto could not help but think of what action he should take if the Kaiserhof station was overrun with Russian soldiers. He had no alternate plan. He could not go back. He pressed forward, hoping it was without the enemy.

His arrival at the Kaiserhof station went unnoticed. With the station stop in near sight, he slowed again to observe the platform before climbing up from the track. Great, Otto chuckled to himself. It's quiet again. I am very mistrusting of all this quiet. Better to have sound. Then at least I can devise a plan for how to get around it. It's always the not knowing that gets me into trouble. But up I must go. Otto grasped the edge of the concrete platform, and with a slight hop, he pulled himself up onto it. Dust, debris, and the detritus of the floor greeted him. Seems the janitorial staff is quite remiss as of late. I shall have a word with Ekkehard, if I ever see him again.

A sliver of light from above the platform caught Otto from his torso up as he rose from his knees. "My goodness," he whispered to himself in disgust as he noticed the grit and grime of train brake residue and the overall filth of the tunnel that he now wore about his body. "Momma would be mortified. This is surely a bit dirtier than my playing down by the creek. Lucky for me, I have never fancied the subways as a place of play."

Otto looked for a cloth or rag, anything to use to lessen the dirt from his hands and clothing. There was none. Any piece of fabric he found was soiled far worse than he was at present. Frustrated, he moved quickly into shadows in case the soldiers that had attacked Ekkehard had followed him. Quiet remained in the lower plat-form, which continued to make Otto uneasy. He soon moved towards the stairwell leading to the upper platform. The dim light that had revealed Otto's disheveled self continued its glare down the stairwell. Keeping to the left wall, Otto sidestepped the light as he climbed the stairs. He came to the top and knelt down on his hands and knees, arranging his eyes level to the floor of the sta-tion. Slowly, he raised his head, offering a view of a large room with entrances and exits coming from all directions. Quiet reigned, as did the emptiness. An emergency flood light had proven the cul-prit of the sliver of light that now lit up the entire station platform. His eyes searched the room, working in an up and down grid pat-tern from far to near. The room was in disarray, the floor holding littered train tickets, schedules, and other paper debris he could not identify. The indications of war once again made itself physi-cally known. Bullet holes pockmarked the blackened white ceramic tiles. Blast scars from grenades randomly found homes around the room, adding a perverse color contrast to the blood splattered walls here and there.

"The enemy is near. Damn, this last effort to the bunker will be more worrisome than expected. Admittedly, for once I certainly wish I had the aid of some despicable German soldiers to guide me."

Otto finished his observation of the room and moved to stand with the intention of hurrying across the room and out the entrance, followed by a swift run across the Wilhelmplatz and on to the bunker. No sooner had he taken his first step into the full light with his lungs beginning their first inhale when a patrol of Russian soldiers entered the room from his right. They were preceded by ten German soldiers with their hands bound behind them.

"Halt! Legen sie ihre hände hinauf!" the Russians yelled, their demonic voices echoing off the tiles of the station. Otto stopped his forward move and raised his hands high over his head, not batting an eyelash. His muscles froze, as did his mind. No thoughts came to him. No plans or observations for escape filled his head. He was empty. It was as if a rush of fear had stripped his soul, vanishing into the littered floors below his feet, awaiting hell as their home. Within seconds, he was overcome and forced to the ground and onto his knees, his face smashed sideways to the floor. His exhales troubled the dusty floor particles, spewing them into the air, swirling freely, only to enter his mouth and lungs upon inhale. His musette bag and satchel were ripped from his shoulder, and he could feel the rope being tied around his wrists tearing into his skin. The pain outmatched the cigarette burn still accosting his flesh. As quickly as he was forced to the ground, he was equally forced back to his feet, lifted by his bounds and adding to his pain. Dirt from the floor let go its grip of his face except for a pebble that had ground its way into his skin, indented into its new home.

A Russian soldier, who appeared to be a sergeant, came into Otto's eyesight and was quickly in his face. He smiled at Otto, his yellowed teeth, hollowed eyes, and warped sense of humor coming to bear. "Ihren unglücklichen Tag. Ha, ha, ha." The other Russian soldiers laughed in agreement as the sergeant pushed Otto forward.

Otto tried not to show his fear; the wetted trousers of his uniform were informing enough. Well, Otto thought, cringing from his newfound pain, at least these Russians speak German, but how is it that now I wish not to understand what they are saying? Although, I can't disagree with the sergeant's comment; I do feel ugly. Otto stumbled forward ahead of the other German prisoners. They were a mixed lot, he noticed. Young, old, all equally as distraught, lifeless, and fearful, just as Otto had now become. He was now a ghost too. Hope had forsaken him.

The Russians moved off the main station room and continued down a wide hallway. The sergeant walked speedily ahead, his rifle at the ready as he searched left and right for what Otto could not understand, although he had his ideas. The sergeant stopped, turned, and motioned his comrades to move their captives into a room to his left, waving them quickly along.

"Macht schnell, macht schnell," the sergeant commanded.

They entered the room, which looked to be a waiting area for passengers. A flood light to the right offered definition, casting across the floor eerie shadows created by broken and distorted furniture strewn throughout the room. The soldiers quickly pushed away the furniture, throwing it aside and further causing its destruction. They moved the prisoners to the opposite wall from whence they had come, turning them around to face them.

Otto sighed, knowing what was to come. Well, here at last is my end. After all I have been through, it has come to this. And they don't even give us a blindfold. He smiled to himself ever so slightly, shaking his head side to side. Otto Kaufmann, aged eleven years. I always thought I would have time to fold my paper boats properly and sail them with Annie again. A tear coursed down his cheek, stopping to go around the pebble still imbedded in his skin.

The Russian soldiers quickly moved back from the wall, turned, lined up, and raised their rifles. The sergeant walked to the end of the line formed by his comrades. His face offered no expression.

In the dark to the right of the passenger waiting room was an entrance to another room. It had not been cleared. The quickened pace of the Russians' intended deed had been at fault. It had remained unnoticed. A small hand, the size of a child's to an adult's eye, slowly retracted the bolt of an MP-40 machine gun. The searing slide of metal grating metal announced its intention. Its whereabouts did not go unnoticed and caused Otto to suddenly look up. That sound was not made by the locking bolt of a Russian rifle, he thought, as he could plainly see the Russian soldiers still awaited their sergeant's fire order. Off to his left, Otto recognized the darkened foreboding end of the weapon, its operator hidden in shadow.

In a mocking inner voice, Otto chuckled. Well, well, how glad I am to see this infamous weapon of the mighty Wehrmacht. I give you the MP-40 Machine Pistol, the weapon of choice when you certainly must put multiple holes into a human very, very fast. I should think everyone in this room is about to die with a horrible end. Hmm, this should prove interesting. Perhaps there is an angel on my shoulder. I just hope that whomever is wielding this weapon is a very good shot.

Otto stood still, preparing for his own quick course of action. His eyes traveled without moving his head. He looked back toward the line of Russians, finding the sergeant's eyes. Then he looked back at the machine gun slowly rise out from its shadow. He quickly looked back towards the Russian sergeant, who was slowly raising his hand to start the order. Timing was everything, Otto thought, keeping a close watch as both events took shape. How ironic that the sergeant's command will order his own death unbeknownst to him. Yes, there is an angel on my shoulder.

Time did not stop for Otto's thoughts. The Russian sergeant's hand thrust down with force, and his firing squad pulled their triggers, calling upon their rifles to do their bidding. At that exact moment, the machine gun came to life from its quiet place. Otto kicked his legs sideways, crashing his body to the ground, the intended bullet from the Russian firing squad striking with anger into the innocent white tile above him. The room erupted with the sounds of ferocious machine gun fire, deafening the world and screaming to that of a mighty fireworks display. The nine millimeter bullets swarmed like angry yellow jackets disturbed from their nest, finding their mark, ripping and burning as they brought death to life. The Russian soldiers crumpled into a pile as they made the floor their final resting place next to the saddened carcasses of destroyed and abandoned furniture. Gun smoke filled the room, dimming reality as anarchy took its grasp. The German prisoners next to Otto did not fare well or benefit from his discovery. Their paths were decided differently. They, too, found the ground in death.

Otto wasted no time on the floor. He turned from his side and came to his knees, his hands still bound. He rose to his feet and kept low as he tried to discern the exit seemingly hidden from this grim, maddening event. His ears were ringing and his balance was off, shifting his walk sideways. He stumbled forward towards the opposite wall, the gun smoke still swirling and menacing the air. He could hear faint, disturbing moans and the gurgling of blood being spewed from dying men.

Otto coughed and gasped as he moved from the room, his lungs begging for less tainted air. When he was almost to the end of the room, he tripped on something soft, and looking down through squinted eyes, he recognized the body of the Russian sergeant. Otto spared no time to be fascinated by his death. It bothered him none. Stepping over him, however, he couldn't help but notice the stunned look on the sergeant's face, his eyes still open, still not accepting his own death.

Otto made his way back to the main room of the station and began searching for the exit onto Voss Strasse, which would put him in the right direction for the bunker. He paused in the middle of the room, turning left, then right, looking up and down, covering the room in all directions. His eyes stung from dust, sweat, and the smoke of the gun fire, making it difficult to read even the largest of words. How many times have I passed this way over the years? I could have navigated my way blind, he grumbled to himself.

Otto walked to an object on the rubble-strewn floor, a plaque with exit designations written on it. "Ah, yes," he said as he bent over to read the sign. "Here it is. Silly me." He swiped his foot, revealing what he suspected. "Right where it should be, on the floor, literally under my nose." Otto lifted his eyes, drawing a straight line from the sign to a large set of paired doors. Kicking the sign to the side, he quickened his pace to his intended exit.

Chapter 5

Otto lightly pushed open the door with his foot and was greeted with a whimsical, pinkish hue fading to ink as the sun rose to the heavens. Morning was just about to show itself. He stopped at the top of the stairs leading down to the street, caring not about the enemy, good or evil, nor did he give a thought to the identity of the person behind his escape from the firing squad. It mattered not. He closed his eyes, tilted his head back, and took in a huge breath, filling his lungs with the sweet offerings of spring.

"Ah, to be alive and free. I am more than through with the subway and its stinky underworld. What a beautiful day. Even war itself cannot ruin the presence of its grace from moving forward. All I can imagine is being with Annie down by the creek, having a most splendid time."

Otto opened his eyes, and the burning of flesh, wood, and oil as it surrounded him brought a darkness to his face. The destroyed buildings, fallen and splintered trees, downed telegraph wires, and rotting figures dirtied his world.

"Oh, war, how good of you to join me again. Still not finished with your task, I see. Very well then. Let's get back to work." Otto fidgeted with his bounds, his hands still not free. "I most surely will not be as quick running with my hands positioned as such, but nonetheless, here I go."

Otto double-jumped down the steps onto Voss Strasse and began picking up speed again, dodging the droppings of war and its havoc. His run was awkward, and it frustrated his moves. He kept his eyes straight and focused. He did not need unwanted things, human or not, to distract him from reaching the Führerbunker.

"I am quite sure there is a sniper watching all of this through his scope, laughing too damn hard to shoot. I had better make haste before he rights himself."

Otto came into view of Wilhelmplatz and, without hesitation, darted across the open for the Reich Chancellery. He could hear small arms fire and cannon bursts from all directions. The coming of morning brought the onslaught of hate to life. He moved past the open square without event, entering the ruins of the ill-fated Reich Chancellery.

The return to the bunker brought new thoughts of purpose and people, particularly Herr Bormann. He will not be pleased with my failed mission. Otto's mind drifted to the major from two days past and their sharing of better times. I will hope for a pleasant outcome, besides, Corporal Huber will protect me. He passed into the bunker garden and ventured halfway across the grounds where he was immediately halted by two sentries, rifles at the shoulder, bolts locked.

"Halt! Erhalten sie zu auf dem boden!" demanded one of the sentries.

Otto stopped his movement and fell to the ground on his knees as instructed. He bowed his head and awaited his capture. One of the two German sentries came to Otto quickly; the other held back with his rifle still trained. Why they did not shoot upon seeing Otto was a mystery to him, but he was thankful. The soldier pushed Otto over with his boot, sending him farther to the ground and causing Otto to roll onto his back and on top of his bounds. He winced in pain, his stomach wound still pestering him when disturbed. The sentry hunched over Otto, recognizing him with delight, his rifle fixed upon his chest.

"Otto! It is so good to see you! Where have you been?"

Otto looked up at the sentry, recognizing him at once. "Private Krauss, so very good to see you as well."

Private Krauss helped Otto to his feet and, noticing Otto's binds, moved to cut them with his bayonet. "You are past due, my young boy. Where is Private Volger? Bormann had sent him to find you. He whispers to himself of your whereabouts. Have you succeeded in your mission? The stakes have been high on this gamble, and most of them bet against you. It is rumored that Reichsmarschall Göring wagered seven-hundred and fifty thousand marks. I, for one, thought you may succeed based upon your stellar record."

Otto looked up at the private with a disturbed look, as if understanding his meaning, but passing it off in disbelief. "Betting?" he mumbled to himself.

"Private Volger is dead. Shot by a Russian sniper."

Private Krauss slumped his shoulders and relaxed his rifle to his side, holding it with one hand. "That is sad news. He was a good friend. I'll miss his camaraderie. The war, Otto, is taking us one by one. By the looks of you, I'd say you are next. Hmm. I hesitate to bring you to Bormann in this condition. You, you are a bit disheveled and quite unpresentable. You smell of urine, Otto."

Otto rubbed his reddened and irritated wrists, the freedom very welcome. He left the private's inquiry unanswered and paid no mind to his observations.

"Quiet are you, Otto? Very good then. I admire a modest winner. Come then. We mustn't delay. It is not safe outside in the garden. The Ivans own the day now as well as the night. The Führer won't even leave his quarters. He has forsaken the outside world. What will become of us, I do not know."

Otto started to shake nervously as they approached the entrance to the Führerbunker. Private Krauss opened the large, hinged doors and led him down the staircase. The other sentry remained at his post. Otto's nervousness grew more intense as beads of sweat formed upon his brow, the haunting of the Führerbunker coming to bear again in his mind. He could hear and feel its voices echoing in his head, clouding his thoughts with pain and suffering. He repeated over and over in his head, 'They will not hurt us. They will not hurt us.' All his positive thoughts vanished to take residence elsewhere. He felt alone.

"Yes, you will be most unwelcome in your sorry state," the private commented as they descended the stairs. "However, do not fret. I shall take you straight to Corporal Huber, and he shall clean you up, my little runner."

Otto smiled, if just for a moment, and his heart calmed. Private Krauss led him to the bottom of the stairs and moved him quickly to the machine room in order to hide him while he located Corporal Huber.

"Shh, Otto. Get under the cot in the corner and pull the blankets over you. Do not stir. I shall be but a moment."

Otto crawled under the bed, pulling the woolen army blankets over to complete his hiding. He peered through a sliver of blanket and watched the private hurry from the room. Good for me, Otto thought to himself. I have time, what little it shall be, to think of what to say to Herr Bormann. A failed mission and I am dead immediately. If he learns I have lied by telling him I was successful, he will certainly kill me. He will most definitely ask for the signed papers from General Heinrici confirming that he had been served his orders. Hmm. I could say I lost them upon my journey home, which is not all that untrue since the Russians did take my bags. I'll get a good kick in the rear, but if he's in a terrible mood, I may be killed. Well, everything points to my being killed.

Moments had passed when suddenly two sets of infantry boots shuffled with speed into the room. Otto could hear faint voices arguing, stern and defiant in their replies back and forth, becoming louder as they approached. A hand reached for the end of the blanket and pulled hard, lifting it into the air and flinging it to the side. Otto closed his eyes in fear and prayed.

"Otto? Otto?" Otto opened his eyes and turned his head towards the voice. He saw Corporal Huber come into focus, on his knees, bent over, and smiling at him.

"Corporal Huber!"

"Shush, my dear Otto. Come quietly now. We mustn't delay. Herr Bormann is away but will return very soon. Quickly now. There is much to do and speak about. Yes. You must tell me all."

Otto hurried from his hole and gave Corporal Huber a welcoming hug. Corporal Huber raised his arms in disgust from Otto's rancid clothing and foul odor but slowly dropped them and returned a nurturing, warm hug in kind, his own eyes closing.

"Be still, Otto. If God shall guide my strength, I shall uncover a way to procure safe passage for you." Corporal Huber pulled away and knelt down to look at Otto in the eyes, still holding onto him gently. "But first, we must get you clean. You stink, Otto."

Otto stood, not saying a word. Tears moved down his face as if they were listening to the corporal and began to wash him. Corporal Huber turned to Private Krauss, his voice firm and clear. "Quickly now. Find Bormann and report back to me his whereabouts. We can't linger in here. It's too dangerous. I'll take Otto up into the servants' quarters at the far end of the bunker. There are many generals and High Court officers visiting these days. The hour is nearer than we think. Escape and death are on many a mind. It has weighed heavily on my mind also."

Private Krauss became suspicious, his mind curious to Corporal Huber's rant. "What of the High Court? You work the telegraphs. What do you know? Tell me. Tell me all."

"I have heard many things. The Führerbunker is at its end. The High Court is fragmented, its armies leaderless and ineffective. That is the state of our current situation, Private. It is all you need to know. Enough talk now. Hurry, Otto, we make for the servants' quarters. Keep right behind me; stay in my shadow."

Otto moved behind Corporal Huber as they walked with great intent through the corridors of the bunker. He could hear whispering from all directions, like little armies of mice scurrying about without direction. They came to the stairs of the upper bunker and stopped abruptly. Corporal Huber came to full attention immediately, with Otto squeezed to the wall hidden behind him. From the stairs came General Burghoff walking clumsily. Corporal Huber gave his crisp and hardened salute true of the SS with no facial expression, his eyes glassed and silently poised straight. General Burghoff smiled faintly raising his hand half-heartedly in acknowledgement and with little countenance. He passed by without a further look and continued his stumble down the hallway, an apparition losing itself in the dark.

"That was close," sighed Corporal Huber, looking down at Otto, who nodded as they continued up the stairs. Dim lights guided their way and Otto stumbled as he focused on keeping behind Corporal Huber. "Okay, okay, Otto. Not that close. We'll both look like bumbling General Burghoffs if we keep this up."

Otto couldn't help himself. He was well beyond being frightened, as his mind swam in fear, one hand still clutching Corporal Huber's trousers. Corporal Huber came to the top of the stairs into the open dining hall and again stopped. A hollowed look came to his face as he reached behind and pulled Otto closer. Otto pressed his face into Corporal Huber's lower back, burying his head into the crisp wool of his uniform. Otto's eyes closed, knowing something was in view that he did not want to see. Slowly, his head reached around Corporal Huber's body and peered from its hiding. His eyes enlarged in fear as they came upon the figure of a man at the end of a long, ornate wooden dining table. A wicked ceiling light cast a sinister shadow hiding the figure's eyes while revealing a faint grin of ill intent. On the table before him, a half-drunk clear glass of cognac and its bottle sat in service, a hand firm in its grasp, one finger tapping the table to its own morbid rhythm. Next to this grim display lay another, a 9mm Walther PPK automatic pistol resting on its side. It was waiting for its call to duty.

"Late is the hour in which this young, scurrying, and filthy rat makes his appearance," bellowed from the grinning mouth as it took to speech. "What ill tidings has he brought me? Speak quickly, Jew."

Otto stepped from his hiding place and, with another step, cleared the side of Corporal Huber, who had since come to attention, his hand to his brow in salute.

"Be at ease, Corporal," the figure ordered in a stern voice. "Your acting has little effect on me. It may trouble you to know I was well aware of the boy's coming. For all your cunning, you have not wisdom. I too have my spies. Long have I watched your affection for this despicable Jewish slave. Your ill-contempt for the Reich has not gone unnoticed. I should probably shoot you as much as I should the boy, a decision I have yet to make."

Otto stood silent, his hands shaking, his eyes staring forward, his soul trembling. A tingle shot through his entire body, which should have caused him to urinate, if indeed he could.

"Come to me, Jew," commanded the figure. "Tell me of your mission. Quickly now."

Otto took an awkward step forward, his legs defying his brain's order to move. As he approached the figure, Otto could smell liquor swirl around him like menacing demons taunting a non-believer. Without warning, the figure suddenly rose with speed, pushing down and straightening his tunic as he stood. His hand grasped the pistol from its quiet rest on the table. Otto knew this man well. It was Bormann.

Otto's voice trembled and broke as he started his answer. "Reichs, Reichsleiter Bor, Bormann. I, uh, I come with gr, great news."

At that moment, Bormann faced Otto and thrust his pistoled hand across Otto's face with a loud and demonic smack. With his other hand, Bormann immediately grasped Otto's neck and forced his head to the table with a solid thump that offered no echo. The Walther was now at its best, its barrel dealt firmly at Otto's head, buried under his hair.

"Silence, Jew! Did you really think I was interested in your embarrassing lies? Did you think your whereabouts would cause me to lie on your behalf to the Führer himself so that a man of such high renown as the Führer would question my own loyalties and dedications, which I have all these years sought?"

Corporal Huber took a step forward from his stance as if to do something, but what, he did not know. Bormann looked up from Otto, his hands still at their posts. "Walk no farther, Corporal, lest you find yourself meeting my bullet."

Otto's mind went blank. His face throbbed from the blow to his cheek, the pain calling upon his stomach wound to answer in kind. Otto wanted an end. Fine, he thought to himself. Let it be. I relent.

Bormann turned from Corporal Huber back to Otto, pressing the Walther farther into the boy's head. With his thumb, he cocked the hammer back. Otto could hear the weapon prepare itself for action as he closed his eyes to find Annie smiling at him from the dam they had built together on the creek off the River Spree. Two paper boats gently floated in circles. His own smile came to his face as he relaxed his body into peace, causing the weight of Bormann's body to further press Otto to the confines of the table.

"Yes, yes," Bormann hissed over and over into Otto's ear. "Rest your soul. Go quietly and relaxed, like a man, but understand that there will be no heaven for you, Jew."

At that moment, a boy's voice cried out from the top of the stairs behind Corporal Huber. "Stop! Stop!" Bormann looked up in surprise, seething with anger, his Walther still at the ready. Corporal Huber turned as well with a look of confusion to this new-found devilry. At the top of the stairs was another boy, dressed in a complete Hitler Youth uniform, a machine gun strapped across his back. Next to him was Private Krauss.

Bormann kept his pose but spoke with anger. "What is the meaning of this? How dare you interrupt the business of the High Court?"

Private Krauss saluted quickly. "Permission to speak, Reichsleiter Bormann?"

"By all means, Private. Your timing is ill at best, delaying my work. Be quick."

"Sir, excuse my interruption, but this boy has information that I thought you might find of great importance."

"Yes? Well, speak then if you must, but make haste. My pistol finger is itching for work."

"Permission to approach, Reichsleiter Bormann?" the uniformed Hitler Youth asked politely.

"Yes! Yes, and be quick! Enough of these formalities. Speak now!"

"Sir, the Hitler Youth under your grasp is the one I saved from a Russian firing squad in the train station just this morning. Please, I ask you to spare his life because he saved mine. You see, Sir, I was caught by surprise in the corridor of the subway station with nowhere to run when a Russian patrol entered. They would have seen and captured me, except this Hitler Youth appeared from the stairs and walked into the open area. They captured him immediately and escorted him and other German prisoners to another room. The Russians quickly arranged themselves into a firing squad, but I followed and sneaked around to where I could get a good place to engage them. I acted quickly and lay a burst of fire from my position. I backed away from the room and waited in silence for the smoke and dust to settle. Upon my reentering the room, I found the boy gone. I was a bit delayed in my firing so I could not save all the prisoners. I did, however, manage to kill all the Russians. I immediately came back here to my post to await further orders from my superior when Private Krauss came upon me. I told him of my deed, and he immediately took me to find you. Please, Herr Bormann. I know not what this boy has done, but I ask you to spare his life."

Bormann listened intently as a smile came to his face. He dropped his grasp of Otto, his pistol coming to a relaxed position next to his side. A great evil and menacing laugh filled the halls.

"Ha, ha, ha. You," he stammered, trying to speak as his laughter and apparent drunkenness overcame him. "Oh, this is, is very good."

Private Krauss slowly walked farther into the room to stand next to Corporal Huber, who looked over at him in disgust. "Where have you been? Who is this boy?"

"My apologies, Corporal, but I found Herr Bormann as you instructed. He asked why I was not at my post, and fearing a lie, I told him of Otto's return. Herr Bormann ordered me back to my post. I am sorry, but as you have now heard, I think I have found a better way for our young Otto to survive."

"Ah yes, Private, a way for you to still continue in your riches from his feats? Your intentions do not escape me."

"You have gambled equally, my dear friend Huber. Your love of the boy doesn't overshadow this fact in the eyes of many."

"My intentions are for the good of the boy. You are ignorant not to see that. When this war is over, and the end is coming, we shall all have to answer to someone. Either to the Russians, the Allies, our mothers, or God. Are you prepared, Private Krauss?" The private held his silence, not answering. He turned his head from Corporal Huber, giving his attention back to Bormann.

Otto lay silently on the table. His body was still pressed over and against it, his face hidden from the new guests. He could only hear words every now and again when Bormann was not pressing his ear flat to the table, muffling the conversation. What topics were being discussed and argued over, he could not discern. He was relieved when Bormann eventually retracted his pistol's wishes to fire. The angels are coming again to help me, Otto thought. Bormann continued his newfound comedy show for his guests. He holstered his pistol to free his hand to join the other in offering pronounced gestures while continuing his banter. "Yes," he jeered in a sarcastic and foul-toned voice. "Yes, this is all very good. And I thank you, my young Hitler Youth, for this wonderful and insightful information. Now, you say you saved this young boy behind me? How wonderful indeed. Funny to me to think you have saved a Hitler Youth as equal to yourself. Am I not correct, dear lad?"

"Yes, Herr Bormann, it is true. The events I have told you are true."

"What is your name, my dear boy?"

"My name?"

"Yes, yes. You do have a name, don't you?"

"Sir, my name is Joseph Kessler, son of Rudolph Kessler of Munich."

"Yes, Kessler," Bormann repeated with delighted curiosity and intrigue. He paced back and forth as if he were on a stage in front of his crowd. "Yes. I know the name well. Fine Aryan stock, the name Kessler. Well, your father was a great philanthropist and very generous to the Nazi Party. He was one of our biggest supporters, I'll have you know."

Bormann walked back towards Otto and grabbed his arm, this time with odd gentleness, guiding him to a firm upright stance. "Come to attention, young Otto," Bormann ordered. "Meet in person your gracious savior. Perhaps you wish to offer him your deepest gratitude for the continuation of your life."

Otto noted the sarcasm in Bormann's words, which gave him grave concern. There is more trickery at hand, Otto thought. This doesn't seem likely to play out well for me.

"Please, Otto, speak. Say what you wish to your savior. You owe him your life."

"My name is Otto Kaufmann, courier to the High Court and adjutant of Reichsleiter Bormann. I offer you my gratitude for saving my life. I am in your debt." Otto raised his arm, offering to shake hands with the Hitler Youth soldier as he approached.

"You are welcome, courier of the High Court, adjutant to Reichsleiter Bormann." Joseph raised his arm and the boys shook hands awkwardly with little grace.

"Good then." Bormann excitedly remarked. "Very good then."

The boys finished their greeting and dropped their arms. Both stood silent, their eyes twitching with nervousness and curiosity to what new words would yet come from actor Bormann.

Bormann kept his smile, a ragged grin ear to ear. He was enjoying his tortuous game with the boys and that of Corporal Huber and Private Krauss, neither of whom had uttered or offered a word. Bormann kept pacing and walked around both boys until he stopped just behind Otto. He raised his arms and put his hands on Otto's shoulders, his fingers clenching firmly around and under the contours of Otto's skin and bones. Otto winced, his mind succumbing to the unwelcome invasion.

Quietly, in a distorted tone, Bormann stared at Joseph. "So, would it trouble you, devout soldier of the Hitler Youth who gave your oath and loyalty to the Third Reich and to whom you are beholden, son of Rudolph Kessler of Munich, of upstanding citizenry, wealth, of fine ancestry and solid Aryan blood, would it trouble you to learn you have saved, not one of your own kind, but a Jewish slave boy?"

The room went silent. This was not news to Private Krauss or Corporal Huber. Joseph's face soured upon hearing this news, and an emotion of disgust and betrayal ravaged through his body. His hands clenched into fists, and his eyes darkened.

Bormann stared at Joseph with piercing, glazed eyes. "Ah, yes, it is very true. Of course you know, my young Hitler Youth, there is still time to right your wrong, your being tricked by my young courier's disguise."

Bormann let go of his grip of Otto and reached for his holster, unsnapping the clasp and grabbing the barrel of the pistol. Reaching out, he offered it to Joseph. "Here my fine, loyal friend of the Third Reich, do as you know you must. Hurry now, for otherwise I will have to do it myself."

Corporal Huber came forward, horrified by Bormann's proposal. He took a step to stop Joseph, but Bormann quickly cut him off.

"Stand back, Corporal, or I'll have you shot!" Bormann yelled, his command echoing throughout the upper bunker.

Corporal Huber hesitated, then stopped, raising his hands in the air as if surrendering, eliminating himself as a threat. "This is sheer madness," he yelled.

"Private Krauss," Bormann ordered, "train your rifle upon the corporal, if you would. Should he take one more step and you have my sincerest permission to shoot him. Am I clear in this order?"

"Yes, Herr Bormann. You are clear in your order."

"Now, young Joseph, please take my offer," Bormann continued. "Hurry now."

Joseph walked towards Bormann with a troubled and confused look on his face. The disgust of having learned the truth of Otto's heritage all but vanished for the moment as the thought of shooting a boy of his age and dress came to bear. He took the pistol from Bormann, his distraught mind offering little direction for the gun to take.

"Good, my beloved Hitler Youth. Good. Now come stand behind me and draw the pistol to young Otto's head."

Joseph did as ordered and held the pistol to Otto's head, unknowingly in precisely the same spot Bormann had previously assaulted. Otto grimaced with the coming of the pain, thus drowning out that of his struck face and burned stomach.

"Please, almighty Lord, no," whispered Corporal Huber, closing his eyes to avoid witnessing such barbarism.

Bormann sidestepped the boys and continued his malicious screenplay as he paced nonchalantly about the room. "Perhaps, young Joseph, you wish to learn how a Jewish boy came into such a high ranking? Surely, your mind has asked itself such, has it not? Shall I tell you so you may find it easier to pull the trigger? Yes?"

Joseph nodded wearily at Bormann and his questions, his finger twitching at the trigger. Otto could feel the hesitation in Joseph, the pistol barrel wavering in circles, gouging deeper into Otto's skin and creating a small open wound. Otto wished to be done with this world once and for all. Clearing his mind, he found his strength and stood stoically upright, taking in a deep breath.

"Stop your tedious delay, you weak, timid Aryan," Otto barked. "Be done with me. I have no time for your indecisiveness!"

Bormann laughed at Otto's outburst, rather enjoying his theatrics. "Very good, my young Jew. Glad to see your part in my little production has come to play."

Suddenly from the stairwell came Artur Axmann, leader of the Hitler Youth. He stopped at the doorway but did not seem to notice the events taking shape in front of him. "Herr Bormann, the Führer has called for you. He awaits with urgency your presence. Come, we mustn't delay."

Bormann stood still, his laugh and grin all but faded. His one weakness was the Führer. If he was summoned, then there were great questions and events needing his attendance and counsel.

"Yes, Herr Axmann," he responded, his voice hesitating with obvious nervousness. "Yes, at once. We must get to the Führer immediately."

Bormann reached for the Walther and removed it from Joseph's sweaty, trembling hand. "You won't be needing this for now, Hitler Youth."

Bormann holstered his sidearm, brushed his tunic, and adjusted his buttons as he walked towards Axmann without delay. Axmann turned and proceeded back down the stairs, his boots clicking the steps as he descended.

Bormann stopped just before taking his first step down the stairs and turned his head back toward Corporal Huber. His voice found with ease its malevolent tone as he ordered. "Corporal Huber, take this wretched Jew and clean him up. He is disgusting. I will deal with him later. Private Krauss, back to your post and escort our young Hitler Youth to my quarters for further questioning about the state of affairs in and around Berlin. Perhaps his knowledge of the city may yet help our cause.

"Word has come to me the Führer may sign orders permitting a breakout. I suspect this is why he has summoned me. He looks for my counsel." Bormann turned away and vanished down the dark stairwell with great intensity, his fingers reshaping his hair from a drunkard's disheveled mess to a more presentable state.

Corporal Huber dropped his head, closed his eyes, and upon opening them, quickly exhaled his breath in a great and almighty sigh. "Well, that was certainly not a fun show." He turned to acknowledge Private Krauss, his rifle still trained. "You can drop your guard, Private. I am sure you have convinced Bormann of your allegiance, false as it is."

Private Krauss lowered his rifle, offering a half-hearted, apologetic smile to Corporal Huber. "So what do we do now, Corporal?"

"You heard Herr Bormann. Get back to your post and take this Hitler Youth savior of yours to his quarters. I'll get Otto cleaned and ready for, well, I don't know what. Perhaps I'll hurry him out of this wretched place for good."

Private Krauss motioned for Joseph to come along, and both disappeared down the stairwell to the lower bunker. Corporal Huber walked over to Otto and knelt down in front of him. Otto looked down at Corporal Huber with a blank expression. No words came to him.

"It is time for you to go, Otto. I have many things to tell you, things you need to hear and understand. I am to set you upon a new course, hopefully to safety. Quickly now. We must get you cleaned and prepared. Your journey with the drudgeries of this house has ended, yet others lie ahead for you."

Otto offered a faint smile at Corporal Huber, if only for a moment, but still he did not speak. Corporal Huber rose to his feet and put his hand on Otto's shoulder, guiding him as they walked quickly to the servants' quarters. The firm but gentle grasp of Corporal Huber's hand on Otto's shoulder reminded him of his Poppa, warming a bit of the cold in his heart. They came to the servants' quarters, and Otto hopped up onto the bed in the corner and came to a fetal position.

"Not quite yet, Otto. First you must make for the shower. Hurry now. We mustn't delay. I will try to find you some new clothes. I suspect Axmann will have Hitler Youth uniforms at his disposal. Although not my first choice for this journey, I should think finding civilian clothes these days for an eleven-year-old will be most difficult. Hurry now. Off with your clothes."

Otto sluggishly sat up in the bed and started to remove his clothes. As he unbuttoned his jacket and shirt, Corporal Huber noticed the wound from the cigarette burn. "My dear boy, what on earth?"

"Oh, that. I had hardly given it a thought until you mentioned it. It is the least of the suffering and sorrows in my heart at the moment, my dear Corporal."

"I'll get a dressing and medicine from Dr. Stumpfegger. We'll fix you up, Otto. Mark my words."

Corporal Huber walked from the room without haste. Otto removed his boots, trousers, and socks, causing him to smile as he thought about each piece of clothing, flooding him with memories of his past missions. Each scratch and scuff, hole and tear reminded him again that even after all he had endured, he was still alive. The thought widened his smile. Otto hopped off the bed and was now completely bare. He stared at a mirror on the wall, looking at himself.

"Yes, Annie, I am still alive. And you better be, too."

Otto ran out of the servants' quarters to the bathroom, which held a very small shower. He turned the handle, and sprinkles of cold water drizzled from the shower head. "I suppose having Onkel Hannes fix this now would be out of the question. If I don't hurry, Corporal Huber will be upset with me. Yes, I should think this will have to suffice for now."

Otto got under the shower, which caused an uncontrollable shiver across and down his whole body. Slowly, the water pressure heightened but offered little warmth. He washed himself well enough despite the conditions, soaping his ears with plenty of suds while giggling about how proud his Momma would be. His wounds were not left forgotten, and he grimaced from the pain caused by the soap and water.

"It is better I feel this pain rather than the horrid agony Herr Bormann had in mind for me. Yet, I would be a fool to think this play is at its end."

He finished his washing and looked the room over for a towel. None were near. He ran back to the service quarters dripping wet and jumped into the bed, pulling the covers over his head. Corporal Huber quickly returned to the quarters with fresh clothes, boots, and the medical kit.

"You had better be clean, Otto. Now is not the time for silly child's play or a good game of hide-and-go-seek. Besides, I know all your hiding places, Otto Kaufmann, as they are obvious and not in the least ingenious. Come now, what has become of you?"

Otto quickly pushed the blankets from his head offering a sheepish grin. "Well, that doesn't sound like the Corporal Huber I know. Besides, who's the one who got stuck behind the diesel generator the last time we played? A bit too much of the ale in the belly, I should think. Oh, and might I add, was it not your wish to play this game in the first place?"

"We've had many good days and nights over the years, my dear Otto. I suppose we could sit here for many a night more reminiscing about each hour. However, that time, I need to remind you, is not now. Here, Otto, I have gathered some fresh clothes for you. I shall take a seat, and we must talk whilst you dress." Corporal Huber pulled up a chair and began inspecting Otto's troubled body. He grimaced at the sight of Otto's stomach. "Hmm, yes, we must talk but first let me tend to your wounds. Where else does it hurt, my boy?"

"I am not sure even the great Dr. Stumpfegger has enough medicine to heal my pains."

"I understand, Otto. You have my sympathies, which is why we must talk."

Corporal Huber began cleaning Otto's stomach wound, causing tremendous discomfort. Otto reacted very little except for a few winces and inhales of breath to swallow the bite. The wound cleaned, Corporal Huber covered it well with a dressing and taped it soundly to Otto's body. He looked up at Otto's face upon finishing and softly inspected his cheek, reddened from Bormann's strike.

"Well, that looks to be nasty but will subside its presence in a day or so. You'll have to tough that one out."

"Oh, and what about the wound on my head? Perhaps you didn't notice a pistol gouged into my head, did you, during that little escapade?"

"Yes, yes. Be still now, Otto, and let me have a look. I was aware of many things during that whole insane performance. Quite queer and dangerous it was. It is very tense around here these days. The end is near, which brings me back to what you need to understand."

Corporal Huber spread a dab of ointment on Otto's head wound, ruffled his hair, and began speaking to Otto with a serious but calm and caring tone. "Now please get dressed, Otto, and listen to me carefully." Otto pulled on his new Hitler Youth uniform, sat back upon the bed, and gave Corporal Huber his full attention.

"I have not the time to go into great detail but will offer you this information. This will be very hard to understand, Otto, but you must listen. You were spared, Otto, horrendous tortures and many unjust acts, well beyond what you have endured here these past years. While manning the telephone switchboard over time, I pieced together stories I had heard about places throughout these lands involving horrible camps, work camps, camps where many of your people, Jews, are being massacred and killed."

Otto's eyes widened and his mouth went limp.

"I know what you are thinking, my child, but I do not know the fate of your family. I do not know the reasons for such madness, but you were spared, Otto, for some unknown reason of which only our almighty God knows the answer. You were chosen. Chosen to live."

"I was chosen because I was fast. That's what they told me. If I remained fast, I would live. It was easy. I was given no choice. As for my people, I have also heard stories of such evils. I never allowed these thoughts to come into my head all these years. I was too concerned with trying to stay alive. Now, however, they capture all my thoughts. My family, Annie. They besiege my mind."

Corporal Huber's eyes teared, and a dim light flickered off their surface. He reached out his arms and laid both his hands on Otto's shoulders.

"Many a night have I heard your dreams, Otto, your nightmares coming to bear. Many a night have I knelt at your side, holding your hand in solace. I have heard your cries and torments. I know of your Annie and your parting from the cold, barren days of the ghetto. I know they haunt your every step."

Otto remained still. The very name 'Annie' flooded his mind each time he heard, thought, or felt it. Tears formed in his own eyes, building up enough depth until they could not be held. Like the first drop of rain striking a leaf, his tears rolled down and off his cheek.

"Otto, listen to me closely. I may know where your Annie is."

"But, but, how? She was taken away and put on another wretched train while I was put into a German officer's car. Are you tricking me, Corporal Huber? Are you being like all the other officers? My heart tells me otherwise. Why have you helped me all these years? Please tell me. I can't bear more."

Corporal Huber grasped Otto and shook him into control, his voice becoming sterner. "Now hear this, Otto Kaufmann, do not take me for a huckster. All these many years, I have guided and looked after you. I have treated you as my own, for it is my wish some day to have a son of such caliber, passion, and mind. This I have told you. Do you really not know, Otto? I love you, Otto."

Otto freed himself from Corporal Huber's hold and came to him quickly, wrapping his arms around him. "I believe you, Corporal. I have always believed you."

Otto released his grasp and came to stand before the corporal, tears still playing their part on his cheeks. He admitted softly, "But I am scared. So very scared. I have nowhere to go."

"I know, my dear boy, I know. But you must be strong, Otto. Do not give in now at this final hour. Do not let the evil deeds of these past years weigh heavily upon your life. Do not let them tarnish your mind. You have many good years ahead of you, Otto. These past few will not hold sway. Trust my words."

Otto smiled and wiped his face. "Oh, I suppose you are right, as usual. Besides, I am tired of all this damn crying. Please, please tell me where my Annie is held?"

"Yes, Otto, but I cannot be sure. However, I have done some investigating. I have learned that the High Court kept files for the deportation of Jews and others hidden in a secret vault at the Wolf's Lair. Do you remember this place, Otto?"

"Yes, yes. Very well. It is in Poland near the Russian front. It's where we first started my missions. It's surrounded by a huge forest, and I remember getting lost there many times."

"Good then. You must go to the Wolf's Lair, and hidden in Herr Bormann's chamber is the vault. There you will find the deportation records."

"But, but how will I find Annie?"

"Trust me, Otto. We German soldiers are very disciplined when it comes to keeping records. You must find the files for the Lodz Ghetto, from where we took you. The files will be organized by family names and by sectors where you were housed. They will identify also where your family was deported. There were only so many camps designed and established at that time. I do not know the names, but you will learn of them when you read the files."

Otto sat back down on the bed and continued listening intently. Many questions swam through his mind. Work camps, deportation, being saved? A troubled look came to his face. It frustrated him not having answers.

"The road will be dangerous, Otto. There are many enemies haunting these lands. Your difficult journey out of the city will be much harder than whence you arrived. I don't have to tell you about the Russians. It is certain they occupy Poland now. Whether they hold the Wolf's Lair, I do not know. It is well hidden, as you have said."

"Certainly such a vault is locked. So, how do I unlock it?"

"Ah, yes." Corporal Huber reached into his pocket and pulled from it a tarnished brass key adorned with the eerie, wicked mark of the Wehrmacht, an eagle holding an encircled swastika with its talons. "With this key, Otto. What Herr Bormann doesn't know, won't hurt him now, will it?" They both laughed as Corporal Huber handed Otto the key.

"Now here, Otto, put the key into your pocket for now. We'll find you a new musette bag for your journey. When you have learned of the camp where your Annie is being held, quickly find her and then head northwest. You must get to the British. Their troops are approaching from that direction. They will treat you well. They are proper gentlemen, soldiers of course, but yet gentlemen indeed and will care for you nonetheless. Avoid at all costs the American armies. I do not trust them. Cowboys and playboys, they are. There is this American General, Patton is his name. It is said that he likes to kill the Hun and that he is very good at it."

Otto sat silently. One last question came to his mind as his heart quickened its beat and a swell of fear returned. "But, but aren't you going with me, Corporal Huber? I thought, I thought you were going with me?"

Corporal Huber stood up from his crouch and smiled. "My path holds a different course from yours, Otto. The war is over for me. I care not for this High Court I have so honored and served with dedication and loyalty. Yet, there are many wounded men under Dr. Schenk's care to whom I must attend and give hope. There's a brotherhood beyond your understanding among men at arms. Then, Otto, God willing, I will look to return to my wife, Eva, as you look to return to your Annie and family. She has been my strength and love through all of this.

The corporal looked down at Otto and bent over gently, reaching his arm out, his hand softly carrying Otto's head up to meet his eyes. "Now do not cry and weep, young Otto, as I see that coming to your face. Perhaps in another time and place we shall meet again. Smile, knowing we can both look forward to such a day."

Otto wiped his tears and stood up from the bed. "Then I am ready."

"Good then, Otto. Let's get you packed and out of here, shall we?"

At that moment Sergeant Misch appeared at the door. He did not wait for a salute before addressing Corporal Huber, as he seemed busy of mind. His command was firm and telling. "The boy has been summoned, Corporal. Come now. Bormann awaits in his quarters."

"His mood?" Corporal Huber inquired without saluting.

Sergeant Misch grinned ever so slightly with what seemed more of a frown, his lips twitching, contorting into foul shapes. He raised his arm just above his waist and tilted his hand left to right quickly from a horizontal position. He dropped his arm and vanished from the doorway.

"Damn Bormann to foil our escape."

Otto looked up at the corporal seeking guidance. Although remaining calm, he was inwardly alarmed. "Seems this play has a second act. I was hoping for a longer intermission."

Corporal Huber moved quickly, gathering the medical kit. "Do not worry, Otto. This time I will take action if Herr Bormann proceeds with any mischief. I could not live with myself if

I did not thwart another episode of his."

Otto smiled faintly and followed Corporal Huber from the room. Within moments, they arrived at Bormann's quarters. Bormann was at his desk busy writing, of what they could not tell. Seated in the corner on a small wooden chair with a plain shallow cushion was Joseph. Corporal Huber saluted immediately and stepped aside. Otto was now in full view.

"Yes, yes, my Jew courier. Good to see you are cleaned and presentable. Come in, please. Don't be shy. We have much to discuss. Hurry now."

Otto stepped farther into the room and took a chair next to Joseph in front of Bormann. Corporal Huber came to attention from his salute and remained near the door, his eyes fixated on Bormann's mood and temperament. Bormann continued his writing, his eyes squinting and laboring. There are evil doings at work here, Otto thought to himself as he glanced quickly to Corporal Huber and back to avoid getting caught not paying strict attention to Bormann. Otto noticed the absence of a pistol, and the sinful vapor of cognac was also nowhere to be found. He peered off to inspect Joseph but again thought better of it and quickly returned his head to Bormann's attention. Bormann's eyes widened as he finished writing his last word and scribbled what Otto felt to be his signature at the end. He looked up, placed his pen carefully on the dark, wooden table, and smiled at Otto.

"Yes, good. You are clean, Jew. It seems your heroics have not gone unnoticed of late. Our mighty leader, the Führer himself, has asked about your great feats. Ironic, the man who has condemned your kind to death should ask for your assistance. Despite my severe warnings and counsel, he has convinced himself that you are the right person to fulfill one final task for him. The dark days and disloyalties of the High Court have drowned his mind with treason. At this gravest hour, he trusts no one. Indeed, quite absurd as it is, he has picked a Jew to finish one last task."

Bormann laughed silently to himself, the very thought of Otto carrying out the wishes of the Führer troubled yet also amused him. Perhaps if I had told the Führer about our little Jewish slave and had come clean about our wagering on his life, I would not be in this position. It matters not in this late hour, thought Bormann. He looked down from the table and grabbed a small folder, wrapped and bound with the Führer's official personal mark 'A.H.' pressed and embossed in blood-red ink. He laid the bound article on the table and continued his menacing smile. Furthermore, he thought, I find it to be deeply troubling and unwise that the Führer has not told me of the contents of this official document. I have my suspicions, yes, but I cannot be certain.

Bormann paused and leaned back in his chair, raising his arms, clenching his hands together, and resting them on the back of his neck. He rocked back on his chair, causing an ominous squeak that echoed just enough to be disturbing. The room became tenser, and no one dared move.

"Speechless are you, Jew? Yes, I was too when he summoned me to his quarters to give me this word, the summons that saved your life, once again. I am not trusting of the Führer's plotting. So, to make sure all goes well, I have bought myself some insurance."

Otto's heart became aroused. It appeared there was to be more trickery to this madness, he thought. He wished he had an escape route as he had so often sought during his missions. Bormann seemed remarkably calm and unmoved in spite of being full of animosity and hostility, which always seemed to swirl inside his broken mind.

Bormann nodded off towards Joseph. "Our good friend here, who you have most recently met under terrifying circumstances, will be joining you on this new mission of yours. We've had a delightful discussion, and he is in full understanding that he has the High Court's best interests at heart."

Corporal Huber dropped his attention and approached Bormann cautiously. "What mission? What is the meaning of this? Where is he to go?"

"Back off, Corporal," Bormann barked, standing up and kicking his chair back to the wall with a crash. Furiously, he stepped forward to meet Corporal Huber. "I find your lack of respect rather intolerable. I am a bit at my end with you and your insubordination. I have been very calm, have I not? Have I not been fair and just?"

Corporal Huber became silent and stood at attention. Bormann came within inches of his face, his eyes wide and blazing. "Keep your mouth closed, Corporal, and I will finish. It is well and sad for you I have now remembered your interests in this boy. You know as well as I that you are equally guilty in the taking and keeping of this boy. You know of the gambling at his expense. What newfound riches have you won because of him? Please, go on. Tell us of your riches? Tell us of the extravagant gifts given your beloved wife."

Corporal Huber stepped back and to the side of the room. His face was angered, but in looking at Otto, it offered embarrassment and disgust in himself. Bormann calmed, turned, and stepped back to his desk. "Have you nothing to offer? Then I expect you will keep your mouth shut."

Bormann turned, found his chair, and twirling it around, he sat back down. He took a deep breath and continued to speak to Otto. "Now, where were we, Jew? Ah, yes, your new mission. You are to go with Joseph as your guide and guard to see Grand Admiral Dönitz at his headquarters up north in Schleswig-Holstein near the Danish border. The Führer has indicated to me the admiral awaits your presence, but I suspect otherwise. The great admiral was just here not five days past. Why he did not give him such an important document then is beyond reasoning. Perhaps my Führer forgot, having so much on his mind. Stranger still, when I pressed him to simply send a wire rather than order such a burdened journey, he snapped and forbid such an idea, which was again quite troubling."

Bormann paused and became silent, his mind playing out what the secrets hidden in these documents before him would mean for his future. His head began spinning, his twisted imagination conjuring multiple theories. He began tapping his finger on the wooden desk before him as he compelled his mind to work. Otto remained poised with perfect posture, his eyes locked onto Bormann's every move and his ears attentive to every word. Joseph remained silent, and Corporal Huber stood stoic and stern. They, too, kept their eyes on Bormann.

Bormann suddenly snapped from his trance, halting his finger tapping. His head sprang up from thought, and he finished relaying his orders. "Needless to say, you are to deliver this document, or whatever it may contain, to the Admiral hand to hand. There is no further order. You needn't await a reply. The documents contain all the information and direction required. Upon the completion of this transaction, you are to return at once to this bunker. Do I make myself clear, Jew?

"Ah, yes. I almost forgot. One more thing." Bormann bent over and picked up a musette bag and satchel and placed it on the desk in front of Otto. "You can thank your new friend Joseph for bringing back your possessions, which you so carelessly discarded when surrendering to the Russians, an act that would have brought you before our firing squad under other circumstances."

Otto stood up from the chair, his new uniform falling from its seated position. "Yes, Herr Bormann. I will meet my objectives and report back to you upon my safe return."

Bormann sat back and smiled. "I am sure that will be the real trick. Yes, my speedy little one?" Bormann did not wait for a reply. The wretched sarcasm was felt by all in the room. He turned and addressed Corporal Huber. "Prepare these boys for their mission. See to it my Hitler Youth friend has plenty of ammunition. The Jew? Get him whatever he needs."

Corporal Huber saluted and motioned for the boys to come to him. Bormann reached out over his desk and handed the documents to Otto. Otto carefully put them in his satchel, turned, and followed Corporal Huber from the room. He could feel Bormann's hatred and ill-will rise and follow him from the room. Bormann sat silent, his head still and his eyes staring straight ahead. He was deep in thought, his twisted mind returning to the scrutiny of his theories.

The boys followed Corporal Huber into the machine room just outside Bormann's office. They both sat down on stools in front of a high work table. Corporal Huber paced back and forth, deep in thought. Otto watched him but did not offer any words. Joseph had a peculiar look on his face, and his mind was also working.

Corporal Huber halted his pacing and came to a stand, addressing the boys in a stern voice. "Joseph, you will find 9mm ammo for your MP-40 in the munitions room near the guard quarters. If you see Private Krauss, ask him to help you. Do not burden yourself with too much weight. Take eight sticks, and be done with it. I'd much rather you have enough food and water. Hurry now. Be off with you, and do not delay. The day is more than half spent, and the hour grows late."

Joseph hopped off the stool and hurried from the room. Corporal Huber watched him leave and paused a moment. Convinced of their privacy, he pulled up the stool where Joseph had been sitting and faced Otto.

"There is trouble here that escapes me. This newfound mission of Bormann's taunts my mind. I suspect something gravely afoul. Otto, you must carry out our planned journey, for it is not safe for you to venture to Admiral Dönitz. I know of what I speak. The Führer's business with the admiral is well beyond complete. He must be the trusted successor of the Führer. I can feel it with my very being. Bormann suspects this and will work to side with him, as I believe these papers cast Bormann and his High Court in an ill light. While I do not dare open them, I am certain of their telling. Besides this Hitler Youth that joins you, Bormann will have many eyes and ears watching your every move."

Otto listened attentively as Corporal Huber fidgeted to find comfort on the work stool. "I have also felt something queer in the air, Corporal, but what shall I do? Bormann will have me killed immediately if I don't complete this mission."

"I have no answers for you, my young son. I do not trust this Hitler Youth. He is dark in mind. Yet, there is hope. If you remember, Otto, I was not unlike Joseph at the very beginning of our meeting many years ago. Good can prevail and find its way to the hearts of even the most terrible of beings. It is up to your kindness, Otto. You are your only ally. Joseph is just a boy, the same as you. Innocent and precious, yet twisted under dire circumstances. War brings out the very worst in men, Otto, yet also the very best. Find the best in him. You will need him on your side if you are to find Annie."

"I shall try, Corporal Huber. I shall try." Otto looked up at him with a peculiar glare, a thought and a whim had plagued his mind since his conversation with Private Krauss in the garden. "What of this gambling and playing upon my life, Corporal Huber? I have not heard this for the past five years, and then surprisingly, this shadow and a doubt overwhelm me."

Corporal Huber rose from his stool and patted Otto on the shoulder. "Do not trouble yourself with this thought." He pulled from his tunic an envelope and handed it to Otto. "All that is truth will be answered in this letter I have written to you. Trust in my words. Please promise me not to read it until your journey has come to an end and you are safe."

"Yes, my Corporal. I shall honor your request and read it at the end. I will trust you and speak of it no further." He took the envelope and placed it in a side compartment of the satchel.

"Good then, Otto. Now, let's get you some more provisions. I have already set aside a medical kit and a number of tools, some thread, and needles, but we'll need to get you some iron rations, a new canteen, and a map. I am worried about your route out of here, my boy. I cannot hold my concern from you. It will be treacherous."

"I know. It's always unsafe on these missions, it would seem. I am no stranger to the unknown and the unforeseen. I agree. The route from here will be overrun with risks, but I have no other choice." Otto paused and jumped from the stool. "Please, please get me the iron rations with turkey. The horse meat is disgusting at best."

They both laughed, if but for a second. Corporal Huber stepped from the room to fetch Otto more provisions. Otto opened his satchel and removed the letter given to him by Corporal Huber. He held it up and inspected it. It is quite heavy for a letter, Otto thought. The corporal must have written quite a story. "The curiosity is killing me." Otto frowned and placed the letter back into the satchel.

Corporal Huber returned with the agreed provisions and filled Otto's musette bag. "Well, I got one turkey and the rest are horse meat. Pray Joseph is fond of horse meat."

At that moment Sergeant Misch walked in with Joseph. Corporal Huber stood up and started to salute him. "Quiet your mind, Corporal. Since when have we saluted each other down here these past few days? No, be at ease, my friend. Herr Bormann has alerted me to a new mission, one of grave importance. I do not know the details, but will trust in its cause, for good or ill. It will be a difficult road. However, I bring good news to this occasion. I have heard over the wire that there is a small army group, the Volksturm, leading a break-out attempt down the Friedrichstrasse towards the River Spree. They will have a few Tigers, support artillery, and antitank rockets. I suggest our little squad here load themselves with two. They are not heavy and very deadly at close range. They will need them in this fight, I should think. The Ivans will have tanks. If these boys are to leave, they must make haste. See to it, Corporal, that they find their way to the staging area. Look to the east. They will be staging in and around the Wilhelmplatz."

Otto rose, offering his counsel. "Sergeant Misch, I just came from there not a day ago. The area is swarming with Russian patrols. I dare not go that way."

"Do as you must, Otto, but the road is threatening in all directions. This will at least give you a fighting chance out of the most dangerous part of the inner city."

Corporal Huber nodded. "He is with sound advice, Otto. I trust in his judgment. Sergeant Misch was a combat soldier long ago at the start of the war, before he came to this job. Trust in him."

Otto smiled, believing in the confidence of the two soldiers. Sergeant Misch excused himself and left the room. Corporal Huber finished packing Otto's musette bag and helped him secure it and the satchel around his head and shoulder, testing their comfort. He looked at Joseph and inquired of his status. "Are you well-prepared, Joseph?"

Joseph nodded but offered no speech.

"Fine then. Let's get moving, shall we?"

"What of these rocket launchers?" asked Otto.

Corporal Huber laughed. "Ah, too heavy for you, Otto. They will slow you down, to be certain. Besides, you have to be uncomfortably close to your target to use them effectively. Trust me, you don't want to be that close."

Corporal Huber led the boys through the emergency exit to the upper gardens. The sound of war slowly raised its volume with each step. A soft rifle report made its presence known, cackling and vibrating until its end. Then a louder cannon burst committed to the scene, its sound drowning all else that cried out.

"Well, do you hear that?" Otto asked. "War is alive and well."

At the top of the stairs, they met Private Krauss at his guard post. "What have you seen and heard of late?" Corporal Huber asked.

Private Krauss frowned. "I have been down in the bunker arming Bormann's little warrior here, running the errands of the Führer's adjutants, and have just now begun my post. I can tell you, however, it's not the sounds of war that concern me. It's the quiet that has me awake in my mind. For a besieged city, it's eerily silent. Silence means no fighting, which has me believe the Russians have laid waste to all."

Corporal Huber nodded. The private's theory was just. He took a careful step into the garden and surveyed the area with the eyes of a hawk. Bomb craters pockmarked the landscape, disrupting its peace. Trees and plants lay mangled and contorted. Bodies bloated and gaseous were slowly becoming one with the ground. The buildings around him were in shambles, skeletons of once majestic structures that exuded the very finest of empire architecture. Now they struggled to keep their poise as they came rumbling and shaking to the earth.

Corporal Huber sniffed the air and found that the smells of cordite, sulphur, burning oil, and mixtures of other unknown vapors, human or not, were on the rise, swirling about and wreaking their annoying havoc on those that breathe. Not convinced the area was safe, he knew he had no other choice. He sighed heavily, shrugged his shoulders, and turned to face Otto and Joseph.

"It is time, then. Darkness is coming. Use its cover. Find a place to hide and await the Volksturm's assault to begin. These are my last words."

Otto fought back his tears, an enormous feat holding a tidal wave of emotion. His lips trembled and his eyes glistened but still offered no tear. He took a step and then another until he was one step past Corporal Huber in the garden. Joseph followed, turning around and around as he walked, not trusting the area's vacancy. Otto glanced up at Corporal Huber, who was now saluting him. Otto mouthed the words 'I love you' as he took another step farther away. Corporal Huber ended his salute and spoke softly, "I do too, now run."

Otto turned away and began to run, picking up speed as he increased his distance. He ran to the end of the gardens and stopped. He wanted one last look. He turned and saw nothing. The garden lay empty. "Yes," Otto whispered quietly. "Let it begin."

Chapter 6

Corporal Huber turned abruptly after watching Otto break across the garden. He walked past Private Krauss, entered the bunker, and began descending the narrow, dark hollows of the stairwell. Suddenly, he heard a hoard of people hurrying up the stairs mumbling and struggling as if carrying a cumbersome load. Coming into view, he could see two SS officers carrying a body wrapped in a blanket.

"Out of the way, Corporal!" they ordered in a hot, flaring temper.

Corporal Huber squeezed himself to the wall, reaching his hands back and flattening them to the cold concrete, stabilizing himself as they passed. He noticed the iconic black trousers only worn by the Führer, and he gasped suddenly at the sight. Behind the SS officers came Bormann, Goebbels, and General Burgdorf.

As Bormann passed in front of Corporal Huber, his demonic voice broke his surprise. "Corporal, forget what you have witnessed here and meet me in my chambers. We are to discuss matters of grave concern."

"Yes, Herr Bormann, I shall be in your chambers at once."

The corporal's eyes followed Bormann and the others as they rounded the stairwell out of sight. His head turned back down the stairs when another body came into view carried by one lone SS officer. It was easily recognizable as the Führer's mistress, Eva Braun, carelessly wrapped in a blanket. Her legs were bare and shoeless. Passing quickly up the stairs, the officer withheld his face from the Corporal, completely ignoring him. Corporal Huber again watched them pass until out of sight, the echoes of both parties continuing their haunting of the stairway. Corporal Huber turned his head back and stared mindlessly at the wall in front of him, his hands still flat upon the wall behind him, now clenching and searching to grasp something solid.

"It is done then. My freedom awaits."

Corporal Huber turned and stepped down the stairs, picking up his pace upon his descent, his mind filled with anxieties of the unknown. "What does Bormann want of me? Surely, he will not play out my end? It won't be without a fight for my part. He has seen his last days of such treachery."

Corporal Huber came to the lower bunker, where he found adjutants, SS officers, secretaries, and servants scattering about frantically. They were carrying papers and moving clothes and other unknown provisions. Looks to me the breakouts are well on their way, he thought. I suppose my tasks here are complete. I shall make my way towards Dr. Schenck's bunker hospital after seeing Bormann.

Corporal Huber came to Bormann's chamber and sat down in the same chair that Otto had when facing Bormann at his desk. The papers Bormann had written were nowhere to be found. His desk lay empty except for a single pen. It was gold, encrusted with diamonds, and engraved with delicate scenes of mythological creatures and deities. As was common with Nazi design, an eagle gripping a swastika in its talons adorned the top. A gift from some High Court official, the corporal supposed. He sat back, relaxed, and sighed heavily. A tiny bead of perspiration began to form on his right temple, slowly caving to gravity. He looked down and noticed his hands had begun to shake. He did not feel frightened, but uncertainty enjoyed producing the same attributes.

Bormann quickly entered the room. Corporal Huber jumped to attention and saluted Bormann upon his taking a seat in front of him. "At ease, Corporal," Bormann ordered, pausing to look around the room. He picked up his pen and began tapping on the desk. "Have the couriers been seen off?"

"Yes, Sir. They are well equipped and on the move."

"And their direction?"

"They were to follow an Army group across the River Spree as part of a breakout attempt. From there, they travel to Admiral Dönitz."

"Yes, very good. Have you any questions for what you have seen? Surely, you are curious?"

"I have suspected such an end would come. Seems fitting. He now steps into martyrdom."

"I don't subscribe to such mysticism. Power is only relative when you're alive." Bormann stopped tapping his pen and laid it down. He rested his elbows on the table and clenched his hands together, laying his chin upon them.

"Yes, Admiral Dönitz has been appointed the new Reich's President and Goebbels as Chancellor," advised Bormann. "This was the wish of the Führer, which I have suspected. Himmler will obey Dönitz, as shall I. A new government will form, this you can be certain, but escape is our only means to that end. There are ten groups formed for the breakout. My group will consist of Stumpfegger, Axmann, and my secretaries and adjutants. Thus, I require your assistance. I need you to remain in the bunker with Sergeant Misch and Hentschel to operate the telegraph station and receive messages after our leave. Anything of military or political importance must be kept secret, as well as the death of the Führer. I give you this highest responsibility and a chance to reclaim your loyalties and fulfill your oaths. Do I make myself clear?"

Corporal Huber offered a slight smile, the threat of his life vanishing his thoughts. "Yes, Sir. I shall stay and renew my loyalties and duties to the utmost."

"Good then. Take your leave."

Corporal Huber stood up, saluted, and walked from Bormann's chambers. He turned down the corridor and entered the machine room. He began whispering to himself, exploring his course of action, and laying plans for his own escape. "Good then? Your manipulation and ill will against me, Bormann, has not gone unnoticed. You know very well this city and bunker will be over-run, as do I. You may not have the authority to shoot me anymore, so you wish me to stay here to rot and die or, worse yet, be held captive by the Russians and submit to their torture and death. I shall do no such thing. When you have left, Herr Bormann, I too shall depart to help my fellow comrades and make for my home and my wife."

Bormann grabbed his pen and placed it in his tunic. He got up and walked from his chamber with his mind racing with curiosity. He walked down the corridor, passed the conference room, and went towards the Führer's chamber. He turned and looked around. Satisfied that he had gone unnoticed, he turned back, entered the Führer's sitting area, and walked through to the Führer's personal study. He stopped at the doorway and surveyed the room. It was sparse. It had a small sitting area for receiving guests and a plain, four-drawer wooden desk with a simple reading light at the corner. Over the desk hung a portrait of Frederick the Great, a figure the Führer admired and held in esteem, often times holding conversations between the painting and himself.

"I know it is in here. Where did he put it? I warned the Führer of this document, warned him with my every being. If it should fall into enemy hands, it will surely mean the end to those of us in the High Court."

Bormann went to the Führer's desk and quickly and carelessly opened the drawers, reaching in and pulling the Führer's papers and personal effects out, eyeing their contents, and then throwing them aside if they did not meet his interest.

"Curse you. Where is it? Where is that damn document? Where did he hide it? Where has it..." Bormann paused. Slowly, his mouth opened and his eyes widened as his skin whitened. He stood up straight then turned and sat down in the Führer's chair. "It, it has left here."

Bormann sighed heavily, anger and twisted hate coming to his thoughts. "It is with that Jew. Right under my very nose. That despicable Jew. My Führer has left us to a grim end without martyrdom. He has deceived us. We will be made a mockery."

Bormann quieted his rage, his skin now finding color. He rose from the Führer's chair and walked with speed from the study. His strides stopped for nothing, either human or concrete. He came into Goebbels' personal chamber unannounced and found him there, quiet and reflective at his desk. Bormann stood in front of Goebbels, his manner stern and desperate. He was breathing heavily, and his rage reappeared.

"We are in grave danger, Reich Chancellor."

"Yes, and how so?"

"The document, the one we all signed, has gone from the bunker. I fear it will fall to enemy hands. If found, we will be held accountable, responsible. Condemned. The lower classes of the world. The West. The Russians. They do not subscribe to our necessary acts. They will not understand the work we have done, work that was given to us by the Almighty. The Prophets of the next coming. Our escape and continuation of the Nazi way, our new government will be compromised. We must act quickly I beg of you!"

Goebbels sat back, still relaxed, his elbows on the edge of the chair arms. His hands held his chin; his index fingers came to a point upon his lips. He listened, but he was more intrigued by Bormann's performance. His voice was quiet with little worry.

"Ah, that document. Yes, we've all signed it. No matter, Herr Bormann, it concerns me not at this late hour. Our great leader has chosen his path into a valiant and mighty ending, one that will live in infamy to be sure. The truth is that he insisted that I follow his orders to live, to carry out the prophecy and further its philosophies. However, it would be treasonous to abandon the Führer at such a great moment in history. My family and I will join him."

Bormann stood utterly shocked. His little performance had had no effect upon Goebbels. Having one last arrow in his quiver, he pulled his bow to a draw. "My great and supreme Goebbels," he appealed, "our signatures, they will condemn us for our deeds."

Goebbels remained motionless and silently laughed to himself. "My, my dear Bormann, your manipulative plays have no bearing upon my mind. Be done with your conniving chants. Word has been sent to Admiral Dönitz of the Führer's death. Perhaps you should take your performance to him."

Bormann relaxed his stance. His mind found a new strategy to play. He turned from Goebbels, beginning to take his leave. Goebbels stayed seated, his eyes following Bormann to the door.

"Bormann," Goebbels softly beckoned. Bormann stopped, raised his head, but did not turn to face Goebbels. "Remember this. We are but the puppets in this production. Nothing but crudely painted wooden dolls with strings attached. When the world has its voice again, it will remember one figure after all this comes to a conclusion. That will be the Führer. You and I? We are fleeting personalities. History will write nothing of us. We are not worthy of remembrance. Historians will relieve us from our part in this vicious life. Go. Find your end in whatever way you must. Write your own tale, Bormann, if you so choose."

Bormann continued his leave of Goebbels' chamber and hurried down the corridor back to his office. "Fool of a mystic," he huffed from his pursed lips. "What is power and the greatness of a deity if you're not alive to reap the spoils and bathe in its gifts? Does no one understand this? No. I will live to see that my name reigns with great power."

Bormann entered his office and set himself down into his chair like a sack of potatoes dropped from the shoulders of its laborer. He scowled and clenched his hands, his anger contorting his face. He pulled a bottle of cognac from the bottom left drawer, pulled a glass from another drawer on the other side of him, and poured it to its edge. The meniscus of the glass kept it from spilling down the side. He sat back in his chair, not taking a drink, and mumbled to himself with ill-intent.

"Admiral Dönitz is a loyal Nazi but a rational one. He will not continue this fight. He is a soldier, not a stately politician. He will take counsel from his generals, many of whom have no will left to keep the Reich alive to its victory. Traitors, they are. All of them. If that Jew gets to Dönitz alive, he will have the papers. Dönitz will surrender Germany and the document, using it for his own bargaining chip. I am sure of it. And that will be the end. I will be brought to the satisfying trigger hand of a firing squad or hanged with the hangman's last laugh. No, that shall not be my end." Bormann's eyes grew callous. His voice ominous. "This Jew. He must be stopped."

Bormann stood up, his mind coming to a quick solution. He stepped from his desk, ignoring his drink as he left the room. He called down the dark, hollow corridor left and then right, "Müller! Müller!" Coming upon Major Günsche, one of the Führer's adjutants, he barked, "Have you seen Gestapo Chief Müller? I request his presence."

Startled, Günsche answered without hesitation. "No, Herr Bormann, his whereabouts are unknown to me. Perhaps you should check with General Krebs."

"Very well. Continue on, Major." Bormann turned and walked back towards the conference room where he found Müller speaking with two SS officers. Bormann disregarded the conversation in progress and interrupted them. "Gestapo Müller, I request your presence at once. Please follow me to my quarters, if you will. I have urgent business that needs your attention."

Müller looked up, breaking his sentence and discussion with the two SS officers. "What talents of mine have you need of, Herr

Bormann? Do you need me for a military matter or one of your scandalous pranks?" Müller laughed quietly and turned back to the officers, both of whom found the humor satisfying, joining in on his little stab.

Bormann became furious and jumped towards Müller, slamming his hand upon the table. "Your insolence fails to be entertaining. How does being responsible for the annihilation of millions stand with your future success, Gestapo Müller? You know of what I speak. You were given the task of carrying out such plans under Heydrich. Certainly, you remember all of this? Perhaps now you may want to hear me out? Is that entertaining enough?"

Bormann stood up and straightened his tunic, pushing it back down over his waist and tidying up the dishevelment caused by his tirade. "I suggest you follow me, Gestapo Chief. There is work to do."

Bormann turned and walked from the room. Müller sat wide-eyed, without speech. He froze, numb for a span of a few minutes. Without warning, as if acknowledging his fears, he snapped back to the present. He gathered his belongings, stood up, set his SS visor low over his brow, and followed Bormann's order without bidding the SS officers farewell.

Müller entered Bormann's office and found him sitting motionless with drink in hand, his glass near empty. "Come, sit, Müller. Cognac? I find it helps revive the soul."

"No, Herr Bormann. Keep that filth to yourself." He sat down in front of Bormann and studied his behavior. "While I disapprove of your manners, your outburst being quite vulgar, I find your words to be of interest. Speak freely, if you must."

Bormann smiled with a devilish grin, his foul breath spreading its fingers across the desk and searching for clean air to spoil. "I am in need of creating a death squad. A valiant task for your Einsatzgruppen, I suspect. I request only four of your most loyal and malicious men. You will send word to whom you choose with instructions to track and apprehend two boys dressed as Hitler Youth. They are to kill the one boy, Otto, a Jew. His companion, Joseph Kessler, is to be set free. Unless, of course, he resists. The Jew has on his person a very, very important document. They are traveling to Admiral Dönitz, stationed in the North. Upon the seizure of the document, they are to bring them to me in Lubeck.

Müller sat back dumbfounded. "But how, how did this happen on our watch?"

"This is not of importance. Can you do as I ask?" Bormann carefully set his glass down and leaned forward on his desk towards Müller calming his voice. "All these years, Gestapo Chief, the tireless discipline you have shown in your work, your devout loyalty, never taking a holiday, your relentless commitment and dedication, have now come to this most critical assignment. The Reich is at certain risk. Our very own legacy. Well, I need not share with you that path. If you must know, I have always particularly admired your ruthlessness. We must partner, Gestapo Chief. Again, I ask you, can you see to this one last task?"

Gestapo Müller sat straight up, eyes fixated on Bormann, as if hypnotized. "Yes, Herr Bormann. I shall see to it at once. Unfortunately, the Einsatzgruppen are scattered, most of its members having been filtered into the regular army this late in the war. However, there is one group, a very nasty bunch they are, an evil mixture from many units. I shall reach them by telegraph. I am curious, Herr Bormann, not to disrespect your authority, but does Goebbels know of this matter? What of the High Court? What of Göring and Himmler? Have they been notified? Surely, the guilt is shared."

Bormann sat back, a sinister grin misshaping the air. "Treachery is afoot, Gestapo Chief, as each partner in the High Court seeks to further himself from the Führer's legacy or, in contrast, delve deeper into his psyche following him into a great end. Reichsmarschall Göring stays away, hiding at his grand palace, hunting, hoarding treasures, and courting grand parties, living the life of luxury as a wealthy man. He despises Himmler, fights with Goebbels, and mistrusts me in his quest for power. The Führer was his only saving angel. He cares not about the war as a whole.

"Himmler is conniving, constantly playing all of us for his own greed. He pays no mind to the possibility of Göring as the successor since his confidence in Göring wavers. In his mind, he feels he is the one needed to guide and police the new Germany and make all the decisions of the state. Little be known, he conceived a plan of surrender, speaking with Count Bernodotte, a Swedish diplomat. He tried to bargain Germany into submission for his own benefit. He is a traitor and a thief.

"Yes, Goebbels knows and cares not of this new information. His egomaniacal self tarnishes his duties as the Reich Minister of Propaganda. True, his devotion to the Führer is unwavering in furthering the fight and drive of Germany. I rather admired his idea of 'Total War' among the German people to use all available resources in rendering the enemy into submission. He believes in a war won, of a great empire, of a superior Germany. He believes his own propagandist self, but in the presence of the bunker, he knows the war is lost. More often than not, he is eerily quiet. Escape never comes to his mind. He fears for his children, and I suspect he will seek the same ending for his family that the Führer has taken. Lastly, that leaves me, your Reichsleiter. I should think you know of my power, beliefs, and capabilities. It is, therefore, up to us to save the Fatherland. I will be leading a breakout by early evening. We shall not have contact. I'll await your group's success. Go now. Make haste."

Chapter 7

Otto ran hard from the gardens into the decrepit remains of the Reich Chancellery, through doors from room to room, down long corridors, jumping mangled corpses of furniture, decorations, and the final resting places of building debris. He came to the exit for Voss Strasse leading to the Kaiserhof station from whence he had come less than a day ago. He stopped to inspect the grounds as his breathing caught up to his heart's beat. Forgetting he had a companion, Otto turned to learn Joseph was not in sight. Several moments passed before he at last heard the scuffing of boots as Joseph appeared from inside the Chancellery. Otto turned back around and continued his surveillance.

Joseph stepped up beside Otto, a nasty expression on his face. "Let us go, Jew, now that I have found you."

"Jew? Really, is that how we are to start? During all the harrowing events we have shared thus far in the bunker, not a word was spoken by you. When you finally do speak, all you have to say is 'Let us go, Jew?' Well fine. Perfect. Then I shall call you 'Hun.'"

Hardly amused, Joseph stepped in front of Otto. "You don't dare. Father will not hear of that word. We are not the peasants and barbarians of that age. We are wealthy, prestigious, and highly regarded aristocrats, loyal to the Nazi regime."

"Well, what am I to call you then, 'Hun?' If you are to call me 'Jew,' then certainly it's fitting to address you as 'Hun,' seeing you are using the word Jew in a derogatory manner. Or, you could call me 'Otto,' for that is my name."

"But you are a Jew, are you not?"

"Well, I am Jewish, if that's what you mean. That is my religion. I don't know what being Jewish has to do with any of this. If it's equality in name recognition you seek, then what is your religion, Hun, and I shall call you that?" Otto stared at Joseph waiting his reply as Joseph stood silent, trying to follow Otto's reasoning.

"Hurry up then, Hun, we haven't got all day. War is knocking on our door and wants to play. Quickly now. We have a long road ahead. We must end this banter and sort this out here and now."

Joseph relented, if just to appease the situation for the moment. "Fine, Jew. I mean Otto. Let's be done with it for the moment." Joseph turned to follow Otto's eyes upon the landscape. "What is it? What do you see, Je..., I mean."

"No, no, no. My name is Otto."

"I know. I know."

They both stood silently once again, still staring out across the decimated landscape.

"It's quiet, despite the noise. It troubles me."

"Yes. It's very unsettling, this air. Perhaps we had better keep moving."

Otto took a step from the doorway and down the stairs. He looked back, not hearing Joseph following. "What is it now, Joseph? My movements not slow enough for you?"

Joseph smiled with an evil grin as he stepped towards Otto. "I am the leader here my, uh, my Jewish religious friend. I make the decisions. We go when I go and where I go. You forget Herr Bormann's orders."

"Um, fine then, my, uh, Hun barbarian friend. Just make sure you keep up with me."

Joseph stepped in front of Otto and sneered at him as they made their way down the street, hugging the nooks and crannies of the tangled landscape and following the shadows created by the sinking sun.

"Darkness is coming, Joseph. I don't see this assault group as told by Sergeant Misch. Perhaps their action is delayed."

"Or destroyed, Jew."

Otto sat down to remove an object from his boot. "I suggest we move quickly to the River Spree under the cover of darkness as counseled by Corporal Huber and await this so-called breakout assault. We can move under its cover as it unfolds from there."

"Or we can move under the shadows of the subway tunnels, hidden from the enemy, and resurface at the River Spree."

Otto stood up after removing a small metal fragment from his boot, tossing it aside to find its end elsewhere. "No, Joseph, I would not venture back into the tunnels unless I had no other choice. The enemy is swelling, and the tunnels hide their menace. The Ivans have now found its value. Besides, the road looks vacant for now. Let us take advantage of its silence."

Joseph nodded. "While I agree with you, Jew, please know that it will not likely happen very often, if ever again."

"Ha, Joseph. It makes me smile knowing I am right and that your mind is tormented because of it."

Joseph's grin soured. "Just keep moving, Jew."

They came upon the Kaiserhof station but suddenly were stopped in their tracks. They looked at each other with a surprised expression, as if not expecting what they were hearing. Notes of music drifted and swirled in the wind from the other side of the station. They continued their investigation, and from around the corner, they came across four men. They were sitting on the upper platform in front of the entrance to the station. All were wearing pressed and clean tuxedos, appropriate attire for the chamber music they were performing. Two were playing the violin, one a viola, and the other a cello.

"They're playing a work by Joseph Haydn, Jew. He is the Father of the String Quartet."

Otto nodded and continued his steps, the moment passing while Joseph stood still. "Father would sit us in the parlor after dinner. He would have a smoke and play this piece on the phonograph. Father fancied music. It was the only art form he accepted. This music is very old, Jew. I forget what the name of the arrangement was, but it had to do with the meaning of life and such."

Otto walked back towards Joseph. He stood next to him and gave Joseph time to reflect. He remembered what Corporal Huber had said to him. 'Find the good in him.'

"It's very beautiful. I, too, have known many nights around the hearth listening to great composers. Is it not amazing, Joseph, that there is still such joy as this gathering before us, finding its place among these ruins? Perhaps the world has started its healing. It is spring, as you know. Perhaps at another time, you can share these stories. I should like to listen, but we mustn't linger any longer. We must move now."

Joseph nodded. He took one last earful of the music's delight, grasped his MP-40 tighter, turned, and quickly followed Otto back to the shadows of the street. They turned up Friedrichstrasse and could see an army group ahead scattering about as if planning a maneuver. Joseph pulled binoculars from his musette bag and, from a hidden position, scouted the grounds.

"Well, they're German alright. Seems the staging area is farther than Sergeant Misch proposed. I see five Tiger tanks and a PaK 37 field gun. Not a lot of artillery and armor for an assault of any magnitude, but there may be more hidden from my sight. I see twenty troops in the open, but they're crouching. There is fire upon them. The battle lines are near."

"May I have your binoculars? There are other things on my mind I wish to search for such as a good hiding place and an escape route, should we need it. I have not been down this road in many days."

Joseph wiped the lenses of the binoculars and handed them to Otto.

"Hmm. The Weidendammer Bridge is too far away to see, but it is my guess that the bridge is this army group's quest. There's enough cover for us to reach them, hopefully without the enemy seeing our movements. We can move methodically in and out of the contorted rubble, using the shelter and passages of cellars and alley ways. We cannot be sure where the battle starts or ends. The lines are very grey these days."

Otto handed the binoculars back to Joseph as they continued their move. Silence reigned their steps with the stealth of a cat stalking its prey. They weaved in and out of the skeletons of war-torn buildings and damp lifeless cellars, climbing up and over unrecognizable debris. They came to the left-side corner of a four way stop, a small street that crossed Friedrichstrasse. Joseph looked both ways up and down the street, not for coming civilian cars or buses, for they had not existed for quite some time. Instead, he searched for army groups. Off to the west, he could see troops scatter across this very street. For whose side they fought, he could not tell. It did not matter. They were taking their danger elsewhere. With the way seemingly clear, Otto and Joseph ran for the other side, continuing their dance of jumping wreckage and waste.

"Well, Joseph, this is much simpler than navigating the darkness of the subway tunnels. And perhaps even less dangerous."

"Hold that thought, Jew." Joseph pointed to the sky near the street corner.

Otto looked up, following Joseph's finger. Hanging from a lamp post by a crude wire noose was a German private not more than nineteen years old. His neck was snapped like a dead tree limb. His head slanted ninety degrees sideways. His tongue drooped from his mouth, and his glazed eyes bulged. Otto stood emotionless. It disturbed him little.

"A deserter, Jew. I have heard the stories that have reached our ears these days. The High Court has given orders to shoot or hang anyone not carrying a weapon to the victory of this fight."

"Better give me your gun then, Joseph. Best I not be taken the wrong way."

"Ha, ha, Jew. Very funny. It will take much more than your subtle wit to persuade me to agree with such an act. No. You'll have to do better to rid me of my presence for my allegiance is strong-willed."

"As strong-willed as that officer motioning to us from up the road?"

Joseph turned quickly to see what Otto was referring to. "Yes. We better move towards him, or we might find ourselves hanging next to this poor fellow."

"Good idea. Yet I fear we'll be folded into whatever sorry ranks he has at his disposal for this futile assault."

"Perhaps. We'll have to try to play along then take our leave as an opportunity arises."

Otto and Joseph ran double-time to where the officer was positioned. From this point. they could see the Weidendammer bridge a few blocks away. The sounds of war grew heavier with the menacing staccato of machine gun fire and increased calls of artillery. They came up to the officer, who was taking cover in a bomb crater by the side of the road, and jumped in alongside him. There were ten other soldiers around him. Otto could now tell he was a sergeant in rank but gave little attention to the conditions or descriptions of the others. Joseph made a quick scan of the area, which divulged fifty or more soldiers scurrying about making ready for some kind of action.

The sergeant sat motionless with a dumbfounded scowl upon his face. "Two Hitler Youth? That's all? I ask for reinforcements, and all I get are two scrawny youths? This assault is folly. To our deaths we go. Well, youngsters, welcome to the SS Nordland Division. We have today for our specials, which are now attached to us, the Volksturm, a raggedy lot of old men and boys, whom I expect are not quite toilet trained. You just missed a quick lesson I gave the little ones on close-quarter combat and the use of this wicked little device next to me called the Panzerfaust. Now hop yourselves closer to me, my young lads, and listen closely. I have patience for only one more lesson."

Otto and Joseph quickly obeyed, not wanting to open more discussion after hearing the sergeant's questionable psychotic rant. Best to keep quiet. So far, so good, they thought.

The sergeant pulled the weapon to his side and began his lesson. "Now this crudely constructed weapon I hold here before you has a long, hollow metal shaft with an oversized warhead on the end containing an equal mixture of TNT and hexogen explosives. It's correctly fired from the crook of the arm. See? Like this. Along the side of the tube is a simple folding rear sight and trigger. You line the rear sight up with the target, pull the trigger, and boom! Its effects are simply devastating. Now, you have to be relatively close to use it. I am sure your courage and fear are unwavering. Is that not so, my little warriors?" Motioning to Otto, the sergeant observed, "Seeing how, my friend, you seem not to have a fine weapon, as does your comrade, I give you mine. It's either that or find yourself next to that poor soul of a private who ran from my little class a few days ago. He now finds himself waving high in the wind. I am sure you saw him as you approached."

Otto grabbed the Panzerfaust from the sergeant. "Now, I hold it like this? Is that right, Sergeant?"

"Perfect, my boy." The sergeant stood up, secured his machine gun, stuffed two grenades into his belt, and lifted his head high into the darkening sky. "Ready yourselves, my little ones. The show is about to start as soon as the grim reaper gives us his twisted signal. If indeed this is to be our end, let us make it such an end as to be worthy of a song."

Otto and Joseph sat looking at each other, made suspicious by the behavior of the sergeant, who moved out from the crater and scurried off. A few of the soldiers followed, leaving the restless others behind.

"What a strange person, don't you think, Jew?"

"Yes, Hun. Thank goodness for our sake he heard the reaper call him away."

Otto looked down at the Panzerfaust as if wondering what to do with it. "This thing is heavy. I should think I'm supposed to fire it at armor, yes?"

"That's the idea, Otto."

"Wait a minute. Did you just call me, 'Otto?'"

"Well, that's your Jew name, isn't it?"

Otto smiled to himself, closing his eyes and then opening them as he shook his head. "And to think we were so close."

Joseph ignored Otto's response. "You speak German, Jew, so you would know the word 'Panzerfaust' literally means 'Tank Fist.' So yes, the idea is to fire it at tanks. Don't worry yourself. We won't be getting that close to combat."

"So you think, Joseph. I have learned combat calls you like a mother to her child. It wants to be found. Nevertheless, I have scanned this entire area and cannot conceive of a way to get around this army group or the other one holding in wait across the river. As you know, there were small Russian patrols in the subway tunnels not five hundred meters from the Chancellery. The front is in all directions. Where are we to go?"

"Into the river."

"What?"

"You heard me. We shall go into the river."

"I heard you, but you've lost your Hun mind, Joseph. It may be spring, but the river has not warmed, not yet freeing itself from its winter chill. We'll freeze. We'll be unable to move and then we'll surely drown."

"You offer no better solution, so it's into the river. Don't fret, my Panzerfaust-toting companion. We'll swim to the opposite shore and hurry along its banks, moving south. We'll find a place to warm ourselves far enough away from the fighting and rest for the remainder of the night. Then, we'll swing around to the north and back to our original route."

"What of my important document? How shall it stay dry?"

"Hmm, good point. You'll have to keep your satchel over your head as you swim."

"So I shall drown, then? Glad your plan has my interests at heart."

"Oh, I get it, more sarcasm?"

"Yes. And well deserved."

"Enough of this. Let's get into position. Darkness threatens."

Without warning, screams echoed through the air, disturbing the smoke that had laid claim to its space. Rocket and mortar fire burst around Otto and Joseph, shaking the earth from its tortured rest.

A soldier sitting across the crater from the boys yelled out, "It has begun!" Quickly, he and the other soldiers moved out of the crater and into the streets, finding positions for the assault. Otto stood up slightly and could see two of the five Tiger tanks moving steadily up the street towards them, making for the bridge. Soldiers ran here and there from hidden places as the tanks crept forward. Machine gun fire erupted suddenly with heavy bursts following the call of the artillery. Ricochets spewed dirt and grime from the streets and buildings searching for something to kill.

"Quickly, Jew. Make for the bridge and down to the river's edge!"

Otto looked up from the crater to his left and right. Convinced the coast was clear of that woolly sergeant, he dropped the Panzerfaust, swung his musette bag and satchel around his head and under his shoulders, and lurched from his position, following Joseph. "No time for shooting things. I've got a river to cross."

They ran to the east side of the street, swinging behind the first Tiger tank and cutting through a huddled line of soldiers, using the steel behemoth as cover. Bullets whizzed past their heads creating hollow, whistle-like cracks through the air. The first Tiger drew near the bridge, the second following closely behind. Looking back, Otto could see the other three tanks arriving and finally getting into the battle. The tanks fired their enormous 88-millimeter guns upon their approach. The noise around them was deafening. Otto's ears began ringing and his head pounding. His eyes teared from the smoke and dust as he tried in vain to continuously wipe them clean, only aggravating them more.

Joseph moved with the speed of the tanks, trying not to get ahead and not wanting to draw suspecting fire. Better the tank drew all the attention. Suddenly from behind them, they heard the sergeant from the crater yelling at them to press on across the bridge.

"Damn, Joseph, if that crotchety old sergeant sees us head to the riverbank, we'll be shot."

"I know. He thinks we're leading this assault. We'll have to get to the middle of the bridge, fake being shot, and fall from the bridge into the water. It's not a far drop. Just land in the water going feet first."

"What? Did I hear you correctly? We are to jump from the bridge?"

"Yes. That is correct."

"Okay, I thought you said something crazy."

Joseph and Otto moved to the entrance of the bridge. Wrecked armor and the dead lay silent from the battles of old.

"Hmm. This area looks rather familiar. Well, Joseph, I am glad your plan is coming together so well.

"I have no time for your sarcastic jabs, Jew. Quickly now. The soldiers are almost upon us. We are almost to the middle."

At that moment, a rocket came screeching from high above with an evil grin and struck the lead Tiger tank's turret on the left side. The explosion ripped its top 26-millimeter steel hull to shreds as if it were tissue paper. Hot steel fragments launched from the hit tore into all those around it, decapitating heads and severing body parts. The concussion from the burst threw Otto and Joseph hard into the side of the bridge's iron guardrail. Otto's eyes clamped shut, and his head spun, dizzy and confused. He could hear a whipping of wind, voices yelling, and a high-pitched ringing. Joseph was knocked out cold, limp and frozen, his legs and arms lifeless. Otto fought to gain control and clarity. He struggled to open his eyes, wiping away the effects of the blast, a black and hot film that covered his face. He finally forced his eyes to open, his first sight being the Tiger burning with rage and viciousness. It was far enough away not to scorch them but close enough that they could feel its heat. Luckily, the tank's ordnance had not exploded or they would surely have been obliterated upon the bridge.

Heavy weapons fire was constant, and Otto could feel the rounds being traded back and forth, cutting the air before him as they traveled. German soldiers in disturbed positions lay dead around him. Those who were alive used the dead as cover for their advance. None of them gave any attention to Otto and Joseph. They were left for dead.

Struggling, Otto came to his knees from a flattened position. He grabbed the guardrail and pulled himself up. At this point, he did not even remember being on the bridge. His head was still spinning. Otto felt for his belongings, trying to remember what had happened. He looked down at Joseph still sprawled on the street to his side, his body pressed against the bridge. For an unknown reason, he bent down and shook Joseph, not really understanding who he was. Joseph's body shook freely, but he did not respond.

"Get up!" Otto yelled to him. "Get up!" Otto reached into his musette bag and pulled out his canteen. He twisted off the cap and poured the entire can over Joseph's head. "Wake up!"

Joseph shuddered, his eyes opening slightly to let in the disturbing light from the burning tank. He turned his head slowly looking up and into Otto's eyes. "I'm wet. Are we in the water, Jew?"

Otto smiled faintly, his mind finally clearing so that he recognized him as Joseph. "No, Hun, we are still on the bridge."

"Then why am I wet?"

"Well, funny thing about that. I, uh..."

"Never mind, Jew. Let's get the hell off this bridge!" Joseph helped himself up and grabbed his machine gun. "Hmm. Seems we are in the midst of a huge battle."

"Good of you to notice, Joseph. Shall we go?"

"After you, Jew."

Otto grabbed the guardrail, and with a swift flip of his legs to his side, he tossed himself from the bridge yelling at the top of his lungs, "My name is Ottooooo!"

In less than a second, Otto hit the ink-colored water with a mighty splash. He closed his eyes, bracing for the impending cold. He sliced deeply into the water, his shirt and jacket becoming undone and covering his head as he fought for the surface. Reaching the air, he gasped and coughed, spewing water from his nose and mouth. He took a deep breath and kicked his legs violently to keep above the water's surface. Immediately, he remembered to bring his satchel above the water in an effort to keep the document dry, knowing very well they followed him deep into the water upon his entrance. He struggled to brush his jacket and shirt away from his face. Suddenly, a hand came to his aid and swiped the clothing from his head. Joseph was next to him, motioning for Otto to follow. They swam frantically, the cold water proving awkward to navigate. Otto's teeth began to chatter, and his breathing labored. His arms slowed, and he could feel his heart pounding, struggling to pump warm blood throughout his body.

"Hurry, Joseph, my swim is failing. Please, please find the bank."

"Stand up, Jew. You can stand now. You're in the shallows."

Otto thrust his legs to the bottom of the river and stood up, the water falling to his waist, his mind quite relieved.

"Oh, well look at that."

Joseph shook his head in bewilderment. "Silly Jew."

Otto joined Joseph on the bank and immediately felt inside his satchel. "Amazing, but I don't think it got too wet in here."

"Well, we have no time to ponder the reasons. We must create distance between us and that bridge. Hurry. Let's be on the move. Now stay close behind me, Jew, but not on top of me, and for heaven's sake, don't gallop ahead of me. It's like constantly running a marathon with you." Otto smiled, and the boys leapt quietly into the darkness.

Chapter 8

Otto and Joseph darted through the trees along the river bank, awkwardly at first until their eyes adjusted to the darkness. The deathly sounds of the battle raged behind them, slowly fading as they pushed for distance.

"Ouch!" cried Joseph. "Damn. I hate these mosquitoes. They must be drawn to my damp clothing and the heat of my body."

"Funny, they're not pestering me. They must be drawn to that pure, superior Aryan blood I have heard about on and off for the past five years."

"Ah, good of you to recognize my saintly qualities, Jew. Father would not share in your sarcasm lest it not be the truth."

"Yes, quite. Oh, by the way, we are one for one in saving each other."

"How so?" asked Joseph, halting his lead as he turned to confront Otto.

"Well, technically, I saved your life on the bridge. Yes, Joseph, don't make that face with me. I woke you when you were knocked out cold. The way that battle is still polluting the air with its grip, I'm sure you would have been killed by now."

"Ah, yes. Perhaps. Except your math is faulty, as I have saved your life twice. Once in the subway station and again in the bunker from Herr Bormann's wrath."

"No, no, no, Joseph. Both of those times you did not know who you were saving, so they don't really count. Technically, that is. I, on the other hand, more or less knew who you were on the bridge. I chose to save you. I gave you a point because you hesitated in shooting me in the dining room with Herr Bormann. You had the time. You hesitated out of choice. Circumstance intervened and was the decider in saving me, as we were interrupted."

"I was confused. You were wearing the clothes of the Hitler Youth. Well, sort of. You were in the bunker, and you are a Jew. The excitement of the situation clouded my judgment. Under different circumstances, we would not be having this conversation." Joseph moved close to Otto's face. "You would be dead." He paused, letting his sentence linger, then he turned and moved on.

Otto whispered to himself softly, so that Joseph could not hear, "Well, so much for trying to start getting on his 'good' side, Corporal Huber. This is like meeting a brick wall. Perhaps I need to go around the back way." Otto continued to follow Joseph, speeding his steps to catch up to him.

"We need to find a place of warmth, Jew. The air is crisp, and the wind howls, spreading its chill and slowing our steps."

"Agreed. We must get off this river and rid ourselves of its dampness. We need to find concealment that allows not only warmth but a good escape route, should we need it."

Darkness grew upon their path as Otto and Joseph worked their way inland, heading on a more northernly route. They came upon the outskirts of Berlin proper, a more rural part of the city. The story was more of the same. Destruction had had its voice. Homes were in a shambles. Wreckage, both civilian and military, shared the same fate. Animals of all kinds, dogs, cows, and horses, littered the ground rotting, their bellies bloated with internal gases not yet finding their way to less disturbed air. Fires burned sporadically, some larger than others. Some smoldered, their fate almost complete.

"Looks as if everything has been left for dead, Joseph. The Russians have moved through here quickly."

"Yes, so quickly that their own graves registration unit has already gathered their own."

"They must have piled the German dead and set them ablaze, which would account for some of the foul stench wafting through our noses."

"We must be cautious, Jew. Patrols will likely be alert, mopping up any smaller resistance and protecting the ground already won."

"Agreed, Hun."

Joseph turned his head away and continued moving down a wooded tree line. "This arguing about how we address each other is petty."

"Petty? It's simple. Just call me by my name. Is that so hard? I call you 'Joseph,' and you call me 'Otto.'"

Joseph stopped and turned to face Otto, again getting closer to his face. "Except you are a Jew, an inferior, worthless human being, wasted upon society. So accept it, and we shall move on."

"I certainly will not. Why? Why am I so less of a human than you?"

Joseph walked away, muttering under his breath. "Because father told me so." Joseph held his machine gun up to his waist as he walked, firming his grip. "Quickly, Jew, there is no time to waste. We've been walking for hours, and I am tired, too tired to have this conversation. On top of that, I am freezing in these damp clothes."

"Fair enough, Joseph. Let's seek our shelter, but this conversation is far from being finished."

Joseph and Otto moved off the tree line and down a small dirt lane with high hedgerows on both sides. The night sky proved darker on this path, making their sight strained and recognition of objects difficult. Otto moved to the opposite side of the lane from Joseph and put his hand out to his side. He noticed the obvious shape of a building in front of him and reached to touch it as he moved. His hands shook from the cold as they pressed against a wooden surface.

They searched and felt their way up and down, looking for a sign of something to grasp. Joseph stopped walking and stood waiting for Otto to offer a word.

"Ah, this feels like a door." Otto continued his search and came upon a handle with a latch mechanism. "Yes, I think this is a barn of some sort."

Joseph walked over to Otto, and they both entered the structure. Joseph pulled his MP-40 up from his waist to his shoulder, setting it into firing position. He strained to see what was inside and whispered to Otto. "I can't see a thing. How do you know this is a barn?"

"It smells like manure, and there's hay on the ground."

"Ah, right Jew. Your kind understand that sort of thing."

"Ha, ha. While not funny, I'll take that as a compliment. We are not known to be farmers, so my knowing what this place is must be a miracle."

Otto walked farther into the room, his arms stretched out, his hands open, fingers spread apart. Suddenly, he bumped into something, hitting him at chest height. He dropped his arms down and searched the surface.

"Hmm, this feels like a platform of some kind, and it's full of hay for as far back as I can reach. Might make a great bed. Better yet, a great fort." Otto turned his head and called quietly to Joseph. "Pst! Pst! Joseph. Joseph. Come. I found us our bed for the night."

Joseph walked towards Otto's voice, and as soon as he had taken a step, he bumped into Otto. "Ouch! Fool of a Jew. Watch where you are going."

"Me? I wasn't moving. You were. Silly Hun."

"Stop calling me that."

"Fine. I think I have a worthy place for our bed tonight. Help lift me up. I think this will work out rather well."

Joseph stretched his arms down and out, clenching his fingers together to make a step for Otto. Otto grabbed the edge of the platform, and with his foot set in Joseph's hands, he hoisted himself up onto the platform.

"Now how am I to get up, Jew?"

"I don't know. You're the superior Aryan race. Why don't you figure it out?"

"Really, Otto, you want to do this now?"

"Okay, I'll help but only because you're tired."

Grunting, Otto struggled to pull Joseph to the platform by grabbing his woolen trousers by the back. He pulled hard, and with one big 'humph,' Joseph was on the platform.

"Great, Jew. Now my under drawers are all wadded up around my privates."

"Stop your complaining. Look at this great mound of hay we have for our bed. I suggest we dig underneath and build a small fort. It'll help keep us warm and aid in drying us."

Otto and Joseph quickly tunneled under the hay, creating a small cavity around their faces from which to breathe. In no time, the heat generated from their bodies warmed their little hiding place quite well. Exhausted, damp, and hidden, they fell quickly to sleep.

Suddenly, Joseph's eyes opened, his mind alerted to an unknown presence. "Pst! Pst! Wake up, Jew! Wake up!"

Otto moaned and turned his head away, still in his dream. "No, Momma, no. I don't want to see Grandma. She smells."

"Stop your dreaming and wake up!"

Turning his head back towards Joseph and forgetting he was in a war zone, Otto snapped at him in an annoyed voice. "What? What is it?"

"This, this great hideout, fort, whatever you call it. Well, it's moving. So what now, my courier to the High Court? What now? We could be in a Russian convoy, for all we know, heading to the Gulags or worse. We could be going back to Berlin and into that mess!"

"Calm yourself, Joseph. My word. We have not been found out as yet. Thus, we are quite safe under this hay. My hiding place has done well to conceal us. Let's just pray we go unnoticed until we figure out what to do."

"Yes, well that's the real trick." Joseph reached for his MP-40 and slowly cocked the loading hammer back, the metal on metal sliding with a metallic glimmer of evil. "Well, whatever decision, I am ready."

Otto lay on his stomach as he had been all night, thinking of their next move. Hmm. It is obvious we are in a wagon of some sort. Why would a wagon full of hay be of any use to the Russians? They can't eat it, and they won't be hauling livestock around so they won't need it for feed. There's only one way for an answer. "I'm going to have a quick look, Joseph, to the cause of our moving fortress. So, please, stay calm and keep that damn gun pointed away from me."

Otto slowly began to move the hay from his body as he tunneled to the surface. The hay was light and as airy as a feather, making little sound. He neared the surface, the bright rays from the early morning light blinding his eyes. He shuffled a few strands of hay aside to shield the light and offer a better view of his surroundings. He could make out the silhouette of an old man sitting at the reins of what looked to be a horse-drawn wagon. Slowly, he popped his head up just as the wagon hit a hole in the road, bumping Otto off balance. "Whoa!" Otto exclaimed while reaching his arm out to brace himself from the jarring ride.

The old man turned abruptly, startled and surprised. "Well, what have we here!? A soldier boy?"

At that moment, Joseph popped his head above the hay, spitting out a mouthful of hay strands.

"Oh! Good gracious me. Two soldier boys." The old man tossed up his reins and stopped the wagon, shouting, "Hold up now, Gerty, my girl. Let her rest." The old man turned back around and rested his arm on the back of his seat, offering a whimsical smile. "Well, it seems my journey has just become quite a bit more perilous. Now, who might you young soldiers be?"

"Greetings, my good sir. My name is Otto Kaufmann, son of Solomon Kaufmann of Nord Strasse. This is my companion, Joseph, uh," leaning into Joseph in a whisper Otto asked, "What is your last name?"

"Kessler."

Otto turned back to the old man. "Uh, Joseph Kessler, from uh."

"Oh, for heaven's sake. I am Joseph Kessler, son of Rudolph Kessler of Munich."

"Deserters, are you?"

"No Sir," Otto replied. "We are on a mission of great significance. Our business is our own, which is safer for you if kept that way."

"A mission? Yes. Leaving this area safely, that is of grave significance. Much harder to do these days. There are very nasty-minded Russians all across these lands. A constant menace, they are."

"Yet you have survived?" Otto asked curiously. "Not much has lived past their notice."

"You are very observant, young Otto, son of Solomon. It would seem the Russians have little use wasting a bullet on a worn, portly, white-bearded old man. All I have had has perished. My farm, wife, sons, and grandchildren. Everything. Stories not of your needing. We must go. I am heading north to be with my sister. Where might you two adventurers be going?"

"We are heading north as well," Joseph answered sternly. "However, we do not ask you to take us. As my companion has said, our business is our own."

The old man turned back around towards his horse, "Very good, then. We'll address that matter soon, but for now we are still too close to the war. Let us be off. Hi! Ho! Come along, Gerty."

The old man snapped the reins, and the horse gave a stuttered tug, smoothing out as she came to her pace. "My name is Christoph Hartmann, son of Gotthard Hartmann. This was my farm, the burned, charred, and desecrated lands around you. Not much to see any more. Thus, I would drop back down into your little hollow you

151

so fondly created. No sense drawing the attention of the enemy. I will not stop until evening when I find a suitable place to conceal our presence for the night. Keep low, keep secret, keep silent."

Otto and Joseph nestled back down to their sleeping positions, recreating a cavity in which to breathe.

"Great! Just great, Jew. Now we have Saint Nikolaus at the helm of our sleigh being putted by an old, raggedy horse as a reindeer. To where? We have not an idea."

"Yes, and we're his two little helpers, stowing away for the journey."

"It troubles me that you are finding humor in this, Joseph."

"Actually, I am not, Joseph. I am quite worried. We have lost our control in this situation and the ability to move freely and set our own course at will. No. I share in your concern. You must admit, perhaps for a second, it is quite amusing this character we have come upon. Saint Nikolaus? That was funny, Joseph."

"Yes, quite amusing, but now what?"

"I am sure our dear Christoph has been thinking the same as we have. His journey is now much more dangerous having the two of us tagging along. The Germans would see us as deserters and the Russians as the enemy. Neither would find any humor if we are discovered. Thus, I am sure Christoph is choosing smarter, alternate routes in order to avoid such an entanglement. He seems odd, I give you that, but he is wise. Let's revel in this safety for the time being. Let him help us put some distance from here, and in time, we'll say our goodbyes."

"As much as I don't agree, based upon our predicament, I'll agree."

"Just be prepared to run hard if it comes to that."

Otto and Joseph lay still in their fort as instructed by Christoph. The road was bumpy and rutted, making for a very uncomfortable ride. The sound of the wooden wheels upon the graveled road drowned all knowledge of their whereabouts. Otto could not discern if he was hearing voices, nature, or the calls of battles still raging from afar. It was the not knowing that was causing more discomfort than the ride itself.

The warmth of the hay and the morning sun quickly shed the dampness of their clothes. The hay, while soft, scratched and tickled Otto, moving him to tuck his shirt back into his trousers, which were still disheveled from his water landing. Joseph had fallen back to sleep, leaving Otto in silence. He thought of how to persuade Joseph to delay their mission and set a new course in search of Annie. Unfortunately, he knew he had made no progress in befriending Joseph, only earning some, if any, trust.

Suddenly, the wagon came to an abrupt, jarring halt. Joseph flinched, awakened, his fingers clenching his MP-40. Otto shook back and forth, planting his hands flat against the bottom of the wagon, bracing himself against further disturbance. They listened for the cause but could hear very little from under the hay.

"Good day to you, my Bolshevik friends!" Christoph offered in a delighted and unassuming voice. "What a fine and prosperous new day we enjoy here. The revolutionary working class are together again as one unified power conquering the sinister greed of Nazism."

"Save your mischievous and petty placating, old man. Your words have little effect on whether my comrades here choose to let you live or not," the Russian soldier barked.

Christoph had come upon a large Russian group of a hundred men leading thousands of worn and deflated German prisoners east towards Russia, many of whom Christoph realized would never be seen again. "Yes, yes, my good sir. I meant no offense. I was merely excited upon your presence. It has been a long time that I have lived under such doubtful rule, and now I finally see some hope."

"Where are you off to, old man?" snapped the soldier. "Where are you taking this artifact of yours?"

"Oh, my horse and wagon? Well, we are moving to the north to visit my elder sister. She is not well and calls for my aid. I will work her farm and tend to her care."

The soldier eyed up and down and all along the wagon, looking under and around. Two other soldiers with fixed bayonets peeled off from watching their prisoners. They curiously walked up to join the lone soldier by the wagon and stood beside him.

"Lucky for you, my comrades and I have no time to quarrel and the thought of shooting you concerns me not. If your wagon is vacant, we'll let you continue with little worry. As for other Russians you may meet, well, we cannot promise you the same courtesies."

The soldier motioned for his two comrades to bayonet the hay. Without delay they began to thrust their rifles, their bayonets thumping to the wood of the wagon floor with a loud 'thwack'. Otto heard the wooden floor rattle, but could not identify its cause until upon another thrust. A shiny bayonet suddenly parted a clump of his hair as it plunged in front of his face, digging into the wood. His eyes bulged in disbelief at its sight, and fear swallowed his heart. He felt Joseph begin to move, and he quickly grasped the end of Joseph's machine gun, halting its temper.

Christoph snapped quickly to thought and action. "My good men, surely you must be hungry? How about some fresh milk and eggs for this glorious morning, yes?"

The soldiers paused their search and stared at one another. One soldier with his rifle at the ready to begin another thrust into the wagon slowly lowered it.

"Yes, old man," barked the leader. "We should enjoy that after we have thoroughly scoured your wagon." The soldier at the rear of the wagon raised his rifle again. His bayonet, while worn, having seen many battles, was still razor sharp, glimmering from the bright, morning light.

"No, no, no!" cried out Christoph. "You'll break the eggs if you go pummeling about my wagon like that. Quickly now, be at ease. Let me get you those eggs." Christoph scrambled from his seat, wrapping the reins around the wagon's brake mechanism. He stepped over the back of his seat and began digging through the hay.

"These are the best eggs in all the farms of this land." Christoph boasted excitedly, lifting up three wooden boxes filled with eggs.

Reaching over the side, he beckoned, "Here, here. Come and have a look. Take them. Take them all."

The Russian soldiers lowered their rifles and shouldered them to help hold the boxes of eggs. Christoph reached back down and came up with three small bottles of milk, fresh and inviting.

"I am sure it has been a long time since you lads have had fresh milk. Yes?" Christoph reached out and stacked a milk bottle upon each of the soldiers' boxes of eggs, further weighing their load. Christoph stood up proud, his hands at his waist.

"Ah! Look at you three. Soon you'll be feasting like kings. Now, before we create too much of a scene, I shall be off, okay?" Christoph quickly stepped back over to his seat and grabbed the reins, calling out, "Onward Gerty. Hi! Ho!"

The horse tugged, and the wheels slowly creaked back to speed. Christoph continued down the road, making a sharp left turn away from the soldiers' direction of travel. He took one last glance behind him for but a second. He chuckled to himself, his robust belly rolling with each breath upon seeing the three Russian soldiers, dumbfounded, standing motionless, arms full of eggs and milk.

Otto and Joseph moved not an inch. Otto's hand was still firmly gripped around Joseph's machine gun. Sweat poured from their faces, the hay creating an oven inside their cave. Joseph pushed his hand to the surface and brushed the hay from his face. Otto followed, hoping to convince Joseph to stay hidden. They gasped for air as they came to the open. Joseph spit pieces of hay from his mouth and shook his head.

"I am tired of this hiding, Otto, and let go of my gun."

"Quiet, child." Christoph barked. "We are not out of range of the soldiers yet. They will hear you. Now shush."

Otto released his grip on the machine gun and turned to face the back of the wagon. His eyes widened as he saw a spectacle unbelievable to his mind. Thousands of German soldiers were being led east. Many were lame, using tree limbs as canes to aid in their bitter march. A group of Russians singled out three obviously wounded soldiers who were seemingly holding up the march. They pushed them to the side of the road, forced them to their knees, and got behind them. The soldiers unholstered their pistols and shot the Germans in the back of the head. They fell limp to the ground, their heads with gaping holes flowing red. Smoke swirled and mushroomed from the wounds as the bodies lay in deformed shapes upon the ground.

Otto felt little pity or fear. He looked over at Joseph, who had a tear running down his cheek. Although Joseph had made no sound, the pain was deafening.

"Do not worry, Joseph. That will not be your end. We will make it through this. Believe in me."

Joseph turned and nodded, accepting Otto's words. He stood up, brushed off the hay, and sat back down fully exposed. The wagon rolled down the road, turned a bend, and the scene was out of sight. Otto raised himself also. Holding the sides of the wagon, he worked his way forward past Joseph, stepping over the seat and plopping down next to Christoph.

"You stink, young Otto," Christoph kidded, smiling down at Otto.

"Why does everybody keep saying that to me? Hmm. No matter. So what of the Russians? I take it we escaped a close one?"

"To be sure, my young boy. The allure of a strange and eccentric old man has a way of going unnoticed. Strength of mind wins over strength in arms every time. There are other ways of winning than fighting, dear boy."

"Brains over brawn? Yes, Poppa would say that to me often when my brothers were sure to antagonize me."

Otto sat calmly, his head falling towards his lap in an apologetic state. "Sorry we have brought this upon you, Christoph. We had no intention of bringing you this trouble as we stumbled upon your wagon merely by accident."

"Oh, no, my boy. Do not think of my abrupt words as means for anger. I suppose some of this is meant to have happened. Perhaps the understanding of it may never be known. However, every little step in our lives equals the greater piece of the outcome. Judge it then, my boy, when you have arrived and found yourself whole and as one. At that point, if you can stand tall, smile, and have happiness, then our meeting surely was a small contribution to your life."

Otto sat and listened. He enjoyed the old man, and his words felt strong and nurturing. "I am also sorry we cannot tell of our journey. We have great need to complete this mission, one last great deed for whose benefit I have no idea."

"I guessed as much, seeing that your satchel has hardly left your side. Military matters mean little to me, Otto. You have my trust and word to keep its secrecy."

The wagon crept slowly forward, its very own being weaving and tossing back and forth through field after field. Otto was correct. Christoph was steering clear of main roads, choosing back country lanes and farm roads, which did not appear on any army's map. Yet all around them, the land was scarred. The Russian army had been through this area upon overrunning General Heinrici's defenses, following its own scorched earth policy. Every town they passed through was damaged to some degree or burned to the ground altogether. Women stood lost, without their families. Their clothes were torn away and covering little, an outcome only the profiteer of a Russian man could smile upon. Children were crying, left vacant and alone. The men were killed. In the Russians' eyes, the men had once been soldiers or could become them.

"The fighting through this sector was vicious, Otto," explained Christoph, "with no quarter given to either side. I lay hidden in a secret room off the main part of my basement for many a day and could hear little, which is perhaps the reason you boys went into my barn unnoticed. Usually, the animals would have given an alarm. They would have rustled in a frenzy if someone other than my myself had entered. They know my smell, you see. The Russians had other ideas as they moved through. They pillaged my home, taking whatever fancied them. They shot my cows and feasted on their meat while encamped in my pastures. They stole my horses, except for ole' Gerty here. I have not a clue why, as the Russians were mechanized."

Christoph stared straight ahead while talking with Otto. He became quiet for a moment and then suddenly continued his thoughts. Otto could hear his voice change, knowing well he was about to offer words he did not want to hear.

"When they first arrived, they took my wife. I was not at home. I was in the wood lot felling trees to create more pasture land. They beat her, and they had their way with her. What kind of animal? What, what kind of beast does that to an old woman? To the rest of my family? I have not a clue. I speak no more of it."

Otto kept silent, his own eyes fixated upon the road ahead. Christoph's words hit hard, and a deep, sickening feeling sank to his stomach. Suddenly, he felt an eeriness and uncertainty about his mission.

Unexpectedly, Joseph stood up from behind the seat and poked his head in between Otto and Christoph. "Seems you two are getting fairly well acquainted. What news have I missed?"

"Nothing, Joseph. Christoph and I were merely reminiscing about brighter days of the past. Nothing that would concern you."

"Very well then. Let's speak of the future. Where are we to go, and when are we departing this ancient mode of transportation?"

"Forgive my bumbling companion, Christoph. Joseph's manners are tardy as of late."

"If you had been listening, young Joseph, when we started our journey," advised Christoph, "you would have heard that we are not to stop until nightfall. I will get you to the outskirts of Eberswalde, a ten hour trek. Seeing we have gone about four of those, we have six left. So I suggest, my young soldier, that you quit belly-aching, turn back around, plunk yourself deep down in the hay, and enjoy the scenery."

Christoph turned to Otto with a big grin. Otto could plainly see his smile through his long white beard. Otto chuckled back at Christoph as they continued their travel.

"I should think you may need to jump back there as well, Otto, for it is too dangerous for you to be in the open dressed as you are."

"I agree, Christoph. It is for the better. Let us know of our day's end as you see fit." Christoph nodded as Otto jumped in the back of the wagon.

"Oh, found time for what is important, have you, Jew? I was beginning to wonder what new thought you might have concerning our mission."

"There are none, Joseph. Our minds are one. Come morning, we shall seek our original route. Now, we had better bury ourselves again to aid in our concealment."

"Yes, but I am not making any more forts, Otto. I am tired of spitting up hay and dirt. Besides, you snore when asleep."

"Ha!" Otto snickered. "Well, that should help keep you and your metal traveling companion awake and on your toes!"

"You laugh, Jew, but this gun has already spared your life, if you recall, and I'll bet it will spare it once more before this mission is over."

"I believe that to be true, Joseph. Let us hope we are not near enough to the enemy for its use. Quickly now. Under the hay."

Otto and Joseph sank themselves deeper into the wagon. The sun had reached high into the sky, clouds passing harmlessly by on a whim, dimming its presence. Otto continued his thoughts and decided he would try and learn more about Joseph upon their stop for the night. He had heard under Joseph's breath something about his father telling him something. Otto wanted to further investigate what that might be. He was running out of time. He would have to convince Joseph to alter their route tonight or sneak away on his own. While that thought gave Otto peace of mind, knowing it was easier to care for himself alone, he was rather liking Joseph's company. He sensed a struggle within Joseph and knew Corporal Huber was right. There was good in Joseph. He would find it.

The sun followed its course, dipping behind the tree tops and creating long shadows and dark pockets within the woods. Christoph turned off the road, guiding Gerty across a rolling field into a hole in the thicket just in front of the tree line. He came to a small opening within the woods and stopped the wagon. Christoph set the wheel brake on the wagon and wrapped the reins around the handle. Looking behind his seat, he saw both Otto and Joseph asleep. Reaching down, he shook Otto's shoulder. "Come to life, my dear Otto. We have stopped for the night."

Otto stretched his arms wide, opened his eyes, and abruptly sat up as if he were startled. He turned his head up at Christoph and smiled. "Not having sleep and then all of a sudden having it, it becomes hard to let go."

Otto turned back to see Joseph still sleeping. He took a strand of hay and crawled quietly over to Joseph as Christoph watched with a grin.

"Ah, boys."

Otto raised his arm and delicately ran the end of the hay on Joseph's nose. Joseph rustled, shifting his position as he swatted his nose. Otto began to laugh. "This is almost too easy, this is." Again, Otto softly tickled Joseph's nose, and as expected, Joseph swatted his face.

"I must warn you, Otto, he is the one with the machine gun at the ready. I would hate to think of our end together gunned down because of your little prank."

"Hmm. Oh, I guess you are right," Otto answered annoyed. "I keep thinking of Annie. She and I would not stop taunting each other."

"Good to know then, my boy, you have not lost your innocence."

"Perhaps, but don't think for a minute, Christoph, that I have forgotten this wretched war. I still have work to do."

"Yes, the business you have that stays with you. Seems like such an overwhelming burden for two small boys. I hope some good comes of it."

"Me too, Christoph, me too."

Otto slowly nudged Joseph on his shoulder, putting his other hand firmly on the barrel of the gun to keep it from coming alive. Joseph squirmed and stretched, his eyes awakening slower than his body. "I am hungry!" he let out with a loud yawn. "What do we have to eat?"

"Funny you should ask. I have some of the German army's infamous iron rations. Otto reached into his musette bag and pulled out a tin. Forgetting to read the label, he passed it on to Joseph.

Joseph thanked Otto and removed the lid with his knife. He took a big bite and a smile came to his face as he chewed. "Yum. Turkey. My favorite."

Otto stared at Joseph with a blank expression. "Damn."

Christoph jumped from the cart and removed a few supplies and other items from beneath. He stood up and leaned over the side of the wagon, checking on Otto and Joseph. "Oh, well it looks as if you lads have your dinner. Okay then, I'll just help myself to this delicious chicken I've been saving."

"Damn," Otto repeated.

Christoph walked around to the back of the wagon, his arms carrying a sleeping roll and a basket. "You boys, do not trouble yourselves. I know the road is long for you, so stay in the wagon and sleep well. I will take my leave but will be close by, near that thicket at the edge of the woods, which overlooks the field. I will be on watch. I have put a small oil lantern for you on the seat of the wagon if you need light, but keep it dim. We do not know who or what is listening or crawling around out here. Good night, my boys. Smile; you are alive. You are both blessed." Christoph turned and walked into the dark.

"He's a crazy old man, I tell you, Otto.

"Perhaps, but he has been true to his words. He's gotten us to safety for now."

"I suppose, but I'll feel better when we are by ourselves come morning as we continue north.

"Yes, Joseph, I agree. I like holding the control of our own actions."

Otto stood up and lit the lantern, adjusting the wick to its lowest setting. "I don't like eating in the dark. Not sure why, but it feels unnatural. Perhaps it's because Poppa, Momma, my brothers, and I would gather around the table and share our day's stories while we ate." Otto sat back down and opened his tin. He took a bite and grimaced.

"So how's your food?" Joseph asked.

"Disgusting, I got horse meat."

"Yuck! That's the worst one."

"Yes. I'm quite aware of that."

Joseph leaned against the side of the wagon, facing Otto. He could not help but stare at him, a confused and strange look coming upon him. Otto could feel Joseph staring, his gaze fixed. It made him terribly uncomfortable. Otto continued eating, and without looking up, he confronted Joseph.

"Now, as I have noticed in the past, since we very first met, you have looked upon me with wonder. Tell me, Joseph, what troubles you about me? What goes on in your mind?" Caught off guard, Joseph stopped chewing his food. He squinted his eyes, furling his brow, and slowly continued to finish his bite. He took a hefty gulp from his canteen before responding.

"I find it odd, Jew, that your hair is blond and your eyes are light, as are mine. That is not the look of the common Jew from what my father has related and what I have observed. So I am wondering, as I sit here and enjoy my turkey ration, sorry by the way that you got the horse meat, that perhaps you are not a Jew after all. Perhaps I have it wrong. Maybe even your own parents have it wrong. Perhaps that is how you came to be such a distinguished courier of the High Court. That would answer Herr Bormann's question to me. It all makes sense now."

Otto smiled faintly, the dim light flickering, casting distorted shadows across his face. "Ah, my dear, dear Joseph," he began, shaking his head slowly. "I have so much to tell you, so much to help you with, but the question is, where to start? Hmm. I had promised myself not to go on with more storytelling."

Otto sat back and pondered his decision. Now was the chance he was looking for to confront the mind of Joseph and sway his thoughts for the good. "Okay, except I must first warn you that every time I share my story, someone gets killed. Perhaps my life is cursed. Think you are ready, Joseph?"

"You forget, Jew, who has the machine gun and the orders. Go ahead. Speak. Let me hear your words. The night is young, and the moon has been added to the night sky. It wants to hear as well."

"Yes, I shall share, but the same goes for you. I too have noticed many things about you. My questions are few but of importance. Agree to share?"

"Yes, yes. All very good. Get on with it, Jew, before I change my mind and fall asleep. I am more than content to go on living with you as a Jew and letting it be. Yes. Go on. I would like a good story over dinner."

Joseph continued with his eating. He nestled down farther into the softness of the hay and reached into his musette bag. He pulled from it a small drawing tablet wrapped in leather with a charcoal pencil wedged under its binding. He unwrapped the tablet and began drawing, stopping to take bites in between thoughts. Otto watched Joseph curiously as he began his story.

"First, I suppose I need to clarify your ideas once again about my faith. You are quite false in your thinking. Perhaps a quick history lesson may apply here. Judaism existed in Germany dating back to the 4th Century and well before Christianity arrived here. As the religion and teachings spread, it attracted many types of people in this area, who were obviously mostly fair skinned. So there lies your answer. As a matter of fact, my grandfather was quite fair, his hair blond as well."

"I was hoping for a true story, Jew, not some fantasy of made-up myths. However, I'm amused, so please continue."

Otto frowned, and his eyes dimmed. His voice became solemn yet stern. "I have learned that there have been many things, Joseph, hidden from my eyes after all these years, things I did not know. The journeys of my family and neighbors, the forced march and relentless travels, the abuse and horrible acts committed towards my people were enough to haunt a thousand lifetimes, let alone one. I have heard of these secret camps, ghettos, and the like. Miserable places they are. I have not seen the camps but have been told of their existence. The ghettos? Ah, I can tell you of that. Jews, mostly. Poppa would tell me nothing more, only that Jews were there. I know not the reason behind this. You say, Joseph, that it is because we are unwanted, low-lifes without the right to your type of existence. Perhaps that is the reason, unsatisfactory an answer that it is. But I ask, based upon what I am to tell you, who is the animal? Who belongs in a cage? It is not for me to judge. That day will come in its own time."

Joseph looked up from his drawing, stopping the swift movements of his charcoal. He stared at Otto but said nothing.

Otto continued his story of the ghetto at the point where he had left off with Ekkehard. No need to retrace old words, he thought. The part he wanted Joseph to hear was near the end of his story.

"Poppa and the other fathers of each family had been called away when we first arrived at the ghetto. He returned from wherever they had taken him to our cold, dark room many hours later. He was followed by a number of German officers in dark, crisp uniforms wearing devilish, mystical pins and patches, some glowing as bright as the waning moon. Some looked like lightning bolts hugging each other, and others were of a skull and cross bones. Scary looking, they were. They frightened Annie terribly. These uniforms were strangers to my eyes, and I felt great evil from their presence.

"We stood up as Poppa came to us. He raised his index finger to his lips again, just as he had done when he left us earlier, a sign for us to listen and obey. He spoke softly but with a stern voice. 'We are to be moved into a house. I am told it will be shared with others.

How many, I do not know. I am to choose those fit for labor, and they will be given work assignments. This, I have done. Momma, Yoram, Samuel, and I shall work. This will be our means for food. Otto will go to school because of his age. I do not have any information beyond this. I am told nothing else. Quietly now, follow me.'

"We followed Poppa willingly as we were all tired of this wretched room. Its decor was displeasing and dead to me. I took one last look at that light on the ceiling and wished it goodbye forever. An officer that wore the skull and cross bones pin joined us, and with the Neumanns and other people I had never seen before, we walked from the building. The moon continued its journey to black, and morning threatened. Time never seemed to matter to anyone. We moved when told. Whenever. I came to learn that in the ghetto, we had no need for a calendar. Our lives were divided into periods based on the distribution of food. Bread was every eighth day, the rations once a month. Each day fell into two parts, before and after we received our soup. In this way, the time passed.

"We were led from the school house down the side of the street. A huge barbed wire fence separated us from the road. We came to a rough-hewn wooden staircase, which was very steep, and Poppa and Yoram helped Momma climb it. This staircase directed us over the barbed wire fence and the street below to the other side. I was beginning to feel like a caged mouse and soon realized, days later, that's exactly what I was. We all were.

"We continued down many more streets, all within barbed wire fences to the street that would become our new home. Doina Strasse. It was a narrow street with row houses attached to each other. It didn't look all that different than Nord Strasse, where I used to live. The houses were three stories high with steep pitched roofs and dark windows. A five-step staircase lifted us from the littered cobblestone street to where we were greeted by large, thick wooden doors. It was eerie. I held onto Poppa's hand as we stepped onto the top stair. I was very tired and wished this officer would go, but that was not to be.

"With the help of the Schupo we were hurried into the darkness. We were shuffled up another flight of stairs to the second floor and led into a large, vacant room. The light of the morning sun shone its first rays on us, and I smiled at its coming because it would bring us some warmth. The officer made center stage of the room, and we formed a semicircle around him. I could recognize the silhouettes of my family and the Neumanns, especially Annie and her long, wispy hair. I did not find a memory for the others in the room, the people who would share this new home with us. The officer began talking, his voice slow and poised, piercing our ears with venomous words. He told us proudly that we would work for our existence and that only work could set us free. He then went on to say we were the chosen, but to remain that way, we would have to prove our value. We would be on constant watch. He began to tell of the rules when suddenly a small child, a boy not more than four years of age, began crying. He held an apple in his hand, and I was curious as to where he had gotten it. The morning sun had offered enough light to see him clearly. Surely, the long night and coming of day had proven too much for him. His eyes were tear-filled, and his pants were wet."

Otto sat quietly. His eyes did not blink. They remained firm, staring into nothingness as his lips spoke softly, as if dreaming an unbelievable dream.

"The officer walked slowly towards the young boy as he spoke. 'And no Jew shall be allowed to leave their home between five o'clock in the evening and eight o'clock in the morning.' He then grabbed the child gently and cradled him into his arms. His one hand suddenly grasped the boy by the ankles as he violently swung him with all his might. With a heavy and quick 'whoosh,' he slammed the child into the wall, his head splitting into pieces which dangled from his scalp connected only by his hair. The wall became awash in red. The stain remained there for as long as I could remember. The officer dropped the boy to the ground, his broken body lying quietly. Emitting a short 'humph,' the officer adjusted his tunic and straightened his sleeves. He then caught a glimpse of something rolling silently towards him on the ground. He leaned over and picked up the apple that had been dropped by the boy. He wiped it off on his trousers and looking at it with admiration, he took a bite. As he swallowed, he finished his lecture. 'Prove your worth and you shall live. Tomorrow, I shall be back with your work assignments.'

"The room remained silent. No one moved until we were assured that the officer was free and clear of us. No parent. No momma. No poppa came to the boy's aid. No one claimed him as their own. It would have meant their deaths as well. Poppa ripped off a window curtain and wrapped the boy in it. He offered his prayers, picked him up, and took him from the room. He never said where he took him, and I never asked. Curiosity always got me in trouble, and I realized we were in enough of that already.

"Momma tore the curtain from the other side of the window and tried to clean the blood from the floor. It was of no use, as the material of the curtain did not offer itself to soaking up blood. It smeared across the floor in the patterns Momma wiped it. I couldn't help thinking about art class where we did a similar type of project. I had other colors than red to my making. I buried the thought and went to see Annie."

"Who is this Annie you keep referring to, Jew?" Joseph interrupted. "I mean, she can't be your girlfriend. Ha, ha. You with a girlfriend?"

"Have you not been listening to me, Joseph? Have you no heart?"

"Oh, I've been very keen on your make-believe, but I am leery of your facts. Ghettos and secret camps? Nonsense! The Jew is certainly a trivial being, but for my great nation to make up such places and be held to such deeds seems like fabricated Jewish mischief to me. We would not concern ourselves with these matters which are so below us. There are greater things to do than look after you."

"Go on then. Be a fool, but I can prove it and I can take you there. Follow me then tomorrow to the Wolf's Lair. From there, I will find the camp where Annie is held. Then and only then can you speak of a judge. Come with me. I beg you."

Joseph continued his drawing with a twisted smile upon his face. It was neither good nor evil. Just empty. "Is that what you would want me to agree to, Jew? A side journey to chase some false mystery? You certainly take me for a fool. No. We shall continue with our mission to its end."

Joseph relaxed his arm for a moment and looked up at Otto. "By all means, Jew, finish your story. Certainly, there is more to this telling, is there not?"

Otto sat back in a stooped position, his shoulders devoid of strength, his heart deflated, his voice shut down. "Yes. There is more, Joseph."

"Good then. I am rather enjoying this tale."

Otto took a deep breath and found the words to resume his story. "Our new home was very cramped, devoid of furnishings, except for an old, decrepit wooden table and squeaky wooden chairs that had surely seen better days. There was one large room, the one where the officer gave us his lecture. It had high tin-stamped ceilings with a single light hanging from it. The light only worked if you banged on the walls to shake it to life. There were two large windows facing the front over the stoop and main door. It was our only means of light and warmth. We had little heat from the coal rations we were given and no fuel wood for the dormant fireplace, which sat empty and useless. Momma threatened to break up the wooden table many times, but Poppa always talked her out of it.

"We had a small kitchen, but nothing worked there either. A trickle would come to life from the faucet, but it took its full energy to make the journey up the pipes to our hands. There were two smaller rooms in the back, both with small windows leading out to a narrow, gated concrete backyard. These rooms would be our sleeping quarters. We joined with the Neumanns in one room, and the other two families occupied the other one. The bathroom was shared by all. It was a tiny, miserable room that was cold and stale. It smelled of urine and feces, as the toilet was seldom without ice and would not flush with what water it had. Many times, we ended up just sneaking out into the street at night to do our duty, which was very dangerous because of the curfew. Over time, we got to know the schedules of the Kripo very well."

"Kripo? Sounds like more imaginative figures for your story."

"Oh, they were very real, Joseph. The Kripo were mean people. They were the ghetto police. That was their role. They were Germans who spoke both Polish and Yiddish, which made it extremely hard to have secret conversations. The Kripo knew everybody's business. In order to avoid any entanglements with them, we took to speaking in riddles to communicate. The Kripo handed the German officers secrets and information on the people's comings and goings rather than doing any actual police work. They had the Schupo, of course, and Jewish Police for that. Seems like everybody was haunting us.

"Poppa ordered us not to befriend the other two families in our apartment. We got along well enough with them, but Poppa did not want us to be held responsible for any of their behaviors. The plight of the little boy was his reminder to us.

"As promised, we were given our work orders the very next day. Because of his merchant skills, Poppa would work as a bookkeeper at a factory where German uniforms were sewn. This was a privileged position and allowed him extra food rations and kept him off the cold factory floor. Even with his entitlement of better rations, it still wasn't enough. We were always hungry. Momma went to work with Frau Neumann and Annie at the Glazer factory, sewing clothes for dolls sold to German toy stores.

"Annie would sew the littlest of clothes because she had small hands and could more easily maneuver the material. She snuck a piece home one day to show me. She was so proud of it. It was a dog's tooth check-patterned dress, red and black with a white collar and delicate lace. I was thankful for that job. It kept her safe. I sat in a corner of our home listening to Annie speak of her work and looking at the little dress she had made. I was bewildered. Even during all this hellish war around us, there was still this beauty before me, piercing its way to survive, just like that stringed quartet we happened upon earlier. It was a theme I kept noticing. These little things were what kept me moving forward, looking to believe in hope."

"Yes," Joseph interrupted again. "It seems your little girlfriend had it better than you in this questionable tale."

Otto jumped on Joseph's words. "Stop it. She's not my girlfriend."

"Well, what is she then if not your girlfriend? Is it love? Ha. But what would a Jew know of love?"

"I know nothing of love. It is a grown-up thing to me, beyond my years. All I can tell you is that it's a feeling. It's like it sort of hurts when she's not with me. Like a tummy ache type of hurt."

Otto nestled back into the soft hay as he spoke. In listening to himself, he started to blush and glow, the warmth of the thought warding off the coming of the night's cold. He stared at the stars coming into focus, looking for the brightest one upon which to make a wish. There, he said to himself. Yes. That's the perfect star. Otto closed his eyes and made his wish. I wish to be together with Annie again. I wish this tummy ache to go away.

Otto opened his eyes to find Joseph rubbing away on his drawing tablet, trying to erase an obvious mistake. His eyes were nearly shut, concentrating hard and intensely frustrated. "What's the matter, Joseph? What are you drawing?

Joseph kept his head and eyes upon his paper. "Nothing, Jew. Nothing you can possibly know anything about."

Otto became curious and sat up, slowly sliding over towards Joseph. Noticing Otto's coming, Joseph kept to his pad and gave him no mind. Otto sat just in front of Joseph and peeked over his drawing tablet. "Ah! So you are an artist. Seems you are full of surprises, dear Joseph."

Joseph turned his tablet up, hiding his work from Otto. "Yes, so? What do you know of it?"

"Have you always been an artist?"

Joseph sat up, keeping his tablet from Otto, his voice changing, hesitantly welcoming Otto's interest. "Well, yes and no. Father would not hear of it. He said being an artist means to admit defeat in life. To be successful, a man must make himself elite, someone of studied knowledge and power. A great industrialist. A lawyer or physician. Or even a politician. He felt that artists were part of a chaotic order of gypsies and world forsakers. They are people who rot the minds of stability and progress with their free-thinking and uninhibited passions. Except, for me, it's a way to find peace, of creating my own world away from my father's, a place of my own making where I am the king. A place where my father can't follow."

Joseph looked down at his drawing, obviously not happy with his new world. "However, it seems my world isn't looking very good. I think Father was right. I think he can find me in this place I have drawn."

Otto peered over the tablet again. This time, Joseph surrendered his guard and his tablet. "See, it looks a bit of a mess."

"Ah, yes. Well, it does seem a tad busy. Perhaps I may help?"

Joseph was aghast. "What? How?"

"Well, in my family the fine arts were to be embraced. Music, dance, and painting were studied. I was never very good at drawing either, but I do remember Poppa would show me a few things. He taught me this idea that the great masters would practice called 'Divine Proportion.' The practice teaches that there's a certain shape, a rectangle, that is used to develop a well-balanced structure and design that's aesthetically pleasing to the human eye. Here, let me see your pad, may I?"

Joseph hesitantly handed Otto his tablet while Otto simultaneously commandeered the charcoal from Joseph's hand. Otto flipped over a page of the tablet. "Let me see. I shall start with a fresh piece of paper. First you draw a square; then draw a line that divides it in half. Um, then you draw a line going from one corner to the opposite corner. Then, uh, rotate the top point of that diagonal line downward until it extends the square. Hmm. Oh yes. Now complete the rectangle using that diagonal length as a guide for the long side of the golden triangle, and it's done. See?"

Joseph looked down at the tablet and then to Otto. "Silly Jew. There's nothing but square shapes on the pad. Ha! Stupid!"

"I am not finished. Pay attention, Hun. Now, I can use this formula infinitely to help stage my drawing and the objects I wish to place in it." Otto flipped the page back to see what Joseph had drawn. "Okay, so you have trees, a building which looks to be a castle, and a wagon pulled by a horse. Is that Christoph? You do like him."

"Just keep going, Jew."

"Yes, thanks. Okay. So, taking these objects and creating a few more triangles, just give me a second." Otto began drawing and erasing and drawing some more. His hand moved quickly, and he pouted his lips, his eyes fixated upon the tablet. Joseph tried to peek, but Otto would shun his eyes and drop a shoulder to hide his creation. He made one last gesture with the charcoal and sat up, turning his head slightly to admire his work. "There, that should do it." He turned the tablet around and held it with both hands on its side, his head framed the top, and his smile grew wide.

Joseph gazed at the drawing, and his eyes grew brighter. His mouth slowly opened, not wanting to believe or admit to what he was seeing. He was simply stunned. "How on earth did you do that? I mean, I've been working that drawing for the past few hours."

"Well, see, that's the problem, Joseph. You don't listen. I explained step by step how to do it."

"Yes, I know. But, um, can you be so kind as to show me how again? Please?" Joseph's manner changed. His eyes softened and his words sweetened. Otto smiled at Joseph. He had found his kindred spirit. He sided up next to Joseph and began his lecture again. They laughed and giggled together as young boys should.

"You may continue your story, Jew. I mean, well, you know. I am having trouble understanding much of what you say. These ghettos and your fair colored skin and hair. I admit my mind is troubled. I love my father. He's a good man. It seems the more we age, the more the facades of those we hold true fade. The truth always finds a way. It worries me to what else I may learn."

"It's sort of like when my Momma would feed me the cabbage dishes for supper," Otto offered. "Oh, they smelled rotten, but Momma would say, 'In time you will come to love them.'"

Otto continued his story for Joseph from where he had stopped. "My brothers, Samuel and Yoram, worked at a munitions factory. They moved crates and supplies into trucks. I never saw them much. I can't really even see their faces anymore. Filth and hate have infiltrated my soul and washed me of their memory.

"As for me, somehow Poppa got the Jewish officials governing the ghetto to allow me to go to school. Class, as much as I dreaded it at home, was a horrid place at best here. I got the feeling there was less emphasis on learning than there was on survival. The instructor, a miserable old soul, was looking to sort us out. Many of the kids were hungry like me. Others were sick, too ill to stay focused on lessons. Everyone seemed to have a cough. One boy would wheeze and vomit repeatedly. The next day, he was not at school. Actually, I never saw him again. Slowly, kids faded and were gone, yet new kids always seemed to fill the desks. I never thought to start friendships with anybody for that very reason.

"I would go straight home from school. Annie and I had a meeting place, as our schedules coincidentally matched. From there, we'd walk home quickly. It was dangerous to be wandering the streets because rules on when you were allowed to be away from your home changed often. We were caught one day, and it terrified us. Annie was late leaving her sewing job, so I waited at our meeting place. She finally arrived, but there was no time for talk. We were well past the hour we were to have been home. We made great haste, keeping our heads down to the littered streets. Suddenly, from around a corner, two German soldiers were moving towards us. There were no alleys to escape down or hiding places to seek, and they would surely see us.

I quickly motioned to Annie to start picking up bricks and garbage and put them in a pile. I have learned well over the years, my friend Joseph, that the German soldier is a sure bet to always follow orders and never question them. I had a plan for such an intrusion. I followed Annie's lead and began furiously picking up bricks, adding them to the pile she had begun, and moving debris from the street to the side. The soldiers approached and slowly drew their rifles level to meet our eyes. Their faces were stern and dark. They meant to kill us as ordered.

"I noticed from the corner of my eye the soldier on the left was a corporal in rank. He would speak first. The other, a private, would follow his lead. As predicted, the corporal spoke, 'Was tun Sie?' Annie kept silent piling the bricks, not wanting to face the soldiers. I could sense her fear and saw her fingers tremble. I begged that her poor little heart would not crumble. I stood up with my arms full of bricks and answered, 'Us, Corporal? We were given strict instructions from a sergeant with a very stern demeanor to rid these streets of bricks. We finished the task on a street a few blocks down and have just started on this one.' I was betting, Joseph, these two would not question my given orders and move off. If it had been found that they altered these orders by killing us, surely they would have been severely punished.

"The soldiers stood silent for a moment, their rifles still level and aimed at our heads. Their eyes moved with a small twitch to read each other's thoughts and then returned to me. I noticed the private come off his trigger and slowly extend his finger straight across the trigger guard. A sigh of relief came to my heart, but the beating did not slow. The corporal slowly lowered his rifle ordering, 'Setzen sie ihre arbeit fort.' I answered him quickly, 'Yes, Corporal, we will continue our labors and do a fine job for your sergeant. Tell him we are still at work, won't you?' The soldiers shouldered their rifles, turned abruptly, and walked off past us and up the street. We kept working until they rounded the corner out of sight. I noticed Annie had tears running down her cheeks. Lucky for us, the soldiers did not see her or they would have shot her then and there. Their report to the sergeant, if asked, would have been that we were ill, weak, and not working fast enough.

"Annie and I walked briskly as the sun closed its light for the day. We ran up our stoop to be met by Poppa and Momma and the Neumanns. Poppa scolded me and shook me hard, which was how he showed his love these days. Poppa was very cold. I was beginning not to recognize him anymore. Momma hugged me tightly, happy for our safety."

"It would seem your father also was mean at heart, Otto. Yes? Perhaps this war has turned good men bad."

Otto was not in the mood to challenge him. He doubted Joseph's father was a man of good will, but that story, he believed, would come in time.

"So tell me, Jew, I mean Otto. Darn! That's hard to change. So again, how did you earn the right as courier of the High Court? We have yet to hear that story."

"I was leading to that, Joseph. Now sit back, listen, and draw with what I have taught you."

"Very well, Jew, continue."

Otto took a deep breath, scratched his itchy head, and continued his story. "Well, starvation was upon us despite Poppa's extra food rations. Our bodies changed, becoming frighteningly thin as hunger continued its menace. It was then that Annie fell sick, and I feared for her well-being. Momma said it was because she was malnourished. She said Annie would not last. I had to do something. One day at school, I learned from my wretched instructor of a German barracks not far from here. She would constantly threaten to send us there to be punished if we were disobedient. I found her threats queer, as no one had the strength or will to misbehave.

"Curious as always, one day I did not go straight home. I had another idea. I knew that where there were barracks, there would be a mess hall supplying the soldiers with their meals. So I followed a group of soldiers after school one day. While they didn't immediately go to the barracks, I knew in time they would. And they did. I watched them stop at the sentry's post, show papers, and continue into the compound. I knew I had to get in there and steal some fruit, meat, or at least bread. During the warmer months, the mess area was just a tent with no sides. I could see a large number of soldiers at ease, eating their meals and talking. Surrounding the mess area was a high barbed wire fence with sentry posts at each corner. I walked all the way around the fence, looking for any way for me to sneak into the compound.

"My curiosity was eventually rewarded. Located on the side where the cooks would receive their supplies, the fence was lower and the gate unguarded. The delivery trucks would enter and exit at this gate, which was left open when the trucks were parked and supplies were being unloaded. This was where I would have my opportunity. I would just simply wait until a truck entered and the gates opened, sneak in, and crawl under the tables where the cooks would serve the soldiers. Then I could reach around and grab food from the trays as it was placed at the very ends of the table.

"Now, I say simple, but a skinny, filthy Jewish boy lurking around was a very easy thing to recognize. So, I thought to convince my brother Yoram to scrounge together a German uniform from where he worked. I told him my clothes were torn, ratty, and quite soiled. I said I needed better clothes for school or I was to be punished. He agreed without further question, which I found to be strange. While not as smart as me, Yoram had a quick wit. I'm sure he suspected another intent for the use of the clothes. Not a day later, Yoram had brought me German trousers and a simple shirt worn under a tunic. The days were warm, and it was not unreasonable for a soldier to not have a tunic on at the mess area while eating. The next day, I stuffed a grungy knapsack that I had found and used for transporting my books with the German clothes and hurried to school. After school, I slipped away to a side street near the barracks and mess hall and changed into the German uniform. I waited in hiding for a truck to appear, which it always did exactly at three-thirty each day. Evening supper was always served at five-thirty. Interesting thing about the German soldiers, they were always punctual. I was happy for that because it would give me enough time to get in, take some food, change back into my normal clothes, and run home before our curfew, when the patrols would have their orders to shoot anyone on the street. I tell you, Joseph, the first time was nauseating. I was so very terrified of being found out."

Joseph sat working desperately on a new drawing to show to Otto, paying little if any attention. "Yes, Jew, I am here. Please continue. You were saying how you stole from the mighty German army."

"Ah, that's the Joseph I remember. Mean and spiteful. Wherever did that sweet and caring voice I heard not ten minutes ago make off to?"

"Yes, I am humbled by your drafting skills and, quite frankly, this story of yours. Let me remind you of my mission again. It shall not be swayed."

"Should I continue my story then? It would seem it is a waste of breath and my time for sleep."

"No, Jew, continue or I shall have been robbed of a good story to tell my friends when I see them again."

"Very well then. The German uniform was not of a perfect fit, understandably, as I was but four feet tall. It would be rare to find a German soldier of this height. It was not a Hitler Youth uniform but a German regular issue one. I wore it the best I could, tucking in excess shirt and pulling my pants way up high. It looked out of place but only if carefully inspected. Hopefully, hundreds of hungry soldiers would not find it of importance.

"The supply truck pulled up to the gate, and the passenger got out, opened the gate, and climbed back into the truck. I took my cue and walked with speed through the gate to the back of the cook's tent where they prepared the meals. Leaning my head around the tent and seeing the way clear, I walked with confidence to the front of the tent and crawled under the serving table. At this time there were many soldiers and personnel around. I was quite certain I had been seen but apparently went unnoticed as I ducked under the table. I scurried on my hands and knees down the line of tables to the end where the bread and other food would be, passing many soldiers' feet and legs, following each other in line as I went. There was a great deal of noise from the stoves, cook's yelling, and soldiers talking to each other that I worried little of my own noise as I hurried along. I came to the end of the table and, still on my knees, turned to face towards the soldiers. I looked at their boots and followed their movements, waiting for a break in the line to peek over and grab whatever I could.

"I succeeded in doing this every other day during the week for nearly two months. Poppa asked bluntly where I had gotten the bread and other food. Sometimes it would be fruit, other times slabs of meat. I hated to lie, but to tell the truth would have been a certain scolding that I didn't want to bear, so I told him that the students who did well in their studies received gifts of food rations. I suppose he suspected otherwise, but he did not inquire further of my story. Annie was still sick after many weeks and I…"

"And you never once got caught?" interrupted Joseph abruptly, stopping his drawing.

"Well, that was the trick, Joseph. But yes. Actually, I thought I was more cunning than it turned out. Little did I know that the cooks and officers had noticed their food being taken, so they set up a trap using bread and fruit which they put out on the very edge of the table. I wondered why it was so easy to grab but paid little mind to it. I learned later that they were betting each other on who could capture the thief, so it became a game to them. That day came soon enough. That was the day, Joseph, when my world came to an end and a new world began. That is how I came to be here, in front of you, on a secret mission.

"I had reached up to grab the food when suddenly a soldier ducked down in back of me and screamed, 'Got you, thief!' I sprang up from my hiding and jumped up onto the serving table. Other officers joined in the chase and tried to grab my feet and legs, but I was too nimble and leaped over them as they lurched at me. Many of them crashed to the table, upsetting the food and drinks and making a terrible mess of their uniforms. Soon it seemed like I had the entire German army chasing after me, yelling and laughing, and some actually cheering for me. It literally felt like I had run a million circles all around the entire mess area, escaping their advances and capture, but that was to end. As I sprinted back towards the open gate, a cook appeared from out of nowhere and grabbed me in a bear hug. I was frantic and screamed, 'Let me go. Let me go. My family is starving.'

"Some of the officers who had chased me started slapping my face and choking me by the neck and demanding my name, which is surprising, because how can you speak when you're being choked? Suddenly, I heard a loud, demonic, and commanding voice boom over the chaos. The cook let go of his grasp, as did the other officers, and they all came to a full and crisp salute. I fell to the ground, my head dropping down in an effort to catch my breath. The air became silent, but from my sight, I saw approaching me a pair of splendid, gleaming, polished black boots that rose to the upper calf. From what I could see, the trousers were well-pressed with not a hint of a wrinkle. I closed my eyes as this unrecognized threat stopped and stood in front of me. Then he spoke. 'Rise, boy, and do so quickly for my patience is altogether lessoned of late.' I slowly rose from the ground, my uniform sloppily surrounding my body and showing its true age. Looking up to face the voice, I saw a smallish, if not somewhat portly, man, taller than I, but a giant by no means. He was dressed in an officer's uniform, a rank of which I had never seen. I looked into his dark eyes, as one could not help doing so. His hair was just as dark, neatly parted, and a bit slicked back. His face was perfectly shaven, showing its roundness with age. Sinister, he was, and I felt great evil from his presence. I could feel my soul retract in fear."

Joseph listened intently now, his curiosity peaked, his voice excited. "Who was it, Otto? Tell me. Who was it?"

Otto paused, staring off into the stars. He slowly dropped his head to look Joseph directly in the eyes. His voice was soft but stern. "It was Bormann."

Joseph's eyes lit up, and he sat back slowly, nestling deeper into the corner of the wagon, the hay falling in from behind him, enveloping his body. He knew of this fear. Most did, especially during the final hours in the Führerbunker.

"He looked at me, Joseph, seeking my soul. Oh, he was seeking it with ill intent. He asked my name, and while my voice cracked in fear, I did not hesitate. 'Otto, Sir. It is Otto, son of Solomon.' I offered no other information as I'd already learned to never surrender anything that wasn't asked. 'Well, Otto, son of Solomon,' he asked softly. 'What, may I ask, is going on here? Speak quickly now and with truth, for I have watched the entire incident from my staff car with great interest. I find it amusing to see my army made a mockery of by a Jewish boy, not to mention one dressed as a German soldier.'

"I answered him as he asked, 'Yes, Sir. Well, my family is starving, and my friend Annie is sick and needs food. So I thought it no harm to take a little of what seemed plenty here. I did not think it would be missed.' Bormann did not immediately respond to my answer. I could tell his mind was swimming in thought. Then it came to him. A strange question, I thought. 'You are a fast runner, are you not, boy?' he asked.

"'Yes,' I said, offering a hint of a proud smile. 'The fastest in my class.' It was at this point I noticed the ghetto police arrive. They walked up to me as if to grab me and cart me away. 'Wait.' Bormann yelled, as if coming back from his thoughts. 'No. Leave him as he is. I have better plans for this boy.'

"That's when I met Corporal Huber. Bormann called for him to take me to his staff car. We sat in the car and said nothing as we waited for Bormann to come. Peeking out the window, I could see him speaking with a number of officers. Moments later, Bormann returned and got into the car. He said nothing, and we sat for what seemed a very long time. Suddenly, a number of similar staff cars pulled up, and one of the officers motioned to our driver to follow. As we drove along, however, it became clear to me that we were driving to my home on Doina Strasse. I was excited because I thought Bormann was being polite by offering a ride. Little did I suspect otherwise.

"We pulled up to my house, and the Schupo Police were out front, surrounding my whole family and the Neumanns. Corporal Huber opened the door, and I ran to them with open arms. I was almost crying but trying really hard not to. Momma knelt down and gave me a big hug. Poppa did nothing. He stood straight up staring with a curious and fearful eye at Bormann as he approached. Annie was with her mother, engulfed by her arms as if to hold her quiet. I could see her out of the corner of my eye while hugging Momma. Annie had an alarmed face. A queer and unsettling thought came to my mind. There was something strange at work here. Momma released her grasp, and I stood full, slowly turning to see Bormann, who was not less than a step away from us. His smile was foreboding and contorted into an ominous shape. His eyes set upon Poppa's, and then he spoke while holding the same sinister look.

"Bormann spoke, 'It seems, Herr Kaufmann, son of Noam Kaufmann, you have raised a little thief. I suppose that would trouble you, would it not? Don't speak. It is fine. However, what are we to do about this matter? Well, I have thought long and hard about it. As you know, his actions cannot go without punishment. Would you not agree? Yes. Well then, I have an honorable solution. As payment for his treachery and the gifts from the Reich, that being our food,

Otto shall come with me and work for the High Court. He shall be more of a slave than a worker. However, if he follows certain rules and responsibilities as our slave, we will allow him to live. Now, as for you and your family, you will fulfill the punishment part of the solution. You and your family and friends will be sent to a unique type of camp, shall we say, for rehabilitation.'

"He stopped speaking after making this last remark, then turned and walked back to his staff car. As he was walking, he called out to me without looking back. 'Come, Otto, there is much to do.' My heart fell to the ground, and I felt my life slipping quickly from my body. My knees grew weak, and my eyes teared. I screamed out to Annie as I could see her frantically trying to escape her momma's grasp. Her screams were ugly and desperate, her voice turning hoarse and then quiet. Her face went blood red, and her breath fought for control. Corporal Huber wrapped his arms around me and hoisted me over his shoulders like a worthless sack of grain. I reached out to Annie but caught nothing. The Schupo herded my family and the Neumanns into a truck that I had not seen pull up. My mind became blurred, and I could no longer see. I screamed Annie's name at the top of my lungs with whatever energy I could muster. 'Annie!' And then my world went black."

Otto sat back against the hay-filled wagon nestling into the opposite corner as Joseph had done. He was finished with stories. There would be no more. Joseph was without an expression. He had no words for Otto. In his mind, Joseph thought no one could fabricate such a story about Bormann without actually experiencing him. It troubled Joseph. He began to question Otto, his character, honesty, and worth. He started to further question his own beliefs. Perhaps his own father was the same as these very men, as Bormann, Goebbels, and Himmler.

Otto stared to the stars in the heavens. A small tear came to his eye, perched at the brink of falling but not wanting to let go. It wanted to stay a tear. Otto enjoyed the stars. He admired their freedom, brightness, and cheerfulness as they sparkled in the night. They gave him hope. They gave him permission to carry on. It was then that Otto decided to wait until Joseph fell asleep to slip away and continue his journey, a course set as directed by Corporal Huber.

Chapter 9

"Where is it? Where is that damn key? Curse the fools who have tinkered with my office. This staff is out to destroy me, but it will be I who enjoys the entertainment of the last laugh." Bormann chuckled as he rummaged through the drawers of his desk, shuffling through papers and objects only to discard them to the littered concrete floor.

"Damn!" he screamed, the menace of his voice echoing through the dark corridors of the bunker. He flopped down in his chair, raising his hand to his mouth in thought, his sinister mind playing through the scenes. "Hmm. I think I know what became of it. Müller!"

Within moments Chief Müller appeared, his eyes shady yet alert, his body confident and poised. "Yes, Herr Bormann, your cries can be heard throughout Germany. What news are you in need of? Is it about my task? Well, I have four of the most loyal, most vicious, and uncompromising of the Einsatzgruppen equipped and on the move per your order. I chose them myself. I was actually on my way to you with this very report."

Bormann snapped, "That news is to be expected, but the plans have been altered." Bormann rose from his chair and quickly passed by Müller, the wash of his walk causing Müller's eyes to shutter. "Quickly, Müller, follow me and my lead, but say nothing."

Bormann and Müller dashed down the hall, their leather boots crinkling and moaning as they struck the concrete floor with great force. The bunker through which they walked was in chaos. Adjutants, secretaries, and military officials of all ranks were scurrying about preparing for a breakout from the bunker. Uniforms were traded for civilian clothes; weapons and provisions for travel and survival were secured.

Bormann and Müller continued their pace and entered the machine room. Bormann yelled, "Everybody out except you, Corporal Huber."

Hentschel and Sergeant Misch stood to attention, slowly stopping their work with open, cautious eyes. Corporal Huber followed, slowly removing his telegraph headphones and placing them carefully on the desk in front of him.

"Quickly now, take your work elsewhere." ordered Bormann again. Hentschel and Sergeant Misch obeyed and quickly exited the room. Sergeant Misch glanced back at Corporal Huber with a forgiving expression. Müller slammed the door and followed Bormann farther into the room.

"I am at my end with your backstabbing, Corporal." Bormann lifted his hand from under his jacket, brandishing a pistol but not the same one that threatened Otto. This was a new gun, a Walther P38. It was clean, crisp, and as black as the darkest depths of night. It was about to be christened. Corporal Huber stood facing Bormann, motionless and hypnotized as he stared down the dark barrel of the gun.

"To your knees, Corporal." Bormann approached him, placing the tip of the barrel perfectly horizontal to Corporal Huber's forehead. The barrel indented his skin, which folded around it as if wanting to embrace its intrusion. Corporal Huber closed his eyes and winced, knowing his end was near.

"Where is my key? I will not ask again, I grant you that, Corporal." Silence came to the room. Nothing could be heard except for the hurrying of frantic people through the halls and the garbled transmissions from the battle fronts coming through the headphones.

"I shall have you tell me where the key is, although I suspect I already know its new owner. Your wisdom escapes you, Corporal. Now speak." Corporal Huber kept quiet, kneeling at attention, prisoner to Bormann's words. "You offer nothing? Then I offer you this, tell me where the key is to be found and I will not have Chief Müller's death squad execute your new wife."

Chief Müller's eyes lifted with question but remembered his orders to follow Bormann's lead. "Yes, Corporal. They are at her doorstep as we speak. I would obey Herr Bormann's command if you want a choice in her future."

Corporal Huber began crying softly. Tears formed, knowing their own end. He knew in his mind he had to answer in order to save her. Otto will be far along, much too far for these swine to have an effect, he thought. Besides, with the battle for Berlin at its end, they will have little hope of catching him. I will save my wife. Sorry, Otto, I know you would have me do the same. The corporal opened his eyes and lifted his head to Bormann, the pistol rotating upwards, lifting off its perch and revealing a reddened round imprint on his forehead. "The boy has the key. This you know, but now you have heard it. So dishonor your threat and leave my wife to me."

Bormann turned to Müller with a proud, ominous smile. "Ah, you see Müller, when dealing with men, love is always a well-chosen threat in seeking information. Men are weak." Bormann suddenly cocked back his arm and like a catapult, turned, and with all his might, smacked the corporal across the head with his pistol. Corporal Huber hit the concrete floor with a forceful and wicked thump. He lay motionless.

"Surely, Herr Bormann," queried Müller, "you are not going to leave him lay there without an end? Surely, you will shoot him, won't you?"

Bormann snickered as he holstered his pistol. "Ah, Müller, I foresee a nastier end for this coward at the hands of the Russians. They will know what to do, and I grant you, it will be something far more hideous than anything you and I could ever imagine."

Müller smiled with a sinister crack of his warped teeth. "I can imagine something quite evil."

Bormann opened the door, and they both left the room, Bormann giving orders as they walked. "Müller, the Einsatzgruppen must now head to the Wolf's Lair. That rotten little Jew has the key, but he will have a hard time finding passage for its use. Do not worry if he does. There are many secrets protecting what he seeks."

Chapter 10

The light of a new day had not yet shown itself. Darkness kept its reign, forming a good disguise for Otto to silently slip away. He gathered all his belongings, checked his satchel and musette bag for all their contents, and slowly lifted himself from the wagon. The soft hay drifted from Otto's legs as he rose and then settled back to its warm slumber. He shouldered his gear and quietly climbed over the wagon to the ground. A slow fog drifted across the surface of the land, distorting and hiding the landscape. Dew fell from the woods around him, tickling the leaves and creating an eerie sound through the hollows. Otto stepped to the back of the wagon and peeked in at Joseph, who was sound asleep. He offered a faint smile, pausing to look at him but for a moment.

Otto turned and followed the path from whence the wagon had come, nimbly passing where Christoph was on watch. "My dear Christoph," he whispered, smiling as he tip-toed past. "Your guard is as telling as your snoring. Sleep well, my friend, and I hope you find safe passage."

Otto looked across the field in front of him, the road leading north and into darkness. The moon offered little light but enough to give form to his path. This is a much more welcoming landscape than the hell I've endured for the past few months, he thought. I can actually inhale a breath of cool, crisp, and clean air. Now off I go. It will be a four-day journey by foot to the Wolf's Lair if it is left uncontested.

Otto hustled to the road from where they were camped in the woods. He turned north, convinced this was his direction, and crept back towards the woods again, following the same direction as the road. His courier skills flooded his movements, as he would not travel on the heavily rutted path or even beside it. He would stay hidden in the bushes and trees of the woods that followed the contours of the road. He knew this offered him not only concealment but also an escape route if needed. It was a difficult and slow way to travel. Crossing fields left him physically exposed and vulnerable, requiring a stealthy approach and execution. They were best left for the night to navigate. The woods demanded the greatest challenge, as they did not always cooperate in offering a leisurely and relaxing walk. There were creeks to ford, marshes to slog through, and thick bushes of thorns and briars to maneuver around.

Otto followed the north road for a number of hours before coming to a crossroad. He chose the east road leading towards his objective and followed it unchallenged for two days. The roads were clear with no signs of confrontation, battle, or war.

The sun teased the sky, offering its light and warmth. The shadows that hid the land started to disappear and reveal its keep. Otto awoke from a night's travel weary and exhausted from scraping across the challenging terrain. He scratched his head and then checked his stomach wound, which he had let go unnoticed since its happening. The wound had scabbed and itched him. Otto changed the bandage, pulled his shirt down, and packed up his possessions. He was ready for a new day.

Otto peered through the woods in front of him with a sharp eye as the day broke. He could see the trees thin in numbers and fade away, exposing what appeared to be a vast field where he thought the road must continue. As the sun gained momentum in the sky, further light revealed the road did indeed cut through the land, but it was not a field. It was a densely entangled city of twisted brush of different sizes and species that covered a murky swamp. Otto stood at the edge of the woods just a few meters from the swamp's edge. His mouth collapsed, and his heart sank. He let out a sigh, and pulling a handkerchief from his trousers, he blew his nose quietly.

"Well, this is a fine way to greet the day. How am I to get through that? It must be two kilometers across that pile of worthless scourge. Swamps. I detest these bastard children of the land. They stink of wet horses and suck the boots off your feet when trying to maneuver their grip. It's as if the very demons of the underworld are grasping at your life, pulling you towards their end. It gives me chills."

Otto sat down to think of his strategy for moving across the swamp. His stomach growled, reminding him that he had skipped breakfast. He pulled an iron ration from his musette bag, and his face sank. "What a surprise. Horse meat again." He shook his head in disgust as he carefully opened the can with his knife, staring out across the nemesis before him. Well, he thought, I suppose I can wait out this day until its end, get some more sleep surrounded by my little wooded fortress until darkness swallows me again, and then face it with a full on sprint. Or I can take my chances exposed to the light and possibly run into Ivan and his merry bunch head on. Hmm. I think I'll stay put.

Otto pulled his blanket back out of his musette bag, and propping his body up against a tree, he nestled in for a long day. He found little solace when waiting in silence. It gave his mind the freedom to think, remember, and feel. Annie came back to him. The retelling to Joseph of his leaving the ghetto reawakened his feelings, and he played over and over the shrilling sounds of Annie's cries for him as he was pulled away. Otto covered his head to try and drown the sounds, but he could not escape the noise until something else did.

Coming up the road from the other side of the swamp, Otto heard a high-pitched whining, similar to the sound of a convoy of trucks revving through gears to keep speed. He slowed his eating, raising his knife from the tin can back to his mouth. Hunger still controlled his body, but his eyes ruled his actions. The sound grew closer and louder, revealing a worthy Russian convoy. Otto watched as they came closer to his position, his eyes following them as they began to pass. Then without warning, they stopped abruptly, the brakes squealing and throwing dust and rubber to the wind. Orders were thrust here and there, and commotion ensued. Something had disrupted this nest of yellow jackets as they swarmed the grounds heading for the woods. Otto's heart pumped hard, and an alarm resonated through his whole body. They are after me, he wondered? But how could they have detected me? Otto tossed the blanket from his body, his head looking desperately in all directions for a cause. He then looked at his hands and quickly up to the sun at his face. Damn. The sun has cast a glare on my knife and tin. Ah, careless, I have been. They indeed have been alerted to me.

The Russians moved methodically yet with speed towards Otto. Their swarm massed with stingers exposed. Otto dropped his tin and pocketed his knife. He stuffed his blanket back into his musette bag, and with his satchel, he slung them both over his shoulder. He kept his body low and, with haste, made for the swamp. His mind began to work on an escape route. The woods would not conceal him, and the Russians would surely track his path. He came to the swamp's edge and sighed. It looks like my escape is reduced to one option, but what to do with my satchel? The documents within may have lasted a quick splash in the River Spree, but they won't survive an extended stay in this muck.

Otto searched the grounds for a place to hide the satchel. He could hear the Russians disturb the forest floor, the leaves rustling from foot to foot. It gave him an idea. He dropped to his knees and swept away an area of leaves under a small fir tree. He placed the satchel flat and covered it with a thick layer of leaves, being careful to blend them with the ground around them. Not convinced it was well hidden but not having time to find out, Otto raised to his feet and swiftly entered the swamp.

The Russians came to the spot where Otto had been lying down against the tree. A Russian sergeant knelt to his knees while motioning to his comrades to come to him. His eyes pierced the grounds around him like a detective mulling over a murder victim and looking for clues. Someone had been here recently, he thought. A private called to him excitedly, "Sergeant, I have found something of interest."

The sergeant came to his feet as more soldiers entered the area and surrounded the position. "What is it? What have you found?" The private lifted the tin can and gave it to the sergeant, who inspected it with a queer expression on his face. He raised the tin can to his nose and took a sniff. "Ha!" Laughing he turned to share his findings with his comrades. "Horse meat. Barbaric German rations. No wonder they have lost this war. How could they win eating such peasant food?"

The patrol around him laughed in return, easing the scene as they lowered their weapons. "This one lonely German is not a threat," said the sergeant. "Quickly now. Search the area from here to the swamp and off to that bluff and then back to the road. Our talents are better used in mopping up larger groups of resistance than this peasant. Let him be. He'll surely die out here on his own." Snickers from the sergeant's words continued and faded as the patrol scattered per his orders.

Otto sank to his chest, quietly fighting the mud, thorns, and dark murky waters around him. He zigzagged in and out of the brush and bogs, finally nestling in under a small briar. He moved far enough within the swamp as to thwart any attempt to be followed but close enough to be within sight of his hidden satchel. He ducked under the muddy cold water to wipe the sheen off his skin and to camouflage his human form. His whole body lay hidden under the water just above his top lip, leaving his nose to breathe. His eyes squinted yet fixated on his satchel.

The Russian patrol spread out in search of what they thought was a German deserter looking for safety. Otto could see a few of the soldiers fade in and out of sight, the woods acting as a blind. However, one soldier acted more curiously than the rest. He walked toward the swamp and searched its edge. Otto became more alarmed as the soldier's snooping clearly threatened his hiding. The soldier's bayonet was attached to his rifle, and he began poking around the bushes in random order. Then he suddenly stopped. Otto could see he was upon his satchel. The soldier swept the leaves away as Otto had done and pulled the satchel from its hiding place. Otto's eyes widened as he raised his head out of the water in saddened anger yet remaining hidden. Damn. No, please. Leave it alone.

The Russian soldier pulled the satchel to his eyes and then called to his comrades. "Here. I have found something." The soldier shouldered his rifle and ran to find the sergeant. Otto could see the other soldiers run to their comrade as they reported back to the road and their convoy. Still remaining hidden, Otto slowly rose from out of the water to rest upon a bog still under the briar. He lost sight of the soldiers but listened intently for further movement. The Russian soldier called out to the sergeant in charge of the search as his comrades followed him with curiosity.

Otto realized this was not a normal patrol of a dozen or so soldiers as he had first thought. It was a considerably large advance force with a number of troop carriers, small fighting vehicles, and stolen and repurposed German combat vehicles.

The soldier came to the road where the convoy was stopped and found the sergeant near a jeep speaking with other soldiers. He saluted and offered his captured item to the sergeant, grinning, proud of his find. The sergeant looked puzzled, hesitantly receiving the satchel from the soldier.

"What have we here? It looks very official as it is marked with the Waffen SS eagle." The sergeant opened the satchel and pulled from it an envelope-sized letter, the one that Corporal Huber had given Otto, together with the larger document given to him by Bormann. "Well, this looks to be of great importance." Suddenly, another group of soldiers approached. The sergeant and his men quickly snapped to a crisp attention in full salute.

"Sergeant Mozarov, what is the cause of our stall?" The voice was stern and confident, that of a higher ranked officer.

The sergeant spoke quickly, if not nervously. "Yes, Major Koshechkin, we have found something that looks to be of great significance and offer it to you."

The major's eyes widened. "What is it you offer me, Sergeant?" The sergeant did not speak as he handed the major the satchel with the SS mark in full view. The major judged it with surprise and delight. "Well, well, what have we here? Documents? Yes, this case looks to be of importance, yet we have not the time to inspect it now. Our advance is late, and we must push on. There is greater work to be done as ordered, or I am to be relieved and found treasonous and made a mockery upon the gallows pole."

The major laughed for all his comrades to hear. They shared cautiously in his amusement, offering shallow smiles and soft snickers in kind. "Come, my comrades, we chase the Hun!" The soldiers raised their weapons and let out a mighty cheer in devilish unison. "Sergeant, keep this satchel at your side. I'll deal with it later."

The sergeant saluted and motioned to his aid. "Corporal Markov, take this bag to my vehicle."

Otto could hear the convoy gather, soldiers climbing onto trucks, doors slamming shut, and engines shifting to first gear, their whining again echoing slowly though the swamp until it faded completely. Silence returned. Otto pushed off the bog and slipped back into the water. He slowly and cautiously entered farther into the swamp, the water becoming shallower, reaching up to his knees in places and back to his chest in others. He thought of moving from the swamp and taking his travel to the road, the chances of another convoy following in this one's tracks being slim.

The cold of the water mixing with the chill of the air caught up with Otto, and he started to shiver. He and all his belongings were soaked to the core. He was caked in mud and soon covered with the first of spring's mosquitoes. "Damn, I despise these unfettered creatures. More of the devil's grasp on my path. There is no end to them." He ranted as he swatted at the air around him in hopes to rid himself of their madness.

Otto cursed himself for leaving the satchel behind to be found by the Russians. He thought of Bormann and the coming of his wrath guaranteeing Otto's own end. "One last and failed mission. I will surely be shot now. I am lost with no further purpose. I am alone and without a place to go." He began crying as he pushed along in the swamp while still keeping an eye on the road to his right. He wiped his nose with his muddy arm, smearing his face with dark sludge as he negotiated his way around the thorns and briars covering the swamp.

"When I get home, Poppa is going to scold me for being wet again. He will think I was down near the River Spree playing in the water, but I haven't even any paper to make any sailboats worthy of the punishment. Worst yet, I have failed my Annie."

Otto came upon a small knoll offering a dryer perch. It was covered with fir and a tangled group of smaller trees. He sat down and rested underneath, hiding his head within his arms upon his knees. His sobbing lessened as he rose his head to gain his courage. "What am I to do?"

Chapter 11

The Russian convoy came up to speed with force and vengeance, putting miles and miles between it and Otto. The sergeant peered down at the satchel next to his feet, wondering its true nature and what to do with it. "If Major Koshechkin takes it, he will only use it for his own glory. I have seen too many of my comrades die in vain at the hands of these officers who would even shoot their own men for failure in combat. Cowards and reckless, they are. No. This satchel will work for me. It will be of my making. It will clear a path for my glory and the glory of my men. I will see to it.

Suddenly, in the road ahead appeared a human figure on a bicycle. The lead scout vehicle came to a halt and confronted the figure, the rest of the convoy coming to a stop behind him. A private called to the figure now obvious to them as a young Russian soldier.

"You, there. Comrade. Where are you going? The war is to your back. You are going the wrong way!" The private laughed with his comrades in the vehicle over his line of questioning, but the laughing ended as quickly as it had begun.

Sergeant Mozarov appeared from their rear unannounced and unamused by the cause of yet another delay. "Stupid. You are all stupid. Why have you stopped this convoy yet again? What is it this time that set you off? Surely it was not another glare from the woods? Answer quickly before the major appears and has our heads."

The private and his comrades came to an abrupt salute, the private answering. "Sergeant Mozarov, this young soldier on a bicycle in the middle of the road was our cause. I thought to question him about his direction of travel, his apparent retreat."

The sergeant glanced at the young soldier with a discerning eye. "Retreat? Come here comrade. What are your orders? Why are you delaying my advance?"

The young soldier dismounted his bicycle and, pushing it to the side of the road, walked to the sergeant with a firm salute. "My name is Vladimir Fedotova, Sir. I am the Divisional Courier for the Second Belorussian Division under Marshal Rokossovski. I am in travel back to his headquarters with intelligence from the front lines. He awaits my return."

The sergeant's eyes became brighter, his eyebrows stretching to his hairline. His anger turned to a conniving query as he paused to think. "Well, we are a part of the Marshall's Division also. Seems strange a young soldier of a boy's height would be sent on an errand of such importance, and by bicycle no less. Even more suspicious is why you are carrying the enemy's weapon." Tension spread as quickly as a virus among the soldiers surrounding the sergeant, and their suspicion aroused their weapons.

Vladimir answered quickly. "All men of fighting capability are at the front. No vehicles or weapons worthy of combat can be spared, and this gun is a trophy taken from a soldier I killed. I serve Mother Russia, my homeland, my people. I will see to the destruction of the Hun and his cities!"

The sergeant smiled slowly as his scheming mind completed his thought. "Yes. Very good, my young comrade. Come with me. I have further use of you."

Vladimir followed the sergeant, who put his arm on the young soldier's shoulder as they walked quickly back to the sergeant's vehicle. "I have another honor to bestow upon you, my son. It is one of great importance that will shape the future of all of us here." The sergeant reached into his vehicle and pulled Otto's satchel from the floor. He turned and held the satchel up to the young soldier. Vladimir studied the satchel with great curiosity and suspicion. "Here, my young divisional courier, you must not fail me in personally delivering these documents and handing them directly to Marshal Rokossovski himself. I am off to the front lines as ordered and will not have the opportunity to do it myself. You must use my name and rank in telling the marshal how I found the satchel. This is of utmost importance. He must know it came from me." Vladimir took the satchel from the sergeant's hands and shouldered the bag.

"Now, you must make haste, and that bicycle will not give you enough speed. Follow me quickly." The sergeant walked past Vladimir to the rear of his vehicle, and Vladimir followed as instructed. The sergeant stopped in front of a German motorcycle with a sidecar. Vladimir saw it was a BMW painted Waffen SS Camo and equipped with an MG-34 machine gun on the sidecar. The sergeant ordered the driver and gunner out of the motorcycle. The driver removed his goggles with quieted anger as he dismounted.

"Now, my young courier," said the sergeant, "this will be your new mode of transportation. Hurry now. Climb aboard. Corporal, give the boy your goggles. You won't be needing them."

Vladimir climbed onto the motorcycle, swinging his right leg around to the other side and mounting it like a horse. Firmly planted, he found it awkward to reach the handlebars or anything else for that matter, a fact that posed no worry to the sergeant.

"Now all of you back to your vehicles," the sergeant ordered his suspicious comrades, not wanting to draw further attention. The soldiers did as ordered, and quickly, the convoy continued its drive to the front. The sergeant came closer to Vladimir and whispered his message into his ear one last time. "Now remember, my courier, you must deliver this bag to Marshal Rokossovski himself. Understood? You must use my name and rank."

The sergeant raised his head smiling and then ran to his awaiting vehicle while peering back at Vladimir. His vehicle roared to life and lurched forward to catch up with the moving convoy ahead of him. Vladimir sat upon the motorcycle, acting as if he knew what he was doing, and watched the sergeant until he was far from his sight. The rest of the convoy had to drive around Vladimir, who was still seated on the motorcycle. He received very suspicious glances but none resulting in a move to halt the convoy. Vladimir turned away to avoid any eye-to-eye contact except for one very confused Major Koshechkin who studied Vladimir from his staff car with grave suspicion.

Vladimir watched the convoy as it roared down the road and was finally out of sight as it rounded the corner. Vladimir sighed heavily taking a deep breath. He looked down at the motorcycle and put his hands on the throttle. "Hmm. Now, how does one operate this thing?"

Chapter 12

Otto stood up. He remembered he had something very special still in his possession. He fiddled in his pocket and pulled from it the key given to him by Corporal Huber. Otto clenched the key in his hand with all his might. He lifted his head and rose to his feet, strength returning to his heart. This was not the end.

The sky was giving over to the oncoming evening. The light dimmed and turned warmer in hue, surrendering the brightness of the sun. Otto picked up his damp musette bag and wiped his nose. He stopped his weeping, pocketed the key, and became fixated on the road. "I am tired of this wet, dreary, and putrid place. Time to get on with it. Time to get to the Wolf's Lair. Time to find Annie."

From his dry perch, Otto stepped back into the swamp, unaffected by the chill of the water as he entered. He came to the swamp's edge where the bank was short and rose steeply to meet the road. "Well, this is it then. I am exposed and will simply have to make a run for it."

Otto peered through the thicket and looked in both directions down the road. It was empty. He could not see to either end or find the beginning of a more suitable landscape. Otto stepped from the swamp for good and into the clearing of the bank alongside the road. He paused to listen for any sounds of vehicles, soldiers, or anything else that would cause alarm. There was nothing. He secured his musette bag and started slowly down the road. He jogged lightly at first to build a rhythm and warm up his body, saving energy for an all-out sprint if something warranted it. He peered back every so often, watching for anything unnatural upon the road's surface. The longer he stayed on the road without incident, the more confident his mind became. He smiled at the coming of a new change in the landscape that now allowed him to see further into the distance. The swamp began to fade, its waters retreating and giving up its grasp to dryer grounds. Briars and thorns traded places with fir and taller trees holding higher branches. The road was longer than Otto had thought, but he kept his pace calm and controlled, his breathing regular and efficient.

The wind's direction was at his face when he began but suddenly subsided, unmasking the sounds around him. Suddenly, Otto stopped his run. A distraction in the air alerted his ears. He stood still, his breathing heavy, his heart pulsating. He slowly turned his head to the direction of the disturbance. A high-pitched sputtering noise, apparently coming from something of great speed, approached. He stood up high on his tip-toes to get a different perspective, straining his eyes to give form to this intrusion. Otto could discern no shape but only a twinkling light moving vertically as if bouncing up and down with the surface contours of the undulating road. Something was indeed coming.

Otto turned and, calling upon his saved sprint, pounded up the road as fast as his legs and lungs could take him. The sound drew nearer and louder. Otto gasped for more breath and richer air to give him more speed, but there was none. He could see the end of the swamp and the coming of firmer ground, an easy escape route, but it was proving beyond his grasp. Otto ran hard, not looking back at the surprising attack. He could feel the intruder at his back, and he awaited a gunshot or perhaps worse, being trampled. The sound grew louder until it was upon him. Otto knew that whatever was giving chase, it was now right beside him flashing ever so slightly in the corner of his eye. He feared taking another glimpse, but he was running out of energy. He would have to confront it.

Thinking by now this new threat would have overcome him, Otto turned his head to face it while slowing his pace. He was caught quite by surprise at what he saw. His attacker seemed less threatening, a small figure engulfed by a large motorcycle. The rider threw Otto a wide, shiny-toothed grin from behind a set of huge goggles that enveloped his entire face. Otto offered an inquisitive smile back as they both moved along side by side, sharing glances. Thinking this scene quite comical and less threatening, Otto stopped altogether. The motorcycle rider met Otto's movement, the droning slowly changing to a low growl until it came to a stop at his side. The rider switched the motorcycle off and swung his leg around so as to be sitting and facing Otto.

Otto stood still, confused, quietly staring at the rider for a moment until it finally came to him. "Joseph? Is, is that you?"

"I prefer the name Vladimir, but yes, I am him. I mean he is me. Oh, good gracious. I'm Joseph, my dear captured Jew."

Otto paused, observing the entire picture in front of him. He brought his hands to rest upon his waist. "You look like a big, ugly bug with those goggles on."

"I think so too, but they sure keep the flies out of my eyes. As for my mouth? Well, I can tell you they don't taste very good."

Otto laughed between catching his breath and creating questions that now filled his head. "Vladimir? Seems you have had quite an adventure these past few days. I would have you explain."

Joseph nodded proudly. "Yes. I have a few tricks of my own, Jew. You are not the only one with abilities and secrets. Quite a convincing disappearing act you pulled a number of days past. You should have seen my furious and angered face when learning of your departure. Had I caught you then, well, I would have been down a clip of ammo, I expect. Then Saint Nikolaus awoke from his snoring, and we had a little discussion. Oh, you should have heard us, Otto, arguing back and forth over my next course of action, to either hunt you down and dispose of you or leave you be and let the Russians have at you. Then, I pulled out that drawing you had done for me, and I began to think. There are too many things, too many stories of yours that have my curiosity. Besides, Christoph made some very solid points. Perhaps you and I are destined for something greater. Perhaps I need to see this through. Somehow, I feel there is going to be something awakened in me that will change many things. There's also another thing, Jew, I mean, um, Otto. I, well, I rather missed you not being there in the morning. I felt a bit alone. There, I said it. Curse that Christoph, he made me say it!"

Otto stood silent, a smile creeping slowly across his face. "You know, Joseph, it's weird. While probably still very inappropriate and wrong, I somehow don't mind you calling me 'Jew' anymore. It seems less upsetting to me now. It's just a word. It seems the hate, anger, and evil behind your emotions have ceased in escorting it anymore. Um, and I missed you also. Much has happened since venturing off on my own. I've come to think I'm not good at it anymore. I need you too."

Joseph sat motionless listening to Otto. "I suppose we need each other, but don't take me for a fool, Otto. I am still only partly on your side. I still must honor and uphold my mission. We must get that document to Admiral Dönitz."

"I have failed us there, Joseph. I need not say how, but I'm afraid the Russians have seized my satchel and its contents."

Joseph smiled and turned to the sidecar, grabbing the satchel and tossing it to Otto. "Ah! My troubled courier of the High Court, you need not worry."

Otto's eyes grew bright. "But, but how is this possible?"

"Well, as Christoph said to you on the wagon, and yes, I was listening to your conversation, the Russians are half-wits. Feeling there was a great possibility of encountering them, I had brought a Russian uniform with me from the bunker, something I had thought might be needed for just such an occasion. I put it on when I decided to come find you, knowing where you were going. I found a bicycle in an old, decaying barn just off the road to complete my courier disguise. It seemed a natural fit for my charade. Despite a rusty chain that squealed terribly and a road not even fit for swine, my travels went quite uninterrupted. Well, it was until that Russian convoy approached. While confident of my ruse, I was very nervous, to say the least. However, I felt it would be easy to manage my way through their ranks and continue on with my quest. As I have said, they were not the smartest lot. There was this sergeant. He had ideas. A strange man he was, having some scheme to elevate his stature. He gave me the task to deliver a satchel to the Russian High Command. I recognized it the second he pulled it from his vehicle. I feared the worst, thinking you were shot, but knowing you, I theorized you would be alive somehow, the only casualty being the loss of your satchel. The rest was really quite easy. The sergeant gave me the satchel and this motorcycle. Then he drove off with his convoy to the German front, I suppose. Either way, they're far from us now, I can assure you." Joseph sat back still wearing a grin, quite proud of his mini adventure.

"You are very clever, Joseph, and I thank you for returning this satchel. So, what are we to do now?"

Joseph reached up and pulled down the bug-eyed goggles covering his face. He turned, grabbed the handlebars, tossed his leg over the bike, and started the engine, bringing the motorcycle back to life. "Hop on. Off to the Wolf's Lair!"

Otto smiled widely. He sprang from attention, and with his satchel tightly held in his arms, he leaped into the sidecar. "Yes. To the Wolf's Lair!"

Chapter 13

Otto sat huddled in the sidecar, shivering. The air had turned unpleasant and added its chill against him. Joseph glanced down at Otto, noticing his trembling. "You are cold, Jew? Yes?"

Otto looked up at Joseph and shouted above the droning growl of the motorcycle. "Yyyes!"

Joseph smiled, "Well, my arms are rather mushy from trying to hold this damn contraption straight, so I make a motion to find a place to rest for the night."

"Th-th-that would be n-n-nice."

They came upon a small village with a number of stone-walled structures attached by adjoining walls that created narrow passages and corridors. The village was vacant and lay in rubble, its inhabitants having abandoned its skeleton and moving on to find solace elsewhere.

"This place looks to offer us much seclusion and safety, my dear Otto. I shall find a structure that will hide a fire and give us an escape route for our motorcycle." Joseph pulled the motorcycle around to the back of a burned-out building. Its roof was gone, but all four walls were still erect and mighty.

"Yes, this shall do very well," Otto offered confidently. "Pull the motorcycle in and swing it around facing the outside. It'll offer a quick getaway."

Joseph entered the wide double entryway, its wooden doors having been burned away. He swung the vehicle around as instructed and parked it, blocking the entrance. Otto hopped out, keeping his satchel and musette bag in the sidecar. Joseph dismounted, noticing Otto leaving the bags in the sidecar. "Knowing what troubles we've had with that satchel, I would suggest you keep it close, Jew."

Otto nodded, as if not admitting his absent mindedness. "Yes, yes, I was just stretching, Hun." Otto reached into the sidecar and grabbed the satchel, swinging it around his head to rest on his shoulder. He looked around him for wood, as a warm fire was on his mind. "It seems fire has already laid claim to the wood in here. I suggest we look elsewhere. I am wet, cold, and getting irritable, Joseph."

"Agreed. You are irritable and forgetful, Jew, and you smell like a filthy pig in its trough!"

They pillaged the grounds for burnable wood, fumbling in the dark in their search. Joseph came across a pile of broken rafters not yet consumed by flame and waved to Otto for help. "Well, this wood should do fine. I'll get a fire roaring in no time."

They began breaking and snapping the rafters into smaller pieces and, in minutes, created a pile where the fire was to be started. Otto reached into his musette bag and grabbed his blanket. It was damp but had always done well in providing a soft bedding. He kicked and swept away the splintered and rubble-strewn ground, making for a flatter surface. Hastily, the wood gave up its warmth, yielding a small but constant flame as the young couriers sat beside the fire. Otto removed his clothes, hanging them next to the fire on a charred beam and spreading them out to dry. Joseph sat across from Otto on the other side of the fire. He pulled from his own musette bag his drawing tablet and began to cover his paper.

"What are you drawing this time, Joseph?" Otto asked curiously with a facetious grin. "Now make sure to draw in your guides, and then see to your subject as I instructed you."

Joseph looked up at Otto with an ill-favored look. "Yes. I remember, Jew."

Otto sat back and laughed quietly to himself. The fire was inviting, bringing him back to life. Joseph peeked up at Otto from over his drawing tablet. "What is that look on your face, Jew? You always seem to be wearing that same look, a smile with glazed eyes, as if you are off somewhere else. You dream with your eyes open."

"I am off somewhere else, Joseph. I'm with Annie, and we are playing by the River Spree, like we are not supposed to do. It is a warm and embracing summer's day, and laughter is contagious and plentiful."

"Then my fire is working. Yes?" offered Joseph.

"It is."

"Glad to see that irritableness drift away. I was hoping not to have to shoot you."

"Speaking of which, why did you come back to find me? Why are we going to the Wolf's Lair? It is not our instructed mission. Well, not yours anyway."

"Sometimes, Jew, I don't think you listen when you're in your dream land. To repeat, my curiosity is aroused. Don't worry, we shall complete our mission."

"I am listening, but what specifically draws you to pursue this curiosity?"

"Well, if you must know, it is my own father. He is a respected man, and I admire his prominence as a successful businessman, political figure, and patriarch. However, I also remember many nights when he dressed in dark suits with an ill-looking icon on his lapel. He would be stern with mother and abrasive with us. It frightened us greatly. We wondered where his heart was being led. Whatever it was, it was how I came to be in the Hitler Youth Corps, thrust into the training and classwork and constantly learning deeper philosophies and mythologies. I was proud to be a part of such a fine group of people. I still am. The brotherhood and participation we all shared and believed in was very inspirational. It helped give my family power and strength. Father would guide us and picture for us a great people in a great land for all the world to see and revere. He said we were superior and we were to act superior. There was no more concerning ourselves with certain people, those of less fortune, power, or placement. Jews were one of them, Otto. Oh, how father spoke of the Jews. I need not remind you of this."

"So you are coming along in hopes to prove your father true?"

"No, Jew. I am coming along because I am proving to you that I'm destined for greater things, to uphold my fine qualities in my father's name."

Otto listened intently, noticing Joseph's words succumb to a hypnotized mindset.

"It is late, Otto. I am tired of this talk. Let's find our rest. We are but a half-day's distance to the Wolf's Lair. Let us hope we get there unnoticed."

Otto nodded and pulled the end of his blanket over him, propping his weary head upon his satchel and musette bag like a pillow. He closed his eyes and whispered to himself, "I should hope dear Joseph's heart is not disenchanted when this comes to an end." He breathed a sigh and soon fell asleep.

The fire crackled as embers swirled freely into the night sky. An owl swooped down and rested upon a charred branch that had grown too near the burned out building, a victim to war's hand. Its head swiveled from side to side, alerted to a crawling delicacy below. With one magnificent force, the owl launched from its perch and plummeted to the ground, its talons sharp and poised. It clenched its prey and silently ascended into the darkness.

"Pst! Otto, wake up!" Joseph frantically shook Otto's shoulder to greet him to the new day. "Quickly, we are not alone. There are strange voices coming to us from over the wall."

Startled, Otto awoke and rose to an upright position as he noticed Joseph with his MP-40 slung tightly around his shoulder, his finger itching the trigger. The fire was out, with not so much as an ember giving up a plume of smoke. "What is it? Should we escape?"

"No. We have not been discovered. Quiet. Let's investigate."

Otto dressed and donned his satchel and musette bag. He followed Joseph to the wall, creeping slowly and following its borders to a hole that exposed the voices they were hearing. In the narrow corridor between two destroyed buildings, they could plainly see four German soldiers confronting two men in civilian clothing. Their rifles were at their captors' heads. One soldier was yelling and demanding answers in stern fashion. Off in the distance, they recognized a staff car painted the basic German field grey with an MG-34 machine gun mounted on the top in the middle between the front and rear seat.

"I recognize their uniforms, Otto. They are SS men. Two are wearing pea-dot pattern camouflage smocks over their tunics, but I can still discern their SS runes on their right collar tabs. The left tabs look blank. Those are storm troopers. They are very wicked. The other two men are wearing Waffen SS green-grey tunics with SS collar tabs. The one on the left, farthest away and next to the storm troopers, has an SD sleeve diamond and police-style toxic green shoulder boards. I have not seen this uniform before in all my dealings with the German army."

"I have. In the ghetto. He is a Schupo Officer."

"The soldier closest to us, the one doing all the yelling, he looks to be of a higher rank. I see three diamonds and what looks to be two silver strands on his left collar tab, which indicates he is a Chief Assault Leader, basically a captain in other armies. That mark, I mean pin, on his side cap, it's like my father's pin, the skull and cross bones."

Otto became alarmed at this finding. He knew these marks as well. "Yes, the skull and crossbones. That's the Totenkopf death head, Joseph. Now shush. Let's try to listen to their words."

Otto and Joseph peeked back through the small irregular shaped hole that had been blown out of the wall. "I can't understand anything they are saying, can you, Joseph?"

"No, Jew, but when you keep talking, it makes it..."

Suddenly, rifle shots blasted into the light of the morning and the two captors fell to the ground, their entangled arms and legs slumping over each other. Blood was set free from its path and greeted the day, steaming in the coolness of the air and glistening vividly in the light of the sun.

Otto and Joseph flinched but a little, with a slight quiver of their eyes that were still fixated on the uninvited guests. The soldiers shouldered their weapons and, with little expression, walked towards their vehicle. They lit cigarettes as they approached the staff car and seemingly joked amongst one another. They jumped into their car and packed their weapons away at their sides. One of the storm troopers with the camouflage smocks stood up behind the MG-34, checked its belt of ammo, and slammed back the cocking lever as if readying it for a burst. The captain motioned to his men, signaling his readiness for departure as the driver found first gear. They sped off down the road in the opposite direction from where Otto and Joseph had come, their cigarette smoke still drifting carelessly in the air and disturbing its purity. Otto and Joseph fell, slumping to the ground behind the wall, mimicking the dead civilians. They were both shaking silently.

"There are angels on our shoulders, Joseph. It is but a miracle we were not found."

"Yes, but the real question is, what are four SS men doing in these parts?"

"A good question. The Eastern front is no longer in German hands. Men of that stature would surely be in Berlin fighting or more likely hidden extremely well in some Bavarian mountain bunker far away from here."

Joseph nodded. "A strange mix of ranks, don't you think? Two storm troopers, lower men in rank, a police officer, and a captain, who was the most vicious of the group. His voice breathed fire, and his eyes had a very sinister glow."

"Yes, a very strange group indeed. I am not sure of their objective, but they have been gathered for a purpose, I can tell you. I would guess they came upon those two civilians just before conducting a thorough search of the village. After their deed, they may have thought it wise to leave quickly, leaving this mess for someone else to find."

"Maybe they were not civilians but were German soldiers. Deserters?"

"That could be. It would explain much, but enough contemplating. We mustn't linger. We must move from here. Their gunshots will not go unnoticed."

"Agreed. I will ready our ride." Joseph sprang to his feet, running to the motorcycle. Otto followed closely and hopped into the sidecar. Joseph looked down at Otto while sliding on his bug-eyed goggles. "You know you are secretly jealous of my goggles."

Otto sneered, looking away and forward from Joseph, answering him aloud at first, then his voice quickly tapering off so that Joseph could not hear his entire sentence. "No! Good gracious, no. Well, maybe. Okay. I want a pair."

Joseph started the motorcycle, spurring it to life. He revved the throttle slowly in neutral, and the beast was soon roaring. "You may need to get familiar with that machine gun. We may find it of use during our travels."

"I don't think so. Only a peasant would succumb to such a thing. Now, driver, please proceed onward and be quick about it." Otto waived his hand nonchalantly, sitting back in the sidecar as if preparing for a leisurely Sunday ride through the countryside.

Joseph shook his head in disgust, whispering under his breathe, "Silly Jew."

"I heard that, Hun. Now on to the Wolf's Lair."

Joseph jammed the bike into first gear, then coming quickly on the throttle, they lunged forward. They circled around the village until Joseph found their direction. Third gear created more speed as they tore down the road. Otto peeked back at the lump of dead civilians now drawing flies to the colorful springtime landscape.

The sun clipped the treetops, individual slices of rays defining the boys' silhouettes as they motored along. The way was bumpy and rutted, forcing Otto to grip the edge of the sidecar with great intensity. The wind from the speed of the motorcycle blew his hair back and contorted his face.

Joseph glanced at his companion with an inquisitive, if not queer, look. "What on earth, Otto? Again I ask, how are you to man that machine gun, should the occasion arise, if you have that death grip on the sidecar?"

Otto turned his head to Joseph, the wind continuing its sculpture of his face. "Well, if you must know, again, I mean not to use this thing. For one, I am not versed in its operation and two, as a result, I may shoot you by accident." Otto finished his comeback with a very fitting and hearty grin.

Joseph thought about Otto's answer while looking at him and leaving the motorcycle to navigate on its own. "Hmm. Well, I should think we'll be leaving that gun alone then, yes?" They both nodded and went about their business, Otto grasping the side and Joseph steering the machine for dear life.

The road held empty as they traveled, but Joseph's mind swirled with thoughts. "I've been thinking that we may need a plan if we are to enter the Wolf's Lair without any, how shall I say it, military engagements?"

"You know, my dear Joseph, you are getting very talented at this sneaking around, planning, and such. Perhaps you have the blood of a worthy courier. While I should not enjoy seeing your head swell beyond the round lenses of your bug-eyed goggles, I think it best we stop and do as you suggest. How far away are we?"

"A bigger head? I would just get bigger goggles. You see, I always have an answer, Otto."

"Very well, then answer my question."

"Alright. We are but a half day away, I suppose."

"Good. Let's find a place to stop and talk of a plan, Mr. Big Head." Otto turned to face back toward the road, searching for a place to seek hiding. "Let's see. Over there. Yes, that shall do very well. Pull into that shady lane of trees."

Joseph nodded and maneuvered the bike towards the hiding place. He stopped the bike and switched off the ignition. The motorcycle burped and gurgled to a quieted state under a thick canopy of dense trees surrounding them and offering little light.

"It's like a little fort in here, isn't it?"

Joseph shook his head in bewilderment at Otto's christening. "This is not the time to play. We have to seriously discuss important matters."

Otto jumped out of the sidecar. "Did you say something, Joseph? Good gracious. I can actually hear now, even though my ears are ringing from all your yelling over the whine of that mechanical behemoth."

Joseph dismounted the saddle. "It's this behemoth that brought you back your satchel, my dear Otto, and it may very well save us again before this is over."

Otto nodded. "Point taken. Let's get on with our work. I suppose we could use your drawing tablet and create a map of the Wolf's Lair. From that, we can devise a plan of entrance and exit."

"Yes. Good idea." Joseph withdrew his drawing tablet from his musette bag. He and Otto cleared the ground on the opposite side of the motorcycle leaving it as a barrier to the road should an uninvited guest come by. They gathered brush and dead branches to hide the facade of the motorcycle. The shady grove was comforting and offered them an exit into a field should they need an escape route. Otto and Joseph sat down, legs crossed, the tablet opened on both of their laps. They went to work and began to put what was in their minds to paper.

"We've both been to the Wolf's Lair, Otto, so this should not be difficult to plan."

Otto nodded hesitantly. "Yes. I was there many times but was never allowed to go into certain areas. For the most part, I stayed with Corporal Huber in the engineering or communications building. On occasion, I was stationed in one of Bormann's rooms in his bunker awaiting his missions for me. I was blind-folded when entering and leaving the Wolf's Lair. My stay was not as regal as yours, I must admit. I think it best you speak of the Wolf's Lair and what our possibilities may be. I can jump in if an experience I've had lends to the plan. Basically, I know little. I don't even know why it was called the Wolf's Lair."

"Aha! You mean the all-knowing Otto, the courier, has nothing to lend? I, Joseph, the know-it-all, have information you don't? Ooh, please, Otto, I beg of you to give me a minute to cherish this delightful fact."

Otto raised his eyes. "Oh, gracious me. I thought you'd fancy that. Yes, by all means, gloat."

"Well, that's not very rewarding if you give in without objection. Okay, let's move beyond this." Joseph began drawing on his tablet, marking the positions of key structures, buildings, and the general layout of the compound.

"The Wolf's Lair, dear Otto, was the Führer's eastern front military headquarters with its main objective to direct and command the war against Russia."

"Yes," Otto interrupted excitedly, "Operation Barbarossa. I've heard Corporal Huber speak of it many times while here."

"Ah, see? You do know of this place. Now sit and listen. We haven't got all day for interruptions."

Otto's excitement sputtered as he hunched his shoulders like a scorned puppy. "Yes, continue on mighty, big-headed one."

"Sarcasm will do you no favors, my dear Otto. Now, as I was saying, I've heard that the name Wolf's Lair was given by none other than the Führer himself. It was a nickname, of course. He fancied the name 'wolf' because of his name, Adolf, which means in old high

German 'noble wolf.' From what was told to me, he only permitted the High Court to address him by this nickname, which I'm afraid leaves you out, Otto."

Otto snickered saying nothing.

"Now, Otto, this compound is built deep into the very impenetrable Masurian Forest amidst the lovely, humid, and mosquito-infested lake region of Poland. It was told to me that even the Führer himself condemned these little flying terrors, although they weren't the only thing with which he took issue. Often he could be heard ranting and festering about, feeling trapped in this dreaded humidity and living in bunkers with no light, air, or space. Self-deserving, some say, but it's the price for creating a heightened sense of security, I suppose. To enhance that security, the compound is naturally surrounded by swamps and lakes and is far from major roads and cities. What nature couldn't provide, we did. I can remember many times my Hitler Youth squad would help the work crews and engineers in camouflaging the bunkers. We'd drape camouflage netting from building to building and to the surrounding vegetation. We even fabricated artificial trees, brush, and grasses on the flat roofs to further create a network of dense canopy that I should think was quite undetected by air. I can't remember any allied threats of bombing throughout the time I spent there."

Otto opened his mouth as if wanting to contribute a thought but wisely concluded quickly that his interruption would be viewed as distracting. In truth, he rather enjoyed Joseph sharing his knowledge and experiences. It brought Joseph that much closer to him.

"When all was completed, Otto, although I'm not sure any of it was truly finished, the compound contained over two hundred buildings. It was quite a self-sufficient village, I should think. It made its own electricity, had a sound water supply with a complete sewer system, and had an independent heating plant." Otto's question begged him, and he raised his curious hand slowly as almost not to be seen. "Yes, Otto, by all means, interrupt again."

"All very good information, but what of the security? What information have you about what's guarding this technical death machine?"

Joseph shook his head left to right, smiling with his eyes closed. "Yes, silly Jew, I was just getting to that part. Now remain quiet while I get through this lecture of mine. Now, as you have suggested, Otto, this compound is very well-armed and protected. Imagine, if you will, a tight, impenetrable fortress of sorts with three distinct security zones. Zone One is where the High Court's bunkers are located. Ten in total, to be exact, consisting of our Führer's, Göring's, Bormann's, Chief Keitel's, and Chief of Operations Jodl's. I should think you've been in this area?"

"Yes, Joseph. I have. I do remember the bunkers being an endless labyrinth of rooms, halls, and passageways with few windows and very little light. It reminded me more of a prison than a command center for Germany's High Court. I also remember security around this area being very strict. There was one incident where a German private had not correctly given the required papers and password. He was whisked away around the corner, and no sooner had he vanished when I heard a rifle shot ring through the compound."

"I too have heard of similar events, of forced laborers wandering off by accident to meet the same fate as that private. Now, Zone Two contained military barracks and housing for other important court figures. However, the people I fear most in this zone, besides now the possibility of occupying Russians, are the Führer's personal escort battalion. We can only hope that they have been called on for the protection of Berlin. If not, then we are to face them and their tanks, anti-aircraft guns, and other assorted heavy weapons, all of which I assure you, Otto, you are not well-versed in operating.

"Finally, my friend, there's Security Zone Three, a vast network and maze of guard houses, entangled walls of barbed wire, trenches, machine gun nests, and if that isn't enough, the hundreds of thousands of land mines." Silence came to Joseph as he continued drawing, which for him now became more the subject of drawing than devising a plan.

Otto pondered Joseph's lecture before adding a touch of quick-witted cynicism. "Oh, is that all? I suppose that leaves us to deciding a plan then? A good one, I should hope. A very, very good one."

Otto sat quietly thinking. Joseph paused his artistry as if he'd been thinking all this time. "Yes, Jew, and an escape route would be a lovely touch, I should add."

Otto pointed to a line on the drawing tablet with smaller cross hatches down its center. "What is that, a barbed wire fence?"

"No, that's a train track that runs through the middle of the compound for the most part."

A bright smile came to Otto without delay. "I have an idea! What if we were to abandon our motorcycle on the outskirts of the compound and follow the train tracks to its center? From there, we could follow the road north that runs through Zone One to Bormann's bunker."

Joseph stopped drawing and stared straight into the air, his mind calculating. "Well, there surely wouldn't be any mines on the tracks, and I suppose, except for a few machine gun nests and infantry to attend to, it may actually be a good plan." Joseph turned to face Otto in a cheery voice. "You may have good ideas yet."

"Seeing how that gun has been quiet of late, you should have plenty of ammunition to ward off such threats." Otto lifted his side of the tablet and rose to his feet, brushing off the leaves and dirt from sitting. "So, shall we go?"

Joseph closed the tablet and stood next to Otto. "Yes, but I am in the dark, Otto. You keep too many secrets to yourself. That aside, you say your answers are to be found in Bormann's bunker. How are we to enter? Surely, the possibilities of it being locked or well-guarded are high or, I would suggest, altogether blown to pieces after the possible advances of the Russians. Furthermore, what on earth are we looking for?"

Otto turned from Joseph and sat upon the edge of the sidecar. "Yes. Well. Quite a feat, yes? If you must know, I'm looking for where they have taken Annie and my family. You are correct. Corporal Huber told me the answer lies within Bormann's bunker. Where, I do not know. I'm not sure what we'll find." Otto dug into his pocket with his hand, pulling out the key given to him. "But I have this."

Joseph's eyes widened, and his mouth opened in excited surprise. He reached his arm out slowly, his hand delicately and somewhat tentatively taking the key from Otto. "Where did you get this? I have heard of but have never seen such a thing. A key in the form of a golden eagle, encrusted in diamonds and jewels and grasping a snake entwined around a swastika. This has come from the High Courts."

Otto flipped his legs around into the sidecar, still sitting on its edge, as if teasing their leave. "We are still going, yes? You are still curious?"

Joseph broke his gaze from the key. "Yes, Otto, we go. While I have suspicion of your stories, this key is very real. This is no ordinary door key to an ordinary bunker, or any door for that matter. It is rumored that only a few such keys exist and hold the great wealths of the Third Reich. The great mythologies surrounding such a key were taught to us during our Hitler Youth schooling, but we were never shown one. Now you and I have one. So yes, let us go!"

Joseph handed the key back to Otto gently. Otto took the key and put it back into his pocket. Joseph walked around the motorcycle to prepare its departure, removing the branches and bushes camouflaging its facade. "You understand, my dear Otto, this means that whatever secrets lie with that key are of great importance to all of Germany. Our mission now has stepped up in its significance. What we now do shall change and alter the history of time, and we shall be a part of its making."

Joseph hopped on the motorcycle with excitement and vigor. He started the engine and donned his big-headed goggles, throwing the bike into first gear and revving the throttle. Otto slipped quickly into his place and stared straight ahead as he held onto the edges of the sidecar. Joseph eased off the clutch, and the machine roared to life lurching forward, the engine still quite cool. They turned around within their little fort and exited whence they came.

Noon came to pass as dark clouds flirted with the sun, threatening to dampen their afternoon travels. War had left its signature, still spreading ugly scenes and twisted stories. Dead soldiers, mostly German, lay in all sorts of disrupted and contorted positions of final rest along the roads. Smoldering machines created for battle lined the ditches, some overturned, blackened from attack. Women, children, and things unrecognizable as man or beast lay scattered. Buildings lay crumbled, distorted in shape, begging to be hidden among an equally disturbed landscape. Grasses and trees were turned ashen, bare earth muddied, eroding into streams now browned and choking. Not even the fish could escape war's grasp as they lay stiff along the shores, eyes sunken and rotting. Ravens swarmed the skies, but not even these picky eaters would welcome the free meal. It was an unsettling vision when contrasted with the newly born blossoms of fruit trees and warming days.

The motorcycle came to a stop. The road had ended with a choice of traveling either left or right. Otto extended his head, looking for a hint. Not convinced of that view, he raised to his feet for a better look but was rewarded with nothing further.

"Well, what way then? Nothing comes to my sight."

Joseph raised his big-headed goggles and squinted to make shapes of the terrain in all directions. "Well, I'm not sure which way to go as I have always arrived from the west or by rail. Our approach from the south is strange to me. Although, that looks to be something human-made off in the distance. I'll get my binoculars out and have a look."

Otto slumped back down into the sidecar as Joseph scanned the countryside.

"Oh, Otto, this is good news. Very good news!"

Otto quickly jumped upright excited. "What then? Go on. What is it?"

"I see a rather well-equipped Red Army convoy milling around a train station, the very one where the tracks are that we need to follow."

Otto looked up at Joseph with a questionably ill-favored smile. "What do you mean good news? That's terrible news."

Joseph dropped his arms, resting them against his chest while holding the binoculars. "No, Otto. That is good news. It means the Russians have most likely been through the Wolf's Lair and are pushing forward." Joseph raised his binoculars for another look. "I'd say they're a bit tardy for the spoils of Berlin. Looks to be an armored division with infantry, probably holding the most northern front."

Otto stood up from the sidecar and swiped the binoculars from Joseph. "Hey! Give those back!"

Otto raised the glasses and adjusted the lens to bring the horizon into focus. "Yes, it seems you are correct. However, I suspect the Ivans have left a detachment for us at the Wolf's Lair. They will not let it fall to an advancing Allied army or to be left to German soldiers trying to destroy it upon their abandonment."

"Agreed. What else do you see? Is there a way around them at our front?"

"Yes. There appears to be a narrow dirt farm road leading to the tracks to the east, which answers our question. We should go right, then a sharp left. Hopefully that will get us to where we need to be." Handing the binoculars back to Joseph, he added, "But I still say our original plan is a good one. However, since the Russians aren't playing fair, we'll have to move closer to the Wolf's Lair to start our travels down the railroad tracks."

"Fine. Quickly now, let's move from here. Surely, if we can see them, they can see us."

Otto nodded and sat back down into the sidecar. His hand brushed the machine gun as he reached for the edge of the sidecar, and a menacing feeling came to his face. Perhaps he would have to become well-versed in its use, he thought.

Joseph throttled the gas and steered the motorcycle in the direction Otto scouted, guiding them to the farm road he had spied with the binoculars. It was indeed narrow, the dirt having turned to mud, rutted by spring rains and the thin wooden wheels of farm wagons. The way was slow and proved to be a menace as Joseph tried to navigate the uncooperative machine around the scarred road. His sour face easily proved his efforts. Suddenly, the engine sputtered and the bike lost power, jerking back and forth as Joseph tried to keep the throttle upon it. Then it simply coughed and stalled altogether, coming to a rolled stop. The railroad track was near, but they were now left exposed except for brush edging the fields to their sides.

"Well, this certainly is most unwelcome, Joseph. The Ivans would have to be as blind as bats to have not witnessed our intrusion now."

"Very good, but your quips will not help our being left out here in this field. I suspect all this incessant rattling has rather challenged the temperament of our motorcycle."

"No, I just think we are out of petrol."

Joseph frowned and unscrewed the cap from the gas tank. He peered inside and could see little. "Well, it does appear as if we are low on fuel."

"You mean to say we are out of fuel?"

"Something like that, Jew." Joseph screwed the gas cap back on with a disconcerted expression on his face. "I am afraid we are near our end with this machine, Otto. My guess would be that there isn't enough petrol for even half a kilometer at best, and the Russians have all but taken what was contained in the vehicles left by the Germans. Our road from here looks to be on foot."

Otto threw his satchel and musette bag over his shoulders, readjusting himself for a long walk. "Well, good thing we made it to the railway somewhat close to where we needed to be. I should think that three-wheeled machine would make for an awful ride on the tracks.

Only our feet need lead us from here. However, let us hope a fast escape is not warranted because we won't have one."

Joseph pushed the motorcycle into the brush alongside the railway and camouflaged its shape. He grabbed his own musette bag and strapped his MP-40 around his shoulder, coming to fall in perfect alignment with the front of his body. "Let's be off. Darkness will come soon, and putting distance in before we lose light would be wise."

Otto and Joseph crouched low, staying out of sight as they scurried down the farm road coming to the railway. They stepped onto the tracks and stopped, both looking into the horizon up and down the tracks for anything suspicious. They were in the open now, except for a few trees lending a canopy that sheltered them with shadows.

"I don't like being in the open like this, Joseph. It's unnatural for me."

"Yes, well, let us go then. We should walk in column patrol formation to give ourselves distance from each other. I know that'll be hard for you because you fancy listening to my brilliance and words of wisdom, but if we were to be surprised with a burst of machine gun fire, our distance would increase the challenge for our enemy to get us both. At least one of us would have a chance to escape."

Otto stared at Joseph with amusement. "Patrol formation? But there's just two of us. That's not much of a patrol now, is it?"

Joseph walked past Otto, not answering, his eyes brimming with frustration.

"Alright. Fine. Patrol formation it is."

The way was awkward as the railroad ties did not synchronize well with the walking stride of a boy. It forced them both to remain cautious of their steps to avoid a twist of their ankles. Otto began talking to himself as he timed his steps, creating a rhythmic beat. He thought of Annie, wondering what adventures she may be having and hoping she was safe. He closed his eyes as he walked in perfect cadence of his steps to railway ties.

Joseph glanced back at Otto, checking on his march, and noticed his eyes closed. He stopped to let Otto catch up. "You are off with Annie again, are you not, Otto?"

"Ah, Joseph, you are getting to understand me rather well, I should think."

"Perhaps, but do you think it wise to go off and be with her now? Surely, when we stop for the night would be a better use of that time."

Otto opened his eyes and stopped his march in front of Joseph. "Time? No, there is never a better time. There is only all the time."

Joseph turned and continued his march. "You sound like a victim of Cupid's games."

"Well, I really think of Annie as the very best of friends. It could just as well have been a boy, I suppose."

Joseph stopped again and turned to Otto. "Boys do not make other boys' tummies ache when they miss them. That could only be love."

Otto pondered this thought for a moment. "Okay, perhaps it is love, but not that kissing kind of love."

Joseph smiled to himself as he marched forward.

Travel left them undisturbed, and the way remained clear. The sun faded beyond the trees, and darkness crept back upon their travels. The damp air brought with it the mosquitoes, which proved to be an added menace in their steps. "Blasted little weapons, they are," Joseph lashed out.

"Interesting that they still fancy you but have no need to bother me."

Joseph scowled as he swatted in all directions of his body, hampering, if only temporarily, his new enemy's approach. "I suppose I'll have to use my musette bag as a head net of sorts for my sleep tonight. I'd like to see them get in there."

"I expect that musette bag over your head all the time would be a welcome advancement to your facial features indeed."

"Oh, so you are the clever one this night, yes? Fine, let it be then. Now be serious, Otto. We are close to our objective. My counsel is to find rest tonight and regain our strength. We'll go fresh into the Wolf's Lair tomorrow."

"Well, it looks like any place off the tracks would be suitable for our rest. There's not much around but woods and mosquitoes. How about over there, by that downed tree? It would make a good hiding place and give us protection if so needed."

Otto and Joseph moved off from the railway, ever cautious of where they were stepping. At this point, they were near or on the outer security zone of the Wolf's Lair, and the threat of mines was becoming real. They nestled down against a large fallen tree. Otto removed his satchel and musette bag and set them next to him. He reached in and grabbed an iron ration. "Oh, good for me. Horse meat. Well, I suppose I could pretend it's chicken."

Joseph cleared his ground and took out his drawing tablet. He lit a candle and began scratching around the tablet, his brow furrowed, his mind focused.

"What are you drawing, Joseph? Many a night have I watched you wrestle with that paper. Do tell?"

Joseph looked up from his tablet but did not face Otto. He was still very much a part of his drawing. "I am sure if my answer does not satisfy you, you will surely antagonize me all night with your questions. Then we'll both have no rest. So, in that regard I shall tell you. It's a surprise for my father. I shall show you when I'm done and not before. It is not ready for viewing."

"Oh, very well. I suppose I should respect the privacy of an artist, but I won't promise you I'll obey."

"Fine then. Do as you see fit. I'm going to sleep."

Chapter 14

Morning found the boys in full light with threatening skies. Dew had settled, and they awoke damp and in discomfort. Otto stood and shook out his clothes, spraying the dew drops upon Joseph, who was still coiled in a fetal position on the ground.

"Blessed me, Otto. Did you have to do that? Surely a few steps into the woods could have been arranged, no?"

Otto chuckled but for a second as he secured his belongings. "Yes, I considered the idea, but the thought of throwing an S-mine into the air and having it explode and tear through us overcame such thinking. No, I should think we'll walk delicately and retrace our steps to the railway without adding any new ones."

Joseph sat up. "Well, I suppose that makes sense when you put it that way. I detest those wretched little menaces."

Otto and Joseph meticulously retraced their steps back to the center of the tracks, again looking in both directions for anything suspicious, anything that was now there that was not there the day before. Convinced all was clear, they continued towards the Wolf's Lair. The quiet was not to endure. Without warning, Joseph stopped ahead and motioned quietly for Otto to come forward to meet him. Otto ran to Joseph, stopping but two paces away. Joseph said nothing.

He stood silent and frozen, his eyes staring into the air, his nose twitching as if something made it itch.

Otto looked upon him with suspicion. "What is it?" Do you smell something?"

Joseph stood silently, not answering.

"Are you wondering why we have not come to some sort of a gate, Joseph, some kind of fortified entrance to the Wolf's Lair? I have wondered the same. Surely, they would have stopped a train at some kind of gate before allowing it to pass."

"Quiet, Otto!" Joseph barked. "Do you hear that? A droning sound, but not of a train's making."

Otto searched into the sky as the droning became louder. His eyes bulged as from out of the clouds jumped two Russian Yak fighters. "Cover!" Otto yelled as Joseph turned to face the oncoming threats.

The boys leaped from the tracks into the grassy ditch lining the railway just as a burst of strafing fire reconfigured the landscape around them, sending adrift dust, rocks, and pieces of wooded railroad ties. The fighters continued down the railway line unchallenged and committed to further destruction should anything greet them. Otto lay in a fetal position with his arms and hands covering his head, his eyes nearly welded shut, creating new wrinkles to the side of his face. He listened to the fighters tear off into the distance, their menacing drone returning from whence they came. Otto opened his eyes to spiraling clouds of dust breaking apart and beginning to settle upon the tracks.

"Joseph, Joseph, where are you?"

Suddenly, something wiggled underneath him. "I'm under you, Jew. Now get off me."

Otto smiled and came to his knees, giving Joseph freedom to move. "Well, I suppose that's another score for me in saving your life."

Joseph brushed himself off spitting dirt and grass blades from his mouth. "How so, Jew? I didn't need saving. Obviously, their machine gun bursts were well out of our line of fire, and just because you landed on me doesn't mean you were consciously trying to save me or that I required saving. So no, that doesn't count."

"Very well. I wonder what those fighters were doing around here?"

Joseph stood up and checked his MP-40 for dirt and debris lodged in the recoil spring chamber. "I'd say they were air support for that Russian convoy we came upon a day ago. They're no threat to our mission."

Otto stood up and adjusted his possessions to their original position. "They're a day late if that was their orders."

Joseph walked back up to the tracks. "To answer your earlier question about there being some sort of a gate, I agree, but I have never seen one. I expect we came in down-track of it somehow. Looking ahead to the left, I see a road that looks like it crosses the track. I think we are here already."

Otto met Joseph at the track, and together they approached the road, abandoning Joseph's mandated patrol formation. "This is familiar to me, Otto. I see a number of buildings and bunkers." Joseph pointed off deeper into the wooded compound. "I think that's the vehicle garage there and the radio building next to it."

Otto strained to see into the area, the sun's rays dappling bits of light and shadow making it difficult to tell shapes and sizes. "I've been to the radio building, but I can't be sure that's it. I've never seen the tracks from there. Everything looks very different when there's no personnel buzzing about. The quiet is unnerving. We should be approaching this mission by darkness."

"I agree, but we haven't time for tip-toeing and dancing around. We are days delayed because of this side-trip, and Bormann will surely have our heads if he finds out. We must hurry. As curious as I am, we must hurry."

Otto took a step off the tracks into the compound. "Fine. Then let's stay off the road and make for Bormann's bunker through the trees."

"As you wish. Lead on, but behind me."

Otto glared. "Joseph, I have no idea how to even begin following that order. So much for not running into tanks, machine guns, infantry, and land mines, yes?"

"Hush. We are not through this yet. There's nothing guaranteeing that we shall be coming out the same way we entered. Besides, that's the one thing that's bothering me. Where is everybody? I am not aware of this place being abandoned, but it seems it has been."

The first building they came to was indeed the vehicle garage. They passed off to the right side and slipped around to its rear. "Should we check the garage for petrol, Joseph? Surely we'll need it upon our return to the motorcycle."

Joseph nodded. "Yes, I suppose a quick look would not hurt." Joseph peeked around the corner and found the whole side of the building destroyed and its interior unrecognizable. "Hmm, this is not battle damage. This was deliberately destroyed from within."

Otto moved off to the next building with Joseph following closely behind. "The radio building has suffered the same fate. The interior is wrecked. Blown to pieces. I fear the Germans have retreated and, in doing so, left us nothing. There is litter and trash everywhere. I suspect that Bormann's bunker may have received similar treatment."

The boys dashed from tree to tree, bush to bush, as they approached each building and pushed deeper into the compound. The forest was dense, the ground dark, the atmosphere damp, and the mosquitoes on high alert.

"This is more like a cave than a fortress. It gives me the creeps, Joseph."

"Me too. I would guess the Russians have been here and moved off without delay. We must be on the lookout for rear guards. If they have learned what this place was used for, they would not be so inclined to give it up. The Russians enjoy their war trophies."

Suddenly, Joseph stopped mid stride and backed off, reaching out to grab Otto and holding him from moving forward.

"What is it this time?"

"Shush, Jew. There is something up in the trees swaying. A guard, perhaps."

Otto leaned into Joseph and peeked around him to offer a clearer view. It was a strange shape, but it seemed to be of human form. "I think it's dead."

Joseph let go of his grasp of Otto and stepped closer to investigate. "I do believe you are correct, my dear Otto."

Joseph and Otto moved into the light, hoping to identify the victim. "Russian," Otto whispered with surprise. Otto turned his head looking above and beyond. "Look, there's another, and another. We are not alone."

Joseph stepped backwards and spun around, his hands clenching his MP-40 and raising it to firing position. "Quickly Otto. We leave here now. We go no further. Back, back to the tracks."

There was no answer.

Joseph lowered his machine gun, his head darting in all directions. "Pst, Otto, where are you? Where have you gone? Don't make me. I will find you. Damn that Jew! Fine. Let us be done with this soon." He took a deep breath and ran towards Bormann's bunker, thinking Otto headed that way.

Otto came to a road at his front, and with a quick look, he darted across it towards his objective. Tears began to swell in his eyes as he ran back into the woods. He reached out in front grabbing branches and brush, forcing them from his body. He came into a small clearing, and before him lay Bormann's bunker. It was a huge, dark, and foreboding concrete structure two stories high and just as wide. Windowless, it reeked of evil intentions. A single steel door was all that greeted Otto's eyes. He got to one knee, putting his right hand to the ground for support. His breathing was heavy, not from his moving but from his mind swirling with emotions. He was at his answer. He would find Annie.

Joseph popped out of the bushes behind Otto and crawled to his side. Otto gazed straight ahead, sarcasm not far away. "Do you mean to tell me you crawled all this way?"

"An answer is wasted upon you, Jew. Now let us..." Joseph paused, noticing a tear slowly falling from Otto's eye. His tone changed and his voice softened. "Um. So, we are here then, my dear Otto. I guess we will find your answer. Shall we go?"

Joseph stood up and gripped his MP-40, holding it at the ready. He walked towards Bormann's bunker, slowly turning as he approached and checking for signs of enemies. Otto followed, wiping the tear from his eye. They came to the door together. Joseph stood guard as Otto grabbed the handle of the heavy steel door. He pulled the key from his pocket and tried to slide it into the keyhole, but it would not fit. He tried again and again, changing the key's position upright, backwards, and even sideways. This was not the right key.

"Quickly, Otto. What is the delay?"

"The key. It is wrong. It does not go here."

Joseph stepped towards Otto, his eyes still fixed upon his surroundings. "Well, did you just try opening the door? Maybe it's not locked."

Otto grabbed the door latch and pressed it hard. The door mechanism clunked with a metallic echo and popped open. Otto's eyes became bright. "Oh, well look at that. Uh, Joseph, the door is open."

"Silly Jew."

They entered the bunker, squeezing through the doorway and not opening it farther than necessary. They were immediately greeted with the smell of foul air. It was unlike any they had ever witnessed, seemingly a combination of excrement, dampness, and decaying rodents, creating one pungent odor to dim their spirits.

"I know this bunker well, Joseph, but this air is unknown to me. This will not be a pleasant visit for us, not that it ever was in the past. So to your point, follow me to Bormann's chamber and let's be done with what we seek."

"Yes, but what are we seeking?"

"I'm not sure."

Joseph shook his head in frustration. "Very well, but we must hurry, Otto."

The corridor from the door was dark, and the thick concrete walls were wet to the touch, emanating an evil that reigned these halls. Otto followed the passageway using his hand, which he slid against the wall as a guide. They could see very little, operating mostly by their instinct and the occasional patches of dimmed sunlight creaking through fissures from the concrete. Other corridors intruded into the one they were navigating and moved off into many directions.

Otto thought hard about where he was going, playing visually in his mind the direction he was to follow. Warped memories flooded his vision as they portrayed past events. He could hear Bormann's tirades and angry banter. He could smell the air juiced with the smell of cognac and women's perfume. They entered an anteroom and found it to be ransacked. Chairs once used for waiting and receiving guests were turned over, were broken, and lay silent. The area rug was flipped and tossed into a pile, and papers littered the floor. Dirty and wet, they were pasted upon their resting places like wallpaper.

"I have waited many an hour in this very room, Joseph. Off to the right is Bormann's main office. We are here."

Joseph entered behind Otto, tripping on a splintered piece of chair taking up residence on the floor and causing his MP-40 to sway side to side, rubbing against his stomach. "Otto, this bunker, while a mess, looks to be quite intact. I suggest the German soldiers at the time were thwarted from their attempts to blow up the place."

"Yes. An order from Bormann, no less. I would think Bormann and his legion had not been here to close it. This mess is of the Russians' doing. It has been searched, hopefully not thoroughly."

Joseph removed a candle from his musette bag and held it close enough to his eyes to see where to light the wick. Once lit, it offered very little evidence. Its brightness flickered as it came under the effects of eerie drafts from all directions, as if demons themselves were breathing on it. Yet, it was enough to surrender a glimpse into Bormann's chamber. The room itself was smallish with high ceilings and heavy walls that were devoid of any precious art or decorate fixtures but riddled with cracks that reached across their expanse like veins. Water dripped from some of the cracks, slowly wetting the floor and soaking the papers that lay scattered around the room. At the far end was a simple oak desk that was turned at an angle and had obviously been disturbed. The drawers were extended out to their limits and hung open. Two chairs that were perhaps once in front of the desk for guests lay on their sides, discarded and abandoned. A lone iron-shaded ceiling light captured by the drafts swayed gently left to right, its purpose forgotten.

Otto stood next to Joseph just within the doorway troubled. "I don't see where this key may be used. If not for his desk, then what?"

Joseph stepped past Otto. "Well, we haven't looked hard enough, Otto. True, you have been in this room many times, but your previous observations can't remember a use for a key of this make. It is foreign to you."

Joseph began searching the room further for the key's master, moving the chairs and desk, disrupting them into new positions. Otto joined him, slowly searching all four walls for any signs of a keyhole. There were none. Moments came and went, seeming more like hours, but nothing revealed itself.

"This is folly. There is nothing here. What if Corporal Huber was wrong? What will become of us then?"

Joseph stood up from his bent over position while examining the desk drawers. "It would seem there is nothing of stature requiring this key's making. Perhaps we are thinking about this incorrectly. We are thinking like commoners. Well, you are anyway. Bormann is of the High Court. He would certainly have had other plans and reasons for this key. We need to think as Bormann. What did he fancy? What did he think about more often than life itself?"

Otto stood still, a grin slowly covered his face as his eyes glistened with excitement. "Cognac!" Otto took a step towards Joseph. "It is the cognac!"

Joseph looked at Otto confused. "Cognac? How does a key have anything to do with that?"

"You said think like Bormann. Well, that's how he thinks, with his mouth and his loins! The answer is in his library where he keeps his most precious spirits on a hand-carved oak bookcase."

"Well then, where is this room?"

"Very close. Bormann would not be far from his lusts, I can attest to that. It was one of my duties, bringing him his cognac. The library is off the anteroom opposite this chamber. We passed it as we entered here."

Otto and Joseph quickly moved from Bormann's chamber and crossed the anteroom into the library. The same condition was found here. Papers covered the floor, sharing the role with hundreds of books, maps, and unrecognizable objects. Their uses were at an end.

"It is here, Joseph. That is the bookcase I remember."

On the right side of the room from where they were standing was a very old, large, wooden bookcase with eight long shelves. It was ornately carved with two demonic-looking stags across the top with their heads turned meeting each other. Adorning the sides was an entanglement of intricately carved vines and leaves intertwined with the mythological deities of Dryads, the nymphs of the woods and trees, and Fauna, the goddess of animals, and most fitting, Harpies, the creatures employed by the gods to carry out punishment for serious crimes.

"That is certainly an oddity."

"Yes, Otto. Mediterranean mythologies were highly regarded by some of those involved in higher Nazi philosophies. I do remember studying some stories and adventures in my Hitler Youth Corps training."

Joseph and Otto slowly approached the bookcase and inspected its craft from different angles, holding the candle close to reveal the many intricacies of the carvings.

"I don't see any keyholes on the shelves. Are you sure it's here, Otto?"

"I don't recall there being any, and I have sought many bottles from these shelves in the past. I think it must be hidden."

Otto gently placed his hand on the carvings, moving his fingers in, out, and around the shapes, feeling for anything unusual.

"Here, Otto. Take this candle. I think it's best if I go and check the entrance for our safety while you search. Call if you need my attention. I shouldn't be long."

Otto nodded but said nothing. Joseph left the room leaving Otto in the dark, the candlelight revealing a hint of his face, his hands, and the wooden shapes of the carvings. He continued his inspection from the left side of the bookcase, starting at the bottom and moving to the top. About midway at the top, he suddenly stopped just under the carvings of the two stags. His fingers alerted him to something of suspicion. A groove crossed horizontally above a strange figure of a man with a face on both sides of his head. The body was svelte, robust, and strong, obviously a god, but its identification was foreign to Otto. He followed the groove as it made a right turn and then another and another, forming a perfect square around the strange figure.

Otto stood back and refocused on the figure, staring at its form. Then it struck him. Something caught his attention that caused the very hairs on the back of his neck to rise in suspense. The figure was holding a very recognizable key. He suddenly took a quick, anxious breath and held the candle closer, the light dancing off his eyes as he made another discovery. Could it be that simple? He pulled the key out from his pocket and held it up next to the carved wooden key. It was the same design, that of an eagle grasping a snake wrapped around a ring containing a swastika. This must be it.

Otto tilted his head at many angles, carefully examining the grooves around the figure. He gently grabbed the wooden key the two-faced man was holding and felt it to see if it would move. As he put pressure on the key, he felt a wiggle. He pulled his hand away startled, fearing it would break. He hesitantly grasped the key again and firmly held it, his fingers gently wrapping around the eagle. With one quick motion, he turned the wooden key to the right. To his surprise, the key turned with his movement. He let go quickly, and suddenly, the figure surrounded by the square groove popped open on a hinge, revealing a keyhole. Otto's jaw dropped with anticipation and excitement, his breath and heart following.

Joseph appeared from around the corner and entered the room. "All seems to be clear. What have you found?"

Otto turned to face Joseph. "It is here! I have found it!"

"Good. Then unlock that which is locked, and let's be done with it. We'll still have light enough this day to further our travels to the end of this mission."

Joseph turned from Otto, waiting for him to put the key into the keyhole, but his eyes soon became fixated on something very out of place. He noticed directly across from Otto and the bookcase a large grouping of familiar-looking pock marks resembling the makings of bullets on the concrete wall. Joseph stepped closer to investigate. He extended his hand to feel the marks, and suddenly, his eyes filled with fear. At the same time Otto raised the key, inserted it into the hole, and gave it a twist, Joseph quickly turned and yelled, "Otto! No!"

A violent mechanical crash echoed through the room as the bookcase suddenly slid sideways along the wall like a tornado. Otto and Joseph instinctively dropped to the floor, covering their heads as a deafening barrage of machine gun fire blasted from within a dark corridor hidden behind the bookcase. The bullets struck the wall furiously and ricocheted all through the room. The burst emptied after nearly a hundred rounds. The ear-splitting sound echoed through the bunker, finally droning off to its end.

Otto opened his eyes to a room spinning with gun smoke, dust, and millions of concrete particles spiraling through the air determined to add further hell to the stench that was massing in the room. He came to his knees squinting, fighting the polluted air for sight and for a clean breath.

"Joseph, are, are you there? Tell me you are not hurt."

There was no response. Otto strained to make shapes in the room, his mind entangled with fear. He slowly crawled to where he had last seen Joseph before the rage came to bear. As he crawled across the room nearing the far side of the wall, his hand stumbled upon a foot. He kept crawling, his hand following the foot up a leg until he came to a body leaning against the wall. Otto crawled to the wall and mimicked the position of the seated body.

"Joseph?" There was no answer. All was still. Otto sat not moving, not wanting to reach and feel for a cold body drenched with warm blood. He kept his hands at his side. The air calmed, and the heavy dust started to settle. A dense fog hovered across the room close to the surface, now revealing Joseph next to Otto, his head pressed back against the wall, eyes closed, mouth shut. He did not move. Otto continued to sit quietly without so much as a flinch. The silence gnawed at him. Then a soft voice drifted to Otto's ears.

"That's a point for me. A very, very big point."

"No argument from me, Joseph."

Joseph's head lazily fell to face Otto, a smallish grin coming to his face. "We Germans, oh how we fancy our booby traps."

Otto blew a huge sigh of relief. "Whew. Yes, booby traps. I did not see that coming. In all my years, in all my travels, I just did not see that coming."

Joseph turned his head back straight. Both boys were now staring forward down the deep, dark corridor from whence the machine gun fire had come.

"I swear to you, Otto, if we find nothing, I will shoot you."

"Agreed. Well, I suppose we should have a look."

Otto and Joseph slowly lifted themselves up, each helping the other. They were rattled, frightened, and mentally exhausted. They adjusted their possessions and turned to face the passageway. Joseph picked up the candle Otto had dropped and relit it. He walked to the opening of the newly revealed corridor and stopped, examining the mechanism of the sliding bookcase.

"It looks as if you set off a trigger much like that of a rifle. The recoil caused by the gas of the ignition of the round forced the bookcase to slide. Crude, yet I must admit ingenious nonetheless." Joseph entered the corridor with Otto trailing closely behind. "See, here along the wall is the mechanism that I would suggest leads to whatever took a disliking to us."

Joseph and Otto walked slowly down the corridor, following the device. They hugged the wall cautiously to avoid straying to the middle. The corridor proved to be short as it abruptly ended with a wall in front of them. Joseph followed the mechanism from the floor up until it vanished into a hole in the wall. He moved the candle to his right, and there in front of them was a well-planned rectangular opening in the wall with two MG-42 machine guns mounted side by side, their demonic barrels protruding into the corridor. Smoke still spiraled from their barrels. The sight of the guns was pure evil. Otto flashed Joseph an eerie frown as he and Joseph ducked under the guns continuing their journey down the corridor. Otto could still feel the heat from the barrels as if they were still alive and breathing. Joseph extended his candle into the air disclosing the continuance of the corridor in front of them. It then abruptly turned left and disappeared into the darkness. They followed the path chosen for them by the light. As they turned left, they were greeted with nothing. To their front was black.

Joseph looked to the floor for answers. "Ah, stairs. Our path is down. That would explain this damp, musty smell tormenting my nostrils." Joseph turned to face Otto. "We are going below grade. Be on your guard. I suspect more ingenious German booby traps."

They slowly began to step down, navigating the flights one cautious move at a time. Their little candlelight offered nothing to what may lay beyond. The steps were dusty and littered with small pieces of rubble, crunching like frozen snow under their feet, crackling and popping.

"Ah, I see a floor. Let us hope this is the end to our descent. I do not fancy going underground into the unknown."

They reached the last step and hesitantly moved into the room, the walls washing away from their sides. They paused for an instant to feel out their new space.

"We must be in a very large room, Otto. I can feel drafts creeping around me from all directions."

"Yes. They haunt me as well. Unfortunately, this candlelight will not help us learn of their origins."

"There must be a light switch somewhere. It will be better if we search as two. Here, I have an idea." Joseph broke the candle in half, giving the lighted piece to Otto. "Now, light my half and we can be off."

Otto followed his instruction, and new light spawned to life.

"Perfect, Otto. Quickly now. Search the walls."

Splitting up, Joseph retraced his steps, expecting that a switch would be logically located near the entrance to the room. Otto moved farther into the unknown, carefully inspecting his steps as he approached nothingness. He reached his arm out straight, swaying left to right to capture anything that would surprise his presence. Suddenly, flickers of light from low hanging ceiling lamps slowly illuminated the room one by one, buzzing as they came to an ominous, subdued glow. Otto closed his eyes to the brightness at first and then slowly opened one eye at a time. He gasped at the sight.

Joseph's voice echoed from outside the room. "Ha. I knew the light switch would be found at the entrance."

As Joseph ran into the room, Otto turned to face him, not wanting to believe what his eyes had seen. Joseph stopped short, his eyes too drawn wide, his jaw dropping in disbelief. Otto turned from Joseph, his head tilting up to follow a tall, stout oaken bookcase an arm's length before his face. The room was cavernous. The ceiling was high, twenty feet or near. Before them were twenty rows of fifteen foot-high and three foot-wide solid oak bookcases packed tightly with what looked to be some sort of folders. They could not see the room's end. The rows of bookcases, in their eyes, went on to what seemed infinity. Otto stepped forward and then around the first bookcase to its front in order to examine the contents weighing heavy on the shelves. His mind swam in anticipation and query. Lured by his suspense and intrigue, his heart picked up a beat. Joseph followed, passing Otto without a word, and walked slowly down in between the rows, his arms stretched out wide, his fingers gingerly flowing over the folders. The folders bent and then quickly snapped back to attention, leaving a finger trail line from wiping away the dust. Otto watched him until he came to the end of the long row. Joseph paused, glanced both ways, and then proceeded to the left and vanished around the corner.

Otto turned back to the bookcase and placed his candle, now near its end in life, on the shelf. He pulled out a thick brown folder wedged between thousands of the same likeness. He glanced at the cover, which read 'BERLIN - 1939, District I, Sector 14.' He became excited and opened the cover. The paper was damp to the touch, and a putrid, moldy smell blasted his nose. Otto frowned and looked away, but it did not sway his interest. His eyes drew back to the page. Suddenly, his heart pounded and picked up its beat. His body followed as his knees weakened and his hands trembled. In three neatly flushed rows were names listed in alphabetical order. His mouth whispered the names as he read down the list fighting to keep pace with his heartbeat and breath from his lungs. The names were all of Jewish origin listed by family starting with the patriarch and finishing with the youngest member. Next to each name was a date of deportation and a location. Otto stood confused, mouthing the names of the locations. "Treblinka, Dachau."

Otto looked up and called out, "Joseph. I think I found something."

Joseph strolled nonchalantly from behind Otto and tapped him on the shoulder.

"Ah! Must you do that?"

"Come, Otto. I too have come across something."

Otto closed the folder, packing it under his arm, and followed Joseph to the left side of the room. Joseph pointed up to the first bookcase in the row forming the corner.

"Look up, Otto. This is the first bookcase as it is numbered. It reads 'BERLIN 1939 - District I, Sector 1.' Now follow me. There is more. You see, I walked to the end of these monstrous bookcases. They are thirty deep and twenty wide, making for six hundred of them. Each is marked accordingly by place, year, and district going from 1939 to 1943. It's broken up by country at certain points as well, but always with the city, date, district, and sector."

Otto grew more excited. "That would certainly be consistent with the information formatted in this folder and perhaps the rest within these bookcases, but that would mean with these many cases, plus the number of folders per shelf, the names per page..." Otto began to quickly do the math in his head. "That would mean there could be over five million names here."

Joseph listened to Otto, but he was not convinced of anything suspicious in these bookcases.

"We have found the vault, Joseph. This is as Corporal Huber explained. My Annie, my Poppa and Momma, are perhaps in here somewhere." Otto smiled, his dimples blossoming from a buried, cold, and hidden place, not having been seen for a very long time. "We have found them."

Joseph stood stern, his voice silent.

"All of these bookcases are filled with people who've met a certain fate. They were taken away and cast to some unknown land and —"

"Quiet, Otto. These bookcases prove nothing. There's no proof of wrongdoing here. They're just names in a folder. How are we sure your Annie met with an ill fate? Perhaps she, as with all these people, was simply transported to safer locations outside a threatened war zone."

Otto's smile grew hard, his dimples fading once again. "Have you listened to none of my stories?"

"Do not start that again. I don't believe such horrid places exist. There is an explanation. It just escapes us at the moment. Now quickly, if your Annie is here, find her and let's be off. We have lingered far too long. Do you not remember the dead Russian soldiers hanging and swaying in the trees?"

Suddenly, an eerie clicking sound echoed down from the stairs and expanded its menace into the great room. Otto and Joseph startled and rose up and towards the noise. Speechless, they froze.

Joseph wore fright on his face as he struggled to force a sentence. "Those are the sounds of hobnail boots. We, we are not alone." His eyes grew large, and his breath heaved, expanding his lungs. "Quickly, Otto, find her and let's move from here. I will see what is coming and thwart their visit. Now please hurry." Joseph slammed the cocking lever of his MP-40 back, freeing it to slide furiously forward, and loaded the weapon for its designed intent.

Otto sprang to life, going over in his mind what bookcase might hold his answer. "Let's see. Twenty bookcases. Folders for Sector I was over there. This case is number four. Oh, here's Berlin, Sector, is that a five or an 'S'? Looks to be 1939." Remembering he had a folder with him, he quickly opened it and read the names to gain a bearing, "Okay, 'Fayvel.' So that would mean Neumann would be..." Otto's head turned, spun, and dissected the bookcases, feverishly trying to decide what case would shelve Annie's last name.

"Hurry, Otto." Joseph yelled from somewhere at the front of the room.

Otto became confused and frustrated, beads of sweat trickling from his temple and forehead, pooling in his eyes. He wiped his brow and continued his search.

"There are too many." he yelled back.

"Well start somewhere. Open everything."

Joseph slowly crept towards the sounds now offering clues to their threat. The same popping and crunching sounds came down the steps, entered the room and Joseph's ears. He sunk down low at the end of the bookcase, facing in the direction of the stairs. He held his weapon up to his face, the cold stamped steel of the receiver embracing his cheek. He readied for the first sight of anything entering the room. It would die then and there. He would not give it time to present itself.

Suddenly, a shadow grew from the stairwell, becoming larger as the angle of the light and the intrusion moved closer. The shadow invaded the room and swelled, creeping across the floor to attack Joseph's position. Then Joseph saw it, a boot planted upon the first step he could see from the entrance. Then another boot firmed its stance and continued until it formed one leg and then another. The glistening of a barrel sparkled as it too entered the story, a hand firmly grasping the weapon with ill will. Joseph took intense aim as another figure showed itself. His finger felt for a comfortable position on the trigger. It caressed the hard metal and began taking up the slack. Pressing until the mechanism gave way, the beast sprang to life, welcoming the intruders with a vicious blast of automatic fire erupting the room in a fury. A half clip of maddened yellow jackets found their mark. The two shadows slumped, dropped their weapons, and piled up in awkward, grotesque shapes at the bottom of the stairs. Ricochets of bullets not put to hell's use pinged and sprang off in other directions. Dust fragments from strays and gun smoke spiraled and danced.

Otto jumped, startled upon hearing the surprise of Joseph's gun go off. His fear engaged and propelled him to speed his search. He began opening folders, reading the first name on the first page, and discarding it to the floor if it was not a name beginning with a 'K' or an 'N.' He ran from bookcase to bookcase, checking both sides of the row, throwing folders aside when not meeting his requirements.

The dust settled, and the thunder quelled. Joseph raised his head from its fixed position, lowering his weapon. He stood up slowly and focused on the dead, making sure they stayed down. Then someone spoke, a foul voice from the stairwell.

"Good show, my boy! Those were two of my best storm troopers. Their overconfidence killed them. Surely, they laughed at the thought of two paltry boys ending their stay in this world. However, you'll have to be much smarter if you are to end my wrath."

Joseph's heart sank. His mind raced. He recognized the voice. That would mean there are two dead, but there were four when last we saw them. Then there are two left. These are the death squad's elite. The Einsatzgruppen. They are after us. Joseph became more frantic, his eyes twitching, his cheeks pulsating with air as he drew and expelled breath.

Otto picked up his pace, flipping through folders at the speed of light, until suddenly he opened one folder to find the name 'Mukel.' He frantically continued his search knowing he was closer, his hands moving faster than he could think. He moved to the bookcase across from where he found the 'M' names and grabbed a handful of folders. He opened the first in the pile and came across 'Neumark.' Yes! Can this really be happening?

"Hurry, Otto! Where are you?"

"So the Jew is with you? Good. Yes. Very good! So tell me Joseph, Hitler Youth, son of Rudolph Kessler of Munich, to where has your allegiance vanished? Have you become a Jew lover? I suspect so. It matters none to me, Jew lover. My quarrel is not with you. I'm here for the Jew. My instruction is to kill him and take what he carries on his person. You may be set free, but if you wish to pursue me, well, that is another matter. So how would you like to proceed?" There was a long pause, but it did not last. Joseph's ears were alerted, and his eyes bulged in fear at the sight of four hand grenades tumbling and clanking down the stairs and launching towards him.

"Otto!" he yelled at the top of his lungs as he leapt further down the row of bookcases. A deafening explosion from all four grenades ripped through the front of the room. The blast percussion splintered wood from the cases, shredded paper into confetti, and shattered the glass bulbs from the ceiling lights directly above him. The room shook and creaked. Echoes ricocheted from wall to wall, ceiling to floor, covering every nook in the room.

Otto sank to his knees, dropped the folders, and sheltered his ears. He crushed his eyes closed, scrunching his nose and contorting his face. Dust and particles bellowed down the rows of bookcases approaching his position. He held his breath as he was enveloped by the filth.

Joseph desperately searched the floor for his weapon. He stretched out his left arm. His fingers clawed the ground, scraping wood splinters and concrete dust. He had been blown flat onto his stomach and into an awkward position. His arm was twisted behind him, pressed against the bottom of the bookcase and his body. His left leg was bent at the knee, caught under the right leg, unable to stretch out before the detonation. He blew grime from his nose and coughed dirt from his mouth, the slobber oozing with particles to the floor. He slowly sat up but felt no pain. The bookcase had sheltered the full brunt of the blast. Joseph quickly came to his knees then to his feet. He took a step and inadvertently kicked his machine gun. Startled but happily surprised, he quickly grabbed the gun and fled to find Otto.

Otto opened his eyes. Halos formed around the ceiling lights that had remained on, but were muffled and somewhat obscured by the dust, their glow diluted. He rose to his feet and searched for the last folder in his hand.

Joseph appeared from around the corner and grabbed Otto. "Come, Jew. We must find our escape."

"But what about finding Annie? I have to..."

"Fine then." Joseph grabbed a random group of folders off the shelf and stuffed them into Otto's musette bag. "Let's hope your Jew girl is in here."

They ran to the rear of the room, distancing themselves from the threat. They paused for the moment but heard no followers.

"How are we to escape, Joseph? We are sealed in."

"I don't know, Jew. Come. Let's move farther. There may be more rooms in this cave we are in."

They ran to the last row of bookcases and came across another passage at the end of the great room. "Hurry, down that corridor," Joseph ordered. The corridor was well lit and led to a large steel door. "Pray that it opens, Jew, or our time here is ended."

Joseph grabbed the handle and flicked the latch. He pulled with all his might, and the door sprang loose, fighting to stay shut. Otto joined the fight, and together they pushed the door open against its will. Joseph flicked up another switch, and the room came to light.

Otto gasped. "My word." There before them was a room of similar design to the great room. It was filled nearly top to bottom from front to back with thousands upon thousands of treasures.

"No time to be enamored, Jew. Find an exit."

Otto entered the room, turning and spinning as he passed their newfound discovery. "There are jewels, paintings, sculptures, and antiquities of unknown origins here. This is a hoard of great wealth and historic importance." He came to a large wooden case stacked upright with canvases. He thumbed through them coming upon one he recognized. "This, this is a Van Dyke, the Dutch master. I've seen this in books. It should not be here. It, this was stolen, Joseph."

Joseph turned to face Otto from the back of the room. "Stolen? No. This was not stolen. This is the great wealth of a superior nation. It lay hidden here from the threats of war and the ills of foreign people. It is as I have learned and was told. Enough, Jew. I think I've found a way out. Look up there. It's an air shaft. I have seen these all around the Wolf's Lair. Above ground they look like covered conical smoke stacks, but I've never seen smoke coming from them. They must be used for ventilation."

"So back to calling me 'Jew' then?"

Joseph wore anger on his face and his words turned ugly. "I'm in this mess because of you. I tried to believe your stories. I want to believe your heart, but I can't. The Einsatzgruppen are here, Otto. Now. Those men we saw not a fortnight ago? They are here for us. The soldier in the stairwell, the leader I suspect, offered me sanctuary. Do I trust him? No. I know the stories. I've witnessed their deeds. They will kill anybody, even their own. So quiet, Jew, and let's get out of here."

Otto became deflated, but the emotion would not last. "That ceiling is twenty feet high at best." He looked around at anything high enough to reach the air vent. "Quick! That case holding those paintings looks to be nearly fifteen feet tall."

Joseph questioned nothing. He ran to the case and tested its will to move. "Hurry, Otto. Help me tip the case against the wall. From there we can climb to the top. Perhaps with a small leap to the bars covering the air vent, we'll be able to find our escape."

Otto positioned himself next to Joseph, and with all their might, they freed the case to their will. Paintings bent, frames warped and crumbled, and canvases tore as the bookcase fell against the wall and made a rather easy climb. Joseph did not hesitate and climbed up the case to the top using the paintings, shelves, and anything else for footings. The air vent was four feet from the bookcase, three feet if balancing on the top and reaching out.

"I hope you don't mind heights, Otto. You'll have to wedge your-self between the case and the ceiling. Then if you balance on the edge of the case, you can jump for either of the two bars covering the vent. From there, you can pull yourself up and through the bars into the shaft." Before Joseph could finish his instructions, Otto was nearly to the top of the case.

"Okay, Otto, here I go." Joseph's eye's widened, and after three great breaths, he stretched out his arms and sprang from his perch to catch the bars. When he stopped swaying from his leap, Joseph pulled himself up and into the shaft. "Good news for us, Jew. There is a ladder of sorts fashioned from iron bars leading us to the top. I can smell the fresh air."

Otto readied himself and began to balance near the edge of the case, waiting his leap. He secured his musette bag and satchel for the jump and, without hesitating, reached for the bar. Suddenly, he lost his balance, his foot slipping from the case as he leapt. "Joseph!"

Otto frantically swatted at the air and caught the bar with one hand, causing him to twist and turn in the air as he held on. Two hands thrust below the bars and grabbed Otto's other arm. Joseph stopped Otto's sway and helped pull him into the shaft.

"That's another point for me, Jew."

"I think you are winning."

Joseph and Otto started their climb to the top. The way was tight and filthy with muddied water finding its way into the shaft through cracks in the concrete. Joseph came to the top and used his elbow to loosen the cone-like roof of the air vent. It ground and shook, resenting being forced open, but after a series of sharp jabs, it fell sideways and tumbled to the ground, revealing a warm sun and a bright sky. Joseph pulled himself out and jumped from the concrete shaft to the ground. He passed on cleaning himself off and swung his MP-40 around, readying it for use and surveying the area for any threats. Otto followed, squeezing through the opening, jumping to the ground, and planting himself next to Joseph.

"Well, that wasn't very much fun in the least, but we are free, Joseph. I suggest we quickly look for cover and safety."

"Obviously, but the real question to mind is, where are we? I can't see any of the bunkers."

"Perhaps we are north, farther north than Bormann's bunker, near the outskirts of the Wolf's Lair. There's nothing here but swamps, dense woods, and mine fields."

"And, I would add, mosquitoes."

"Yes, Joseph, quite right. I forgot about those nasty buggers."

"That and an enemy intent and committed to killing us. We shall make for the refuge of the thicker woods, assuming we are north. Then we can circle around to link up with the train tracks again. From there, we head east and then north towards our objective. Bormann will have it for me for sure. We are very delayed."

Otto said nothing. He felt Joseph's anger, his frustration, and even his contempt. Joseph was returning to his meaner self.

"Hurry now. We go, Jew."

Securing their belongings, Otto and Joseph stood up and searched for darker cover.

Chapter 15

"What's that sound?" asked Otto, his voice cracking with fear and doubt.

Joseph slowly turned his head from left to right, lending his ear to the air. His eyes bulged as his ears took notice. "There is someone approaching through the brush, and I sincerely think it is not of the four-legged kind."

Joseph grasped his MP-40, his fingers twitching to start its mechanism. Otto watched Joseph transition into fight mode while he himself naturally prepared to run.

"There is no time for offense, Joseph. We must run. We must put distance between them and us."

Otto turned and, without waiting for a reply from Joseph, began his sprint. He came to speed quickly, dodging trees, twisted thickets, and an uncooperative ground strewn with dead branches and exposed, gnarled roots. He could hear Joseph behind him gasping for breath, his weapon's worn metal sling clanging against the steel receiver as he ran with abandon. A single rifle report burst from their rear as a shot echoed through the forest. Otto could feel the snap of the round pass his right shoulder as he leapt left to right to dodge further shots. His reflexes for escape had returned. Blood flowed with more intensity as he ran. His breathing labored, and his pace quickened. Another shot entered the race, finding a tree branch as its end. The branch splintered and spun viciously to its newfound resting place on the ground. Otto jumped and cleared its fall, not missing a stride. Joseph picked up his pace and was now running next to Otto. The gunshot also quickened his feet.

They came to the edge of the forest and were greeted by a vast field overgrown to knee height. Otto looked left and then right. The field was narrow, no more than fifty meters wide, and ran both ways until it fell off into the distance. The forest picked up again on the other side of the tall grass.

Otto turned to Joseph, his lips twitching and his cheeks pulsating from his breathing. "This is the outer perimeter of the Wolf's Lair, I should think. To our front hidden in the grass is a minefield."

"How do you know that?"

"It is written on that sign at your feet."

Joseph's head dropped as he slowly turned to look down to where Otto was pointing. He was greeted by a poorly constructed, painted wooden sign. Its white paint was all but faded and lifeless. Upon it was a crudely painted image of a human skull. The black paint that formed its shape was chipped away, creating an even more menacing image. Under it in capital letters of different sizes read, 'MINEN.'

There was one choice in Joseph's head. "We go, Otto." Joseph stepped into the field offering methodical steps one foot in front of the other. Otto murmured in frustration to himself in fragmented Yiddish as he followed directly behind Joseph. Their pace was quick but decisive. Otto focused intensely on placing his foot exactly where Joseph had stepped. However, the grass sprang back to its original place, making the feat nearly impossible. He thought about adding space between them, but it was not an option. If Joseph were to step on a mine, then that would be their end.

They reached the center of the field and then heard a foul voice speak. "Halt! Waffen fallen lassen!"

Otto stopped. His heart sank as he took a deep breath and closed his eyes. Joseph turned slowly and faced his threat. He hunched over and carefully laid his weapon to the ground as instructed. Otto turned as well, raising his head to lay eyes on what evil plague had been nagging them.

"Good. You listen well. It may surprise you to know that my two shots were a warning. One would have thought that two young boys would know enough to halt. Now, take two steps from each other. I wouldn't want one of you to get too close to the other's possessions. Perhaps there is another weapon hiding that I might not know of, yes? Move now. I will only ask once."

Otto glanced over at Joseph and nodded with a jittery motion. Joseph obeyed and took two steps to his right away from Otto. Otto closed his eyes and clenched his teeth as Joseph took his first step. Nothing. On his next step, however, the ground spoke. Click! Otto's heart sank. He knew that sound. It was an S-mine. Joseph heard it, too. He turned white, his knees shook, and his heart plummeted.

"Do not move, Joseph. Not one tiny little spec of a centimeter."

"Very good, my boys. See? This is easy when you cooperate." The soldier approached the field leaving the forest's edge.

Otto whispered to Joseph, "Pst, Joseph, look at me. We will be okay. Do not warn him of the mines. Did you hear me? The mines. Do not tell him of them."

Joseph nodded back, not quite sure what he was agreeing to as he eyed the soldier's approach. The soldier came to within a few meters of where they were instructed to freeze and stopped. His rifle was at the ready, his hands clenching it with fury. Everything about his being was demonic. This was a very different kind of evil. Otto could feel the soldier's darkness, and his presence shuddered his skin.

"A very good escape from Bormann's bunker. It was amusing to watch you both dangle from the ceiling. So much so that I couldn't hold my rifle up steady enough to shoot. Quite amusing. Now I suppose we should properly introduce ourselves, don't you think?

Allow me first. My name is Wilhelm Jager, Chief Assault Leader of the Einsatzgruppen and leader of this noble quest to find you both and to kill one of you. And perhaps the other. That still remains to be seen. Actually, I care not in the least who lives. I would have figured that four hand grenades would have done an admirable job, but you are very clever.

"My name is fitting, I suppose. Strange I have not thought of this until now. Nonetheless. My surname does, as you might know, mean 'hunter.' Yes, truly fitting. Feel free to call me Chief Jager. It's shorter, easier for a child's mind to remember. Now, as for you two adventurers, I think I have you both identified so I shall not waste your breath, of what little time it has left."

The Chief rotated his hips, his rifle following. He turned his intimidating gaze upon Joseph. "You, my little machine gun-wielding Hitler Youth, must be Joseph Kessler, son of the mighty Nazi Party official and philanthropist Rudolph Kessler. I'm quite sure he'd be wonderfully surprised to know of your fond caravanning around all of Europe with this sad case for a human next to you, a young, frowning little elf of a Jew."

He turned towards Otto and spread his arms wide, his rifle in his right hand as he leaned back and raised his head to the sky in a mocking display. "I give you the Jew boy Otto Kaufmann, slave courier of the German High Court. It pained me to learn of this from Chief Müller when assigned and briefed for this mission. Here I am, an exquisite example of Germany's fighting elite, privileged with extermination of the detritus of the Fatherland. Then I find out that those who chose me for my talents have now spared you. Disheartening. I suppose that at this phase of the war, what does any of it matter? I should think a little bit of fun is in order, and that is exactly how I view this noble assignment, a fun little cat and mouse game. What a splendid way to end the war. I shall do my very best killing yet."

Otto's frown straightened, and his eyes froze.

"Don't look so surprised, Jew. Wish to know what end came to your family? Let's replay a bit of your history, shall we? You do remember the day you were taken by Bormann? You remember watching your family immediately escorted away? Well, they were then transported by rail to a small town just outside of Kulmhof in Poland, which is not terribly far from here, a five day journey by foot without rest, I should think. In Polish 'Kulmhof' would be pronounced as 'Chelmno.' As one of the first extermination camps, I've had the pleasure of a personal one-on-one tour of its facility and operation. Your family would have been transported to a stately manor. Here they would have been escorted to a special room and met by SS officers wearing white coats. The officers pretended to be doctors interested in examinations, health, and well-being, but that was not to be the case. Your family would be asked to disrobe for bathing and told their clothes would be disinfected before further transport to other facilities. They were stripped of their possessions, riches to never again reach their hands. From here, it was on to the final act. From upstairs, they were guided into the cellar and onto a ramp into a confined compartment. The door behind them was shut and the way locked. They were now inside a specially designed vehicle and, well, I need not explain what happened next. It was a disgraceful death that not even my trusty rifle could rival."

Joseph flinched in disbelief as he stood listening to the soldier. "What you say is untrue. These, these places do not exist. We are a great and superior people. We would not concern ourselves with the lesser of the world."

The Chief grinned and shook his head. "Is that true now? How do you know? Have you seen these places? Been there? No. How could you possibly think such places exist? But I assure you, my young, naive Hitler Youth, they do exist."

Joseph and Otto were speechless. A small tear welled in Joseph's eye. He heard and digested every word. Curiosity now turned to hate and deep betrayal. He glanced at Otto and his breathing intensified.

"Yes, yes, my dear Hitler Youth. Now that's the emotion of the SS. I see your allegiance returning. Very good indeed."

Otto eyed Joseph's movements, worrying about any imbalance on his stance that would set the mine to explode. He would worry about Joseph's emotional stability later. If the Chief's words were true, then his next journey would be to Chelmno. His search for Annie and his family would continue there. He would have to hope the latter part of the Chief's story was untrue.

Joseph wiped the tear from his eye. "So what is our next move, Chief Jager?"

"For you Joseph, depending on your cooperation, there would be life. We take the satchel the Jew carries and the document it contains to Bormann. I suggest to Bormann what an outstanding and fine soldier you are. You are rewarded, given medals and praise, and sent back to the front to continue the war or, depending on the war's status, released from duty and sent home, back to your aristocratic way of life. Either way, you win for the Fatherland."

"Now as for the Jew? Well, it is very simple. He dies. Perhaps you are the one to do it, my proud Hitler You..."

Otto broke silence and interrupted the Chief. "My goodness. I mean, not this again. Why can't you just do it, Chief? Surely your cat and mouse game has come to its end. There must be other evil errands for the Fatherland requiring your attention. Must you really offer to a boy a man's work? I suggest you come to me, plant the end of the rifle barrel to my head, and splatter my Jew brains all over eastern Poland. As you say, what a fun day. One of your best killings yet."

The Chief stood expressionless as if not believing what he just heard. Joseph, too, had little reaction, staring at Otto in disbelief. He then quickly glanced back at the Chief.

"Fine then, Jew." The Chief raised his rifle towards Otto's head and took a step forward. 'Click!' The Chief's eyes widened. He glanced down at the ground in front of him, his rifle still at the ready upon his shoulder. "What, what was that?"

"That, my dear SS Chief Assault Leader of the great and almighty Einsatzgruppen, was an S-mine." Otto offered a slight grin and repeated Joseph's words. "So what is our next move, Chief Jager?"

The Chief smiled wide and let out a roar of a laugh. "Well played, Jew. Well played! You think this changes anything? Joseph will come to my aid. He'll simply disarm the pressure sensor plate per my instructions, and I'll be free. Then I'll shoot you in the head as you requested."

Joseph's voice cracked. "Well, not exactly, Chief. I'm standing on a mine also."

Otto stared at the Chief, his grin widening. "You see, Chief, here's how our next move will work. I'm going to ask for your rifle. Then I'm going to free Joseph. Yes, I also know how to disarm these mines. After that, we are going to cross the remainder of this field and onto our next objective. You will be left here to your own devices. I believe you have one of your comrades left. He may save you. However, I ask you to listen closely. Our mission is of no more use to you. The war is lost, and I have seen the crumbling of the mighty Third Reich. The Russians own these lands now. Better you should worry about them. Take your misery and hate elsewhere. Leave us be."

The Chief chuckled. "Leave you be? Disregard a direct personal order from the High Court? Dishonor the Fatherland and my oaths? You Jews know nothing of such matters, and that is why you must be eradicated. To think I should follow a Jew's instructions. I should shoot you right here and now."

"You could do that, but while you were carrying on, I have taken two steps towards you. Shoot me and I'll simply lunge at you, and in my death-throw, we'll both be turned to ash. You'll watch your death and feel its gnawing paws clenching your legs from a fiery hell. You will die knowing you were killed by a Jew."

The Chief's smile slackened. "Yes. Live to fight another day? There is no shame in that. However, Jew, be warned. My wrath will be swift and vicious. You have now made this personal indeed!"

The Chief lowered his rifle and turned its butt-end to face Otto. Otto reached for the weapon and grabbed it by the rear of the stock. While he detested guns, Otto was very familiar with most small arms, even one of this make. Without hesitation, Otto took the rifle and racked the bolt back, ejecting the chambered round, letting it find a less dangerous position in the deep grass. He pulled the ejector housing to the left and pulled the bolt straight back from the receiver, tossing it as far as he could back towards the forest. Everybody hunched over expecting an explosion upon its landing, but none came. Otto gently placed the weapon on the ground and swung his musette bag around to his front. He opened the bag and pulled from it a small canvas pouch. Fishing inside, he pulled from it a sewing needle. He reset his bag to his shoulders and slowly approached Joseph. He gently knelt down in front of him and dug away the dirt and grass around Joseph's foot. Otto brought his head to the ground, revealing the S-mine. He secured the needle into the hole of the pressure sensor plate and looked up at Joseph.

"You are free again, my dear Joseph. A point for me."

Joseph shook his head and clenched his teeth. "You have gone mad, Jew."

The Chief's face reddened, and rage came to his words. "My Hitler Youth, take up arms with me. Remember your oath. Grab your weapon and rid this Jew of breath. Do it. Do it now, or your future will be his."

"We have no time for talk, Joseph," warned Otto. "Quickly now. Grab your weapon if you must and follow. I will not ask again. If you shoot me, you will never know the truth. It will stay hidden the rest of your life. Come with me, my dear friend."

Joseph glanced at the Chief and then to the sky. He sighed heavily and reached for his weapon, pulling it to ready position at the hip. He pointed the gun at Otto and raised the receiver to his cheek, his finger dancing with the trigger. The barrel site was at Otto's head.

"Promise me, Otto. Promise me there will be answers. You will disclose the contents of that satchel. Promise me."

Otto's shoulder slumped in relief. "Yes, Joseph, I promise."

Joseph came off aim and withdrew his ready position. He slung the machine gun around his shoulder and secured his pack. "Then let us find the truth."

"You have sealed your fate, young soldier. There will be no trial for you. You will hang like those Russian scum near Bormann's bunker. A fitting and agonizing end by a wire noose for your treason."

Otto turned and took a cautious step towards the edge of the forest. Joseph followed closely behind. The Chief yelled to them at each step, at each breath and beat of their hearts. "Death! I shall bring you both to a horrid and vicious death."

Slowly, Otto and Joseph safely reached the edge of the forest and stopped to wipe sweat from their brows. "Let's circle around the mine field, Joseph, and back south towards the train tracks. From there, I know the way."

"The way? What way, Otto? To where?"

"To the truth. To Chelmno. You heard the Chief. My family and Annie are there. Perhaps they are waiting for us with sweets."

"Sweets? Did you hear nothing, Otto? He spoke of the camp as some sort of killing place. There are no sweets there."

"It doesn't matter. That is our road."

"To death! He will know we are to go there. It's a trap. They have been one step ahead of us. Perhaps the other soldier of the Chief's group has already been directed there. He'll be waiting. No, no, we shall not go there."

"But Joseph, that's..."

Joseph suddenly lunged at Otto and swung a rounded punch that found Otto's cheek. Otto's head jerked sideways as his knees buckled under him. He piled to the ground, spread out on his stomach. He was out cold. Joseph started shaking, his hands and knees chattering bone against skin. He bent over and ripped the satchel from Otto's back. He tore the flap open and pulled the envelope bound document from its safety. His eyes were numb. On the cover it read 'Verboten! Offizielle Dokumente.' It was signed in blood red ink with the initials 'A.H.' at the bottom, the official mark of the Führer.

Joseph ripped open the document and sat down under a nearby tree. He leaned up against the trunk, rubbing his back against it to find a satisfying position. Joseph began reading and tossed caution to the wind. The potential chase from the Chief bothered him little. He would have his truth now.

"Die endgültige Lösung der Judenfrage," he whispered. "The final solution? To what?" Joseph read slowly, hanging onto every word of the document. His eyes would widen and then squint. His breathing heaved and then stopped. His fingers quaked, and his heart raced.

Otto opened his eyes, blew out his nose, and inhaled. He spit out dead leaves and dirt lodged in his mouth when he collapsed to the ground. He clamped his fingers into the earth and slowly raised his chest. He swiveled his head and was suddenly met with a jolt of pain to the left side of his face. He quickly flipped sideways and raised his hand to his cheek checking for blood. There was none. He gently touched his cheek again, and another jolt of pain attacked him. He could tell the left side of his face was swollen. He raised his head and spotted Joseph under a tree motionless. His manner was sullen, and his eyes seemed lost, fixed in a forward position with a ghostly haze. The papers he had been reading were strewn across the ground, some blown by the wind and captured in a briar. He had one piece of paper in his hands that he held tightly, crinkling its shape. Otto came to his feet and slowly approached Joseph.

"Ow. You punched me."

"It is here, Otto. Written in cold, black ink of the darkest kind. He signed it on, uh, on the bottom."

Joseph handed the paper to Otto. There on the bottom, the top line with many signatures below, was written 'Rudolph Kessler.' "He did it, Otto. These papers speak of horrible things, places. He, he killed millions. Jews, gypsies, everybody and anyone. My father is a murderer."

Otto knelt down next to Joseph. He too rubbed his back against the tree to find an agreeable position. "We don't know that yet, Joseph. A signed paper is just that. A signed paper."

"Then we must go to this camp. That will convince me once and for all."

Otto stood up and offered his hand to Joseph. Joseph grabbed his hand and stared into Otto's eyes. They scurried about the forest floor and gathered the papers, tucking them back into the folder without paying attention to their order. Suddenly, off in the distance, an explosion rang past their ears. Otto looked up and turned to Joseph.

"That's either the sound of war finding us again or the Chief has met a certain fate."

"Let's hope the latter, Otto. That would leave us with only one to face. The odds would then be in our favor."

"Yes, we can hope. Have you found this town where that camp is on your map?"

"I have. I should think it's a five-day journey from here if we are uninterrupted by enemies. Let's hope we go unnoticed."

The sun started to sink, yellowing the sky and muting the landscape. Evening cold crept in and stole the day of its spring warmth, casting it aside. They came to the train tracks and located the position of their hidden motorcycle, but it was no longer hidden. It had been tampered with, the engine wires pulled and tossed aside, the tires flattened, and the spokes of the wheels dented, twisting the rim. The sidecar mounted machine gun was missing, and there were multiple narrow punctures from a knife stabbed into the gas tank.

"You see, Otto. They have been one step ahead of us. I would offer they were even following our moves and plotting our actions. It is as the Chief said. They are toying with us as a game."

"You are correct, but we have no choice. We know our path. We'll have to outwit them."

Otto and Joseph continued south from the train tracks, creating distance from the Wolf's Lair and following a rearward road to Chelmno. Their run turned to a walk, which turned to a slow and a tired drag of their feet.

"Light is leaving us, Otto. Perhaps we should find rest for the night."

"Rest? I should have you know many of my missions during my service were often operated at night. I suspect I've grown cat eyes."

"Cat eyes? You have a silly mind, Otto. I'm impressed you survived any of your missions. They sounded never to be quite what they were made to be."

"I have been thinking about that quite a bit since Bormann had been so kind as to make it known. I have heard that before, and it doesn't matter for my part. I'm not of a military mind. I don't subscribe to the honor, glory, and brotherhood philosophy of soldiering. For my part, I did what I had to do to stay alive. So I could eat."

"Yes. I'm quite sure you enjoyed many a feast during your tenure with the German High Court. That's not ordinary soldier food that we elite of the Hitler Youth were subjected to."

"I suppose, but I am curious, seeing you are a Hitler Youth, that there have been many times your oath has been questioned and you did not obey. I am not so sure I understand why you joined."

"I already told you. Father instructed us. I didn't want to go, but he said it was our duty, my brothers' and mine. I have not seen them since the defense of Berlin was thrust upon us. I fear they are lost. Father would lecture us and say that this time in this war he would make his mark, that he would not follow others like in the first world war. Other than this, I have no other justification. Yet he had gentleness and kindness also. I did as he asked and tried to be the best soldier for him. Is that wrong?"

"Only you can answer that, Joseph. Seems we have both been victims of doing what we deemed to be necessary to survive. In that case, you were not wrong."

"A very well-played political answer. I do think we've uncovered your future career."

"It would be a very different world if I were in charge. There would be no more running with fear, just skipping with smiles."

The forest turned to farm country where fields surrounded them, providing little cover for hiding. They stopped at a crossroad where two dirt roads met.

"There are no shadows, Joseph. We are open to all and anything, enemy or friend alike."

"We shall not find friends here. Poland, as you are aware, was invaded by Germany many years ago. This country will not have forgotten such an act. No, we shall not find kindness here. I have heard of small Polish militias and organized armed marauders that go stalking in the night for German soldiers."

"The fields are high with grass, and tending them with plows is not yet upon them. I would suggest we find the thickest cover and lay low in its nest."

"Agreed. Over there. That field to our east. We'll be downwind from there. Sorry, Otto, but you stink."

"Yes, I suppose I have aborted my bath of late." Otto jumped the wooden fence entering the field and waited for Joseph to follow. He then straightened any grass or brush that crushed under their weight to hide any sign of an intrusion. The grass was at knee height, and they searched the grounds for thicker and taller cover.

"I've got it, Otto. There's a drainage ditch off to my left. It is dry to my eyes and should allow us to sink deeper below grass height."

"Very good."

They sank into the ditch and uncluttered their possessions from their bodies. Otto pulled his woolen blanket out and covered himself up to just past his mouth under his nose. He looked up into the darkening of the night and closed his eyes. "Sleep well, Joseph."

Chapter 16

Otto suddenly awoke and gasped for breath. He sat up quickly and searched his surroundings. His eyes met the tops of the field grass and an orange sun teasing the horizon, not yet chasing away the stars to find new darkness to light. The night had brought him fragmented dreams of twisted happenings and horrid events. Annie flashed in his mind, crying, paralyzed in fear and doubt, captured in a dark and cold cement-walled room. She shivered and cowered in the corner. Her once free-flowing hair, now twisted and mangled, lay cover to her face. Her once large, warming, and innocent eyes were now empty and dull and gazed blankly at the floor. Her arms were wrapped tightly around her body, warding off the chill playing upon her mind. Then, in a snap, she would vanish to be replaced with the sounds of his tortured family. He could feel his Poppa and Momma screaming in agony and pain, on their knees, naked and crumbling. They, too, vanished. However, this was not the dream's end. Suddenly, the horror of millions of wailing voices had echoed in his mind.

Otto glanced at his trembling hands. He grabbed his left hand with his right to try and calm its quake, but it proved fruitless. "A dream. Yes, just a dream. Manufactured from the evil words of the SS Chief. It was just a dream."

Otto leaned over and grabbed his satchel. He was curious to know each word written on the document he carried. He was curious to know what frightened and angered Joseph. He hesitated opening and reading them. His order was to deliver, not read, the papers, whether their content was of great military importance or not. The game was still being played. He took his hand off the cover of the satchel and brought it to his lap. He would not read them. He turned his head away and found Joseph still asleep, sucking all the air from the sky and exiting it from his nose.

"Oh, for goodness sake. A boy snoring? That is something for an old man of wise years beyond his knowing."

"Shush, Otto. I hear you. It is not polite to make fun of the sleeping. However, I applaud your knowing me as a wise man."

Joseph adjusted his blanket and turned over, bringing his knees to his chest. "Besides, you tossed and turned and murmured bizarre things all night. How was I to sleep?"

"They were not dreams of children. I was haunted."

Joseph opened his eyes and sat up, still covered by his blanket. "Yes. Bad dreams. I've buried mine since we've started this journey. Although, honestly I think I buried them many, many years ago."

"We have a long road ahead of us. Best we make our way."

"Agreed, but after an iron ration, of which I suggest we have one each." Joseph removed his blanket and reached for his musette bag. He foraged inside and pulled a tin from its hiding. Damn, horse meat."

"Ha! Well, it's about time for you, Joseph." Otto likewise pulled a tin from his bag and joined Joseph for breakfast.

Joseph consulted a map while eating, mulling over which road they should take. "Hmm, a five-day journey. Taking smaller roads will cost us time but will be safer. I suggest a longer trip, Otto. Unfortunately, this map is of military making. It does not list many roads except for a few major ones, larger towns, rivers and train tracks. I cannot be sure of our way."

Joseph set his map to his side on the grass. "And now, I am wondering if such an unsanctioned journey is needed. We must get to Bormann. However, the SS Chief, assuming he survived that blast, and his lackey will be at our throats. Perhaps Bormann will offer us the same plight as the Chief. From what I've read in the document, it seems, well, I just don't know what to believe or what to do. All is not clear to me, Otto."

Otto swallowed his last bite of horse meat and tossed the can aside, licking his fork to the last scrap of food. "It is hard to know what is the truth, but let's take one step at a time. We are in enemy territory so we must travel slowly and with caution. That's an unsettling fact no matter where we go. As to Chelmno or to Bormann? I'm going to Chelmno. That is where my heart is telling me to go. I think yours is of the same mind. I am weary of Bormann. While our mission as ordered leads us to him, I am leaning towards surrendering to the British. Corporal Huber counseled me to that end. From there? I do not know what is to happen to me. The British are gentlemanly soldiers, I am told. They will not harm us."

Joseph ate while listening to Otto's words. His eyes concentrated on his eating, his fork navigating the tin, but suddenly he glanced at Otto when a word took his attention. "We agreed on Chelmno because, as you promised, there we'll find truth. I understand I waver and often wander from that decision at times, but it is difficult not to. As for me, from there I will go to Bormann and I will go with the document. The SS Chief is after you. If I can get to Bormann before him, then my words and success of the mission will hold sway over the Chief. I will be spared. Besides, Bormann knows of my father and he will not harm me. As for you, we will part ways and you can find your British. I'm sure your story, truth or not, of being a slave boy will find their fancy. You will not be harmed. We will both find our safety."

Joseph tossed his tin into the tall grass and wiped his mouth with his sleeve. "I think it would be wise to change into my Russian uniform. I would think we'll have better luck with you as my prisoner."

Otto snickered at Joseph, his nose crinkling with wrinkles. "What?"

"Well, is it not a sound idea?" asked Joseph. "I suspect there are many more chances of a Russian patrol finding us than a German one. The Germans have abandoned these lands, cowering to escape or retreating to defend the Fatherland. The Russians would applaud me with you as my captive and revel at my deed. They would not harm us. If a Polish army patrol or militant commoners were to find us, they would see me as their liberator and support my prize. So you see, either way we win."

"You mean you win. What if in either of those scenarios, they order you to shoot me in front of them? Perhaps a raucous sergeant commands you. Your uniform is of a private's rank. You'll have to do as you are told."

Joseph pondered the thought as he raised to his feet, slowly surveying their hideout nestled amidst the field. "Hmm, I had not thought of that."

Otto secured his bags while whispering to himself mixed thoughts, finding Joseph's decision suspect. Joseph quickly began changing uniforms, continuing with his idea. Otto watched, still leery. "And how are you to explain the German weapon?"

"Simple. I secured it from you, as my own weapon was damaged in our struggle."

"What struggle?"

"Well, you are the one with the swollen cheek."

"Yes, and as if you cared, it still stings." Otto felt air tickling his toes as he rose to his feet and looked down at his boots. "Damn. Another hole. Either way, Joseph, our journey must end soon. My boots are deteriorating."

Joseph nodded as he pulled up his trousers. "It would be well for us to find another mode of travel other than our feet. However, nothing comes to mind that offers safe passage."

"Well, then it's our feet again."

They slipped from the field and greeted a new day. Joseph pointed to the south road from the intersection. Otto nodded and led the way. He still questioned Joseph's plan to be his prisoner.

The sun initially greeted them on this morning but soon gave up its brilliance. Dark clouds settled in, and a slow rain embraced their travels. Raindrops became a constant menace as they drowned more than just the two travelers. They also drowned the sounds of anything moving into their path. This gnawed at Otto, and every once in a while, he would turn as he walked to draw his ears to a new air. Whenever possible, they cut across fields, meadows, or a wood and then rejoined their road farther along. They would flank villages or homesteads to thwart any human entanglements. The road was quiet for its part, except for sightings of an occasional farmer readying his work or a lone beggar or vagrant scrapping for food. What troubled Otto more was the long, ragged following of displaced peoples pushing carts and carriages full of their belongings and wares. Their bodies moved in hunched and limp positions, turmoil and agony stealing their shapes. German or Polish, soldier or citizen, their origin was unknown to Joseph and Otto. From a hidden ditch along the side of the road, Otto watched the long convoy of people pass while Joseph kept his weapon at the ready, covering their back.

"Sad it is, Joseph, that war started by just a few could wield such anger and disrupt so many. No one asked these people if they had the heart to fight. No one cared about these people."

Joseph turned from his rear guard, his eyes narrowing. "I suppose it depends on whose point of view it's from, my dear Otto. The winners seem never to worry about such things. It's always the losers who wallow in such thoughts. Best to be a winner."

"Let us move from here. This landscape sickens me."

They held low, following the ditch until well beyond and out of sight of the caravan. Evening was upon them as the rain kept steadily falling. They climbed back onto the road, which twisted and spiraled, following a more indirect line. Otto stopped numerous times to stuff his sock back into the hole of his boot.

"My feet are soaked. We need shelter and warmth, Joseph. Look at yourself, you're shaking with chills. We can't hold this path much longer."

"It's quite a burden, I agree. Not even a steady march is keeping me warm. I detest spring. It is neither adequately warm nor sufficiently cold."

Otto chuckled as he turned from Joseph to continue his path. "I suggest a place to build a fire, perhaps a barn, or better still, a fort in a tree."

"There you go again with your childish enchantments."

"But I am a child, just as you are."

"I am not so sure anymore. Carrying a machine gun, killing enemies, and wandering strange lands while being chased by villains does not sound like the enchanting life of a child."

"True, Joseph, but that is not a choice of our making. It was designed for us by the few."

"Hmm, I see where you are going with this, Otto. Point taken." Joseph stopped without warning, noticing a small shack hidden down a hedgerow.

Otto paused as well, surveying the hedgerow and following Joseph's eyes. "I think that'll do, if indeed we are seeing the same thing."

"We are. Let us go."

They hopped off the road, jumping the ditch on the other side, and like two mice, they scurried down the hedgerow coming upon the shack. They halted their advance ten meters away and held still to assure all was clear.

"Looks to be a farmer's tool shed, Otto."

"Yes. I don't think we'll have any visitors looking for tools at this hour, but by morning, we'll need to be gone. Those farmers are early risers."

Joseph rose from his position and silently approached the shack. He came to the door, which faced from the road to the right. A small path led away into the field and beyond. The shack was well made. Sturdy beams and a solid frame gave strength to a hearty wooden sheathing. It was windowless and had a small stone fireplace, that of a smith's use. Twisted vines, layers of moss, and ages of lichen covered its northern shadowed face. Joseph motioned for Otto to follow. He slowly tested the door's will. It creaked but was ready to be opened. Otto came up from behind and put his hand on Joseph's back in anticipation.

"Really, Otto. Are we that curious, as if there's a candyman in there with gingerbread snaps, pudding, and assorted chocolates?"

Otto quickly withdrew his hand as Joseph pushed the door open. He pulled a candle from his musette bag and lit it, forcing its light forward. The small shack remarkably took to the light and showed its holdings. They stepped inside and quickly closed the door behind them to conceal the light from any intruder's eye.

"Quite a shack, I should think, Joseph."

"Yes, but why does a tool shack have a table, chairs, and a loft with bedding?"

Otto moved further into the shack, his eyes swirling with questions. "Agreed. Why are there cooking pots, utensils, and candles of different burned heights around the room?"

Joseph glanced at Otto, turning from his thoughts. "Someone is living here." Otto nodded, his face becoming alarmed. Joseph continued, "We must not linger here. This place is not safe."

"But it's quite warm. The hour is late, and we have no other shelter. I would guess if this shack were occupied, especially on a dismal day as this, it would have its owner already here."

"That would be my logic as well, but it is still not safe."

"Perhaps it has been abandoned. Look, there is no firewood for the hearth and the table seems to have a film of dust upon it. There are no clothes of a man or woman and not a scrap of food to be seen. Not even a mouse could live here."

"True. All very sound reasoning, but my stance remains."

"You know, my dear Joseph, I've noticed you have not been drawing of late. They say you lose your talent if you do not keep up your practice. It would be a shame to have lost all I have taught you."

Joseph lowered his machine gun from his ready position and contemplated Otto's words. "Hmm. Well I do fancy drawing, as you know. All right. We'll stay, but we must leave before first light."

"Agreed."

Otto and Joseph unloaded their belongings and lay them on the table. Joseph climbed the short ladder to the loft to investigate the bedding. He came to the top of the ladder and instantly questioned the size of the sleeping area. Otto searched the floor for wood to start a fire. The hearth was small, raised to waist height since it had been built more for a blacksmith than a heating source.

"I hope you don't mind close quarters for your rest tonight, Otto. You'll have to keep your tossing and turning to a minimum or risk falling to the floor below, although I may push you."

"I'm sure that would please you. Now on to more serious matters. We have no wood for a fire, and our wet clothes will not dry on their own."

Joseph climbed back down and jumped to the floor, skipping the last two rungs of the ladder. "Break up the chairs. They're dry and will burn hot."

"Five chairs will hardly be enough."

"Then we'll use the table and whatever else is wood that can be devoured by a flame."

"Seems a shame to ruin these chairs. I rather fancy their make. A fine craftsman spent hours crafting these. Oh well." He laid the chair on the floor, and with one hard stamp from his foot, the chair splintered. Joseph followed Otto's lead, and soon the chairs were a heap of kindling ready for a flame. Joseph gathered scraps of straw found on the floor, and with a few of the smaller pieces of broken chair, a fire quickly roared to life. Otto and Joseph peeled off their damp clothes and hung them near the warmth of the flame. They wrapped themselves in their wool blankets, lit candles, and sat in front of the hearth. Joseph pulled out his tablet and began drawing, continuing his secret project.

Otto remembered he had a number of folders from Bormann's bunker stashed in his musette bag. He pulled them out and began thumbing through the pages.

"Why do you look, Otto? It will only cause you despair. The Chief has already solved the riddle for you. Your Annie is at Chelmno."

"Perhaps. In my excitement I believe that, but when the night closes in and the mood swings to the dark, I question that truth. If these camps are what the Chief has made them to be, then my hope dwindles."

"I'm sure the Chief was only trying to scare you. Adults are good at that. I'll bet when we arrive at the camp, we'll find your Annie and many more people safe and secure from the troubles of war."

"Let us hope, Joseph. Let us hope."

"Speaking of the camp, while we are headed in the correct direction now, there will come a point we will have to find someone to ask. We do not know its exact location. As I have said, our map is limited."

Otto did not reply; his head was busy reading the long list of names. Men, women, children, grandparents, uncles and aunts. Row by row, folder by folder he read, until there were none left. "They are not here. Annie is missing to me still."

"Sorry, Otto. Perhaps then you can use the paper for our fire. Our wood runs low, and the hearth could use more flame."

"No. I would not do that, Joseph. These names are perhaps all that is living of these people. No, I will not let them die."

"Fine. Have it your way. It's not my burden to carry."

"I would expect that reply from you. Enough of this gloom. What of your drawing? Can I see it?" Otto's steady frown broke, his mood brightening.

"I told you, silly Jew, it's not for viewing yet. I will show you in good time. Be still."

"Well, then I'm climbing to bed. I'm tired of this day." Otto climbed the ladder and had to crawl into the loft as it was but a few feet in height from its floor to the ceiling. "I expect since we are in such cramped quarters, you'll hold your snoring for another night."

Otto heard nothing from below. He smiled and pulled his blanket over his head. He tucked his knees to his chest and brought his arms and hands into them tightly. The fire snapped below, and he watched the shadows from the light flicker and dance across the walls and ceiling. He lay gazing ahead as long as he could until sleep finally took him.

"Otto? Hurry. Wake up."

Otto shrugged his shoulder, groaning unrecognizable words. "Go away. It's not morning yet."

"But it is, Otto. We have overslept! It is light, and the fire has long since waned. I thought I heard whistling not a moment ago. We must dress and leave here. Quickly now!"

Otto jumped to attention, unraveling his body from his blanket. He sat quietly listening for a whistle or any sound of humankind. Why does it always happen in the morning, some intrusion or dramatic event? This dread of war is constant. Then he heard it. A high pitched whistle. It was not the making of a well-rehearsed song. It sounded fragmented without melody or cadence. It had more breath than sound, almost as if someone were just learning to whistle. In any case, it was an unwelcome intrusion nonetheless.

Otto clamored for the ladder and slid down. Joseph was already dressed and ready with his weapon positioned to the left side of the door. Otto dressed quickly, barely pulling up his socks and tucking in his shirt. He grabbed his bag and satchel and slung them over his shoulder. If he had to escape, it would not be a polished and well-groomed exit.

The whistling grew louder and was nearly upon them. Joseph waved frantically, motioning for Otto to ready himself on the other side of the door from him. Otto moved quickly and took to a flattened position against the wall on the hinged side of the door. If it opened, he would be hidden and would have to wait for the intruder to enter before he could make his escape. His hands trembled and his heart pressed against his clothes as he prepared for his run. Suddenly, the door opened slowly and squeaked as it threatened Otto's space. A small, dark shadow entered the room, and before Otto could make his move, Joseph jumped from his position and wrapped his machine gun around the intruder, pulling him off his feet and catching him in a choke hold. Screaming and wailing, the intruder stamped his foot down hard with one mighty thrust on Joseph's foot.

Joseph cried out in pain, dropping his hold and his gun. Grasping his foot and continuing his cry, he fell to the floor in agony.

Otto leaped from behind the door, but stopped suddenly, bewildered by what he saw. "You're, a, a girl?"

"Stop or I'll shoot you both. I promise I will."

"But you're a girl."

"Of course I am. What else should I be?"

"Joseph, look. It's a girl! She's quite a bit smaller than you, and she has your gun."

"Yes. I'm aware of that, and by the way, my foot is fine."

"Quiet, Huns! What are you horrible, smelly Germans doing in my shelter?"

Otto slackened his shoulders and turned to Joseph lying on the floor. "See, I told you the Russian uniform would fool no one. She figured you out quickly."

"Yes, Otto! Very good. Now what are we to do?"

"Nothing now. She has the gun."

"I said quiet, Hun! Your bickering is annoying. I'll ask you again and not one time more. What are you doing in my shelter? Speak quickly."

"My dear little girl," Otto calmly began, "my name is..."

"I'm not little. I'm nine years old, if you must know."

"My apologies. I meant no offense. We mean you no harm. Please allow us to introduce ourselves. My name is Otto Kaufmann, son of Solomon Kaufmann of Nord Strasse, which is a small, wonderful, and happy street on the west side of Berlin. This one fidgeting on the floor and rubbing his foot is Joseph Kessler. He's my friend and companion, also from Berlin."

Otto leaned forward and whispered to her with a wink. "Good shot on his foot. He needed that." The girl smiled with a slight giggle to herself.

"The uniform, although misleading not to you, was very much needed as his own clothes were ragged and offered no warmth from the elements. We were cold and wet and were trying to find shelter in order to dry out. We are lost traveling south to our home. We have heard word that the war may be over."

The girl stood poised, her newly claimed weapon still holding her captors still. She wore a tattered dress so soiled one could not discern the true color. Underneath were tight, dark wool stockings that were torn and full of holes. They were tucked into evenly worn boots of a boy's make with unmatched laces. Her hair was dirty blonde, falling to her shoulders. It was disheveled and tangled with obvious knots and stragglers. Her face was round, complimenting her round cheeks and pudgy nose. Her eyes were blue, big, and wise. Her mouth was quaint and strong.

"My name is Marzena Gorski. You are on the farm of my Papa and Mama. This is the blacksmith quarters, but none of them are here. They are all dead. Many years ago when the Huns came to intrude on our lands, they burned our house and killed my whole family. Mama tried to hide us all. She hid me in the well by strapping me to a rope and letting me down to the bottom. When I climbed up many days and nights later, I found everything dead. I am all that is left."

A small tear welled up in Marzena's eye, but there it stayed. She did not wipe it or acknowledge its presence. She loosened her grip on the gun and placed it harmlessly on the hearth. She hopped up onto the table facing Otto and Joseph, who was still agonizing on the floor.

"I see you had a nice fire last night. You understand there are many bundles of dry firewood on the other side of the shelter. I actually fancied those chairs."

Otto took a step very slowly and joined her in sitting on the table. "We are sorry. We were cold, frightened, and lost. I promise to replace your chairs. We had thought this place abandoned and did not think our intrusion would harm anybody."

Marzena turned to face Otto. She looked up and investigated his face, judging his character. She gazed into his eyes searching for truth. "I have other hiding places that I use to keep hidden. Depending on what's happening, I decide on where to go. When I feel there is danger, I hide deeper. I have not been here for quite some time. Word from afar about the war has come to my ears too. So I left my deepest hiding place and came here to find the truth. This shelter is the least of my most hidden places. The road you traveled is a worn one, and there are many towns nearby. So while this shelter is close, it is still quite out of the way from an eye's notice. Many army groups have passed this way over the years. Mostly Hun armies. I have only seen one Russian advance, but they moved swiftly."

Joseph finally stood up and walked around the table, limping at first. It was more of a show than any real physical impairment. Otto and Marzena watched with hidden grins.

"I'm sure if you had a girl's shoe, Pole, I would not be in this condition."

Otto rolled his eyes. "Ha! You are the biggest girl here. Now stop your stage show and relax. We have a new friend, I should think."

"Great, just great. A Jew and a Pole. My choices for friends are lacking these days!"

Otto shook his head and looked towards Marzena. "Don't mind him. He's a bit of a bellyacher but quite harmless, mind you."

"Sorry about your foot, Joseph," apologized Marzena. "I was taught that move by my brother. It worked well when the bullies at school plotted ill deeds."

"Yes, I'm quite sure it did, Pole," Joseph replied.

"So tell me, Otto, when does he stop calling me 'Pole?'"

"I suppose after he's warmed up to you. It's hard for him to take being subdued by a girl."

"Yes, all very funny, you two. I should think word of this will not get around?"

"I could have just shot him, Otto, and been done with it."

"That's what I keep saying."

"Ha, Ha. Very funny. If you were to ask me, and I know you will not, I should think the time for laughter has passed. We have a journey ahead of us, my dear Otto, and we don't know our road. Perhaps your new friend could help us."

"He is right in his words, Marzena. I'm afraid I have not been entirely truthful. We are on a mission. I could tell you more, but to involve you is to put you in danger."

"I suspected as much, Otto. The world becomes very different when you are forced to survive. Your senses tingle like never before. Sounds become warnings. An odor becomes a threat. Eyes notice even the smallest of movements. Yes, I have noticed things about you. You wear the uniform of the Hitler Youth."

"Yes. It is true. Joseph is a soldier for the Hitler Youth as well. However, we have no quarrel with your countrymen. The deeds of the past is blood not of our hands."

"I believe you, Otto. Your words are kind and gentle. It's refreshing to see youth again." Marzena scratched her head and pushed back the hair from her face, tucking it around her ears. A dimple found a way to her cheek as she spoke to Otto. "So tell me of your mission?"

Otto looked quickly at Joseph, seeking a reaction and approval to tell of their objective. There was no emotion from Joseph. He seemed disinterested except for his foot, as his head was staring at the floor.

Otto turned back to Marzena. His voice was soft. "We have a document that must get to a very important person, but first we are to go to Chelmno. There are answers there that Joseph and I seek."

"I know this town. It is in the southwest near a small village where my aunty resided. She has passed since the war broke out. It is many days from here by foot or cart, but fortune has found you, Otto. There is a railway not four kilometers from here that takes you to a town near Chelmno. We could be there in two days."

Suddenly, Joseph came to life. He had been listening. "Whoa. No, no, no! You are not coming, Pole. Having two people to watch is a burden I wish not to take. Otto and I travel well and light together."

"You are right, Otto. I should have shot him."

"Joseph, you're being hardheaded. Our map does not give us the way, and as you keep pestering me relentlessly, we are many days delayed from our objective. She could be our guide, and then we can part ways. Besides, she handled you quite easily, I might add."

Joseph sneered back at Otto as he continued his limp around the table thinking. Voices of his father in his mind disturbed his decisions. He remembered the invasion of Poland and his father's terse words about the Polish people. 'Barbarians living on stolen Germanic grounds.' His father despised the Poles. "I have learned to accept you, Otto, these past many days together, and I'm working on trust. However, once again I am challenged, and again, things are not clear. I should do what is in my heart, not what's plaguing my mind." Joseph stopped his circling and sat upon the table. He gave a loud sigh and took a short breath. "She can go."

Otto smiled and glanced back at Marzena. "That is, if she wants to go. Do you?"

Marzena smiled back at Otto and hopped from the table. "Nothing is clear to me either, Joseph. The hate I've lived with these past many years has long since dissolved. One cannot live with such burdens. Thrust upon us has been an adult's life with adult decisions. I don't really know what a nine-year-old girl is supposed to do, or how to act, or even look like. I have not gazed into a mirror for a very long time. I remember my mother would brush my hair at night and I would hold a hand glass up to my face and smile. These days, I have only seen myself when staring into the ripples of a muddied puddle, a warped reflection of a saddened life. I do not see beauty. There is nothing for me here. Just darkness. Going with you, to whatever end, for whatever reason, seems like a chance to live again. So I will go and ask for nothing. I can hold my own and will carry my weight."

"I warn you, Pole, Otto and I are not alone in this journey. We have enemies upon us. Germans, Russians, and perhaps your countrymen. We are with no friends. You may feel alive again, but death will be waiting should we near its path by mistake. We must be smart, swift, and vicious, none of which we have been of late."

Joseph grabbed his machine gun from the hearth and hopped from the table. He stepped towards the open door and turned back to Otto and Marzena. "Gather your things, you two. We leave now."

Marzena walked to a small wooden chest beside the hearth. She opened the lid and pulled from it a hand-knitted blanket. "I'm relieved you two did not burn this chest. This blanket was made for me by my Mama. It's a family blanket. She would come here often to get away from the farm, to find quiet and knit. She loved to knit. I would come to watch and visit with her at times, only to fall asleep in minutes. Mama would cover me up with this blanket and continue her knitting. The blanket never left here. I almost forgot about it until Joseph asked for us to gather our things. This will be all I'll need."

Marzena proudly unfolded the blanket for Otto to see. Otto smiled, his mouth opening in amazement. The blanket was quite ornate, crafted with a kaleidoscope of brilliant colors with geometric patterns of circles and squares, each depicting within them family scenes of play and work. Marzena smiled with Otto, pointing to the scenes and explaining their origin.

"This is me and my two older sisters, Adelajda and Kaja. This little character here is my younger brother, Rafal, and his chickens. Over there next to the garden picking vegetables are my Papa and Mama. That's our dom, the big stone and wooden house, and oh, that's the stajnia next to it with our horses peeking out from the window. You know, I've quite forgotten their names. I didn't care for horses as much as my sisters did. They were very good riders, I'll have you know. I loved our ducks. See, that's Sylwia and that's Ula, the big white one. Mama would always ask me to keep them in their pen. Well, I thought nothing of that and let them out to run free. Mama would scold me, and then I'd have to chase them around the stable yard and put them back."

Marzena turned to Otto, her voice frail and her eyes moistened. "I, I was in the well. And. And the soldiers. I could hear them. They yelled and hollered at papa and mama terrible things. They charged them with holding weapons and food for the Polish army. There were many screams. So very loud. And the ducks were squawking terribly. And the chickens and horses. And me. Then nothing. When I climbed from the well, the soldiers were gone. I found my parents shot in the head and crumpled next to each other near the front door of our dom. They were engulfed in blood, so much so I could not see their faces. I, I, remember horrid screeches from my sisters that plagued my ears. I found them naked, their throats cut, bleeding from where they were violated. They did not last long. I never found Rafal. Never. The horses were gone. To carry the army's wares, I suppose. The chickens? Gone too. Then I saw it. I saw feathers, feet, and wings, but none of them were attached. They killed and ate my ducks."

Otto sat motionless on the table. Marzena's words were no stranger to him for he had lived and seen many of the tortures she shared. He remembered the woman on top of the building in Berlin chased by the Russians, only to be caught and tossed off the roof. He could feel and hear her screams still. They played in his mind over and over and over, so much so that his eyes froze straight ahead looking into nothingness.

"Otto? Otto? Are you with me?" asked Marzena.

Otto's head fell forward and quickly snapped upright, removing his trance. "Yes, Marzena. I'm here with you." Otto smiled, and facing Marzena, he slowly reached his arm out and gently held her hand with assurance. "Come. We mustn't let the war sway our memories. I was told by a friend not many days ago that life is for the living and what we choose to do with it shall be our own making. Let us make it happy."

"Otto!"

"Whoops. That would be Joseph. We best be moving. His patience is lacking of late."

Otto followed Marzena out of the door. They could see Joseph in the field with his arms out to his side, hands on his hips, annoyed. They hurried their feet and caught up to Joseph, continuing past him without making eye contact. Joseph swiveled his hips, his apparent displeasure following their pass. He shook his head but said nothing as he broke his stance and followed closely behind.

Otto's little devil inside was equipped with a comment it wanted to so eagerly share. He thought better of it, but the timing was too perfect and the devil won. "We are nearing squad size, Joseph. Shall we get into patrol formation?"

Joseph continued shaking his head, his voice finding an easy comeback. "My dear Jew, so conveniently you forget who carries the gun. It pains me to repeatedly remind you of that."

The three travelers left the field and came to the road where Joseph had first noticed the shelter. Marzena stopped and turned to consult with her new group.

"We shall follow this road south not more than a kilometer. From there, we head west on a small shepherd's path that will lead us to the rear of the rail station. It is small, more of a reloading and unloading depot for the most part. Army groups use it, although I

have heard of other uses also. Ones not so pleasant. Of ghosts fre-
quenting the rail cars. There is word that strange things have been
seen. Glimmers of eyes peeping through the wooden sides of the
cars. People's arms, hundreds of arms reaching into the thin air,
begging to be let out."

The hair on Otto's neck took notice, raising against his clothes
and gnawing at him. "There is truth to this, Marzena, for I have felt
it. As an animal I have lived it. I will not speak of it now. We do not
seek that train."

"You two, there is no time for idle chatter. We must leave this
open road. The sun is still new. Quickly to the shadowed side of the
road. We must make haste."

Chapter 17

"Look, my new friends," pointed Marzena, "the shepherds' path. It is here."

Joseph walked to the front to have a look. The path had a menacing quality. It was quite narrow, well-worn to bare earth, yet overgrown on the sides with newly sprouted leaves welcoming the dawning of spring. Vines intertwined with trees; brush and weeds yearned to be seen, all of which added to the ghostly darkness even under a bright, warming sun.

"I am troubled by this path, Marzena," Joseph confessed. "You say it is of a shepherd's making?"

"Yes. All the shepherds and farmers use it as a short cut to their fields. It follows a meandering stream in places, then veers away meeting hedgerow after hedgerow and passing through field and meadow. The dark places through the woodlots are few."

"That is what troubles me, Pole. Woodlots are a good place to be ambushed by enemies. What have you heard of your countrymen? Are they formed into killing groups?"

"I have come across such men at times. Mostly, however, they rest and speak of their deeds and then move on. They care not for the matters of an orphaned girl. Their minds are fixed on killing the Hun. Actually, I have not seen them for quite some time. They move often."

Otto stopped suddenly. "Shh! I hear something you two, quickly into the dark!"

"What, Otto, what do you hear? Nothing comes to me." Joseph looked around with alerted eyes.

They scurried into the thicket and hid to the side of the path with eyes and ears pinned to the road. The sound became louder, a droning of machinery, engines drumming and treads grinding as they plodded forward. Otto could feel the earth shake around him. He stretched his head from its hiding, searching for a differ-ent angle in which to see, when a Russian soldier scouting the road ahead surprised his view. The soldier swept the road from side to side with the eye of a hawk alert for enemies. The soldier approached, darting from across the road and coming to the shepherds' path, but paid it no mind. He searched quickly ahead. Then they appeared, a well-armed column of men, tanks, personnel carriers, and miscel-laneous support vehicles.

Otto began counting the equipment, trying to discern their strength. "One, two, three... ten, fifteen, twenty-five..." They dis-appeared almost as quickly as they arrived. Otto slowly sat up from his hiding and glanced out from the path down the road. He could see the last of the column, its dust and sound fading into the land-scape. Joseph snuck in behind him.

"A Russian mop-up group, Otto. Just what I feared. They are combing the countryside for stragglers and devout German soldiers still clinging to the Fatherland. Well, that settles that question. The shepherds' path it is."

Otto patted Joseph on the shoulder and turned back to the path. They met back with Marzena, still hiding off the path. She looked up at the boys with questionable eyes. "So we are to go this route, Joseph?"

"I shall not give it another thought, Pole."

The darkness of the path did not last; as Marzena had described, the woodlot gave way to a small, luscious green meadow leading to a larger field. A quiet stream soon joined them, accompanying their left side. The most pleasant scents tickled their noses, the lures of flowering herbs, pungent fruit blossoms, and the mesmerizing flavor of wintergreen from the ever present Black Birch. The contrast of the different landscapes burst with beauty and brought smiles to their faces. Otto led the way, his lazy steps caressing the newly green world around him. His eyes gazed upon the stream, his feet yearning to run to its shores in hopes of launching a paper boat.

Marzena walked beside Joseph, if for no other reason than he had the gun. It made her feel safe.

"So tell me, Pole, how did you know I was a German soldier and not a Russian?"

Marzena smiled coyly, her head facing the ground and watching her steps as she answered. "Oh, it was quite easy really. You wear the boots of a German's make. Certainly no Russian has such fine leather. Also, your uniform was not quite a perfect fit. A bit baggy in the seat, as Mama would say."

Joseph stared at his steps. "Not a word to the Jew. I'd hate to give him fodder for a joke. He fancies that, as you'll soon learn."

"You have my word." Marzena glanced from her steps and observed Otto's playful presence. It puzzled her, knowing the potential danger surrounding them. "Tell me, Joseph, how does he pay no mind to our plight? It's as if his mind has drifted off somewhere else."

"He is with his Annie."

"A girl?"

"Yes. He says it is not love, but I say differently."

"Oh. A love story. I fancy love stories!" Marzena skipped quickly to Otto's side, her tangled hair somewhat finding life again as it flipped from side to side. Otto paid her no mind but felt her presence.

"So what does she look like?"

"You've been chatting with Joseph, I suspect. Well, you two can go on with your fun if you choose."

"Oh goodness me. Be proud of her, and share with me. Boys and their secrets. What ends can it possibly serve?"

"Do not mistake my intentions. There are times I wish to be alone in thought. Quite, really, I cannot help to be cast off to another place with her. It happens naturally without much effort on my part."

"I was just teasing, Otto. I had older sisters. I know all too well the giddiness of the heart. I have been through too much, and I often wonder will I ever come to such a place in my own heart."

"You have many years left, and I am certain you will. But love? Those are adult things. I just feel a tummy ache when she's around, that's all."

"A tummy ache? Silly boy. That's love!"

The group came to a gate at a hedgerow leading into another field that was quite larger and flatter than the others they had passed. Marzena took a few steps into the field and spread her arms wide as if trying to give it a big hug.

"In late spring, Otto, this field will be alive with corn poppies. They are most splendid in their color, a vivid red with a black dot in the middle. I wish we were here to stay so we could see them."

Joseph brought up the rear and met Otto and Marzena at the gate. His eyes surveyed the grounds for anything suspicious or out of place. "Where to next, Pole? I would think we've covered good ground."

Marzena dropped her arms, turned, and skipped back to the boys. Her joy subsided, and her tone became serious. "The station is two fields away next to a woodlot. I suggest we stay on the path of the hedgerow and skirt the field. It's longer than cutting across but safer than being out in the open."

Joseph nodded. "That would be my course of action also." He stepped through the gate and took the point position. He did not look at Otto, but the air was ripe with concern. "Please, Otto, if you are to go off with your Annie, let me know and I will gladly take the lead. Remember, we are on this route because we are to find her for real. No sense getting killed over dreams first."

Otto sighed, and an unarguable frown came to his face as he dropped his head away from Joseph. He knew Joseph was correct in his words. He had been lazy. He was no longer in his heart the keen survivor he had once been. He knew the Otto of old was fading.

The three moved along the hedgerow, skirting the field as Marzena had suggested. A stiff breeze confronted their direction and played with their hair, tossing and swirling it from side to side. Marzena kept her pace while constantly tucking her dirty locks behind her ears. The strands would not obey, and no sooner had she put her hand down, they would flop back into her face.

They came to the second field, which was bursting with swaying green sprouts, drowning the dead grass of winter's hold. A rickety, old wooden gate greeted them. It was held fast by two fieldstone posts on either side, the wood covered with moss centuries old.

Otto and Marzena knelt to the ground as Joseph crept forward to scout the field and beyond. He spent a number of minutes staring through the openings of the fencing. Convinced there were no threats, he crept back to his companions with news.

"The field is empty, and I can see the woodlot beyond. I did not have a good sight of the station but could discern a rooftop that is not the design of a barn or house."

Marzena nodded with excitement, frantic to share her mind. "That is the train station, Joseph. It sits just beyond the woodlot just as I told you. After we pass through this gate, the way is short."

"She has your energy, Otto, but not your will to interrupt."

"Ha, ha. Joseph. All very funny. Now I suggest we make haste and spend little time in this field. Large open areas trouble me. A good run would be welcome."

"I agree. Let us run then to the shelter of the wood."

Otto turned to Marzena and flashed her a wink.

They secured their belongings and retied their boots tightly. Joseph slowly walked to the gate, and with one last glance across the field, he gently pushed it forward. Otto and Marzena followed closely behind, pouring past Joseph. Otto paid little attention to anything else except for the other side of the field. He came quickly to a run, bounding across the field. With little effort, he came to the far side, stopping before the hedgerow. He came to his knees, turning to greet his companions still running across the field. The sight before him brought him to a laugh. He could see Marzena speeding in front of Joseph. Joseph wore a face of disbelief as his new friend held stride. They came to Otto and dropped to their knees. Joseph struggled for breath while Marzena had none.

"Seems Marzena has a bit of speed, yes Joseph?"

Joseph's head bobbed up and down, offering short gasps of breath. "Ye, yes. She had a, a, lead, Jew."

Otto dropped his head and laughed out loud. "Oh my dear Joseph, you are simply telling a tale. I saw you both leave the gate at the exact same time."

Marzena joined in on the prank. "Yes, and to be truthful, Joseph, we bet each other that I could beat you in a race. Seeing how you would never agree to it, we had to sneak it on you. Oh, what good fun."

Joseph's breath returned to normal, but he was not in the very least amused. "Great fun, you two swines. Do you both not understand I have the gun? I mean, honestly, this is why I am and continue to be the superior race. Yes. Have your fun. I bet neither of you survive this ordeal."

Otto stopped laughing, his demeanor becoming quiet. Marzena's followed. Her tasseled hair had fallen in front of her face.

Otto glanced at Joseph, catching his eyes and staring at him. "You don't mean that, Joseph. Marzena and I were just..."

"Just what? What? Just having fun?" Joseph rose to his feet and stared down at Otto and Marzena as if talking to scolded pets. "I am scared, Otto. Very scared. Okay? We are in great danger. Two assassins are at our heels. There are four armies around us shooting at everything and in every direction. And let us not forget the small bands of Polish fighters ripe with hatred and loathing for anything German. To top all of that, heaven only knows what Bormann may have in store for us if we are to ever see him. By all means, how is any of this fun?!"

Joseph did not wait for an answer. His orders were stern. "I am all for a good joke, well, when it's not about me anyway, but the time for a joke has passed. Now get up the both of you, and let us find our train."

Otto and Marzena returned to their feet and moved from the field into the hedgerow. Otto climbed up, pushing brush and branches aside as he came to the top. He turned and offered a hand to Marzena, pulling her up and over. Joseph followed. He saw Otto offer his hand but hesitated to reach for it. His eyes softened and mind relented as he grabbed hold. Otto leaned back and, with a mighty heave, pulled Joseph up to stand beside him.

"I am sorry, Joseph. We both are. I am scared, too."

"I know. I am trying to be strong for us all, but there are many things in my mind with which I am struggling, my father, you, her, this war."

"Those are heavy burdens. I only ask you to keep an open mind."

"It's so very hard, Otto, when my mind is yelling at me."

"Boys. Come quickly! There is a whistle in the air. There is a train coming."

"Hurry, Joseph. Let us be off. Let us quiet your mind."

Otto and Joseph jumped down from the hedgerow and scurried into the woodlot, following Marzena's run. The whistle grew louder, and puffs of steam bellowed into the air. The three companions darted through the woodlot. The way was unencumbered and easily maneuvered. Brush and small saplings had all been cut, leaving mature fir trees to stand tall, offering wide passages to navigate. The canopy hid the midday sun, creating dark shadows on the earthen floor while providing an element of cover for their movements.

Joseph came to the edge of the woodlot first and rested behind a pile of cut logs. Otto and Marzena fell in behind him. Joseph turned to look at both of them and offered a sneering grin. Otto and Marzena looked at each other, having been conquered at their very own joke.

"Very good. You made your point."

The train was in full sight and slowly pulled passed the station. Steam billowed from under the engine as it came to a full stop. Attached was a long column of wooden covered boxcars. The station was small, as Marzena had depicted. There were wooden crates of all sizes stacked upon the platform that looked to be of civilian use. Nothing military had shown itself.

"That's the train I spoke of, Otto, the one with those wooden slats like coffins."

"The tales are true, Marzena. They are used to escort people to very evil places. I suspect they are returning and picking up either civilian or military cargo."

"I think you are correct. It looks as if there are workers beginning to load the cars with those crates. I do not see any soldiers. Well, at least no one armed with weapons. We may be in luck."

Joseph crept beside Marzena. "Is that the direction we are to travel? Is this our train to Chelmno?"

"Yes, that would be the correct way."

"Good then. I suggest we wait until the train has been loaded and it starts to pull from the station. It looks to be a twenty meter run, so we'll have to be quick if we are to jump aboard the train before it comes to speed. I certainly know I have the legs for it."

Otto nodded. "Okay, Joseph. You won the last race through the woodlot, but there was no bet on it."

"That's just a technicality, Otto. It has no bearing on the outcome."

Otto and Marzena shook their heads in amusement while keeping their eyes on the workers loading the train. It remained still for many hours as workers scurried about loading each car with crates and other items not discernible to the three of them. Midday slowly churned into mid-evening, when suddenly a whistle blew and steam shot from the undersides of the engine.

Joseph sat up and secured his machine gun around his head and shoulders, crossing his back and coming to rest. Marzena again fought with her hair and finally tucked it around her ears in anticipation of her first leap. Otto was equally prepared, his satchel and musette bag well placed so as not to encumber his speed.

Marzena tapped Otto on the shoulder. "How are we to raise ourselves up into the car? I ask you, Otto, because it would seem you are the only one quite familiar with its workings."

"Well, my Poppa helped me back then. Your question poses a considerable issue."

Otto turned from Marzena and tapped Joseph on his shoulder. "Joseph, my dear friend, could you be so kind as to tell us how we are to get into the boxcar?"

Marzena peeked her head around Otto, eyeing Joseph for his answer.

Joseph recoiled his head, his mind deep in thought. "Hmm. Well, I haven't thought of that. It sure does seem like an awfully high platform to climb upon. Let me think."

"Joseph, the train is starting to move." She anxiously pointed out to him. "You had better think a bit quicker."

"Yes. Okay, Marzena. I know. Give me a minute."

Otto tapped Joseph on the shoulder, this time harder, "But, the train is..."

"Yes, Otto, I get it, it's moving. Run!"

Joseph sprang to life and darted towards the train. Marzena stared at Otto and hunched her shoulders, and then she too suddenly bolted from her position. Otto shook his head in bewilderment and launched to speed, forcing his arms and legs to action. The train roared to life and gained momentum fast. The three ran on a diagonal path, attempting to head off the train. Otto caught up to Joseph and looked over at him as they ran. Otto was still looking for guidance from him, holding his arms to his side with palms up waiting for an answer.

"The stairs! Run to the stairs between the cars. Hurry."

The train was moving faster, as the first boxcar passed them. Otto slowed and timed his move to run between the cars and grab the rail of the stairs. Joseph followed. The ground was littered with debris. Rocks, old wooden railroad tie splinters, and scraps of iron all made their plan even more difficult. Otto grabbed hold of the stair rail firmly and pulled himself onto the first flight. He turned quickly to assist Joseph, still running between the cars. With one great leap Joseph swung his body sideways, catching the rails with both hands as his foot met the first flight of stairs. Otto grabbed hold of him around the waist, further securing his stance. The boys quickly climbed the stairs and reached the platform between the cars.

The train was at full speed, and the wind became a menace. Dust and grime swirled between the cars, fouling their air and plaguing their eyes. Joseph pointed to the ladder on the car behind them as if they were to climb. Otto shook his head, not liking the choice, but was met with Joseph's angry eyes. Otto shrugged his shoulders and relented. He followed Joseph up the ladder and came to the top of the boxcar. The wind was howling past them, contorting their faces and flapping their clothes erratically. Joseph lay flat on his stomach and hugged the roof of the car. Otto followed his position, as standing was near impossible. He crawled next to Joseph and turned his head to face him, fighting the wind with his voice.

"Where is Marzena?"

Joseph's eyes bulged with alarm, and he quickly looked in back of him. "I thought she was with you. Did she not follow us up the stairs?"

Otto shook his head and frowned. Joseph tapped Otto on the head and pointed to a raised square door in the middle of the roof of the car.

"I think it's a way inside. I see hinges."

The boys crawled as flat as they could until they came to the door. Joseph examined its form, and feeling around the opposite side, he found a latch.

"Here, Otto, hold the door open while I climb in."

"Who's going to hold it for me?"

They both grabbed hold of the door and flipped it open. A locking mechanism engaged and the door held fast, vibrating in the breeze. Joseph spun around and raised his feet and legs, lowering them down into the opening. The way was tight but still had enough room to squeeze through.

"It's about a four-foot drop if we hang from the roof."

Joseph nudged to the edge of the opening and flipped back around. He wiggled his body further, and with one swoop, he dropped down into the boxcar, grabbing the edge of the opening with both hands. He looked down into darkness with light flickering from the cracks between the sides of the cars.

"Hurry and drop, Joseph. It's freezing cold up here."

Joseph let go, and a loud thump followed his landing. Otto caught sight of Joseph rolling across the floor and into the side of the car. He did not hesitate and followed Joseph's moves exactly. Another loud thump followed his own landing, complete with a roll into Joseph, who was still on his back against the wall of the car.

"That hurt, Joseph."

"Yes, Jew. Now get off of me."

From out of the darkness, a voice greeted them with a precocious laugh. "Silly boys."

Otto sprang from the floor with amazement. "Look who it is, Joseph. It's Marzena."

Joseph rose to his feet slowly, reaching around and rubbing his buttocks. "Yes. I know. How did you get in here?"

"Yes, and before us? Joseph, she got in here before us."

"Yes, Otto. I can see that."

Marzena came into the light, her grin growing wider. "Well, you two bolted off to the front of the train, and seeing how it looked as if I was not going to get an answer as to how we were to get inside, I took matters into my own hands. So, I immediately ran to the second car and grabbed the handle located on the side of the car near the side door. I simply pulled myself up, unlatched the door, and slid in. Just like that."

"Huh, Joseph. She just..."

"Yes. I heard her." Joseph sat back down facing Marzena. "So now what, Pole? What is next? Where are we to get off?"

"Hmm. You know, I can't really remember the name of the station, but do not worry yourself. I remember what it looked like. It is many stops from here. Perhaps a day and a half ride. From there, we can walk to Chelmno, not but a few kilometers away."

"All very good, Marzena, but what if this train does not stop there? What then?"

"You'll have to trust me."

"Trust? I am plagued with such burdens."

Otto sat down next to Marzena, leaning his back against the wooden slats of the boxcar. "Calm yourself, Joseph. Look on the bright side. We are on a train and not walking in hostile territory. We can rest, regain our strength and our thoughts. Let's use this time wisely and put our energies towards a useful plan."

"I suppose you are right, Otto. Let us rest."

Chapter 18

The light flickering through the slats of the boxcar dimmed. Darkness was approaching. The air cooled, and all that could be heard was the mesmerizing staccato of the iron wheels of the train as it sped along. Its pulsating sound heightened and faded depending on objects the train passed and the effects created by the wind's turbulence.

Joseph wiped his nose in disgust. "It smells of urine in here."

"Yes, Joseph. We are not the only passengers to ride this train."

"They are ghosts, my dear boys."

"Ha. Silly Pole. Ghosts do not urinate."

Otto stared back at Joseph, his eyes firm and painful. "These ghosts do, Joseph."

"The both of you are crazy. I am tiring. Enough talk." Joseph shrugged his shoulders, attempting to ward off the cold. He reached into his musette bag and withdrew his woolen blanket. He brought his knees to his chest and covered his body. Tilting his head down, he drew the blanket high, masking his face.

Otto welcomed the idea as well and, taking Joseph's lead, removed his own blanket. Marzena leaned against Otto without so much as a thought of getting her own blanket. Otto reacted with surprise, his blanket not quite wrapped around his body. He could feel Marzena shivering. A quiet smile came to his face as he continued wrapping his blanket, covering the both of them. Otto sighed and exhaled a large breath of air. He stared into darkness, realizing they had not cleared the boxcar for enemies.

"Psst, Joseph. Joseph. Hey Joseph, are you awake?"

"Yes, Otto. It's been only a minute since we last spoke. Sleep has not come to me yet, and I suppose it won't until you've had your say."

"Good then. We have not cleared this room. Should we not wonder about its contents?"

Joseph adjusted his blanket and turned his head from Otto. "I suppose. Except for the space we are occupying, I only see a room full of wooden crates. Feel free to search further if you must. My gun is beside me should you so choose to use it. Yet, Otto, don't you think we would have been overrun by now if there had been anybody on this train?"

"Well, I suppose you are right. No matter. We'll just stay here then."

"Very well, Otto. Good night."

Otto sighed again, his eyes staring straight into darkness.

"Stop wriggling, Otto. I can't possibly rest with all your wriggling."

"Oh, so you are awake as well?"

"Yes. How can one find rest with all this wriggling of yours?"

"Sorry, Marzena, but I cannot rest. My mind is filled and gnaws at me. I can't concentrate on any one thought."

"You have to focus. So tell me of Annie."

"Annie? You wish to know of her?"

"Yes. Girls fancy jabbering about other girls. It's what we do. My sisters were remarkable at it. I feel it's why they never had any boys calling on them. They were too busy gossiping about the other girls."

"Well, that wasn't Annie. I think I was her only friend. We got along splendidly. I knew her fears, and she knew mine. I knew what made her laugh, and she knew what made me laugh. It was more than just feeling comfortable with each other. It's strange, really. It's as if she was the girl version of me and I was the boy version of her, which sounds ridiculous, I suppose. Except, that's the heart of it, I should think. We are one. I miss her so very, very dearly. Have you ever felt that way, Marzena? Uh, Marzena?"

Otto slowly shifted his eyes down towards Marzena without wriggling. Her head was tenderly at rest upon his shoulder, fast asleep. He could hear her soft, precious breaths and feel the weight of her tiny frame upon him, safe and without worry. Otto's mind cleared, and beautiful thoughts came to him. A smile tweaked his face, and his eyes gently shut. Slowly, his mind drifted, faded, and found solace in Marzena's closeness. Silence came to the boxcar.

Steam burst from the underside of the train, and its whistle blew loudly and with great ferocity. The mighty engine dropped its speed and slowed to a near halt. Joseph was jerked from his position and threw the blanket from its sleep. He jumped to his feet, swinging his machine gun to its call in one uninterrupted, masterful swoop. He yelled to Otto, who was now lying flat on the wooden floor with Marzena next to him covered with most of his blanket.

"Otto! Wake up!"

Otto rose frantically with a shiver and looked down at Marzena. "So that's where my blanket went."

"Quickly, Otto, we are stopping."

Marzena awoke but hesitated to join the fray. "What, what is it?"

"We are not sure. Get to your feet and have a look. You know these lands. You said you would know the station when you saw it. As Otto and I open the door, have a look, but be careful not to reveal our presence."

Marzena tossed the blanket aside and sprang to her feet. She frantically brushed her hair from her face and readied herself to peek from the train. Otto and Joseph unlatched the door and pulled on the handle. The door creaked and groaned as it let in light from a new day.

"My word, Joseph. We've slept through the night."

"Yes, we have, and who knows what time of day it is?"

Marzena grabbed the side of the door and slowly glanced from their hiding place. She squinted in the bright light, and no sooner had she peeked out than she quickly retracted her head. Worry caught her breath, and her words fought to form sentences.

"What, Pole? What is it? Speak quickly!"

"Russians!"

"Well, that certainly puts a damper on this morning, doesn't it?"

"Very good, Otto. Now please, get your head in the game. You used to be so very good at this."

"I still am, so keep your quips to yourself. These crates are quite large, certainly large enough for us. May we hide and wait them out?"

"I've thought of that, but I would think there's no benefit to hiding. I suspect the Russians will check every car and crate, and if they are not the owners, they are sure to become so anyway. Marzena, beyond the soldiers, do you recognize the station?"

"Yes, I do, but we are one stop from where we should be. We've another thirty-five kilometers if we are to move back to our feet."

"Yes, and that's exactly what we'll be doing."

"Which means jumping from a moving train?"

"Exactly, Otto."

"First a bridge and now a train. Perfect."

"Stop complaining, Otto. Quickly, to the other door. They will not see us from that side."

They moved to the other side of the car facing away from the train station platform. Slowly, the train cut its speed; the brake jerked and caught the three off balance. They fumbled into each other searching for their footing and grabbed the side slats of the car. Joseph and Otto grabbed the handle and unlatched the door, sliding it open.

Joseph came to his knees and peeked out into the open air. "I'll wait to jump when the train has slowed. After I go, get down as low as possible to the floor and follow me out. During our Hitler Youth training, our instructors taught us to tuck and roll. Basically, tuck your head into your chest and roll onto your shoulders into a little ball, coming to your feet when you land. However, even at slow speeds, I expect you might somersault a few times before that happens."

Otto glanced back at Marzena still clinging to the slats of the boxcar. Her face held fear. "We can hold hands, Marzena, and do it together if you wish."

"No, Otto. I'll be fine. Please worry for yourself."

Otto turned back towards Joseph, who was kneeling at the door looking for a clear spot where he could land. "Luck has found us. There is a small, grassy area uncut and without obstructions. It looks soft. Secure your belongings. You must be quick. One right after the other."

Otto and Marzena nodded and lined up behind Joseph. Marzena grabbed Otto with both hands steadying her feet. Otto reached back and gently covered her left hand with his, rubbing it with his thumb. He could feel her heart quiet in anticipation of her leap. Joseph carefully tossed his machine gun below him and, without warning, pushed off from the car platform into the morning air. Otto followed with Marzena closely behind. All three were airborne at once, coming to an abrupt crash onto the grassy floor still moistened with morning dew. Joseph followed his training and maneuvered his body to somersault across the ground. Otto and Marzena landed nearly on top of each other, rolling and sliding across the wet grass. The train continued another hundred meters and finally announced its final stop. Steam belched from its underside, and its whistle blew in a fervor. Orders and commands echoed from their screams as soldiers scurried about the platform following their master's directions.

Otto opened his eyes and turned from his back to his stomach. A swift pain shot up his leg as he reached down in search of proof of a wound. He pulled his hand to his face and gasped at the brightest red. He pushed his hands to the ground in front of him and came to his knees. Slowly, he drifted to his feet. His eyes abandoned his pain in search for Marzena. He found her face down, the top of her tangled hair choked with dead leaves and scraps of twigs and grass. He awkwardly stepped towards her as she slowly lifted her head. She looked up at Otto, her mouth faking a smile.

"That was not very soft grass."

Otto sighed and flashed a small grin. Pain reminded him of his wound as he sneered at his right leg, bare, missing the cloth that once covered it. A long, deep cut ran from his knee to his boot. Blood oozed and covered anything it could find. He sat back down and reached into his musette bag. He pulled his medical kit and quickly went to work. Marzena crawled from her position and sat down next to him, dusting off her ragged appearance.

"Are you hurt, Marzena? Have you any pain?"

"I am fine, Otto. Just a few cuts and scratches. Nothing like your leg."

"Yes, well, I am no stranger to pain, I'm sad to say. Joseph thinks I've softened of late. Quite honestly, having him as a companion has allowed me to pass on the responsibilities of survival, freeing my mind to other chores. Seeing how he makes decisions, jumping from a train being one of them, I think I shall reinstate my presence."

"Speaking of Joseph, where has he gone?"

Otto and Marzena frantically turned left and right, searching the ground around them. They rose to their feet and spread wide their eyes.

"He is not near. Where did he go?"

"There, Marzena. Down the hill at the bottom near that creek."

"I see him. He is lying still."

Otto and Marzena slowly dragged themselves down the short, steep hill and came to Joseph, who was lying on his back. His eyes were wide open staring straight into the heavens. The left side of his face was caked with blood, slicking his hair back around his ears.

"Joseph, are you hurt? Joseph? It's Otto. Your Jew."

Otto and Marzena stared eye to eye at each other with worry. The silence clouded their minds with grim thoughts. They looked down at Joseph, but his body remained quiet. Marzena put her hand to Joseph's forehead. It was cold and clammy.

"Joseph? It's the Pole."

Joseph blinked. "Am I alive? Am I in some kind of Jew and Pole heaven? Oh, please, no. Say that is not my fate."

Otto grinned, shaking his head. "Well, Marzena, he's perfectly normal."

Marzena chuckled. "Well, you couldn't have gone to a much better place than Pole heaven, my dear Joseph." She raised her arm and smacked Joseph with a hearty thrust to his right shoulder.

"Ouch! Good gracious. Why did you do that?"

"That's for making us worry without cause."

Otto smiled. "So tell us, Joseph, what happened? How did you end up way down here?"

"Yes, well. Funny thing is that I tucked and I rolled as instructed. So that was good. However, when I came to my feet, I was so dizzy that I fell and tumbled down here, hitting my head on a rock by the creek. I've never seen so many stars. My eyes twitched, lost focus, and blackened no matter how wide I opened them. My mind swam, and I seemingly fell asleep. I could hear the both of you but wasn't able to move, and then suddenly I snapped back to the present."

Otto stood up and, clearing his smile, searched the area for any followers. "We mustn't linger, my friends. While we are out of sight, we are not far enough away to be safe. I would imagine this area around the station will have a morning patrol, either beginning their move or soon returning."

"Agreed, Otto. Help me up then."

Otto and Marzena lifted Joseph to his feet. He staggered and, with a firm grasp, held onto them tightly. "Where is my gun? Did I have one?"

"Yes, Joseph. You tossed it out of the train before you jumped. I shall go fetch it."

Otto steadied Joseph with Marzena bearing the weight. "Guide him to the other side of the creek into the woods and hide."

Otto slowly crept up the hill to where they had jumped from the train. He crawled in the wet, tall grass towards the tracks and began searching for the gun. He peeked his head up high enough to survey the station for any oncoming threats. He could see many soldiers and civilians removing crates, some of which were open, but he could not discern what was inside them. He moved farther back down the track from where they had come, and there, covered with dirt and debris, he came across Joseph's gun. The magazine was gone, and the leather strap was torn loose from one end, hanging free from the front swivel. Otto turned over onto his back, and with the gun on his stomach, he slammed the bolt back, flinging a chambered round to the ground. He released his hand, and the bolt lunged forward locking into place.

As much as I hate to say it, Otto thought, this thing seems to be fine. He stared at the gun, his eyes caressing its shape, his mind relishing in its construction. Yet, it troubles me. What possible madness in this world willed men to want to create such a device?

Voices echoed from Otto's right. Men were approaching. He quickly turned from his back and came to his knees and hands. He peered towards the direction of the voices and could see a group of soldiers on the other side of the train walking its length. Otto raised to his feet, and in a hunched over position, he scurried down the hill and across the creek.

"Pst! Otto! Over here!" Otto followed Marzena's voice and came to her and Joseph behind a downed timber, huddled together in its shadow. Marzena was attending Joseph's wound, much to his displeasure.

"Here is your machine gun. It's in sorry condition but functioning nonetheless. Speaking of functioning, how are you doing?"

"He's fine. He has a nasty cut on the side of his head, but the bleeding has stopped."

"I'm fine, Otto, but my nurse here wants to make it not so fine."

"Hush, Joseph. Every time you wriggle, it disrupts my work. I don't understand why you silly boys always must wriggle so much."

Joseph glared at Marzena, turning his head away only to catch a glimpse of Otto's leg. "My word, what happened to your leg?"

"Your tumble and roll didn't go as well for me either, but my wound will not thwart our moving. Quickly, we must make distance from here. I suggest we follow this creek, keeping the train tracks in sight since that is our intended route."

Marzena and Joseph nodded and slowly rose to their feet. They followed the creek south, which played to their favor as it followed the train tracks for a number of kilometers. Their movements were labored and awkward, their wounds having an effect despite their will. The woods were thicker in the valley by the creek, and mosquitoes and gnats pestered their distressed bodies, threatening their moods and adding to their encumbered travel. Otto took on the lead while Marzena assisted Joseph, still spinning from his unintentional fall. They came to a bend in the creek that veered away from the tracks and vanished into the woods.

Otto stopped and turned to his companions. "What shall be our road? Back to the tracks?"

Joseph sat down and rested upon a large boulder by the stream. He reached down and helped himself to some water that was gurgling in circles, spinning round and round like his head as it continued its flow. "Marzena, what are your thoughts?"

Marzena sat next to Joseph and wiped away the hair that was stuck to her sweating forehead. "I think it would be wise to follow the tracks and abandon the stream. The next station is not far. From there, we can inquire as to a route to Chelmno. Perhaps we may find a farmer who knows the way, a back way far from harm."

Otto and Joseph made eye contact and nodded to each other in agreement. Otto reached down and filled his leaky, dented canteen and took a large gulp. A cool spring air was still gripping the lands, but the day wore on more like a heated summer roast. They climbed from the shallow valley and came to the tracks. Otto and Joseph looked in all directions imaginable, to their left and right, up and down, to the north and south, east and west. Marzena was watching them bewildered, catching Otto's attention. "We don't have a fancy for train tracks, I can tell you, Marzena. They are not easily and safely navigated."

Otto turned to Joseph. "Squad file formation?"

"Yes, Otto, by all means."

Otto marched down the tracks, concentrating on creating a rhythm between his steps and the spaces of the railroad ties. It was a laboring chore because of his leg wound. The erratic movements caused certain discomfort, and Otto winced with every step. Marzena followed behind the required paces as instructed by Joseph, who immediately took up the rear. They walked for hours without incident, stopping regularly to survey their surroundings and converse about further travel details. The train they had abandoned did not pass them as the sun followed its path towards dusk. The landscape changed, leaving the small hill area behind and turning into a much flatter terrain from whence they had originally come. They found field upon field separated by woodlots and small streams. The area was dotted with farms and small villages with not more than a few buildings in number.

Otto stopped on the track as the sun dipped beyond the horizon, leaving this day. "We will not make the station in light as it appears there is nothing directly at our front. We should find a hiding place and rest."

Marzena caught up to Otto with Joseph following. "Marzena, are we near?"

"Hard to say. My memory is spotty at best. I do remember the station being near flatter land with farms speckled here and there. Since that is what is upon us, I would imagine we are near. If you are challenging me and my knowledge, then trust that I will know it when I see it."

"Seems that is all I have very little of, trust."

"Stop your pessimism, Joseph. Marzena will lead us as she promised. Now let's make haste and move a good distance from the tracks. The night is clear, and a chill will soon find us. A warming fire would be very welcomed."

They stepped from the tracks and entered back into the woods, distancing themselves about a hundred meters away. They came to a small clearing under a stand of tall fir trees that provided perfect cover for hiding a flame. Otto unleashed his musette bag and satchel, freeing himself to gather firewood. Joseph followed while Marzena brushed away the grounds, clearing it for a fire pit. Soon the first embers burst with warmth as they settled in close to ease the night's chill.

Otto uncovered the bandages around his leg and picked out dirt, small scraps of wooden splinters, and anything else foreign to him. He poured water the length of the wound and washed it clean before applying fresh dressings. He made no moans or pleads of agony. His face remained expressionless. Marzena watched him in silence. She knew men of greater strength and beyond Otto's years who would cry to gods and mothers when having to attend to such acts. It gave her strength and encouragement.

Joseph pulled his drawing tablet from his musette bag and flipped to the project he'd been laboring on for many days. Marzena found this rather peculiar, and a question came to her mind. "I would never have suspected that you are an artist, Joseph."

Joseph peered from over the top of his tablet. "Oh, and why not? Just because I am a Hitler Youth means I cannot be an artist?"

Otto jumped upon Joseph's thinking. "Ha. I got you. I finally got you. So, my dear Joseph, with that reasoning, just because I am Jewish and Marzena is Polish, does that mean we are any less human?"

Marzena smiled and turned her head from Otto back to Joseph. Joseph tipped his tablet higher and hid his face. There was silence for just a moment's time.

"I know your words have trickery in them, Otto, and I wish not to participate. If you must know, history has spoken well of your question. It has proven itself to be true."

"That's your father speaking."

"Keep him out of this, Otto. I warn you. I grant you that it is true that we have learned he has signed a very troubling document. But why would my very own father lead me, his son, down a road of corrupt perceptions and false ideologies? Why? No father would do that to his family, the people he loved."

"I don't have that answer. Please know that I don't see you as a Hitler Youth. Or a monster. Or a killer. I see you as Joseph Kessler of Berlin. Thirteen years old. Likes to draw. Has a funny smile and snores at night. Gets grouchy if he doesn't eat and always gets the good iron rations. He doesn't like my jokes but laughs at them anyway. He calls me 'Jew' when he's annoyed and 'Otto' when he's happy. He's someone I trust with my life and for whom I would give my own to save his if it came to that. Whether you call me 'Jew' or not, I'd do it for you unconditionally."

Marzena nodded. "Me too, Joseph."

Joseph lowered his tablet and frowned. "I don't really snore."

"Yes, pretty much you do. Marzena and I heard it."

Marzena offered another peculiar look, and another question soon found a voice. "So what document did your father sign, Joseph? It sounds like he was important. Please share."

"She is just like you, Otto, very curious at the wrong times. Nevertheless, Pole, I don't know what the document means, but what is written is beyond words. They speak of horrible things and the creation of horrible places, which is why we are to go to Chelmno. Our pursuer has told us such places exist, Chelmno being one of them. For Otto's part in this tale, this is where Annie is said to reside. Otto and I are unsure. We may find a wonderful place where people are being kept safe. Otto thinks there'll be sweets. As to why we are being hunted? I have guessed that if what is written in the document we carry is true, then should they fall into the wrong hands, it would condemn an entire nation, culture, and its people. A condemnation that will last to eternity."

The night quieted. Otto sank into fetal position facing the open flames, staring at its freedom, fading into the darkness. Marzena lay next to Otto and pulled her Mama's blanket over her body, leaving an opening for her face. Her hair flopped down shielding her eyes, which she held still but open. Joseph closed his tablet and leaned back against one of the pines. He pulled his German issue field blanket around him and stared at the night sky counting stars.

Morning arrived quickly but spared the sun. Clouds hid its presence, choking its light and warmth. Rain threatened, and the night's chill remained. Otto awoke and immediately looked for his companions. Joseph still lay beside the tree that he had been leaning against, his drawing tablet next to him. He was snoring. Otto laughed under his breath and turned his head expecting to find Marzena at his side, but she was gone. Her blanket lay next to Otto, carefully folded and ready for him to put back into his musette bag. Otto was not alarmed and slowly rose to see her whereabouts. He followed the trail they had taken from the tracks and found her sitting on an old tree that had fallen many years ago. It was moss covered on its shadowed northerly side but wiped of its bark on top, which made for a clean perch. Otto carefully approached, his ears telling the story. She was weeping softly, her hands covering her face. Otto sat beside her but said nothing.

Marzena raised her head and faced Otto. "I am not scared for our journey or any of its dangers. I feel safe with you two."

"Then what has your little heart troubled?"

Marzena wiped her eyes and sniffled. "I don't have anywhere to go at journey's end. I'm alone."

Otto put his arm around her and pulled her near. "I am not able to speak for Joseph. He has his own path to follow and his own answers to find. Perhaps we shall be a part of it or not as this plays out. As for my part? I, too, am not clear. Some say I was a slave boy, some a courier of the High Court, to others a worthless Jew, which I still have no good reason as to what it has to do with anything. My story is a long one of which I will spare you the suffering. It is not important. What I can tell, Marzena, is that you shall not be alone. You have me, and I shall never leave you. We are friends."

Marzena smiled. "Do you think Annie will like me?"

"Well, I should think if you can fold a paper boat, you'll have her blessings. Yet, I, I have to be realistic. Even while my dreams tell me otherwise, Annie may not be alive. My family may not be alive. It has been five years, Marzena, since I've seen them. I am alone as well."

Marzena sniffled and hopped off the log. "I feel better now. I mean, not that you're alone too. I mean, well, thank you. Come then, new friend, we have much to do. We will find your Annie."

Otto slid from the log slowly, setting foot on the ground. The pain in his leg agonized him, and he was not looking forward to a day on the march. He followed Marzena back to camp and found Joseph still asleep, snoring. They both looked at each other and laughed. Marzena raised her foot and tapped Joseph on the head. He swiftly raised his hand, swatting away the intrusion.

"You two trolls are but a nuisance. It may be morning, but I am not ready."

"And a fine morning it is, Joseph. Marzena and I were wondering if you would move faster if you knew rain was upon us."

Joseph opened his eyes and sighed. "Oh, that type of morning. Yes, well I suppose that'll do it."

Otto secured his belongings while Joseph stood up to stretch. Marzena wiped her face clean using the ends of her tattered dress and retied her boots to make herself ready for a long walk. Joseph swung his musette bag and machine gun around his shoulders, the bag settling on his back and his gun coming to position in front at the ready. He pushed down on the receiver to test the strength of his new rigging of the sling. Convinced of his job, he followed his companions back to the track.

"We had nothing to eat this past day, Otto. We must find food or we will not last long on this march."

"I agree, Joseph, and these fields will not produce for us so early in the spring. We'll have to come to a village or a farmhouse and find our goods there."

"Being a Polish girl, I will have better luck at this chore. Two ill-smelling Germans dressed in, well, whatever is left of your uniforms, will not be well served."

"Speaking of which, Joseph. I see you have changed your dress. What happened to your plan to be Russian and I your captive?"

"Oh, I decided, Otto, that it was not in our best interest after all. You were right. Quite frankly, a Russian uniform certainly does not speak well for the aristocracy I am so accustomed to as one of the German Army's elite."

Otto snuck up to Marzena and bent her ear. "I take it you told him it made him look silly?"

"More like he had potatoes in his buttocks."

"Good for you."

"Stop your chuckling, you two, and move on. Back to formation."

The railroad tracks were empty among a calm and vacant landscape. The wind was faint as a few scattered droplets of rain splattered on the ground. The three companions traveled along the tracks, making good time despite their wounds and going without food. Joseph would pause every so often listening to the tracks and feeling the rails for vibration that would indicate the coming of a moving train. None came. Hours passed without incident and with a cooperating sky not yet unleashing its wrath.

Marzena suddenly stopped as they came around a corner. What the bushes and trees had previously hidden was now revealed. Another train station on the horizon came into view. Otto met her and stopped with Joseph following. Joseph removed his binoculars and surveyed the grounds.

"Hmm. Looks to be vacant of anything. Have a look, Marzena. Is this our intended stop?"

Marzena took the binoculars from Joseph and held them to her eyes. "I can't see a thing; everything's too small. Joseph, I don't think these work."

Otto grinned but held his laugh. Joseph rolled his eyes. "Unbelievable, Pole. And you wonder why your countrymen are the fodder for such ridicule. You're holding the binoculars backwards."

Marzena scowled. "Oh, uh, sure. I was testing them." She turned them around and had another look. "Yes! This is our stop. I remember it very well. We are close. We take the west road from the station and then south to Chelmno. I would think about fifteen kilometers."

"Good then. I see no need to approach the station. Best to skirt around it and meet up with the road farther along. Otto, what is your counsel?"

"Yes, that would be my choice. I also suggest we put food as an immediate need from here. I noticed through the breaks in the tree line a few farm houses in our midst."

"Marzena, lead on. Let us fill our bellies."

Otto held a blank stare at the sky, his mind calculating when the storm swelling around them would strike.

"Quickly, Otto. No use worrying about what is sure to come. Marzena is fast, you know. Let us not lose her."

The boys hustled up to Marzena, who was busy picking her path through the woods and swinging a long arc to the west of the train station. They pushed through small fields not yet tilled and woodlots much like the ones they had earlier navigated in their travels. Suddenly, the most unlikely thing appeared to their eyes as they entered a thick stand of trees. Otto stood dumbfounded. Joseph gasped while Marzena held steady.

"What, Otto, what on earth are these doing in here?"

"Good gracious, Joseph. I have never seen such a thing at any farm I have ever come across. What are all these cows doing here in the woods? Why are they tied to the trees?"

"And why, Otto, have they muzzles over their mouths and blinds over their eyes?"

Marzena stepped forward as she came to a calf, her hand caressing its back and tickling it under its mouth. "When the German army invaded, they did more than kill our people and burn our homes. They stole our food. Most people starved. So the farmers would hide the cows in the forests and put muzzles over them so the Germans could not hear them or find them and take them for meat and milk. At night, the farmers would come and milk the cows when all was silent. Messenger boys, not unlike yourselves, would use their bicycles and go door to door distributing the milk. Everything to survive was done at night, because you learn to survive very quickly during war or you simply don't survive."

Joseph was unmoved. His mind was on food. "So, being one of these night farmers, perhaps you can milk a cow?"

Otto gasped in disagreement. "No, Joseph. We must not take these people's milk."

"The time is not now to argue. The time now is for us to survive."

"He is right, Otto. Please do not worry. We shall take our share and be off. We'll take just enough for a canteen full each."

"Quickly, Marzena. Get to work. Otto, your canteen. Give it here."

Otto quickly fumbled for his canteen, which was stashed in his musette bag. "Here. I suppose it's fine if Marzena is willing."

Marzena sat down next to the cow and gently massaged the utter with her hand. Joseph knelt down next to her with the canteens ready to be filled.

"Uh, Pole, that's not where the milk comes out. You have to pull down on that long piece underneath."

"You do that and she'll be liable to kick you in the head, and she'd be right to do so. Now sit still and listen, you snotty, elite

313

German soldier. First, you have to prepare her so the milk can flow. That means massaging the utter so she knows to relax her muscles. Then, you take your thumb and first finger and clamp off the tit right under the utter. Yes, that piece under the utter you so intelligently named is called a tit. From here, it's quite easy. Just squeeze gently, and the milk will come out. Here, hold the canteen under while I squeeze."

Joseph sneered but did as instructed. Marzena squeezed, and milk shot into the canteen. "See? That's how you milk a cow."

"Fair enough. Now hurry. We've not got all day." Joseph glanced up at Otto for no reason except to see his reaction. Otto struggled to keep from laughing and quickly turned away.

"Go ahead, Jew. Get it out. Laugh all you want. Such peasantries are unfit for my people, as you may already know."

"Well, Joseph, these peasantries, as you call them, may keep us alive."

Joseph turned his attention to holding the canteens still. He did not wait for them to fill, changing them out quickly. "Perfect. Now let's be on the move. We'll drink as we go."

The clouds swirled above and began dropping their contents on the weary travelers. The air was damp and thick with an elusive mist scouring the landscape in search of things to engulf. Their movements became encumbered. Small objects on the ground not ordinarily a thought to navigate around became a nuisance, hidden by the mist. Their wet clothes stuck to their skin and restrained their steps, further obstructing their travel. Tripping and near falls were the norm.

"Ooh, I cannot bare another step with this hair of mine swatting me in the face as I move."

"Why don't you cut it, Pole? I have a knife. We can be done with it."

"Yes, but it's the only thing that keeps me feeling like a girl. It keeps me being Marzena. Without it, I am lost."

"Well, that's silly."

Otto looked up at Joseph from his path. "No it isn't, Joseph. If I were to take your drawing tablet away from you, the item you cherish most, then what are you?"

"But, Otto, that's a thing. I'd still be me. I'd still be an artist. I'd just do something else like sculpting or painting. Marzena would still be a girl, just with shorter hair."

"True, but my point is we all have unique things that make us who we are. Whether that is a hairstyle, a uniform, or an object we fancy. They all give us our identity, and through our identity is the expression of our character and personality. It drives us. How we behave; handle fear, doubt, and happiness; and more so, how we share and project those things."

"That's the fairest argument you've ever made, Otto. Okay. Agreed then. However, Pole, if you're going to keep your identity, then by all means stop your bellyaching about it."

"Seems we are getting to him, my dear Marzena."

"I think so, but he has not given up on calling me Pole."

The rain settled in to a constant and steady rhythm. They came to a road due west of the station as predicted, approaching it with stealth and caution. Otto came to the point and crawled to the road's edge. He lifted his head to survey the directions east and west. Off to the west in the distance, he could discern a farmer on a horse drawn cart carrying an oversized pile of hay that was hanging over the sides, somehow clinging to the main pile, not wanting to be left behind. He wondered if it could be Christoph but thought better of it. They were hundreds of miles from where they last left him.

Otto crawled back to his companions and reported his findings. "We are clear except for a farmer pulling hay. Let us be off."

They rose to their feet and started west, hugging the road. Joseph took point and distanced himself nearly fifty meters ahead. Otto and Marzena followed, putting less distance between them. The day progressed without incident as darkness crept upon them.

Otto and Marzena came up to Joseph, who had stopped in the tall grass beside the road.

"Let us find rest and shelter. This rain will not make for a very welcomed sleep if we remain so exposed, and we have little time before darkness has set. There is a fence row just up the road. I suspect a farmhouse or a barn is near. Let us hope we don't find another companion attaching themselves to us by morning should we use their shelter."

Joseph turned and continued his march with his friends behind him. They soon met the fence and immediately happened upon a small stone barn with a thatched roof. Joseph hopped the top rail of the fence and quickly ran to the side of the barn. He knelt down, his machine gun now on call. Convinced he had not been seen, he rose and slowly hunched over as he stepped to the front. He was greeted by a set of tall, wooden double-sided doors with primitive wooden handles for each side. He shook the right handle, checking for movement. It swung slightly then settled. Joseph paused, listening for movement. Nothing came to the door from within. Reassured the barn was vacant, he motioned for Marzena and Otto to follow as he swung the right door open and entered. Two small windows, one over the door and the other at the rear of the barn, gave enough light to show its wares. Besides a few farm tools, two carts, and some stacked wooden crates, it was empty. Joseph released his musette bag and brought his gun from duty to lay against one of the carts. Marzena and Otto entered, breathing slightly harder from their sprint from the road.

"We won't have fire for warmth, but it will be dry. I suggest we use these carts for our beds. It will keep us from the damp ground and offer somewhat of a temporary hiding place should we require it. I'll take the cart on the right, and you two disciples of tomfoolery can have the one on the left."

Otto and Marzena climbed up into the cart and were unexpectedly greeted by a soft bed of hay.

"How is your cart, Joseph?"

"Otto, if you must know, it is horrible. Just horrible. I am met with a hard, splintered wood surface for a mattress that I should think will call for a most uncooperative rest. Perhaps I'll just draw all night. And your cart?"

Otto looked at Marzena trying not to laugh. "Oh. Ours is equally as bad. Certainly not fit for a nobleman but just right for us peasants."

"Well good then, Otto. I should feel comforted knowing you'll be as miserable as I."

Marzena started giggling, her nose snorting and spewing a web-like discharge all over her hand. Otto gasped and laughed.

"My goodness, Otto, for someone not resting well you sure seem to be having a good time over there. Now please be quiet. I am going to draw and require peace."

Otto and Marzena sank within the hay, nearly burying themselves. Otto pulled their blankets out and unraveled them from their folds. They were more damp than wet but, being made of wool, were still very warming. Marzena slipped off her boots and socks and pulled her dress up over her head. She continued by doing the same with her shirt, leggings, and underwear. She caught Otto's eye and saw he was not wanting to stare but was embarrassed.

"It's okay, Otto. There is no shame in looking. Not much to look at anyway. Not like my sisters. I've learned there's no need for being shy during such times. We have other things to worry about."

Otto followed Marzena's guide. He removed his wet clothes and hung them over the side of the cart as she had done. "I was going to remove my clothes but thought you would be uncomfortable at the notion. Thank you, Marzena."

"It is fine. Besides, our clothes will dry much faster if not on wet bodies."

Otto lay motionless, not knowing what to do next. Marzena crawled next to him, wrapping herself with her blanket. She nestled her head on Otto's shoulder and closed her eyes. Otto moved his hand awkwardly feeling for her hair. His fingers found her ear and pulled away suddenly, frightened of the unfamiliar touch. He let his hand down again, found her head, and gently brushed her hair back from her eyes. Back and forth his hand softly stroked, his fingers finding a place of calm. Otto glanced over at Joseph, who was still upright leaning against the side of the cart. A ray of light found his tablet.

"Are you drawing, Joseph?"

"I thought you were asleep."

"No. No, not quite yet."

"Well, go to sleep because your next question is a 'no' answer. You may not see my drawing. It is still unfinished."

"Good night, Joseph."

Otto secured his blanket, engulfing his travel-hardened frame. He could hear Marzena's breathing, which triggered his mind. He again thought of Annie, hoping she was still breathing. He closed his eyes and began to dream.

Morning greeted Otto and Marzena with Joseph staring over them with a most unpleasant face. "Where did you get that hay? I suppose you find this funny. I with a hard bed and you two peasants with a bed of soft, fluffy hay."

Otto yawned and stretched his arms out wide. "I do recall you were the one who assigned our bedding for the night."

Marzena rolled over from under her blanket fortress. "That's true, Joseph. I heard your orders as well, and as peasants, we followed your orders. I should think that would delight you. Yes?"

"Words are wasted on you two. Fine then. Now back to business. Marzena, tell me. We are close to Chelmno, yes?"

"I suspect that if I am correct, this is the outskirts of town. We need just ask our way from here."

"Good then. Now quickly dress, and let's be off. If food is in our path, then it is welcomed because we won't be making any side journeys in search of it. Otto, I am nervous about our pursuers. Surely they are near. I dreamt of Bormann and his swift punishment. We are beyond delayed at this hour."

Otto stood up slowly, a sharp pain coming from his bandaged leg. He winced and gritted his teeth but made no sound. Pain would not win today. Joseph noticed and did not hesitate to inquire.

"Otto, your wound, it is not well?"

"I am afraid not, but it will not impede our way."

Marzena jumped from the cart fully dressed in her dry clothes, her tangled, frumpy hair bouncing into her eyes as she landed. "By all means, Otto, let us look."

"Very well, my nurses."

Otto slowly climbed from the cart and sat down on the damp ground. He unwrapped his dressing without incident except for the last piece, which had clung to his skin, blood and other fluids having glued it shut. As he started pulling the dressing away, the scab tore off and oozy thick strands stretched out like a spider web. He gritted his teeth tightly as a small bead of sweat started to form on his forehead. When at last he pulled the bandage completely off, a steady flow of puss, blood, and a thick, clear-like substance ran down his leg.

"This is not good, Otto. It's becoming infected."

"I know, Joseph, but I have no medicine for it in my medical kit and have but one dressing remaining. It's nearly impossible to keep it dry, free of dirt, sweat, and grime."

"Clean away what you can. Apply your last dressing, and we'll keep moving. It is the best we can do."

Otto nodded and quickly began cleaning his wound and wrapping a new dressing. Marzena helped Otto to his feet and packed away their blankets into his musette bag. Joseph slowly opened the door to the barn and stole a glimpse of the new day. He turned back to his comrades and motioned for them to follow. His eyes sank as he readied his machine gun and set his musette bag to a comfortable position.

"I'm afraid the rain is still with us." Joseph stepped from the barn and sprinted to the fence, hopping over it in one swift move. He glanced behind him and saw Otto and Marzena at his back. Joseph turned his head back towards the road. He could discern a number of buildings in the near distance, the makings of a town center. To his right and left were fields, barns, much like the one they had spent the night in, and farmhouses, all dotting the landscape. He thought that perhaps at another time it would make for a very picturesque painting.

"Marzena, I think we have come much farther than you suspected. I suggest we are closer than being on the outskirts. Would you agree now that the day is light?"

Marzena crawled up to Joseph with Otto limping behind her. She stretched her head out far and squinted her eyes.

"I see the steeple of the church, so I agree that we are closer than I had thought, but again, I am not sure what we are looking for."

Otto pulled the binoculars from Joseph's musette bag for a clearer look. "Hmm. I see townspeople milling about attending to chores. There are farmers to our right and, uh, nothing at our left. Perhaps we should seek out the farmers and inquire. The Chief said the word 'camp,' so I must assume that is our quest."

"Agreed. I remember the same words from him. I also suspect there is an army group nearby. Hurry then. We shall flank the town to the right and find answers."

The three scurried down the road, keeping low by following in a ditch that ran parallel. They came to a hedgerow meeting the road and turned right flanking the town. The rain was steady and soon altered the solid dirt of their travel route to a quagmire of mud sucking their every step. Otto tried his best to keep clean, but it was of little use. Mud caked his lower body from his knee down. His trousers had little cloth left, which allowed the mud and water to freely have their will to do what they chose.

Joseph stopped suddenly and held his hand up to his friends to halt. Something had caught his attention. Just on the other side of the hedgerow, he could hear someone whistling. The tune was well-rehearsed, a soft lullaby dancing in the rain. Joseph climbed up the bank of the hedgerow and silently peeked through the brush. He could see a small barn with its doors held wide open. A flickering light glowed from within. He could make out the shape of an old man hunched over an object as if repairing its health. He jumped back down and crept to his partners.

"We have company, but it is not the enemy. It is merely a farmer at work. Marzena, these are your lands, your people, and as such, perhaps you are best to find our answers."

Marzena nodded but did not speak. Without hesitation, she hopped up the bank, clawed through the brush, and jumped to the other side.

"Are we not going to cover her, Joseph? How will we come to her aid from this side?"

"You've fallen in love with her, haven't you, Otto? Is not one girl enough that you must add another? Yet I suppose if your Annie is gone, Marzena is a worthy replacement, no?"

Otto's face soured. "You have a troubled mind, Joseph. A very troubled mind."

"Calm yourself. I was just playing with you. I am quite sure your Annie is safe and dry from this rain. But yes, we shall stay hidden up top of the hedgerow at an angle where I can lay a burst of fire if needed. Hurry now. Let's position ourselves."

Marzena slowly approached the barn, her hair tucked behind her ears and her arms stretched out to her sides as if balancing delicately across a log. Her curiosity and suspicions were on full alert. She came to the door and stopped. The old man looked up from his work over his silver-rimmed glasses for a moment and then returned his eyes to his chore. He had a scraggly silver beard, a drastic contrast to the dark woolen jacket and dirtied trousers he wore. He was short, not much over five feet. His hands were rough, firmly grasping a wooden mallet. His work was methodical, stern, and bold. Pressed in an iron vice was a small wooden wheel with its spokes missing. An oil lamp set upon a sturdy, old, thick wooden table offered him light.

"I have no work, if that is what you seek," the old man stated.

"With all due respect, kind sir, that looks like work in front of you."

The man peeked from above his glasses at Marzena and smiled. "You're a very precocious little thing, aren't you? Strange, I do not recognize you. I would have thought I knew everybody in this town at this late age. What is it I can help you with? If it is not work, then surely you're in need of food. No?"

"My goodness, how horrible of me not to introduce myself. My name is Marzena Gorski of the eastern Prussian lands."

The old man stopped his work and put down his mallet. His eyes widened fairly surprised. "Eastern Prussia? Well, that is a long road from here. Perhaps the war has taunted you for a very long time, forced you from your home, yes? Without a papa and mama then? That seems to be the popular story these days. Never in history has there been another war that has done more harm to the very people the soldiers were meant to protect than this one. Well, good to meet you, young Marzena. My name is Stanislaw Pokorny, son of Henryk Pokorny. This is my farm. So tell me, Marzena, how have you come to be here?"

"Good to meet you, sir. I'm sorry, but I have not the time to tell stories of my journey. I have questions. We, I mean I am seeking a camp, such that it is. Do you know of this place?"

Stanislaw walked slowly from his work table and took a seat on an equally old work bench. He wiped his eyes and face with his worn hands and sighed. He turned to face Marzena with great curiosity. "Camp? Yes. You mean the Castle, as it is referred to by the German SS. Why do you seek such an evil and dangerous place?"

"I am sworn not to tell, but it is of great importance."

"I see your eyes hide secrets, and I doubt I will have at them." The old man grasped firmly the tops of his knees with his hands, flattening out his arms to support his upper body. His voice became more intense and serious. "The castle was an old, abandoned manor house altered by the German SS to do their evil exploits. It is a place of death and torture to the likes of which no one in this town speaks of. Our very own mayor challenged its use and met a horrible fate. Many a night, we could hear the screams and cries of those who were meeting a grueling end. Thousands and thousands have come and gone, to where not even their own ghosts could tell. The evil was not to last. The Russians invaded and liberated the town, forcing the SS to retreat. A small Russian force, not more than thirty men, now hold the manor. I have not been to the castle for more than five years. No townsfolk have, I suspect. This war has done enough destruction to this town by enough armies for our liking. No need to seek more evil. It is all behind us now. The war has come to its end. What will come of our lands is uncertain. I suspect it shall fall into the Bolsheviks' hands, a fate some may say is far worse than what we have ever endured."

"End? The war has ended? What day is this?"

"It is the eleventh day of May, if you must know. Word of the war's end has come by messenger to the Russians. They danced and celebrated for a fortnight at the town center. It was quite a show, I must say. I have no cares for the Russians. Just as evil as the Germans, I say, but at least that day they brought us a few smiles."

Marzena stood silent, her mind swallowing Stanislaw's news. She slowly became excited. "I made it. I made it alive."

Stanislaw stood up and walked over to a wooden cart behind him. He reached over and grabbed two loaves of bread. He tossed her the bread and walked back to his work table. Marzena was caught by surprise, nearly fumbling her catch. "What is this?"

"Bread for you and your companions hiding in the hedges."

"They're not very good at it, are they?"

Stanislaw shook his head with a grin, his words gentle and direct. "I understand you have your own way to follow, Marzena. So I will give in to your whims beyond good judgment. To get to the castle, start by passing through my farm and its fields to the south. You'll come to a hedgerow. On the other side of the hedgerow, the fields continue. Stay south and you'll find a narrow gauge railway to your front. Beyond that to the near horizon, you'll see a church. You'll notice the tall steeple at first. Just to its east is the castle, which becomes clearer as you approach. It's a stately, two-story brick building with many large windows. Cross the rail tracks and continue into another field still moving south. Ahead of you at the end of this field there will be a road. When you cross the road, a number of village buildings and doms will appear, but do not worry. Homeless wanderers, adult or child, are the norm these days. You'll likely go unnoticed from townsfolk. However, be on your guard. The Russian soldiers have commandeered a number of doms for barracks to your west, and you'll have to be watchful of patrols. Approach the castle from the southwest, which will position you at its rear, northeast corner. The entrance in front is grand with large doors. You'll know it when you see it. Where you stand now, the castle is nearly two kilometers from here."

"You are very kind, my friend, and I hope you are able to fix whatever it is on your work table."

"Before you go, Marzena, heed these words I give to you. Whatever it is you seek, I hope you find it. And once you do, let it go. It is then you will find your peace."

Marzena nodded. She turned from the barn and ran back to the hedgerow. She climbed up and over holding her loaves of bread with the tightest of grips. Otto and Joseph awkwardly crashed through the brush, meeting her in the field. Their eyes grew large, surprised with her bounty.

"Here, my friends, food." Marzena broke large pieces of bread and shared them with Otto and Joseph. Words were few. All that could be heard were sounds of chewing and attempts at eating with their mouths closed. Joseph chewed hard, trying to create a breath with which to talk. "Have you, um. It's so hard to, um, talk with just bread in your mouth."

Otto nodded but continued eating.

Joseph swallowed, finding his words now to be discernible. "Have you news for us of our travels?"

Marzena's eyes lit up, and she spit her bread from her mouth into her hands with excitement. "Yes! The war! It is over!"

Otto's knees went limp and he fought for a stance, but none came. He crumpled to the rain-drenched ground with his hands over his face. Tears welled and then flowed from his eyes. Not even the most torrential of storms could hide them. Marzena knelt over him and brushed his soaked hair with her hands, as Otto had done to her the previous night.

Joseph stood silent. His mind was still on his mission, focused and unemotional. "We have no time for weeping, my dear Otto. We must keep moving. Our war has not yet ended."

Otto turned from his side, pushing against the muddy earth to gain a hold. His eyes were reddened and swollen. Marzena grabbed Otto from around his back and helped him to his feet.

"I know, Joseph, but I do not cry for myself. I am crying for the good of man, that the pain has ended for the ones who've lived, so that they may all go home to warm beds and soft, feather blankets and begin putting behind them the hell they've endured. I am also crying for the dead, the boys hung from wire nooses, a woman thrown from a building, men dismembered piece by piece from exploding bombs, animals who never had a choice as they were torn inside out, babies left vacant in the streets yearning for their mothers' milk. It is they who I cry for."

Joseph bowed his head and turned from his friends. "Marzena, surely the old man shared a travel route for us. Please lead on."

Marzena walked up to Otto and lightly kissed him on the cheek. She stepped away and took to the point position. Joseph stepped forward and followed her. Otto wiped his eyes and nose. He took a bite of bread and took a step. Then another and another, slowly following behind.

Chapter 19

The three traveled the path given them by Stanislaw, trailed by a damp, relentless rain. Marzena took the lead and followed the fields, hugging the hedgerows, her feet not daring to venture into open country. She glanced upwards looking for the narrow gauge railway and the facade of the church steeple upon the horizon. Trees hid her view, only offering a quick peek. Joseph held ready with overly-sensitive reactions to his steps. He walked and turned like a whirl of dust spinning around and around through a dry field on a windy day. His trigger finger flinched at the slightest unrecognizable sound. Otto watched him go about his antics but cared little. He was lost in mind, his steps lazy and thoughtless. Tears still came to him.

Joseph suddenly stopped and held fast, motioning for Otto to halt. He could see Marzena wave her hand urging them to meet her. Joseph began to run and kneeled at her side. Otto continued walking. There was no urgency in his breathing.

"What is it you see, Marzena?"

"It is the church. There, beyond that tree line."

"Yes, I see it."

"We are near then. The castle should be in our view soon."

Marzena waved to Otto. "Hurry, Otto, your Annie awaits your presence."

Otto looked up but did little to speed towards them.

"What is wrong with him, Marzena? Why is he sluggish? He's been yearning for this so very long."

"The war has finally caught up to him."

"Yes. His running has stopped."

They waited for Otto to greet them but wasted no time in continuing to the castle. They pushed through a small field and a thick patch of brambles and briars to the side of the narrow gauge rails. Joseph came to the tracks first, following his routine of a thorough glance up and down the rails. To his left, he could discern a small station but noticed no activity. To his right, he saw nothing. Convinced the way was clear, he hurried to the other side. Marzena and Otto followed together, finding Joseph hidden in a small patch of brush facing towards the church.

Marzena knelt down next to Joseph. "What is it, Joseph? What do you see?"

"A road ahead surrounded by buildings, many more than I would have liked. The church is in full view, and I am offered a glimpse of a building I suspect is the castle."

"Not to worry, the old man said we would find little confrontation here, but he did mention Russian patrols."

"Perfect. You mention that now. Not even Otto would have withheld such important information."

Otto glanced at Marzena. His grin was telling. "It's true."

Marzena sneered. "Silly, grouchy boys."

Joseph came off his knee, and as he approached the road, his speed quickened. Otto and Marzena followed, and they all came to a full sprint, dashing across the road, not paying it any mind. They jumped over a row of brush lining the road and fell to a prone position, hidden in tall grass. Otto looked around carefully but could see nothing. Only the sounds of his friends breathing heavily held his attention. He lifted his head up and saw Joseph and Marzena doing the same. Surrounding them were tall trees in full spring splendor of luscious new growth. Otto jumped to his feet. Joseph followed, his MP-40 at its ready. Marzena rolled over and hoisted herself up, pushing on the ground with her hands.

Joseph called to Marzena. "What next, Pole?"

"Is he still calling me that, Otto?"

"He is, but I'm not quite sure why. He doesn't seem to be mad at you, which is his usual self. I believe it's his way of showing affection."

Marzena scrunched her face in confusion. "That's silly. Why would anybody show affection like that?"

"It's beyond me, Marzena."

"Although, it makes sense from an immaturity standpoint."

"I suppose. A flaw in communication skills. Yes?"

"Exactly."

Joseph stood calmly, his expression turning sour. "If you two are done, may we get on with the war? Marzena, lead on. Jew, stay here and rot."

Marzena maneuvered through the thick, tall grass under a shaded canopy, pushing aside brush as it met her path. She was greeted by a very unexpected, oppressive, and sinister fence. It surrounded the castle and was constructed of eight-foot high posts cut from pine trees, their branches stripped, leaving a mangled, decrepit ill sight. Rusted barbed wire stretched its height at six-inch intervals, creating a menacing, impenetrable wall from post to post.

Joseph stepped to the fence and placed his hand on a strand of barbed wire, running his fingers lightly across its rough surface. "I have a bad feeling about this place, Otto. It looks deserted. I see little life."

"It is raining, Joseph. Perhaps the people are inside. There must be people here or why else would there be a bus parked against the back of the castle? It belongs to somebody."

"I welcome your unclouded view, but something is not right here. Barbed wire has but one function, keeping things in or out. Let's move around to the front."

They followed the fence line further and continued tracking its shape, bringing them into clearer ground.

"I see a river in front. Did the old man mention it, Marzena?"

"He did not, but I know it as the River Ner. It runs close to where my aunty lived."

Joseph stepped into the open. "From here on, it is all or none, my friends. We are now exposed. There are no hedgerows to shield our steps, no tall grass to lay hidden, no forests to shadow our moves."

Otto and Marzena stepped from the brush and came to Joseph's side. Otto placed his hand on Joseph's shoulder. "Let's be done with it, then."

Joseph nodded, a grin admiring Otto's newfound strength. "Just when I think you've lost your will, Otto Kaufmann, son of Solomon, you manage to find your resolve. Most impressive. You would have made a good Hitler Youth."

"Sometimes I feel death hitting me on the side of the head, telling me it is not my time yet. Even death sometimes plays fair. And when I joke? Well that is me slapping the bastard devil in the face."

They scurried around to the front of the castle and were confronted by two large wooden gates. They lay open, blown from their hinges and leaning to an awkward angle. Barbed wire sprouted from its grasp into the air in warped shapes. A road entered the gates and circled around in front of the castle, spawning a concrete walkway leading up to a gallant stairway and beyond to a small veranda and the doorway to the castle itself. The castle door was destroyed, blown open into scrap, crumbled without further purpose.

Joseph hopped up the steps to the doorway, Otto following behind. "Seems the Russians entered in a hurry, not waiting for an invitation."

"Yes, and it seems the Germans made no haste in leaving."

"Quickly now, let us move inside and have our look. Otto, Marzena, we stay together; no wandering off."

They both nodded and followed closely behind Joseph's machine gun, well-stocked for use.

"Hand me those field glasses, Police Sergeant. It seems our visitors have arrived."

"Yes, Chief, and just about on time. Here, the lenses are somewhat dirty but still quite clear."

"Not to worry. Dirty is fitting for these subhumans."

The Chief raised the binoculars to his eyes and quickly adjusted its focus. "There's the Hitler Youth who's betrayed us and his country. Well, at least his Jew friend knows his place in line behind him. Looks as if they've taken on a straggler. No matter. The more the merrier. Now, you remember the plan, do you not, Police Sergeant?"

"Yes, of course."

"Very well. We must act fast. The Ivans are near. No gunshots. If we are quick, they'll do exactly what I expect them to do."

Joseph came to the front door and peered inside, listening for anything human. He stepped past the entrance just within the battered doors coming into a large foyer fitting for a castle. He motioned for his friends to follow. Otto stepped inside, and his heart sank. There was no disputing Joseph. The castle was abandoned. The architecture was indeed palatial despite its worn appearance. Walls were plagued with holes. Great towering ceilings were cracked and chipped, its pieces only to find rest upon a marred and splintered floor. Curtains and rugs were torn away, discarded and pushed aside against the sideboards. Wallpaper, peeled and torn, draped from the walls and littered the ground. Vacant was furniture or any semblance of life.

Joseph rested his MP-40 from its firing position. He turned and glanced at Otto. "I am sorry, dear Otto, we are too late."

Otto's heart sank upon eyeing the interior. He stumbled around the wreckage, wandering deeper inside. He looked for clues, writings scratched on the walls, anything Annie would have perhaps left him. He entered into the parlor, a grand room brightly lit by large windows that faced out over the River Ner. This room's fate was similar to the others, morbidly desolate, void of any existence. Joseph came into the parlor, looked around, and then exited. He found a

331

stairway and followed it to the second floor coming to a long hallway with rooms to both sides.

Marzena walked slowly to Otto's side, taking his hand. "We shall find her, Otto."

"That is kind of you to say, but it is with a dream and a wish that I hope. I fear the war has taken her. Come. Let us find Joseph. He was not to have explored on his own. Let us leave here. We go to the British now."

They walked from the room and quietly called to Joseph. "Pst! Joseph, where are you hidden?"

"Up here, Otto. I've discovered something quite unusual in one of these rooms."

Otto and Marzena quickly climbed the stairs, finding Joseph on a knee looking at the floor.

"What is it Joseph? What did you find?"

"Here, Otto, in my hand. A strange small pebble, gold in color but of an irregular shape. There are thousands of them on the floor."

Otto knelt down and picked up a handful.

"It is gold. I am quite certain of it. The High Court bathed in it, from jewel encrusted medals to the accoutrements that adorned a prized officer's presentation sword."

"What is it doing here?"

"I don't know, but nothing good can come from it."

"Nonsense. Take up a pocket full's worth. If it's gold, then we may have use for it later."

Marzena dashed into the room, interrupting, desperately seeking a voice. She was visibly shaken, hers eyes wide and frightened. "A soldier approaches the front gate."

Joseph sprang from his knees and followed Marzena to a window at the front of the castle. He glanced out and gasped. "How can that be? I heard it. The mine. It went off." Joseph stepped from the window. "Otto. It's the Chief. He is armed, approaching from the road and entering the gate. Quickly. We leave!"

Otto burst into the room; meeting his comrades as they were running towards the stairwell, he nearly bowled them over. They clamored for balance, skipping every other step as they vaulted down the staircase. Exiting the front entrance, they could see the Chief in plain sight, a wicked grin shooting across his face, his rifle at his front held firmly with both hands.

"Otto, Marzena, there will be no battle here. Quickly now to the east side, around the back from whence we came. We head north."

They jumped down the stoop and sprinted to the opposite side of the castle from the Chief. Otto stopped at a side entrance leading down into the cellar. A poorly painted sign lay at its entrance scribbled with the words 'To the baths.'

"Joseph, we will not be able to navigate the fence in time. It is too high, and the barbed wire will afford no safe passage. We'll be cut to shreds or shot trying. Let us hide in the cellar and confront him on our own terms, concealed in darkness."

"I am suspect. We don't know what will greet us down there. Besides, the Chief fancies grenades. What if he tosses a bundle of those down there?"

"Not with the Russians near. He knows this. His confrontation with us will be a quiet one, if it can be helped. Hurry, there is no time, Joseph."

Otto jumped down the stairs. The way was open leading into the dark. Joseph followed with Marzena close behind. Small windows of light flickered from fissures in the walls and from the floor above. They ran down a long corridor, stumbling along, and used their hands at their sides to provide balance and guidance. They passed side room after side room, opting for sudden glances instead of deeper investigation. Otto moved with abandon, unaware of the hall's end, abruptly smacking into a ramp laid across the width of the corridor. He fell to his knees but quickly recovered.

Joseph came to his side. "Where does this take us?"

"Up, I suppose."

"This doesn't look good."

"I am beginning to agree, but up we go."

They hustled up the ramp into pitch blackness. Otto reached out his arms in search of anything recognizable. He came to an end. To his left, he felt a wall. To his right a step away, the same. Joseph and Marzena bumped into him.

"We are enclosed, Otto."

"I see that. This room is small, encased by cold, solid walls."

Suddenly, a swoosh of steel doors slammed shut, its maddening crash echoing throughout the room.

Joseph's breathing labored. "We are now trapped."

The Chief was most satisfied. "See, I told you, Police Sergeant. All tidy and ready for a very quick and deadly transport as planned and without a shot. I rather miss those days, really. Now, is the mechanism hooked up?"

"Yes, my Chief."

"Good then. Now as planned, drive to the Rzuchowski Forest, not fifteen minutes from here. You know the road. There will be a number of fields within the forest. Go to the farthest field, and park at the very end out of sight. Our little travelers shall have succumbed by then. The Jew carries the satchel with Bormann's document. Waste no time with the bodies. I shall be waiting with the scout car at our meeting point. Do not delay, I fear the Russians swarming these lands."

The Chief patted the police sergeant on the back and darted off around to the front of the castle. The police sergeant opened the driver's side door of the bus and hopped inside. He pumped the gas pedal three times, priming the engine while turning the key to crank it over. The vehicle rumbled and roared being forced to life.

"Damn it, let's go. I have no time for your stubbornness." The engine coughed and sputtered, coming to a questionable idle shaking the vehicle. "Ha!" The police sergeant jammed the shifter into gear, and with a jittery imbalance of gas and clutch, the vehicle lunged forward.

"We are moving, Joseph."

"I see that, Otto. We must be in that bus."

"Boys? There is a foul smell entering from the floor. I feel a heated air pumping violently upon my legs."

"It's exhaust, Marzena."

Joseph and Otto sprang to the back of the bus and pounded on the door.

"It's no use, Joseph; we are sealed shut."

The police sergeant calmed and lit a cigarette. He exited the grounds and found his road heading towards the forest. The rain lightened, and the sun offered a hint of brightness. He switched on the windshield wipers, but nothing happened. "Damn heap of worthless junk. They can build a clever vehicle in which to gas people to death, but they can't make the wipers work. Idiots."

Laughing as he dragged on his cigarette, the police sergeant throttled the gas, knowing more exhaust would pump faster into the sealed compartment. He sped down the road passing homes, barns, and pastures. Farmers went about their business readying their fields for crops as foul weather had not delayed their work. He passed a small side street and was surprised by a Russian patrol vehicle at the stop. He scrunched down in the seat as he passed, hindering their view while checking his passenger side mirror for their follow. He became nervous and frustrated when they did not move.

"Damn you, Ivan bastards. Leave me alone and go the other way." His eyes strained and a small bead of sweat plowed down his temple. "Damn you Russians, move!"

The Russians turned away, and the police sergeant sighed a heavy relief. He wiped the sweat menacing the side of his cheek and regained his normal height in the seat.

"Good. Bastards. We should have annihilated you and your whore woman at Stalingrad." The police sergeant continued down the road unchecked. He slowed his speed and glanced out his window, looking for clues of his turn off into the forest. "There it is."

He spun the wheel and entered a dirt road muddied from the rain. The forest swept him up and shadowed his way. Little sun followed. He traveled the road, following its turns, grinding through gears, and braking when his speed determined. Off to his left, he passed a number of smaller side roads. He counted them as he lumbered by, slowing until he came to a larger opening. Greeting him was a much longer than wider field. He turned into it and drove to the far end. He stopped just within the tree line of the forest, the rear of the bus facing the open field, and shut off the engine. Silence followed but for songbirds enjoying a midday tune. He adjusted his holstered P-38, unsnapping the clasp and readying it for use. Checking his watch while lighting another cigarette, he noticed nearly twenty minutes had gone by since leaving the castle.

He opened his door and straightened his tunic, taking a long drag from his cigarette. "Twenty minutes seems long enough. This is such an inefficient way to dispose of people."

He walked to the back of the bus in a rather indifferent manner and placed his cigarette in his mouth, freeing both hands to unlock the doors. With one swoop, he pushed the heavy steel doors to their sides, coming to an abrupt crash and bouncing once until coming to a quieted end.

"Where's that dead traitor and his filthy Jew?"

Suddenly, a deafening barrage of machine gun fire erupted from inside the bus. The police sergeant buckled and shook as the rounds pelted his body, tearing up his uniform and adding a bright vivid hue of red to its drab presence. He choked and gasped, his cigarette falling to the ground as he continued to belch and cough. The echoes from the firing attacked the forest, disrupting the tranquility of the songbirds' play.

The Chief suddenly raised his head to the air, his eyes twitching, knowing very well what he just heard. "Damn them." He thrust the staff car into first gear and sped off in the opposite direction of the gunfire.

A metallic clatter answered from the floor as a spent MP-40 clip bounced to its end, having served its purpose. Quickly, another clip was fed into the weapon's receiver and the hammer slammed back for more work. The police sergeant lunged forward, stumbling until he fell to his knees. His head slumped over, and all that could be seen from inside the vehicle were his fingers, bloodied and tense, clenched over the ends of the floor. Slowly, they slid down, still trying to cling to life. They held no more and vanished from sight.

Joseph took a step into the light, his gas mask covering his face. "That traitor is right here."

Otto stepped behind Joseph and tore his gas mask from his face. They jumped from the bus and glanced behind them looking for Marzena.

"Where, uh, where is she?" Otto frantically climbed back into the vehicle and quickly found her lying tightly in a fetal position pressed up against the corner at the front of the bus. "Marzena! No!"

Otto dropped to his knees shaking profusely bringing her limp body to his chest. "Marzena, please, breathe! Joseph, she is not breathing. She is not breathing!"

Otto burst into tears, his voice cracked and wavered and his sight dimmed. Joseph hopped into the bus and stepped quickly to Otto, pulling him away from her. Otto fought hard, gripping her hand dragging her across the floor as Joseph tried to yank Otto away.

"Stop, Joseph! Stop! Please, she is not breathing. We can save her. Stop pulling me, Joseph!"

Joseph released his grip. Otto recoiled and again held Marzena tightly. Her face was buried in Otto's wool jacket. His tears welled and dripped on her tangled hair.

"Otto! Stop this craziness. She is dead! Did you not hear me? Dead. She did the job as promised and got us here!"

"No! We can save her!"

"Otto, in minutes there will be very curious Russian patrols on their way here interested as to why a full clip of machine gun fire sprouted into the air. We must leave at once. She is dead, Otto! Do you not hear me?"

"She is not dead."

Otto sniffled and coughed, his runny nose flowing down over his lips into his mouth and hanging off his chin. His breath acted as a spray that spewed into the air around him as he spoke. "Wha, what happened?"

"I don't know, Otto. Everything happened so very fast. It was dark. So very dark. We were all screaming and yelling, pounding on the walls. I, I couldn't hear and became disoriented, and I, I pulled the masks from my musette bag hastily, not thinking clearly. Everyone was yelling. It was terribly loud. I, I gave the mask to her and uh, I put mine on, but she, she must have given it to you. The mask. She must have realized there were not enough masks and gave hers to you. It was very dark, Otto. I, I didn't know what to do. I only had two masks. It was just always you and me. It was only supposed to be you and me. I didn't think I needed a third."

Joseph sank to his knees. He dropped his weapon, and it crashed dead to the floor. His heart begged for mourning, and he began crying. "It's all my fault, Otto. I'm so very sorry."

Otto reached out and put his hand on Joseph's shoulder. "It is not your fault, my dear Joseph. The war is to blame. It forces its evil upon us, and we are unwillingly torn from what is normal to face the abnormal. Even the very brave bow to its claws."

Otto eased his clenched hand and gently laid Marzena down to the floor. He brushed her hair back around her ears and sobbed. "She hated how she always had to brush her hair out of her eyes."

Joseph looked up at Otto, his tears glistening across his face. "Otto, Marzena, she whispered one thing to me in the dark. I could barely hear it over the whine of the engine and the desperation of our cries. She told me that she found the one thing she had been looking for and that's all she had ever wanted out of this life. She said she was happy to let it go."

Otto's frown straightened while he continued brushing Marzena's hair.

"Please, Otto. We must go. There is no time to bury her. We mustn't linger and be captured. It will not have served her purpose well."

"I shall not leave her in this monster. She deserves better. I'll find a quiet tree to lay her beneath its beauty."

Joseph wiped his eyes, rose to his feet, and reached out his hand. Otto glanced up at Joseph and then back to Marzena. He sniffled and shook, his heart pounding his chest. He grabbed Joseph's hand and held on tightly. Joseph leaned back and pulled Otto to his feet. He glanced back down at Marzena lying gracefully on the floor. He sighed and put his hands to his face, hiding his tears. Joseph reached down, grabbed his weapon, and jumped from the bus. Otto knelt down and gently picked Marzena up from the floor. He carefully climbed to the ground, and for the first time in a day, he winced at the pain shooting up his leg into his chest.

Otto glanced all around him, surveying the area. He hardly noticed the police sergeant lying face down, blood stains soaking the back of his torso. Otto walked towards the woods, staring into the treetops. He came upon a small, bushy fir tree, precious and innocent. He knelt down and gently placed her under the tree, brushing her tangled dirty blonde hair from her eyes. He gathered pine duff and placed it around her, creating a bed that embraced her tiny frame. "There Marzena, it is the best I can do. I will miss you dearly."

Otto knelt over her and kissed her forehead. A tear fell to her cheek. He softly brushed it dry with his thumb and quickly came to his feet. He sighed and sniffled. Then he turned and ran fast to find Joseph.

He came to the rear of the bus but could not locate Joseph and became frantic. "Joseph? Where have you gone off to?"

"I am down here, Otto."

Otto followed the sounds of Joseph's voice, but his eyes were still murky with tears that blinded his consciousness. He stepped forward and sank to his knees. In front of him was a sight like no other he'd ever experienced throughout the war. A ditch at nearly two-hundred meters long by ten meters wide and five meters deep lay at his feet. It was partially covered over with unearthed dirt except for the last twenty meters. Half-buried were thousands of mangled, distorted human forms, twisted and piled atop one another. Whether man, woman, or child, he could not tell them apart. The wind was at his back, guarding him against the horrid odor of decaying flesh and bones. He found Joseph in the ditch, down on his knees, his head bowed and silent. Otto climbed down the sandy bank, his tears welling up again. He slumped down next to Joseph, shedding tears, wasting to the sand at his knees. Sickness poured over him. Joseph's head throbbed, and his hands trembled as he slowly turned to face Otto. "It is true then, Otto. These places exist. My very own father is a murderer."

Joseph slumped sideways to the sand crying, his head resting next to what was left of a skull of a decaying corpse. Its flesh shrunk and tightened around dried raw bone. Its eye sockets hollowed and its jaw opened as if frozen in its final scream of terror.

Otto lost his breath and hunched forward, his arms reaching out to stable his lean. His hands crashed to the sand, and his stomach convulsed. He vomited repeatedly, choking and wheezing, panting for air. He wiped his mouth after spitting the last pieces of vomit. Joseph was curled up, his knees tight to his chest, his eyes reddened and closed. He gulped at delayed intervals for air as tears continued. Otto crawled closer to Joseph, coming to his side. He carefully placed his hand on Joseph's head and began to gently brush his hair back over and over in a soft, rhythmic stroke. Slowly, Joseph quieted and calm came to him. Calm came to the forest, and the songbirds' melody sweetened the air.

Chapter 20

Joseph wiped his eyes. "I know where those gold pebbles came from, Otto."

"Shh, everything is going to be okay. Come, let us leave here. We head north and then to the west. We are done with this mission. Let us find our freedom."

Joseph slowly nodded. The boys rose to their feet. Joseph picked up his machine gun and shook the sand from the side that had been facing the ground. "How are we to get there? We are eight hundred kilometers away, and we have no knowledge of the trains or where they run. We will not make it by foot, not any longer."

Otto glanced up at the bus, its cold, menacing facade still frightening. "That's how."

"You dare go back to that evil?"

"It is not my first choice, but it has no markings of any army and may go unnoticed. It has served the evil doings of warped minds taking the lives of the innocent. Let it now take two people to life."

Otto clambered up the ditch and walked to the back of the bus. He stepped over the dead police sergeant to shut the rear doors. Joseph met him at the other side of the bus, aiding him in swinging the doors to a close.

"Otto, I suppose you thought of how we are to drive this thing?"

"No, Joseph. I thought of how you are going to drive this thing."

"Really? You may wish to lend me a few inches in length to reach the foot pedals."

The boys hopped off the back of the bus and ran to the front. They swung open the doors and jumped in, Otto to the passenger side and Joseph to the driver's side. Joseph sat dwarfed in the seat, the steering wheel coming to eye level of the windshield and his feet dangling helplessly inches from the pedals.

"I told you, silly Jew. I'm too short for its operation."

"Here, sit on our musette bags to give you a better view out the window. Search below. Perhaps there is an adjustment for the seat."

Joseph reached under the seat and searched frantically for anything that would move it. He grabbed hold of a lever and tested its resolve. It moved freely rearward, thrusting the seat forward. Joseph sprang with its movement bumping his head into the steering wheel. "Ouch! Damn you, Otto."

"What? What did I do? Now quit stalling and get this thing moving."

"Hmm. Let me think. Well, I push in the clutch, um, this pedal on the left I think, and uh, then put the transmission into gear. Then, I ease up on the clutch as I press the accelerator and hopefully we move. Somewhere."

Joseph followed his procedure, and the vehicle lurched forward and stalled.

"Uh, Joseph, that's heading into the forest."

"Yes, I know. Now quiet and let me concentrate."

Joseph pushed in the clutch, grinding through the gears hoping to find reverse. Each new position he maneuvered the shifter proved fruitless as the bus lurched and stalled again.

"There's one last gear, Otto. Let us hope it moves rearward or we go through the forest."

Joseph jammed the shifter towards the seat and eased up on the clutch, pressing harder on the accelerator. The vehicle chugged and sputtered but moved to the desired direction and rolled up over a bump. "Serves him right for dying in the wrong spot."

Joseph threw the shifter back to the front, and following his last movement, the vehicle lunged forward. It whined and screamed as Joseph awkwardly shifted to second gear. Otto stared wide-eyed out the passenger window, his heart hollow and numb. "We shall never forget such a place exists, Joseph. The world must know of this. Every soul here will be mourned for eternity."

Joseph said nothing. A small tear welled up in the side of his eye. "Let us first live to tell someone." He came to the end of the field, and pressing his foot on the brake, the bus came to an abrupt halt.

"What are you doing, Joseph?"

"Where am I going? We do not have a map of this region, just a field map of military travel routes. It will not supply us with small roads such as this."

"I have my compass, which you are sitting on. It shall be our guide. As to how to leave this forest? I'd follow those fresh tracks in the muddy road that appear to have been made by this vehicle."

Joseph pulled both musette bags out from under him. Otto quickly dumped the contents of the bags and grabbed his compass and Joseph's map. He stuffed everything back inside and shoved it back under Joseph. Otto studied the map and worked his compass.

Joseph brought the vehicle to a slow speed following the tracks from the forest. They twisted and turned as the police sergeant had done, finally coming to the asphalt.

"Now where, navigator?"

"Left. Once we find a more northerly route, we'll be making a right."

"North, Otto? Towards the Baltic Sea? But that is a ways from where we are to go."

"Yes, but we must skirt Berlin to our immediate west. All eyes are upon it. A large flanking maneuver around will afford us more safety. I'll work up a more detailed route once we've settled at speed and danger is behind us."

The day lingered at a snail's pace. The sun fought with the clouds and rain and yearned for summer. The roads held vacant except for farmers going about their business. The bus passed without incident with not so much as a head turning toward them.

Otto sat quietly. Tears would come and then wane as his thoughts drifted in and out with pictures of those in his heart. He began to accept they were lost. Joseph held steady at the wheel, all his efforts focused on keeping the steel monster wrapped around them on a straight course.

"Otto, we are low on petrol. I am at a loss as to where we shall find it." Otto's attention was suddenly captured by something they had just passed on a side road.

"Then we are in luck. We passed a tank not a second ago."

Joseph shot Otto a distressing look. "Was it a moving tank?"

"No, Joseph, it seemed quite still. Its main gun was blown apart, and it was missing a track."

"And you observed all of this as we passed?"

"For five years, my life counted on such observations. I am certain of its status."

"Very good, then. We will have its fuel."

Joseph braked heavily and downshifted the bus. He awkwardly pulled the vehicle around and sped back to the road as Otto directed.

Otto pointed as they approached the tank. "There."

"I see it, Otto. Hmm, yes. It looks quite still."

Joseph pulled around to the back of the tank, hiding the bus's facade from view by anyone traveling down the main road. They hopped out of the bus and slowly approached the ominous steel machine.

"It's a Panther Ausf. D, Otto, one of the German army's best medium tanks, built to combat the Russian T-34. Boy we whipped a few of those back in the day."

"I'm surprised it lasted that long. The Russians had swarms of those T-34s."

"Yes, true, and this one's in very sad shape. It still has its winter camouflage paint."

"It never made it back from its retreat, I suspect."

"Agreed. It looks like it's been here for quite some time. This one seems to have had the hands of the Russians to blame for its demise. As you observed, its main gun has been blown apart perhaps with a few grenades shoved down its barrel. It's missing its machine guns. Seems not much is left of it. Well, too bad for them. Hopefully, its fuel tank has a little left for us."

Joseph slung his machine gun around to his back, freeing his hands to climb up the side of the tank. Otto watched both Joseph and the road for any curious intruders. Joseph struggled to the top, obviously not thoroughly trained for such a feat. Once aboard, he knelt down on the rear engine deck of the tank to locate the fuel tank filler caps. He crawled closer to the rear of the tank and located the two cylinders that emerged from the center plate with two round lids fitted to them. Underneath these lids, he found the filler caps, one for petrol and one for radiator fluid. "I've found the fuel tanks, but I'm going to need the lock key to access them. Hmm, now where will I find that tool on this mess of a tank?"

Otto glanced away from the road, finding an opening to counsel Joseph. "To the rear of the tank on both sides of the exhaust are storage bins. Inside, you should find a mechanics bag with tools and perhaps the lock key. Seems you should know that."

Joseph sat up with a surprised look and glanced at Otto below him. "And how on earth did you know that?"

"Observation, my dear Joseph. Actually, it was a guess. I remember some time ago back when I was talking with this major of an army group. I noticed a mechanic fumbling around in the engine compartment of a tank just like this one. Boy, he was cursing up a storm. Well, he kept barking orders at his crew to get him this tool and get him that tool. His crew kept muddling around inside a storage bin not unlike this one each time an order rose to the air. It was quite amusing, now that I think of it."

Joseph sneered and withdrew his head out of sight. Otto switched his focus back to a steady eye on the roads.

"So, Otto, you being so smart, how are we to draw petrol from the fuel tanks?"

Otto glanced up at Joseph again, raising to his tippy toes. "You'll have to siphon it out. Again, a guess, but there should be spare hoses of all sorts in the storage bin. Then you'll need to stick it down until it hits bottom. The hard part is to suck with deep breaths until the fuel comes to your lips. Be quick to close your mouth and then stuff the hose into a fuel can or whatever you can find."

"Well, we're in luck. There are a few petrol cans up here already. Seems someone had the same idea but did not know how to access the fuel tanks. Not like I do."

Otto shook his head in disbelief. "Oh, my dear Joseph, how you amuse me."

Joseph reached over and unlatched what he thought were the storage bins as described by Otto. He reached down and pulled a large, heavy, dirt-encrusted cloth bag from inside. He dumped the contents on the engine deck, spread them around, and searched for the lock key. "Ah. There it is."

Joseph grabbed the key, inserted it into each lock of the lids, and turned with all his might. The locks were stubborn but were suddenly forced free. He pulled the lids off, exposing the filler caps, and then rotated and opened both caps, not sure which one held fuel. He knelt down closer to sniff each hole and retreated his head in haste with a grimaced look. "That certainly smells like it."

Joseph leaned back over and searched the rest of the storage bin for a hose. It was empty except for some oil-soaked rags and random personal belongings, a pair of socks and an officer's toiletry bag. He crawled to the other side of the Panther and opened the second storage bin. He reached down inside a few times, and with luck, he pulled everything from hoses, bolts, and a number of small spare parts that he could not identify. He discarded everything but the hoses, looking each one over carefully for the right fit. Three of them were too short for the job, and the other was of a larger diameter. "Perfect."

He forced the large hose down into the fuel tank as far as he could, readying the fuel cans at his side. He opened his mouth as wide as possible and began drawing air into his lungs. Immediately, he gagged and coughed, spitting out dust and dirt.

Otto grew anxious to help and slowly climbed aboard. His leg wound caused excruciating pain, and he fought to control its annoying presence. His bandages had all but tattered and left gaps exposing its grotesque status. He knelt next to Joseph and made ready with the fuel can. Joseph sucked harder and harder until finally a flow of fuel filled his mouth and splashed his face. He hastily shoved the hose into the fuel can, and spurt out the putrid liquid from his mouth. "Yuck! My word, that is absolutely terrible."

"It's not for drinking, Joseph."

"Funny, Jew. I'm hopping off this thing to watch the road. When the cans are both filled, drag them to the edge of the tank and lower them down to me."

Otto offered his nose to the air. A foul smell caught his attention. "There's a dead animal somewhere around here."

"No need to search. It's the crew. They've been blown to a million pieces all over the inside of the tank."

"Seems the Russians had many grenades that day."

"Let us pray they have no more."

Otto turned and noticed two more petrol cans near the turret. "What about those cans over there, Joseph?"

"They are riddled with bullet holes and are of no use."

Otto nodded and returned his attention to filling the petrol cans. Joseph slipped down from the tank and swung his machine gun around to a more prepared position. He walked to the other side of the road across from the tank which offered a better angle for observation.

"It will be dark soon, Otto. We should discuss what to do next. Drive or rest. I expect a seven hour journey to our destination."

Otto motioned for Joseph to come assist him in lowering the fuel cans to the ground. "We drive, Joseph."

"Agreed. Then let us go."

Joseph swung his machine gun to his back and grabbed the cans of fuel from Otto as he lowered them. He held one in each hand and carried them to the bus. Otto slid down from the Panther and scurried next to Joseph.

"I suppose you found a funnel from the storage bin as well?"

"Yes, Otto, we German soldiers are very thorough, you know, and always thinking ahead."

Joseph handed him a dented steel funnel. Otto opened the fuel cap, inserting the funnel into the bus's fuel tank. They emptied one can and placed the other can inside the back of the bus for reserve. They hopped back into the bus, and Joseph brought the vehicle to life. He jammed the gear shifter into first and pressed down on the gas. The engine whined, not agreeing with the intended direction. The bus lunged forward, and they came to the main road. Joseph spun the wheel with all his might, and the beast was forced into a fast, sharp right. Joseph flowed through the gears, coming to a near highway speed.

Otto consulted Joseph's map and his own compass, planning their route.

"I've chosen our path, Joseph. It shall be direct and swift. We are to go north from here to Torun and then west to Szczecin on the German and Polish border. From there, we drive through Luneburg on to Bremen. Depending on the British Army's advance, I suspect we shall be in their secure hands at that point."

"And what of the Chief? What of his advance?"

Otto sat silent before answering. Joseph glanced from the wheel at Otto with concern. "He will find us, Joseph."

Otto turned his head from Joseph and faced straight ahead, staring out the front of the windshield and down an empty road. Joseph slowly withdrew his eyes from Otto. He clenched his hands tighter around the steering wheel and exhaled.

The vehicle sped forward as the sun fell, its light fading into a dark world. The rain and clouds had vanished, leaving room for stars to dance across the heavens. Otto had fallen asleep, his body pressed against the side of his door, his head held steady by the glass. His breathing was light but labored. Words from dreams came to his lips, a slurred speech, nothing discernible. Joseph paid him no mind. He fought his own exhaustion, his own demons sharing their place in his thoughts.

The night wore on. If danger was near, they had no intention or will to attempt to meet with it. Joseph stopped the bus, repeatedly consulting Otto's travel plan written down for him on his map. They had passed Torun and were heading west to the German border. Joseph expected resistance coming into Germany. The Russians would have established their front at its borders. "Enough of this. My mind is ill at work. I need rest."

Joseph searched for a place to pull over and hide the bus. He came to a pasture to his left with an opening, an ancient stone wall with a wooden gate. He slowed the vehicle and pulled off the road in front of the gate. He jumped from the bus, ran to the gate and jiggled the latch free, pushing the gate forward. It creaked and hobbled, bouncing upon its hinges as it came to a shuttered halt. Joseph hopped back into the bus and guided the beast into the pasture. He searched for a hedgerow to hide the bus's facade and noticed a clump of trees to his left. He pulled around behind them and convinced he had the trees cloaking the bus, he switched off the engine. He sighed and glanced over at Otto, who was still mumbling in his sleep.

"You are smarter than I give you credit for, Otto, leaving me to navigate this thing while you find rest." Joseph knelt closer to Otto. He sensed something strange about him.

"No matter. He is asleep, as I soon shall be." Joseph reached for his musette bag and retrieved his blanket. He covered his body tightly and leaned back against the door. He exhaled in relief and shut his mind to the world for the night.

Chapter 21

Joseph opened his eyes and jumped from his seat startled. "What the..."

Otto awoke to Joseph's commotion. "What? What is it? Are we dead?"

"No. "It's a beast trying to eat us."

Joseph scuttled away from his door and jumped on top of Otto. He flapped his hands inside his blanket, trying to hide the beast's stare. Otto wiped his eyes, opened them wide, and then squinted, trying to discern what was causing the ruckus. He started laughing, tears welling up into his eyes.

"It's a cow, you silly Hun."

Against Joseph's window was a cow chewing on grass, its hot breath and nose mucus slimy on the glass. It had a most inquisitive look, perhaps wondering what these two intruders were doing parked on its breakfast.

"Very funny, Jew." Joseph pulled the blanket from his face, revealing a sour look.

"Well, I suppose much funnier than the look on that farmer approaching us. Where on earth are we, Joseph?"

Joseph quickly slipped back to his side of the vehicle and turned the key, coming onto the throttle hard. "Oops! I just remembered. I didn't close the gate after coming to this camp."

Joseph jammed through first gear, coming to second with a whine. They sped towards the gate, which had indeed been left wide open and was now surrounded by a large herd of cows meandering freely on both sides of the stone fence.

"Well, I have no retort worthy enough for this, my dear friend. You have certainly outdone yourself."

"Your accolades fall short. Now please hush as I try to, uh. Oh, no!"

Dodging cow after cow and spinning the wheel a hard left, Joseph finally maneuvered the bus out of the gate and down the road. Cows sprinted left and right clearing a path, their eyes white with panic.

Otto sat back, his head pressed against the rear of the seat. Calm slowly found his heart as his giggles owned to his face. "Well, that certainly was a very unexpected morning."

The sun greeted them and followed their day, but the way was not without incident and would not find them rest. They were forced to flank many smaller villages and bridges, having spied Russian patrols and troops from unrecognized countries. Such maneuvers ate up their fuel, requiring dangerous stops to siphon fuel from unlucky civilian or military vehicles. Time passed slowly as the hours tested their safety.

Otto fought the progressing and agonizing pain of his wound. He faded in and out of sleep, his head constantly beading with sweat. Joseph noticed a sign on the side of the road and suddenly pulled the vehicle to a stop with an inquisitive look on his face. He pulled the map to his eyes, not believing what he was reading,

"Neubrandenburg? But that's, that's not possible. Otto, we are in Germany."

Otto glanced over from his relaxed, slumped position. "Oh, well, that's lovely."

Joseph placed his map on the seat and slid towards Otto. He placed his hand on Otto's forehead, retreating it quickly. He rubbed his thumb against his fingers, his eyes becoming alarmed.

"My dear Otto, you are with fever." Joseph knelt down and sniffed Otto's wound. He grimaced, blowing air from his mouth. "It smells of rotted cheese. This is not good at all. It's infected for sure."

Joseph grabbed his blanket from his musette bag and covered Otto. He slid back to the wheel and roared the vehicle back to life. After a few awkward shifts, they were back to speed. They came to an intersection, and Joseph noticed smoke billowing to the north. He pulled the bus over and jumped from his seat, grabbing his binoculars and hurrying to the front of the vehicle. He climbed up onto the hood and peered through the glasses.

"Germans. Damn." He lowered his arms and huffed. He glanced through the windshield at Otto, who was half conscious in the passenger seat. Otto shivered and spasmed. His eyes were drooped and worn, his skin yellowed and matted. Joseph raised his field glasses for another look.

"Surely that army group is in the midst of a fight, a fight with the Russians, I suspect. One that's not in our plans. How unfortunate. Two army groups I wish not to tangle with. It would be easy to skirt past them and continue to friendlier faces. Damn, what to do?"

Joseph glanced back down at Otto and quickly jumped from the hood, climbed back into the bus, and slammed the door shut. He threw the bus into first gear and lurched forward, spinning the bus north towards the Germans. As he approached, he could recognize armor and battle positions. His eyes grew alarmed as a group of soldiers appeared from nowhere in front of him, heavily armed and ready for war.

"Hören Sie sofort auf!" ordered one of the soldiers.

Joseph slammed the brakes, the bus squealing to a forced stop as commanded. The soldiers swarmed the bus from all sides. Joseph raised his hands off the wheel high over his head and shouted. "Nicht schießen! Nicht schießen! Hitler Jugend!"

He frantically rolled his window down only to be greeted with rifle and machine gun barrels. Off to his left upon a knoll, he recognized the menacing facade of an MG-42 cautiously eyeing his every move. He dared not get out.

A soldier approached, swatting his comrades' weapons from the window to greet his new captive. "You are not our re-enforcements then, are you? Surely this bus is loaded with those ready to fight. Speak quickly now."

Joseph did not hesitate to answer. "No. I mean, yes. There is only us, two Hitler Youth, sworn to uphold our allegiance to the Fatherland."

"Fatherland? That has long since passed in our minds. This war is now fought to protect our homes. It is a fight much more personal than one's country."

"With all due respect, Sergeant, what unit is this?"

"Unit? My boy, there are no more units, or regiments, or divisions, or ranks, or soldiers. There are only those who now protect our woman and children." The soldier pointed off into the distance as his troops slowly withdrew their arms. The MG-42 eased its poise, its gun crew swiveling its stinger to patrol elsewhere.

"Look down the road past your windshield. Do you see where the hills on both sides flatten and the fields lay quiet? There in the middle lies in wait the whole Second Belo Russian Army. Soon they will come this way, storm through those fields and down this road, laying waste to anything German. We are to die. As we surely will and as you surely will for the good of our people. Enough talk. Come now. You are armed? Yes? I see that machine gun at your side. You fight now with us to a great and mighty end."

Joseph swallowed hard. "Yes. I will fight, but my comrade, he is wounded and has fallen ill. He needs medicine."

The sergeant swiftly turned back, his eyes grew dark as he reached into the window and grabbed Joseph by the front of his shirt, raising him to his face. His voice was hard and unwavering.

"Wounded and ill? We are all wounded and ill. I have four hundred souls spread too thin on a long front, all wounded and ill. Boys

354

half your age and men six times it. All wounded and ill. Your comrade shall fight or he shall be shot."

The sergeant released his grip and turned away. "Hurry now. Do follow shortly, dear child. The reaper has plans for us."

Joseph slowly opened the door and slid his weapon from the seat. Eyes were upon him, judging his moves, waiting for a reason to intervene. He slowly continued to shoulder his machine gun as he walked around to the passenger side door. He turned the handle and caught Otto as he slid sideways from the seat.

"I have you, Otto. Quickly now. We must go. I promise to get you medicine, but please help me. Do not fight my assistance."

Otto's speech slurred and his body struggled to stand. A soldier walked up to Joseph with a watchful scowl. "What is the matter with him? He can barely walk. How is he to hold a rifle?"

"That is no concern for you, Corporal. I shall follow the sergeant's lead and position him to fight. Be thankful he is on your side this day."

The corporal sneered and walked off with the rest of the soldiers. Joseph stood holding Otto up, lost as to what to do next. He knew the sergeant would be back, barking orders and giving directions.

"I have a plan, Otto. Trust me on this and follow along. I will dig you a trench and hide you in it. I will tell the sergeant I have equipped you with a mine and that when the Russians advance, you will rise from your hole and seat the mine on a tank, sacrificing your life for the greater good. I should think he will fancy that. He will be too pressed to check up on my ruse. Then, Otto, I will leave you to find medicine and hopefully return."

Joseph held Otto tightly, walking him towards the front. His heart sank as he passed the ranks of old men, bandaged, coughing, their heads barely lifted, and boys with cruel wooden splints, unclothed, using their rifles as crutches. The sergeant had been honest in his description. This was no army. It was a waiting room for the dying. Joseph stopped near a small cluster of bushes not thirty yards from the field and the open country where the enemy loomed. He lay Otto down and covered him with his blanket, placing his machine gun at his side with the intention to fool any passerby into thinking Otto was armed and willing.

"Hmm, seems I have not quite thought this out clearly. To dig a trench one needs a shovel. Well, I need to find one. Rest easy, Otto. I shall be but a minute."

Otto said nothing. His murmurs were muddled and disjointed. Joseph ran up and down the battle line asking all he met for a shovel or any tool with which to dig, but there were none. He was breathing heavy and became frantic. He saw a group of soldiers farther to the rear busy at work doing something to the ground. He ran up to them, stopping abruptly at the shadow of a soldier with his back to him. Joseph smiled when recognizing the tool the soldier held in his hands.

"Excuse me, Corporal, may I borrow your shovel? I need it to build a trench for protection. I swear to return it at once."

The soldier stepped aside revealing his identity. "A trench? Sound protection? Strange. That's what these naive minds believed before I was tasked with burying them. A false sense of safety, I would suggest, but why not? The shovel is yours at the end of my task."

Joseph froze, nearly tumbling over with surprise. In front of him were hundreds of fresh graves, the dirt on top marking with newly moist and darkened soil their new inhabitants.

"Forgive me, but you wear a red cross armband. You are a Krankenträger? Yes?"

"Yes, and what of it? Speak. I have little time for your questions."

"My friend, he is ill. He needs medicine. Please come to his aid."

"Sick? Look around you, boy. We are all sick. It would be better to be these poor, quieted souls you see before you."

"Yes, but he needs medicine. Please. You must come. Come at once."

Joseph reached out and grabbed the medic's hand. He turned and pulled him as he furiously stomped off in the direction in which he had left Otto.

The medic retracted his hand hastily. "I shall do no such thing. I have no medicine for you, your friend, or anybody. Now be off. And here, take the shovel, dig your hole, and hide yourself. War will be at our throats again soon."

The medic threw the shovel to the ground before Joseph and walked away. Joseph eyed him at each step. "I have gold, medic."

The corporal stopped, his foot slowly pivoting, his hips swiveling as his head came around to stare down at Joseph. "Gold, you say? How much? Where?"

Joseph reached into his musette bag and pulled out a sizable leather pouch imprinted with the lumps of small irregular shapes of gold he had found back on the floor in the castle. "Here. It is yours. A trade for the medicine you say you don't have."

Joseph tossed the bag to the medic's feet. The medic smiled, stooped over, and slowly raised his head, gazing at his new treasure. "Show me to your comrade."

Joseph turned and started running back towards Otto. He glanced back and noticed the medic walking at a snail's pace. He waited for him to catch up and then ran ahead. Again he stopped and waited. "No sense of urgency from these soldiers. No wonder we lost the war."

The medic caught up and passed Joseph. "Your running will only tire you for our next battle. No sense rushing your impending end. Find patience, boy."

Joseph and the medic found Otto now scrunched up in a fetal position and shaking terribly. The medic knelt down and put his hand on Otto's forehead.

"He is burning with fever. He will not last."

Joseph dropped to his knees next to the medic, frantic. "But you can cure him, yes?"

The medic said nothing. He examined Otto up and down, noticing his leg. He pulled the rest of the tattered bandages away and quickly recoiled. "The leg is gone. Infection has set. We need to take it."

Joseph winced at the thought and pleaded. "No, you must find another way. How will we run together again? There must be another way. Please. Say you can do something."

The medic sank back resting on his heels. He sighed and glanced at Joseph. "There is another way. I was given medicine from another medic who was transferred to my unit. It's American medicine. Penicillin, they call it. Very powerful, I'm told. I was saving it for myself, if you must know, but what of my life these days? I can't see a clear and happy path to a known future. My friends, my comrades, my division. All gone. My death is near. Who knew it would come to this?"

The medic reached into his rucksack and pulled a small, narrow tin. He clicked it open and drew from it a small syringe. He pulled the cap covering the needle and knelt down over Otto, pulling his arm from his coiled position. He removed his belt from his trousers and strapped it around Otto's arm, creating a tourniquet to raise a vein. Joseph moved closer, watching curiously as the medic worked. The medic positioned the needle horizontally to Otto's arm at the appropriate angle to inject, just enough to break the skin and enter the vein at the correct depth. He held Otto's arm tightly and plunged in the needle. Otto did not react.

"There. I promise you nothing. He may live or die, either from reacting to the medicine or from his wound should it not work."

The medic reached back into his rucksack and withdrew a roll of bandages and a packet of sulfa powder. He unsheathed his dagger and went to work on Otto's leg. Joseph flinched at the sight of the dagger. He knew its purpose. The medic began scraping the wound removing maggots. "They have done their part eating the dead flesh, but they have no use now."

He opened the packet and spread the sulfa powder along the wound and then tightly wrapped it with the fresh bandages. He fastened his belt around his waist, returned his knife to his side, and slung his rucksack around his shoulders.

"There. I have done my part. Farewell, my young friend." The medic rose to his feet and walked off.

Joseph watched him vanish into the woods and then quickly made work of the shovel. His plan was not yet finished. He dug ferociously, building a fine trench that was wide, long, and deep enough to adequately cloak a boy. He rushed to a small woodlot and dragged back a number of small logs to create a roof. Tearing limbs from fir trees completed his ruse.

"Very good. I think you should like this fort, Otto."

Joseph gently picked Otto up and helped him into the trench. He sat him up, laying his back against the dirt wall of the trench, and covered him with his blanket. "I know you won't like this, Jew, but here's a helmet. The medic left it behind by accident, I suppose. Better to protect your head now than leave it lying on the ground empty." Joseph strapped the helmet to Otto's head and climbed from the pit.

"Now don't go meandering around, Otto. Stay put. I am off to find that sergeant and offer him my services. I promise to be back. I mean, how else will you survive without me?"

Joseph grabbed his machine gun from the ground and ran off to find the sergeant. He hopped down the German defenses, moving from crater to crater and trench to trench. He happened upon a group of soldiers huddled in a huge bomb crater, one large enough to have been made by an aerial attack. Sitting on the opposite side of the crater, he recognized the sergeant and went to his side. He shouldered his weapon and knelt down next to him.

"I have done as you asked. My comrade is ready to fight."

The sergeant looked surprised, as if not remembering Joseph. His breath was foul and wreaked of schnapps. "Fight? Yes, we shall

all fight and go to the almighty thereafter." The soldiers at his side all sneered, twisted grins cracking their faces.

"I am glad you are to fight, boy. Good. I have a special job for you. I need a forward observer. My first one, uh, second? Third? My sixth one was just killed. No matter, just go into the field as far as you can without being caught or shot. The Russians do horrible things to you if you get caught. They may even look to cut your manhood off then."

The sergeant started laughing uncontrollably and bowled over to his side. Tears found his eyes as he tried to right himself. His comrades joined in, their cackling echoing down the lines on both sides. Unknown faces popped up from trenches and foxholes, wondering with leery feelings what the raucous was all about.

Joseph was expressionless, not understanding the sergeant's humor, but he did understand his new post. The thought was not laughable. He rose to his feet and faced the expanse of the field. He looked down at the sergeant, who was still laughing quietly to himself, and then back at the field. He swung his weapon to a ready position and stepped towards the field.

The day had aged, night hinting its presence. Smoke lingered and swirled from burning bomb craters and destroyed vehicles, all complimenting the day's mood. Crows squawked, adding a gruesome chorus of misery and doubt. Buzzards circled high in the sky, curiously eyeing the rotting humanity below. They would wait patiently until the cries of battle had ceased.

Joseph entered the knee-high grass of the field and crouched low. He consulted his binoculars to find a scouting point to place himself, hopefully one providing safety. He could not see the enemy on the horizon. All seemed calm. To his right, he noticed a small footbridge made of fieldstone. It was not six feet high and had two arches shadowing a narrow, dried-up stream bed below.

"That should do nicely. Looks as though there would be just enough room for me to hide myself while still offering a rather good point for observation."

Joseph stepped forward slowly, each move calculated and mindful. The never-ending threat of Russian snipers plagued his mind. He had no doubt they would be crafty, hidden here and there. A constant menace. Joseph moved like the wind through the field, not crushing or bending the grass but flowing through it. It left his presence quite unnoticed.

He was so effective in his stealth that he happened upon two Russian forward observers sitting and talking just inside of the footbridge, tucked under the farthest arch. They seemed relaxed, their field glasses around their necks, cigarettes in hand. Joseph crouched silently on the ground just across the dried-up stream bed from where they were positioned. I should have known this would be an occupied spot.

Joseph brought his weapon to his cheek and gently pulled the trigger as a short, violent burst erupted through the grass, its demonic scream echoing across the field and down the valley. The Russian observers hardly flinched at the impact. Blood spewed from their mouths as they flopped sideways headfirst to the ground.

"There, now it's unoccupied."

Joseph sprang to his feet and hustled to the footbridge. He crawled through the first arch to the other side, watching for other enemy soldiers either hurrying their escape or searching for the cause of the commotion. The way was clear. He turned and stopped inside the middle of the arch and found an uncluttered perch in which to settle.

"I sincerely trust my little disruption will not pique anyone's interest."

Joseph pressed the magazine release button and ejected the magazine. He checked his ammunition, blowing dirt away from the inside of the magazine and the bullets. Satisfied he had firepower left, he pushed the half-empty magazine up into its receiver and drew the bolt lever back. He grabbed his musette bag and reached inside, feeling for his spare clips. He counted six.

Joseph secured his weapon and slung his musette bag to his shoulders. He had been still long enough. He raised to his feet. If the sergeant indeed cared for intelligence, he would have it. He crouched low and exited from under the bridge. He crept past the dead Russian observers, now a home for swarming flies interested in their filth. The sun fell closer to the other side of the world. He would have to be quick. He raised his field glasses to his eyes and surveyed the field beyond. He could discern artillery emplacements along an impenetrable line speckled with well-concealed armor. Scurrying about were infantry uncountable from this view. It did not matter. They were clearly outnumbered. He lowered his arms and shoved his binoculars back into his musette bag.

"There's too much action on their front. They will be attacking soon. Time to go."

Such warning signs had alerted Joseph's eyes, but the timing was poor. A sudden eruption ripped through the early evening sky, followed by another and another. A series of blistering rockets screeched overhead, yearning to vaporize their intended targets. Joseph dove to his belly, holding his ears with both hands, his head facing the ground. He fought for breath as rocket after rocket ruled the skies. Then he heard it. A repetition of explosions followed, never-ending as they devoured the horizon on the German lines. The torture would not lessen as hours passed with more of the same. It was a vicious onslaught to the likes Joseph had never experienced.

Joseph lay frozen, his mind in turmoil, thinking, trying to draft a plan. The noise was deafening and clouded his thoughts. He knew they would be coming. They always did after a hard pounding of the enemy's front, but his options were thin. To run back now would be suicide. The bombing would surely find him. To fight would be foolish at best. It was not an option. He would have to hide or perhaps trick his enemy.

Joseph raised to his knees and crawled to the dead Russians, now stiff and bloated. He grabbed the one soldier by his hair and lifted his head. Flies buzzed all about, angered by the disruption. Joseph held his hand under the Russian's mouth and pulled his head forward. A pool of blood still fluid and warm poured from his mouth into Joseph's hand. He quickly rubbed the blood all over the back of his neck and head, covering it as thick as he could. He let the soldier go, his stilled body hitting the ground with a hard thump. Joseph positioned himself just in front of the Russians and lay down flat onto his belly, exposing the back of his newly bloodied head and neck. He placed his machine gun to his side in an odd position and spread a light veil of dirt and grass on top of it. For his final act, he spread his arms out wide and clenched his fingers as if gnawing at the ground. He closed his eyes and waited. His thoughts gathered, and he hoped for Otto's safety.

The bombing ceased except for a few sporadic pops from anxious batteries not yet given the order to halt their fire. Silence spanned across the fields, but the war was not to be delayed. Joseph opened one eye, curious as to what his ear had detected, a faint but hellish droning and metallic squeal that announced the lurking presence of armor called into action. The threat grew louder and more ominous as it approached. The louder it grew, the faster Joseph's heart would beat. He closed his eyes and sighed deeply, trying to calm his nerves. It would not be long.

The sky changed from a beautiful burst of bright color to a muted morbid ink. The earth cooled, and a flat, shallow fog infected the field. Out of the mist, T-34 tanks and infantry stalked; bayonets glistened and were ready to turn red. Tank commanders called directions as officers barked orders. Joseph heard them overtake his position, mashing awkwardly through the grass, but he did not dare open his eyes. He lay as still as the dead.

Suddenly, he felt it, a cold sharp blade at his neck slowly enticing his skin and exploring its contours. Joseph had not detected the soldier coming upon him, but now he could hear his breath, panting, and twitching as he examined the scene in front of him. Joseph prayed to anything that would listen that he would not feel the blade sink into his back or cut his throat. The blade continued its investigation, coursing its way down Joseph's back, its pressure getting greater. Joseph prepared for his end. The blade stopped its examination, and the pressure grew. This would be it.

"You there! Comrade. Get a move on or I'll shoot you for desertion. The enemy is in front of you. They are dead. Quit wasting your time and let them be."

The soldier hastily lifted his rifle, bringing the bayonet along with it. It would remain unused for the moment. "Yes, Sir. At once." The soldier turned and ran off towards the enemy lines.

Joseph kept still and his eyes remained shut, knowing his enemies were indeed swarming all around him. He knew by the sounds of battle that the two forces had met. His breath became slow, his lungs arrested. Sleep found him, and the world quieted.

Joseph wiggled his nose and opened his eyes. He was surprised to learn he was on his back and the sky was in front of him, its color azure and bold. He wiggled his nose again and noticed a bright orange butterfly resting upon it. Its wings opened and closed, quite happy with its chosen roost. Joseph sat up and raised his finger to gently hoist the butterfly from his nose. The insect did not challenge the new spot and fluttered as it lifted to his finger. Joseph was enchanted with his new friend, forgetting the events of his long, frightful night.

"Well, it seems you have survived the night, and why not, I say. Who would have the heart to kill something of such beauty? If I had the time, I might just sit here and have you model for my pencil and tablet."

Joseph's attention became distracted as his eyes swayed to his rear. He could see the blackened smoke of war disturbing the blue of the sky. His eyes drew back to the butterfly, not wanting to be rid of its visit.

"You must be off, my little friend. Perhaps another day in another lifetime we may meet once again." Joseph raised his hand to the sky and gently shook his finger. The butterfly guessed its stay was ended and fluttered its wings, taking flight. Joseph watched as his unexpected friend passed from sight.

Joseph sprang to his feet, his eyes fixated on the burning German lines. His heart began to pound as he gathered his belongings. "I'm coming, Otto. I have not forgotten you."

Joseph swung his weapon to the ready and darted across the field. He ran swiftly, not caring about the enemy or finding a stealthy path. He came to the lines quickly, but it was not the same as he remembered. Where there had been trees defining the edge of field and wood, there were none. What was man and man-made could not be discerned. Bodies lay burning, tangled with the bent, twisted metal of armor and weaponry. Craters now occupied the place where the land was once flat. Trenches, gun emplacements, and fox holes were obliterated, their residents torn apart or vaporized. There was no whining, no cries of pain or moans for gods. There was nothing left living.

Joseph could not tell where he had left Otto. His searched all around him and saw no signs of him. He became distraught and started yelling for his companion. "Otto! His steps became crazed and without thought. He kicked burning branches from his path, turned bodies over, and started digging but never finishing, hoping to uncover Otto.

"Otto! Where are you?" He ran further down the line, his mind delirious and his eyes blurred. Suddenly, his foot caught a root forced to the surface from an unwanted airborne intruder. He stumbled and fell to the hard ground, rolling over and over until he came to a still end. He raised his head and spit dirt from his mouth. His eyes widened, and his heart grew full.

"Otto? Is that you?"

There, sitting silently on a blown over tree, was Otto. His knees were tight to his chest with his arms wrapped around, holding them secure and fast. He was rocking gently back and forth, his eyes solemn, straight, and hollow. The medic's helmet was gone. Dirt, ash, and soot caked his hair and darkened his clothes and exposed skin.

Joseph slowly came to his knees as if not wanting to spook a startled deer. "Otto, it is Joseph, your Hun friend. Are you well?" Joseph slowly stood up, lifting one leg at a time until standing firm. "Otto?"

Otto raised his head to meet Joseph's eyes. His portrait was still faceless. "They, they wouldn't stop. All, all night. They, they wouldn't stop."

"Otto, who wouldn't stop? The bombs?"

"They just kept going. They, they wouldn't stop."

Joseph took a cautious step towards Otto, slowly meeting him at the downed tree. He brushed himself off from his fall and hopped up onto the log next to Otto. Then he saw what Otto was stammering over, something previously unnoticed from his view. There lying on his stomach was a small boy about seven years of age. His throat had been cut, and his trousers were torn and wound into a ball around his ankles. His hands were strapped together behind his back. Blood oozed from his anus. Joseph swung his head to the side opposite Otto. He convulsed from the sight but did not vomit. Spit drooled from his mouth as he turned back. He wiped his face and put his arm around Otto, pulling him close. "It's okay, Otto, I am here. It's okay."

They sat following the sun until noon, not moving or speaking. The blue sky kept its resolve and shown all the brighter despite the dark evils below it. Nothing moved, neither enemy nor friend.

Joseph slowly slid from the log to his feet. He bent over and grabbed an empty German helmet with a bullet hole through the side of it. He knelt down and started digging with his make-shift shovel. Otto watched expressionless but soon realized what Joseph was doing. Moments later, he slid off the log and began digging with his hands. Joseph reached over and grabbed another empty German helmet and handed it to Otto. They dug a hole large enough to hold the boy and gently placed him in it, resting him flat on his back. They covered the boy with the freshly dug earth and stood at his feet, staring down at the newly formed grave. Otto turned to find Joseph's eyes. "I am okay now. We should go."

Joseph and Otto gathered their possessions and walked along the battle lines. Joseph glanced down at the dead as he walked, recognizing a familiar scene.

"They were all of them shot in the head, Joseph, both the living and the dead."

Joseph stopped unexpectedly. He turned and faced Otto. "I am sorry for the war, Otto."

"It's not your fault, but you are kind to say it."

Joseph offered a faint smile. They continued walking, dodging the reaper's path of destruction. "Do you remember anything, Otto?"

"I'm afraid my memory has failed. I don't recall much. Not even how I ended up in that hole."

"I put you there. Your wound was infected, and you were with fever. I found a medic and paid him for medicine."

"Medicine? Paid? With what?"

"It is of no concern, Otto, but you are well, yes?"

"I feel very weak. My arm is throbbing, and my leg is sore. I'm hungry, but my stomach is nauseated."

"Are you well enough to travel? I'm afraid we are back to our feet again."

"I am not in the mood to run, if that is what you are asking. What happened, Joseph?"

"What happened is that you are alive. What is of importance is our next move. You have not forgotten we are being hunted."

Otto nodded slowly but said nothing.

Joseph pulled the map from his musette bag and spread it out on the ground. They knelt over it, deciding their next course of action.

"We are in Germany, Otto, on the outskirts of Neubrandenburg."

Otto lifted his head in disbelief. "Neubrandenburg? We are that far? We are in Germany? Where is our bus?"

"You missed much, my friend."

"My friend? You called me 'friend'?"

"I've called you that many times. You just don't listen."

"Not like that, you haven't. There's no hate in it."

"I can add it back in if you like."

Otto sneered and dropped his head to the map. Joseph pointed to where he thought they may be. His finger slid along the map, finally resting upon a town. "Here, Hagenow, just south of Schwerin. I was hoping to make Bremen or at least Luneburg, but it is not realistic in your health. Let us trust the British have pushed farther by now."

"We make haste then, Joseph. The Chief will be at our heels."

Joseph folded the map and stuffed it back into his musette bag. He helped Otto to his feet, securing his belongings.

"Come, friend, to freedom."

Chapter 22

The air cooled, and the day's warmth surrendered. The light of the sky fought for its existence, not ready to succumb to darkness. Otto and Joseph trudged along with little worry of the enemy. Their health made such elusive travel difficult. They stayed in the open, walking the main roads, and while the landscape was mundane, it was easily navigated. They met few farmers and townsfolk as they passed from village to village asking for food and seeking directions. They learned the Russians had not penetrated this part of the country, and little was heard of the British. Still, the whereabouts of the Chief weighed on their minds, and they hoped he was caught or killed by the advance of the Russians or had merely just given up his chase.

"It has been many a day, Joseph, and while the road has been slow, I am feeling rather hopeful."

"Hopeful of what?"

"That we shall see a brilliant and warming sun."

"The night sky approaches, Otto. There is to be no sun soon."

"That's not what I mean."

"Then you mean a glorious and happy ending? I am not so certain."

"If it is the mission that has you worried, it has not failed."

"I am not troubled by that, Otto. Long has it been since that has weighed on me. We have both witnessed many atrocities, the magnitude of which we can't possibly comprehend. No. For me the burden is personal now. I will have to decide how to handle it."

The boys happened upon a small pond and found a cove in which to make camp. The sun shown red, its image mirrored across the water.

"Shall we have a fire, Joseph? It would be fitting for such a picturesque night."

"You must be feeling better. Your child has come to play again."

"No. It's just a good way to quell all my pain."

"I suppose a small one would not be of harm."

Joseph shook his head with a grin as Otto limped off, filling his arms with wood. In no time, a blaze carried light and warmth to their faces. They settled in, secure under their wool blankets. Joseph pulled his drawing tablet from his musette bag and went to work.

"You have been quiet about the battle, Joseph. I suspect you scored a big point in saving me."

"A very big point."

"So please tell."

"You are very chatty tonight, Otto, but I have a drawing to finish and I wish to focus on it."

"Why the rush? We will be in the safe hands of the British soon. You'll have plenty of time to draw when you get home."

Joseph said nothing, his pencil scratching the surface of his drawing tablet. Otto laid his head down, frustrated he was not being entertained with a story. He closed his eyes and forgot his pain.

The night wore on, and they drifted off to a troubled sleep.

Joseph's eyes popped open, alerted by the sound of a stick snapping. There in front of him were two muddied German infantryman's boots. Joseph looked up into the sky and was met by the barrel of a rifle pressed against his forehead.

"Rise, traitor."

Otto awoke and flipped his blanket to his side but stayed flattened to the ground. He saw the Chief standing in front of Joseph, his rifle in a grim position. His tunic was unbuttoned, torn and bloodied. His hair was tousled, dirty, and his face was charred with dark blast marks.

"Good, you are awake, Jew. My game will be short. After my entanglement with the Russians, I have little patience for more. All that drunk sergeant had to do was hold you rotten traitors long enough for me to arrive, but no, he filtered you into his ranks and welcomed me with a battle."

Joseph slowly turned, coming to his knees. "How did that sergeant know of us?"

"He is Einsatzgruppen, traitor. We all know of you. Despite the order of the High Court to fold our units into the regular German army, we still have not forgotten our loyalty to the unit. I radioed to all my comrades operating in your travel direction. That's how I managed to track you all this time.

Joseph looked for his machine gun but could see the Chief had his left foot poised confidently upon it. It wasn't moving.

"Now rise to your feet, traitor. Hurry now."

Joseph slowly did as ordered, coming to his full height.

"Good. Now bend over and grab your weapon. Hurry, I've not got all day. The Chief slowly stepped off the gun as Joseph carefully knelt down and drew it from the ground while watching Otto. Otto's lips were trembling, and his hands shook furiously.

The Chief took a step from Joseph, his rifle still trained on Joseph's head. "Perfect. Now let's try this again. I will count to one, and you will kill the Jew. This deed will then vanquish your past treasonous acts. Knowing you will feel relief of that burden, I will shoot you in the back of the head. If you hesitate upon my count, I will shoot you anyway and then kill the Jew. A splendid game. Quick and easy."

Otto lay quiet; fear held his heart and froze his entire body. Joseph hesitantly raised his weapon, pointing it at Otto. His finger teased the trigger as his arm tried to steady the barrel for its duty.

"I am sorry, Otto."

"Joseph, please. No."

Joseph lowered his machine gun and turned to face the Chief. "I can't do it."

The Chief erupted with anger and swung the butt of his rifle around, hitting Joseph in the right eye. "You filthy traitor."

Joseph hit the ground hard face down. The Chief offered Joseph no reprieve and began kicking him in the back and pounding the butt of the rifle into his ribs over and over. Joseph screamed and rolled back and forth, side to side, trying to protect himself from the vicious strikes.

"I did not count to 'one' yet, and still you defy me. You are a disgusting, Jew-loving traitor."

Otto began crying, imprisoned by fear. He dropped his head and noticed something glimmering on the surface of the ground.

The Chief continued his rant as his beating heightened. Joseph's right eye swelled, and blood caked his face and neck. His nose was broken and bleeding, hidden by the blood coming from gashes in his head.

Suddenly, the Chief stopped, his breathing psychotic, his hands bloodied and bruised, his eyes black and filled with death. He turned his head around to face what he knew he heard, the slow retracting of a bolt skirting across the cold steel of a receiver.

"Go ahead, Jew. I'm already dead inside."

Otto pulled the trigger of Joseph's machine gun and emptied the magazine. The Chief fell lifeless to the ground, riddled with bullets. His neck snapped sideways at impact, contorting his body to an awkward position. His eyes were open, facing his killer. Otto reached into Joseph's musette bag and jammed another clip into the magazine well. He slammed the bolt back with force and pulled the trigger. The Chief's tunic erupted and shredded with each hit, skin tearing and twisting into the air. Otto pulled still another clip and fired away, emptying it into the Chief. The steel of the barrel changed in color, turning a ghostly hue from the heat. As he reached into Joseph's bag for another magazine, a bloodied hand grabbed him. Otto froze, his eyes widening with madness.

"Enough, Otto." Joseph took the gun from Otto's trembling hands and tossed it to the ground. He dropped to his knees. His head drifted downwards, falling, carrying his body forward. Otto jumped to Joseph's aid, stopping his fall.

"I have you this time, Joseph. Please, do not leave me." Otto grabbed his wool blanket and began wiping the blood from Joseph's face. Joseph drifted in and out of consciousness, his words slurred and fragmented.

"It, my side hurts when, I uh, talk."

"Your rib may be broken, Joseph. I, I don't know what to do."

"It's okay, Otto."

Otto gently laid him to the ground and went to work. He dumped his musette bag and gathered any cloth or bandages he could use to dress Joseph's wounds. The fire still smoldered, offering little heat. Otto stirred the embers and tossed on what wood there was left. Joseph began moaning and shaking his head sideways.

"Shh, be calm my friend. I am here. Rest now."

Otto gently poured water from his canteen and began washing Joseph's face and neck. Bruises formed, discoloring his skin in horrid yellows and deep hues of purple. Otto kept to his work, frightened for Joseph.

The day wore on, clouds flirting with the thought of adding misery to Otto's struggles. His own wounds were still agonizing, and he could barely walk himself. He consulted his map and concluded the British were still possibly a day's journey away. He wrestled with their next move, knowing they could not survive here long. He went to the woods and gathered long branches in which to fashion a stretcher. He strung them together using torn pieces of the bloodied blanket and leather strips he cut using the Chief's boots. Otto carefully hoisted Joseph onto the stretcher and tucked what was left of the blanket around Joseph's body.

"There. You look quite comfy, if I don't say so myself. Rest easy, Joseph. Tomorrow we shall leave these dreaded lands."

Night brought its cold, and Otto sat trembling next to the fire. There were no more blankets left for warmth. Flies circled and buzzed around the Chief's lifeless body, pinned to the earth and courting hell. Otto cared not and paid it no attention. He tried to find rest, but uneasy dreams flashed, preying on his thoughts and tiring his mind. Exhaustion creeped in and took him.

Morning came upon them quickly. The fire offered wisps of smoke that danced and spiraled, a light breeze morphing them into fantastical shapes and designs. Otto followed the smoke closely, trying to create his own images. Suddenly, he sprang from his rest and jumped to his feet. Joseph's only good eye was open, and he greeted Otto with a wry face.

"My whole body aches, Otto. I am wound up so tightly in this fabrication of yours I can hardly move. I applaud your efforts, but don't you think it's a little much?"

Joseph started laughing quietly but soon stopped. "Ooh, my side hurts. Don't make me laugh."

Otto knelt down next to Joseph. "You have great resolve, but I was taking precautions."

"Very good, but please free me. I can walk. He beat my face and body, not my legs. Besides, you are in no shape yourself to drag me along."

Against his better judgment, Otto began unwrapping Joseph and slowly helped him to his feet. Joseph winced at the pain gnawing his side. "Now hand me my musette bag and help me secure it to my back."

Otto carefully lifted the bag to Joseph's back, fastening it tightly around his shoulders and gently resting it upon his back.

"Now, where are we to go, Jew? The Chief has started to rot, and his smell is polluting my fresh morning air."

Otto stood proud of Joseph. His resolve gave him strength and hope. "You are back, my friend." Otto cut the straps holding the stretcher together and pulled the poles free. He handed Joseph a pole and took the other for himself.

"I should think we'll be needing a third leg, Joseph."

"And maybe a fourth."

They stared at each other and chuckled.

"No, Otto, stop making me laugh. It hurts."

"As for our way, we go west. There is a road just beyond this pond. I do not know where it leads, but anything going west is good."

Surprising to Otto, Joseph's steps were quick, his wounds causing little delay. Otto lagged behind. His leg throbbed, and he struggled to keep step. They came to a farmhouse, but it was vacant, ransacked, and burned, offering no food or drink.

"There is nothing here, Joseph. We must push on, shall we?"

"Yes. We have little choice."

Otto turned and walked out of the gate of the farmhouse, stepping into the road. He looked left and then quickly right. The sun dipped to the west, guiding their way. Joseph watched Otto step towards the sun and then followed behind. Down the road passing field after field they walked, and while the way was slow, it offered time to reflect.

"I know you despise guns, Otto, but thank you for coming to my aid."

"No need to thank me. I did what had to be done. It doesn't matter why we do what we do. It just matters that we do them. We take care of each other no matter what our faith is, no matter what we believe or how we think. We do these things because that is what being human is about."

The day lumbered on but offered little. Vagrants and the displaced, in their eyes not unlike themselves, added human presence but were not a threat. Their wounds impeded their progress and forced them to rest often, making for an unproductive day.

"We need food, Otto. I am weak, and my head is dizzy."

"I feel it too, but there is nothing around us except woods and fields. Nothing has sprouted as of yet, if indeed farmers have planted at all. The homesteads we have come across have been gutted, burned, and left for the ages to erode into the ground."

They came around a sharp bend and happened upon an elderly couple with a horse and cart at the side of the road. The cart was filled with furniture and other household wares all tightly held into place by a number of different ropes. The old man was bent down looking at a wheel, while the woman was seated upon the top holding the reins. The old man heard the boys approach, and he struggled to his feet, concerned about their intentions. His features were rough and chiseled. He wore a short, scraggly, greying beard and mustache. His clothes were muted, his wool trousers pulled above his belly, held by suspenders. His jacket was ripped and torn at the elbows with patches covering the holes. The woman mirrored him in appearance in many ways but had a more rotund body shape. She wore a scarf over her head, tucked down around her neck into her pilling wool sweater. A long, greyish dress complimented the thick stockings she wore tucked into men's boots.

Otto reached the old man ahead of Joseph and spoke softly. "Good day, my fine sir. My name is Otto, and this is Joseph. Are you in need of assistance?"

The man paused, eyeing the boys up and down. He stood firm and was quick with interrogation. "Are you wolf children?"

Otto looked at Joseph, both shaking their heads at one another. "No Sir, but please don't be alarmed. Although we have seen fighting, we carry no weapons."

"You look like wolf children. Orphans, nomads, in search of food, clothes, and shelter. They travel in packs like wolves. They steal mostly, but some have been known to kill if needed. I have nothing, if you must know."

Otto smiled. "Nothing? But your cart is full?"

The man smiled back, a chuckle finding his cheeks. "Well, it looks like you are both in no shape to cause even a flea harm. Come. Help me fix this cart, Otto, and I shall offer you a ride. My name is Hartmut Strassner, and this is my wife, Mathilda. We are from Berlin. We are moving to the northwest near the Baltic. Help me lift this wheel."

Otto helped the man remove the wheel as Joseph lay to the side of the road. The old woman flashed a shallow smile from her seat but did not speak. Hartmut pulled a wooden box from the rear of the cart, sifting through for a specific tool.

"There it is, a fine hammer."

He began pounding the steel-wrapped wooden wheel back into place. Otto watched, curious of his work.

"You have seen much war, Otto?"

"Too much I'm afraid, but that is behind us."

"I see. So, where are you to go now?"

"We are going west to the British. I haven't thought of my life beyond that. I'm quite amazed I'm still living at all."

Hartmut put away his hammer. "It's not perfectly round but better than it was. Here now, lift with me as I fasten the wheel to the axle." They hoisted the wheel with great effort and slipped it into place.

"Very good, my boy. Much easier with four hands. Well, hop aboard. No time to spare. We will take you as far west as we are to travel before we head north."

Otto yelled to Joseph, "Hurry Joseph, we are leaving." He climbed on top of the cart, wriggling his body around the ropes that held the couple's possessions secure. He looked over at Joseph and saw he was scribbling away in his tablet.

"Drawing? Now?"

Joseph glanced up and saw the cart spring forward. He slowly rose to his feet while shoving his tablet into his musette bag. He awkwardly tried to run to the cart but was a few steps behind, his face showing his pain.

Hartmut looked behind him to check on his new passengers and noticed Joseph's struggles. He pulled back on the reins, halting the horse. "Whoa, Linza! Whoa!"

Otto extended his arm as Joseph gained on the cart. He grabbed Otto's hand, and with a mighty heave, Otto pulled him up. He flopped down next to him with a winded sigh. "That hurt, Otto."

Hartmut leaned his head to the side. "All secure, children?"

"Yes Sir, we are aboard."

"Good then. Hi yup, Linza! Hi yup! Onward, ole' girl!" The horse balked but soon found her stride.

"Here we are, Joseph, the both of us, barely able to make a step and you nearly miss a free ride."

"A free ride it may be, but it sure jostles my ribs around. I'm not certain it's a better choice."

Mathilda turned around and pointed to a sack near the end of the cart. "There is bread there, if you are so inclined. Please, help yourselves. It worries me children are not eating."

Otto's eyes brightened as he reached into the sack and pulled out a loaf of bread. He tore a piece off for Joseph and one for himself. "Thank you, Frau Strassner. You are very kind."

Hartmut leaned over and kissed her on her cheek.

Rain settled in as the day faded towards evening, making for a softer ride as the roads muddied. Hartmut pulled the cart off to the side of the road, stopping under the canopy of a large, sprawling tree. Darkness joined their travels early as clouds swelled.

Otto and Joseph climbed from the cart, crouched down, and scurried underneath, eluding the rain.

"Joseph, look. We have a new fort!"

"Silly Jew."

Hartmut bent down and peeked under the cart. "Well, look at you two. You have a fort under there, do you not?"

"See, Joseph?"

"The both of you are silly."

Hartmut shuffled around in the cart, and bending back over, he tossed the boys two thick wool blankets.

"Here my children, cover yourselves now. Be warm."

Otto grinned ear to ear. He could not be happier being in a little fort and having a soft, thick, wool blanket. "A feather pillow would complete a most wonderful night, would it not, Joseph?"

Joseph stretched out flat and covered his body with the new blanket. He placed his lumpy musette bag under his head as a pillow and sighed. "It would indeed, Otto."

"I suppose we should just be thankful we are alive. I think that's complete enough." Otto closed his eyes and fell asleep.

The bright light of the morning dappled its warmth across Otto's face. He scrunched his eyes and mouth, troubled by the annoying intrusion, and turned his body, preferring darkness in which to continue his sleep. His new position alerted his nose as he sniffed and teased the air. Something was foreign to him. Suddenly, his eyes opened wide and a welcoming smile lifted his head.

"I smell onions! I hear sizzling."

Otto swept his blanket to the side and crawled from his fort. He stumbled over to a tree where he saw a large canvas tent. He stood speechless. There in front of him was Hartmut stirring an iron pan full of eggs, chopped onions, and minced meat. Mathilda looked up at Otto, delighted as she exited from their tent. "Sit, child. Sit. Come. Eat. Eat."

Hartmut handed Otto a fork and dented tin plate which he piled high with the food from the sizzling pan.

"Take your time with your food, child, or you'll get quite a belly ache."

Otto sank to his knees and began eating. He started fast at first, but noticing Hartmut's scowl, he slowed and began to savor each mouthful. Mathilda poured him fresh milk from a glass jar and handed it to him. Taking a long drink, surprising Otto's stomach even further, he licked his lips and wiped his mouth with his sleeve.

Joseph joined Otto not a minute later, his reaction similar. He sat down next to Otto, a wide smile on his face as Hartmut handed him a plate heaped with fresh-cooked eggs. The boys sat together and stuffed their mouths with food, chuckling as they enjoyed their morning's surprise.

After their breakfast, Mathilda ordered them one at a time to take off their clothes and ready themselves for a bath. She heated water over the fire and poured it into a white porcelain tub. Otto went first and sat in the tub with his legs and feet hanging out the side. Mathilda doused a sponge into the tub and went about scrubbing his ears, hair, and entire body with lard soap. She could not help but shed a tear as she washed Otto, noticing the many wounds and scars that covered his body.

"It's okay, Frau Strassner. This is not of your making. Shed no tears for us."

Mathilda's eyes were solemn. After drying him off, she pointed to Joseph for his turn in the tub. Joseph offered sneers but was smart enough to follow her orders. He carefully lowered himself into the tub, his ill body not agreeing with the hot water. Mathilda gently washed him down, not letting her emotions guide her heart.

The boys returned to their tattered dress and sat back down next to the fire. Mathilda gathered a roll of bandages and sat with each boy, attending their wounds.

"Are you done with the boys, my dear? We must be going."

"Yes, Hartmut. They are prepared."

Joseph and Otto eased their bodies back into the cart. Otto looked at Joseph with a strange face.

"I am not so sure what just happened this morning, Joseph."

"I think we were fixed, like a broken toy glued back together."

"Well, I hope she used strong glue."

"So do I, Otto."

"Hi yup, Linza! Hi yup!"

The cart jerked forward, greeting a new day. The sun shone brightly, hinting at the comings of summer. The ruts and mud of the dirt road dried and filled, providing a much more pleasant ride for Joseph. Otto sat back, his head resting comfortably upon the perfect positions of a group of wooden dining chairs that were intertwined with each other. He stared innocently at the sky, his mind deep in thought about what was next for him and his life. The thought intrigued him and yet frightened him all the same.

"After we relinquish this document to the British, I suppose we'll be on our own. What has come of Annie and my family is uncertain, but I suspect they are gone. I'm learning to accept it. I can't help to think something will come of our journey, Joseph. Perhaps something good. What I do know is that we'll have each other."

"I don't know what to tell you, Otto. You'll figure it out."

"Have you decided what you are to do?"

"If you are referring to my father and the document, then no. I have no plan, but I am working through it."

"Good. I am sure you will find the right path."

The light of the sky reached well past noon. Hartmut pulled the cart to the side of the road just before an intersection that traveled north and south. He wrapped the reins around the brake handle and thrust the lever forward, locking the cart. A map trembled in his hands as he turned to face the boys.

"It is time, boys. We are to go north."

Mathilda sat still, her eyes remaining forward. Otto and Joseph stood up and climbed down from the cart. They came around to the front and covered their eyes from the sun as they looked up at the old man. Otto took a step forward and reached up to offer his hand. Hartmut reached down grabbing it gently.

Otto began shaking his hand. "Because of you, we are alive. You have our sincerest gratitude. Your kindness will forever be with us. Joseph and I wish you all the best at your new home in the north."

"Thank you, Otto. For your own travels, this crossroad is just east of Luneburg. I suspect you may find your British there. Farewell, my children."

Otto and Joseph waved and stepped back from the cart. Hartmut pulled on the brake lever, disconnecting its hold. He unwrapped the reins and shot the boys one last smile.

"Hi yup! Linza! Hi yup!" The cart roared forward, dust circling around its wheels as they spun.

"We should not have abandoned them, Hartmut. They are children and need a home. They could come with us."

"Now, Mathilda. Please shed no tears. They are not ours to keep. There is something special about those boys, and they need to find their own end. Feel good knowing we did our part."

Otto and Joseph stood and watched the cart disappear from sight. "Well, we are on our own again, Joseph."

"Yes, and I am quite done with strange, old people that have carts and horses. What was the name of that other fossil we took refuge with?"

"You mean Christoph? He was a jolly good fellow."

"He smelled of cabbage."

"That's the silliest thing I've ever heard. Come now, let us leave here. My senses are tingling again. I hate being in the open like this. According to our map, Hartmut is correct. We are to the east of Luneburg. I suggest we circle around it to the south as we head west."

Otto and Joseph crossed the north-south road into a field. The tall spring grass was a brilliant green and had not yet been plowed. It made for a favorable camouflage as they walked its long length, fading into the horizon. The way was slow as their wounds still thwarted their travel. They came to the end of the field and rested on top of a hedgerow. They opened their canteens and were surprised, for Mathilda had filled them with fresh milk.

"Oh, she was simply adorable." Otto leaned back and closed his eyes. He was quite content despite the condition of his body. Milk residue spread upon his outer lips and accented his smile.

The boys sat quiet for what seemed an age as the sun faded to the west. Otto suddenly opened his eyes as a recognizable sound caught his ears.

"Do you hear that, Joseph?"

They sat still, slowly turning their heads left and right, trying to discern the creator of the noise. "I hear a droning. It sounds like armor. Quickly, Joseph. Hand me the field glasses."

Joseph reached into his musette bag and handed them to Otto. He quickly brought the binoculars to his face and adjusted the focus. Otto gasped, his eyes showed excitement, and he dropped the binoculars in celebration.

"It's the British, Joseph. We've made it. Come. Let's hurry. I do believe I feel a bit of a run left in me."

Joseph crept back down the hedgerow and rose to his feet. "I'm sorry, Otto. I will not be joining you."

"What? What do you mean?"

Joseph pulled a pistol from his musette bag and raised it towards Otto.

"Joseph? What are you doing?"

"You should be very familiar with this pistol, Otto. It's Bormann's PPK, the one he had at your head. He gave it to me for this very moment. I am sad it has come to this. I was ordered to kill you either at the end of a successful journey or if we were to fall into enemy hands. Well, it seems we are in enemy hands."

Otto felt weak, his voice became deflated, his body froze, and his mind numbed, not believing his fate.

Joseph grinned ear to ear as he raised the pistol higher.

"Joseph. What are you doing?"

"I have decided, Otto. This is the only way. I am changing Bormann's orders. Take the document to a government that will do good with them. There is great evil in it that needs to answer for its actions."

"I, I don't understand. There is another way!"

"Please understand, Otto, there is no path to a grand future for me. For what shall I become? A monster? Like the Chief? Like my father? No. That shall not be my fate. If I live, what is to happen fifty years from now, or a hundred years? History has already decided my fate. I have already been judged. I shall not subject my children and their children's children to living a life in fear and embarrassment from a tarnished family, always suspect, always persecuted. No, my dear, Otto. My line ends here."

Otto began crying violently, his words slurred and fumbled, "But, but we, I love..."

"I love you too, Otto."

"No, Joseph!"

The shot rang out across the fields, its enraged echo ricocheting back and forth in all directions. Joseph's knees buckled, and he fell lifeless to the ground, resting to his side. Otto screamed at the top of his lungs, tears drowning his eyes and washing across his face. He grabbed Joseph, held him in his arms, and furiously brushed Joseph's hair, wiping the blood from his face. Otto started convulsing, his lungs gasping for breath between his screams. Mucus poured down his nose and into his mouth.

"No, Joseph! Don't leave me here alone."

Otto raised his bloodied hands and arms into the air; his head trembled and shook uncontrollably. He tried to stand but fell immediately to the ground. He crawled back to Joseph and again picked him up, holding him in his arms. He rested his forehead against Joseph's and continued crying.

The sun's evening light shown bright although subdued in color. The horizon was murky and ghostly as fog crawled across the rolling landscape. Otto raised his head and gently set Joseph to the cold, barren ground. He looked beyond his body and happened to notice Joseph's drawing tablet peeking from his musette bag. He awkwardly crawled to it, tears welling up into his swollen eyes and bloodied face. He sat up and pulled the tablet from the bag. He opened it to the first page, and his heart sank. He dropped his head and offered the earth more of his pain. There, neatly crafted, was a drawing of the two of them, smiling and running together across a vast, rolling

field with majestic mountains in the background caressing a spar-
kling lake at its base. Otto lifted his head and suddenly turned to see
the butt of a rifle. All went black.

Chapter 23

"Nurse! Nurse! The boy. He's awakened. He's trying to speak. Hurry."

The nurse ran down the long, white-tiled aisle and came to Otto's side. She squeezed a white cotton cloth soaked with cold water and pressed it to his forehead. "Shh, my dear child." She placed the damp cloth on his forehead and ran from the room. Otto raised his head slightly from his pillow. His eyes fought to open; his blurry vision greeted the world. He could discern a large, white room with high windows of frosted glass muting the brightness of the day. He could see rows of beds lined up neatly and filled with bodies. People dressed in white scurried about, some passing him, giving him little notice. He laid his head back down slowly and stared at the ceiling. It was very high, a story or more, with large fans rotating endlessly. The nurse returned with a man in a long white coat. Otto could barely see before his face, but he could feel their poking and prodding, lifting his arm and moving his head side to side. He could feel the doctor's breath as he looked deep into Otto's eyes.

"The medication is wearing off, and he will awaken soon. Has he given his name, nurse?"

"No. Only mumbling. It sounds like he keeps saying 'Fanny' over and over."

They turned from Otto's bed and walked off down the long aisle, vanishing through large oaken doors. Otto continued gazing at the ceiling, watching the fan blades spin. He became hypnotized and soon fell back asleep.

Suddenly, Otto gasped for a breath and opened his eyes. He turned his head left then right. He spotted a man next to him smiling seemingly with a chatty mind. "Hello, my friend."

Otto sat up in his bed, his arms securing his movement. He felt dizzy and confused. "Who, who are you?"

"My name is Sergeant Douglas Sikora of the 351st Bomber Group of the United States 8th Air Force."

"I'm in America?"

"Oh, you speak English? It seemed all you mumbled at night was in German or another language that is unfamiliar to me."

"Air Force?"

"Yes, I was a waist gunner."

"Waist? America?"

"Sure was. We got shot down over Germany. I was a POW for more than a year."

"A what?"

"Prisoner of war. I was liberated not three weeks ago. I was shot in the stomach and broke a leg. The Krauts weren't very fond of us bombers, so we didn't get the best of care."

Otto rubbed his eyes, bringing his new home into focus.

"It would seem, my young friend, that you have many admirers. Men of all sorts have been in here watching you closely, speaking of things in secret that I don't understand. They wore nice clothes, and they didn't look like soldiers to me. Must be real high up, those men."

"How, how long have I been here?"

"Not certain. You were here when I arrived. I've only been here a week."

"Where am I?"

Otto suddenly startled as a man approached him from his left side. "I can answer that, my young friend."

The man had an affable smile with reassuring confidence. He wore a dark, pin-striped suit, a crisp white dress shirt, and a bow tie. He was impeccably groomed, closely shaven and with dark hair perfectly parted to the side.

"You are in a British operated field hospital in Reims, France."

"France?"

"You've been here nearly two weeks. Picked up by Dempsey's 2nd British Army. Sorry about the bump to the head."

"I was told you British soldiers were gentlemen."

"Yes, perhaps we do enjoy our tea. When it comes to battle, however, we prefer killing."

"I should thank you for falling short on that part of your character."

"Good heavens me, where are my manners? My name is Agent Hadley Goodwin. I'm from the SIS."

"What's that?"

"It's the British Secret Intelligence Service."

"What do you want with me?"

"Perhaps we may start with your name."

"That would be appropriate for a conversation. My name is Otto Kaufmann, son of Solomon Kaufmann of Nord Strasse, Berlin."

"Strange to find a Jewish boy in northern Germany with a German army-issued musette bag and accoutrements."

"My musette bag and satchel. You have it?"

"We do. They are safe with all of your other belongings."

"So I presume you have read the document in the satchel?"

"We have. Each and every word."

"Is it true, then?"

"I'm afraid it confirms many things."

Otto could not keep his tears quieted. He sat back and wiped his eyes. "I am surprised I have any tears left."

"Rest easy, Otto, son of Solomon. We may speak more when you have strength. You have already shown great resolve. The doctors were mortified upon seeing your condition. They fought hard to keep that leg of yours. They found a needle mark on your arm. Whoever gave you that shot saved your life."

"I know. I miss him."

"You speak of your companion. There's something you need to understand, Otto. It is very important you listen carefully. You have given back honor and dignity to every single boy, girl, man, and woman who died in this despicable war. This document will give them justice. The men named within will be held to answer for their crimes and will forever be disgraced in history."

"Was it worth the sacrifice of my friends?"

"You will have to answer that yourself, Otto, but, yes. It was for my part."

Agent Goodwin softly rested his hand on Otto's shoulder. After a moment, he turned without further words and walked out of the room.

"Wow! So you're a war hero?"

"No, Sergeant. I should think not. I did what I had to do to stay alive."

"Please, Otto, call me Douglas. The war is behind us now for such discipline."

"Okay, Sergeant. Douglas it is."

Weeks passed, and Otto regained his health. He spent afternoons in the gardens surrounding the hospital, sharing tea with Agent Goodwin and other SIS agents, answering questions, providing information, and dispelling tales and myths heard from SIS spying activities. The bunker and the role he played with the German High Court flooded his memories. He gave them names, places, and events as best he could remember them. Otto, too, had many questions, and Agent Goodwin helped him understand the war, its events, and his part in them.

"I have one last question, Agent Goodwin."

"Yes, Otto. I thought you might."

"What is to become of me?"

Agent Goodwin sighed, resting his teacup on the saucer upon the table. He turned his head away and then back to face Otto. "It has been discussed at length, Otto. I am sorry to tell you we have not located your parents. We are still uncovering journals and official registers of the SS. Our work is incomplete. We have uncovered no records that your family were taken to Chelmno as you have stated."

"You have not answered my question, Agent Goodwin."

"You will be taken to an orphanage in the English countryside. From there, we will find a family to have you as their own. I would offer you better, Otto, for your selfless heroism, but it is not up to me. Others in the government preside over such matters."

Otto sat back upon his chair, his legs swinging underneath. "It's okay. I expected worse. I've lived through worse. Even if I were to have had relatives, they would surely have met the same fate as my parents and friends. No. I'm afraid that I'm alone."

Otto sipped his tea, cupping it with both hands and enjoying the heat that warmed his hands this chilly, spring afternoon. "One last question."

"Yes?"

"Was my companion's body, the one you found with me, was he buried properly?"

"We trust he was the Hitler Youth soldier you said he was. Thus, his body was given back to the new operating government under the auspices of the allied armies and buried with proper honors. Strange, however, that he should take his own life when salvation was near. Even stranger is that when we researched his name against the Hitler Youth enlistment registry, Dietrich Schneider was not to be found."

"Sorry, Agent Goodwin. I don't know what to tell you other than what I know. I thank you for taking care of him. He was a fine human being and came to be a good friend. In many ways, Agent Goodwin, he was more of a hero than I in bringing this document to the Allies."

"I suspect you have secrets, Otto. Remember, I am an SIS agent. We know everything."

"And a fine agent at that, Sir."

"Yes, hmm. So is there anything else you wish to know?"

"There is, Sir. When am I to leave?"

"There is one other person who wishes to meet you. That shall likely be tomorrow. After that, we'll be seeing the White Cliffs of Dover and beyond in less than a fortnight."

Otto returned to his bunk. The room was dwindling of patients, most of whom had recovered and been shipped back home or returned to duty. He hopped in bed and opened a book Agent Goodwin had given him entitled "The Adventure of the Lion's Mane," a Sherlock Holmes short story written by British author Sir Arthur Conan Doyle.

Douglas sat up in his bed, noticing Otto's return. "How are you this day, Otto? Those British interrogators keep you busy, I see."

"I am well, Douglas, and yes, I am tiring of them at best, although our conversations put many things that have happened to me in perspective."

"And your dreams? They have not rested."

"No. I'm afraid they haven't. I am sorry for my screams late into the night. My demons have caught up with me. I thought I could bury it all deep into unchecked places."

"You need to make new dreams. Happy ones. Dreams that will push the terrible ones away. For me, when I get home, I'm going to marry my girl and father a bunch of kids. Then, I'm going to craft beautiful homes of stone and rock for people to build their lives in."

"That sounds wonderful. Perhaps I will do something creative also."

"I am sure you will, Otto."

Otto turned the next page in his book and nestled deep within his bed, building a small fort out of his blankets. He and Douglas became close, sharing stories and adventures like two old friends reuniting after many years. They laughed, cried, and healed together. Otto fancied the simplistic viewpoints of his new friend. The innocent pleasures of neighbors gathering for a backyard cookout, a sporting event of friendly rivalries, and charming stories of a land across the sea all fascinated him.

"Douglas, tell me of your country America. I have heard that the cowboys and Indians still roam the woods and that everything is big, houses, cars, and people."

"Oh, my dear, Otto. You have been brainwashed, I'm afraid, by very well-versed propaganda. Cowboys and Indians live in our history books now. Well, actually in Hollywood films."

"I've heard of this Hollywood. That's where all the big cars are."

"I suppose some of that's true, but the plight of the Indians is a scar on our history. A very sad story on our part. I often think our forefathers forgot about their own persecution for their religious beliefs. They forgot what it was like to be treated inhumanely."

"Much like my people, as I have learned from this war."

"Of all peoples."

"It's not that hard."

"What is not hard?"

"Acceptance, Douglas. If people would just listen to each other, set aside differences and just listen, they could find similarities, find each other's beauty. Find acceptance."

"You amaze me every day, Otto Kaufmann."

Otto closed his book. He suddenly became sleepy and started to drift off. He shut his eyes and tried to find happy dreams.

"Otto?"

"Yes, Douglas?"

"I need to tell you I have my orders. I will be shipping back to the States tomorrow. I have known for a few days now, but I didn't know how to tell you."

Otto sighed heavily. "I understand. I expected as much. This floor is nearly vacant. I knew your time to leave would come. I've been prepared for it."

"If you ever get stateside, please look me up. You will have a friend and a home, I promise you that."

Otto sat up and hopped off his bed. He jumped in bed with Douglas and gave him a hug. A tear came to Douglas's cheek as he wrapped his arms around the boy.

Morning shed its light quickly. June offered a warm, glorious day as the skies blazed azure. Otto shuffled in his bed, trying to find a more comfortable position. He turned sideways facing Douglas's bed and noticed him gone. His bed was made, the blankets tight, and the pillow without its case propped up on the iron headboard. In the middle of the bed was a neatly folded flight jacket.

"My word, Douglas, when you said you were leaving, you were not kidding."

Otto sat up in his bed and spun his legs to the floor, slipping effortlessly off the side. When he picked up the jacket, a note fell to the floor. Otto laid the jacket aside and picked up the note.

Dear Otto,

My handwriting is awful, so I hope you can read this! I have enjoyed our time together and have learned many things from you. Truth is, I hated the Germans and how they treated me. I hated everything and anything German. However, you have painted a new picture in my head. I will always remember the word you spoke. Acceptance. And while my body has healed, I am working hard on my mind. I hope you will find the courage to follow. I have left my bomber jacket for you. It is yours now. It has provided me warmth and safety for many years. May it do the same for you. Remember, Otto, fill your dreams with happy things! See you stateside.

Your friend, Sergeant Douglas Sikora

Otto shed a tear and stuffed the note inside the pocket of the bomber jacket. He hopped back in bed and placed the jacket to his side. No sooner had he found a comfortable spot when a large party of men entered the room with two sentries guarding the door. A short, rotund man with a dark suit, top hat, and walking cane made his way through the crowd and approached Otto's bed. Agent Goodwin was a step behind the man, and he motioned to Otto to sit up and be polite. Otto chuckled to himself, and fully understanding the hand signal, he immediately followed the order.

Agent Goodwin slipped past the man and stood firm to Otto's side. "Otto Kaufmann, it is my pleasure to introduce the Prime Minister of Great Britain, Sir Winston Churchill."

"It is an honor to have your acquaintance, Sir."

"No, my dear boy. The honor is all mine. Agent Goodwin has told me your story. The world owes you its sincerest gratitude for your selfless deeds and acts of bravery. Your trials and tribulations were met with resilience and fortitude, the likes of which have seldom been surpassed. I spent the entire war years tirelessly breathing determination, perseverance, and inspiration. You, my dear boy, have inspired me."

The Prime Minister removed his hat and bowed. He smiled, put his hat back upon his head, turned, and walked from the room, his entourage following in kind.

"Well, that was surprising, Agent Goodwin. I would think a bit of warning to dress properly would have been welcomed."

"Typical of Churchill, I'm afraid. It's very difficult staying ahead of such driven tenacity and charisma."

"He could wear you out, I would think."

"It is time, Otto. We are to leave. Our plane awaits."

"Plane? I get to go on a plane?"

"Not unless you dress and be quick about it."

Otto stood up in his bed and jumped to the floor. He threw on his clothes with hurried efforts. He grabbed his bomber jacket and slung his musette bag and satchel over his shoulder.

"I forgot we gave them back to you. Are you still carrying that smelly, moth infested, dirty old musette bag? The least we can do is provide you with a new one."

"I cherish this bag more than life itself. The drawing tablet it now holds is my bible. It is my guide, my remembrance of five years of turmoil, pain, and suffering. Now, in my new days, where the sun shines bright and the rains fade, it brings me great joy and hope. It is my only family now."

"Hurry then, Otto, the car is waiting."

"Yes, Sir. I'm saying goodbye to my bed."

"Silly boy."

Otto stood and stared at the great empty room he had shared with soldiers from many countries. All the beds were vacant. He was the last to leave. He sighed, turned, and walked out of the room. His smile grew, and his walk quickened, coming to a full run. He ran through the long halls, his new leather shoes clicking on the hard granite floors as his strides made contact, echoing down the corridors. He came to two large oak doors and swung them open. There, greeting him, was Agent Goodwin, standing ready with the car door held open for him. Otto hopped down the grey fieldstone steps and jumped into the car, with Agent Goodwin following. The car sped off out of the gates onto the road. Otto stared out the rear car window, his glare wide and bright.

They soon arrived at the airport, passed through security gates, and stopped next to an open airplane hangar adjacent the runway. Otto gasped as he gazed upon a shiny, bright bird.

"Whoa. What is that?"

"It's a de Havilland DH95 Flamingo. It will be a most pleasant ride, as you shall see."

"It sure beats running or riding in horse-drawn carts." Otto rushed to free himself from the car. He sprang from his seat and ran to the plane, stopping in awe under its nose.

"I've never witnessed such beauty."

"Have you not seen an airplane before, Otto?"

"Just the ones either shooting at me or wrecked upon the ground."

"Well, hop aboard then. I'll have the pilot take a more leisurely, scenic route."

Otto was excited and put on his bomber jacket, his arms too short to fill the sleeves, which fell to his thighs. Agent Goodwin watched in amusement. "Looks to be little long around the waist, I'd say."

"Very funny, Agent Goodwin."

Otto spared no time humoring Agent Goodwin and leaped through the door into the cabin. He ran up to the nose of the plane and greeted the pilot and co-pilot, who were going about their pre-flight routine. Seated behind them was the radio operator buried in papers. Otto could not believe his eyes upon his viewing of the cockpit. "What does all this do?"

The pilot was busy flicking switches and checking gauge readings. "Well, my dear lad, all these things fly the plane."

"How fast does it go?"

"It'll do 390 kilometers per hour easily with the two 930hp Bristols working as they should."

"And are they working?"

"Sit back, young man. You'll see."

Otto ran back into the cabin of the aircraft. He found Agent Goodwin sitting in the first aisle seat on the right.

"Here, Otto, take the window. I've seen this view a thousand times during the war, never knowing if I would be pelted out of the air. The view from this aircraft will be splendid."

Otto hopped into his seat and drew his seatbelt as Agent Goodwin had done. In no time, the engines sputtered, black exhaust spewing from each as they came to life. Otto braced himself, stiffening with excitement. His head was planted against the window, surveying anything that came into his view. The plane shuddered as it lurched forward, picking up speed as it rolled down the airfield. It reached the end of the runway and spun around. Otto's heart began beating faster and faster. Agent Goodwin reached over and gently grabbed Otto's hand. Otto hardly noticed his touch as the plane suddenly leaped forward. It came to speed quickly, pushing Otto back against his seat. He snapped his head quickly to Agent Goodwin as they roared down the runway. His mouth slowly opened until suddenly the plane sprang into the air angling up and up. Otto's mouth held wide, his eyes bright and in pure shock, the power, force, and beauty of the craft bearing on his childish whims. He turned his head to the window, his nose pressing upon it, flattening its shape as he watched the landscape beneath him recede in size.

"I, I have never imagined such beauty. The fields, luscious and deep emerald green. The meandering roads, fieldstone homes and straw-topped barns. So very beautiful. I think I know what I am going to do with my life." Otto glanced over at Agent Goodwin. "I'm going to build tall buildings so the world's people can see these things every day."

"An architect?"

"Yes, if that's what it is called."

"A fine profession, Otto. Yes, very fine."

Suddenly, something caught Agent Goodwin's attention flashing past the windows.

"Look, Otto."

Otto cast his head to the sky with wonder. "Wow. What are they?"

"Supermarine Spitfires. The Royal Air Force's best fighters. They've come to escort you to England."

"Oh my word. Is that true? For me?"

"Yes, Otto, for you. Now watch me. Flip your finger around in the window like this."

Otto followed Agent Goodwin's hand movements exactly, and instantly, the fighter pulled a fast barrel roll, spinning over and over until coming back to its original position.

"Spectacular." Otto began laughing and gave the fighter pilot a thumbs up. The pilot returned the same gesture as it sped forward. Otto watched them from both sides of the plane in utter amazement.

The shores of England soon presented themselves as they approached the White Cliffs of Dover. The brilliance of their sheer, chalky faces as they fell to the waters below again pinned Otto's head to the window. The plane swooped low, following the contours of the cliffs. He could see a shepherd walking his flock of sheep high upon the bluff. Otto waved, not thinking the shepherd could see him, but to his surprise, the shepherd returned a high waving hand. Otto laughed as Agent Goodwin stuck his head next to Otto's to have a look for himself. The fighters came back to broadside and wiggled their wings.

"They're saying goodbye, Otto. Wave."

Otto waved and then saluted his new pilot friends. He watched them come together and climb into the clouds above, peeling off until they vanished from view as his own aircraft banked hard right heading inland.

"I think our pilot's taking you over London, Otto."

"Oh. Is he really?"

"A most welcomed sight for us both. This will be my last trip from home."

Otto quieted, his excitement fading. "Agent Goodwin, where am I to go? Where is my home?"

"We are to land in Leeds to the north. A car is in waiting. You are to go to the small village of Kettlewell in North Yorkshire. You will stay at the Abbey. The small orphanage is run by St. Mary's of the Wood. They will take wonderful care of you. Trust me."

"I do, Sir. You would not lead me astray."

"We are above London, Otto. Look there, the London Bridge."

Otto swung his head back to the window, his eyes full of wonder and adventure. "And is that a castle next to the river?"

"Yes. That's the Tower of London. Nice of the Luftwaffe to have spared it."

As the plane circled, Otto could see the decimation of the city, skeletons of buildings ages old drawn to rubble and ash.

"Yes, but I see they have not spared much. I guess I was not the only one to suffer through this war."

"Quite resilient, the British folk. Have no worries. We are already on the mend."

The plane banked left heading west. Otto watched as city streets became pastures that turned to fields and to woods and suddenly to mountain peaks.

"Where are we, Agent Goodwin? Such magnificent mountains and deep twisting valleys."

"We are in Wales, my dear boy. Those are the mountains of Snowdonia. I would hike them during the summer months with my pop, mum, and brother."

"You had a brother too? Like me?"

"I did. He was killed in action in New Guinea."

"I'm sorry, Sir. I too have lost my brothers, but your poppa and momma are alive, are they not?"

"They are. Alive and well, living to the east of London in a small town. Pop is a cobbler. Yes. They are very much alive, old and stubborn."

"Ha. Not unlike my Poppa was at times." Otto eased his head back. He had tired of glaring out the window. His heart became heavy as talk of family still troubled his thoughts.

As the plane began to descend, the co-pilot walked from the cockpit and entered the cabin. "We are in Leeds, Agent Goodwin. The car is waiting as planned."

"Landing is as exhilarating as the lift-off, Otto. Keep your eyes to the window."

The aircraft furthered its descent, the runway just before it. Otto watched, but his heart was not enthused. He knew the excitement was at its end. The wheels touched down, and the plane slowed with the gentle but confident braking of the pilot. They taxied for a moment until a ground crewman helped them navigate to an open hangar. The engines withdrew their whine as they shuttered to a halt.

"We are here, Otto. Let us go."

The co-pilot walked past their seats, unlatched the handle, and opened the door. He dropped out a small set of steps for his passengers.

Otto followed the co-pilot with Agent Goodwin at his back. He exited the plane and walked straight to a waiting staff car, its door already propped open. Standing next to the door was a man as well-groomed as Agent Goodwin but dressed more casually.

"Otto, this is Agent Willard. He is to join us for our ride to Kettlewell."

"It is a pleasure to meet you, Agent Willard."

"Spare your formalities, dear boy. I'm not as stuffy as old Goodwin here. Please, call me Willy."

"Very good then, Willy."

Otto climbed into the vehicle and slumped into the seat. Agent Goodwin followed and seated himself across from Otto. Willy took his place next to Agent Goodwin, closed the door, and motioned for the driver to go. Otto stared at both men, his mind spinning with ideas.

"Agent Goodwin, when I think about the day I awoke at the field hospital in Reims, I found a number of things rather odd. First, two guards were always stationed at the door to my dormitory whilst no others were positioned in any other areas. During our meetings in the gardens, the same guards followed. Then, I am given a ride to England in an airliner, complete with two fighter escorts. Now, please don't think I'm ungrateful. I enjoyed their spectacle, but it seems a little excessive. Finally, we are joined by Willy here, another SIS agent, who I suspect will not be far from me during my stay in Kettlewell, which, if I'm correct, is a small, unimportant, and unassuming village in the middle of nowhere."

Willy offered a sprightly grin and turned to address Agent Goodwin. "The boy is very astute. I have guessed you did not tell him?"

"What did you not tell me?"

Agent Goodwin turned to both of them, expressionless and confident. "It is uncertain, Otto. We are simply taking precautions.

There will most certainly be a trial for these crimes committed by the men named in the document and others we find not named. We have much to learn if we are to build a solid case. Thus, Otto, for now, you are our only witness to the actions of the men mentioned in the document. If we should find no other evidence and no other witnesses, it is possible these men may be absolved of their crimes."

"So why does that put me in danger?"

"The bunker, Hadley. Did you not tell the boy about the bunker?"

"I thought you told me everything."

"What I have told you is the truth, Otto, but perhaps I have not told you everything. At war's end, the Führer trusted no one, not even Goebbels, his second in command. It made sense to give the document to a boy who could possibly go quite undetected in delivering it to Dönitz. The Führer is not mentioned, nor did he sign the document. He had everything to gain by calling out his High Court, absolving himself of any responsibility for Germany's atrocities against humanity. At least in his mind. The Russians claim that the Führer is dead, and they are not cooperating, being very secretive about their capture of the Führerbunker. As the days pass, our intelligence is more certain that the Führer is dead, so we may never learn the truth from him. However, there are still many of his High Court that are unaccounted for, Bormann being one of them. We had intercepted a transmission originating from the bunker around the same time as you started your journey. It is a garbled communication, but we managed to discern a conversation about two soldiers carrying an important document. We assume that it was you. Now, if Bormann is indeed currently alive, he may know that his death squad has been killed since they have not reported to him with the document. Thus, Bormann may have employed others to find and kill you. Who that could be, we do not know. Bormann could have looked as far as contacting German spies here in England."

"I am not following, Sir."

"Simply put, Otto, you are perhaps still being hunted."

Otto slumped farther into his seat. "My word, will this never end?"

"As I have said, we are taking precautions. Do not worry yourself. The Allies have many well-respected officials at their disposal who are gathering information, interrogating prisoners, and authenticating facts. It is the opinion that British Intelligence will have more than enough evidence to condemn these criminals."

"Yes, but that doesn't solve the issue of my being hunted."

Willy glanced over at Agent Goodwin, but received no acknowledgement, for there was no answer for Otto.

Evening hinted its presence, and the cool, damp English air spread across the hollows, misty and elusive, dipping above and below rolling hills. Willy had fallen asleep, his loud snoring nagging the rest of the passengers. Otto stared out the window, his thoughts conjuring many questions.

"Agent Goodwin, you indicated that the Russians overran the bunker. Is there any mention of others being captured or killed? You remember I spoke of Corporal Huber? He was good to me. Is there any word of his status?"

"I am sorry, Otto. We have no word of him for good or ill. If he was captured by the Russians, unfortunately his fate is questionable. It is doubtful he would have survived. As for his wife, the Russians hold that part of Berlin and we have no way of knowing her whereabouts."

Otto dropped his head. "I understand. He was a kind man."

The car slowed as it crossed an ancient stone bridge set above a lazy stream that was flowing carelessly underneath. They came to a town, a small, innocent imprint of quaint fieldstone homes and barns connected with narrow cobblestone roads and paths. Townsfolk milled about, not particularly interested in their passing.

The car turned right at the outskirts of town and entered a short, dirt road leading through a small woods and coming to a rolling hillside surrounded by fields and ponds that were separated by well-crafted stone walls. There, nestled in this little hollow, was an Abbey with a number of buildings at its side. It was a hearty structure, simple in design. Grey field stones were wedged between large, hand-hewn wooden beams. The facade was dwarfed by a steep, slate roof with four grand chimneys rising towards the sky, adding to the building's charm.

They pulled up to the front greeting area, a circular driveway splendidly gardened and manicured. The car stopped, and Agent Goodwin opened the door and got out, adjusting his suit jacket and bow tie. Willy followed, stretching his arms high into the air and taking a deep breath. A nun greeted them. She was a smallish woman, not yet middle-aged, slender and well-poised with a warm smile. Her aura was simply angelic and inspiring. Her habit consisted of a dark robe tied with a gold rope from which rosary beads swayed freely. Her headdress was a simple, dark, translucent veil proper.

"Good evening, Agents Willard and Goodwin. It is so wonderful to see you again."

"Very good to see you as well, Sister Rose. Is Mother Superior present?"

"I'm sorry, Agent Goodwin, but she is off on a mission trip."

"No worries. I wished to say hello as I missed her on my last visit."

"I shall let her know you give her your best. So where is our newest guest?"

Agent Goodwin bent over and peeked into the car. "Come, Otto. It is time."

Otto slowly stepped from the staff car and came to his feet. His face was pleasant yet soured.

"Otto, may I introduce you to Sister Rose? You will be in her care now."

"It is a pleasure to meet you, um."

"You may call me Sister Rose or, if you wish, Auntie Rose, if that's easier."

"Oh, that would be perfect. I fancy Auntie Rose much better, if you please."

"I insist then, Otto. Come. Hand me your bags, and I will show you your room."

"I, I just have this musette bag and satchel. I don't have any other clothes."

"Well, don't despair. We shall remedy that in the morning. Come now. Let us get you settled, shall we?"

Otto followed Sister Rose, coming to her side as she turned and walked towards the Abbey. He glanced back and noticed that the two agents were not following. He took a deep, forced breath as his heart became alarmed and ran back to Agent Goodwin.

"You are not staying?"

"Sorry, Otto, but I cannot. I have other things to attend to. Do you understand?"

"I do, but I am tired of being alone."

"Willy will be near."

"But you won't be."

Agent Goodwin knelt down and put his hand on Otto's shoulder. "My dear Otto, I am British Intelligence. I am always near."

Otto's frown turned, and he gave Agent Goodwin a warm hug. Agent Goodwin opened his arms, pausing at first. He then closed his eyes and wrapped his arms tightly around Otto. A moment passed before he let go and stood up. "Be off now, Otto. Do not worry yourself. It's time to start your life."

Agent Goodwin turned and stepped into the staff car. Willy winked at Otto and followed, shutting the door behind him. The car roared to life and drove off down the lane and out of sight. Otto turned back towards Sister Rose and noticed her hand reaching out for him. Her presence was reassuring and warm. Otto walked up to Sister Rose and took her hand. Together, they walked to the door and entered the Abbey.

Chapter 24

Otto hopped down the stairs, his musette bag bouncing at his side. He entered the great hall of the Abbey and sat down in his usual place, a small nook by a magnificent window next to the hearth overlooking the gardens and beyond. The late morning sun greeted him and shone brightly, offering a warm and cheery day. Sister Rose walked in a moment later, her arms full of cleaning supplies. She rested her wares down on an ancient pine table and made ready her work. She began dusting the oaken furniture and rearranging the cushions and pillows of the chairs spread in front of the hearth.

"It's a beautiful spring morning, Otto, the first we've had in many a day. Why are you not outside with the other children? Looks to me like they have a rather steady game of rounders going."

"They don't pick me to play because they say I run too fast."

"Is that so? And how did your math contest go yesterday?"

"They didn't pick me for that either. They say I'm too smart and blurt out all the answers, not giving them a chance to play. Sister Margaret even had to create her own team with just the two of us so I could participate."

"And how did that fare?"

"Well, you know Sister Margaret. She fancies that burly wooden ruler of hers, always seeming to find the buttocks at the opportune time."

"Oh, stop your fretting, Otto. She loves you as much as I do."

"I suppose so."

"Rabbi David will be visiting today. That should raise your spirits."

"Is it Saturday already?"

"It is."

"I do fancy him, but he smells just like my grandmother."

"Nonsense. You two get on very well with your cackling, incessant laughter, and joke-telling for hours on end."

"Yes, I suppose he is quick with a good bender, but he was not so amusing during my Bar Mitzvah. I didn't care for one part of that ritual at all. I'm not certain why I even had to go through that."

"It is an important part of your faith, Otto. Rituals such as that give us dimension, meaning, creating harmony and unity."

"Is that why you became a nun?"

"No, that would be a calling. It is not a choice, but more of an inherent, inner feeling, when your soul and spirit tells you it is right."

"Well, my calling certainly wasn't to endure that ceremony. I could have prolonged that much longer than beyond my years in the war."

"Stop your complaining, Otto. Now give me a hug and go join the other children. I won't have you moping around inside on such a beautiful day. Hurry now. Be off."

Otto slung his musette bag over his shoulder and slid from his nook. He walked to Sister Rose and gave her a quick hug as he made for the door leading to the gardens. Sister Rose watched as he sauntered from the room, a hopeful smile coming to her face. Otto passed through the garden stopping, every few steps to smell and observe the flowers as they swayed gently in the breeze. A young boy came running by, nearly bumping into Otto as he plowed his way towards the fields where the other children were playing.

"Sorry, Otto. I'm late. Are you not playing?"

"Quite all right, Sydney. No. I'm not playing. Amando says I'm too fast."

"Ha! What does he know? Turtles are speedier than he is. Well, I must be off."

Otto smiled as he watched Sydney bolt to the fields. He continued his walk through the garden and onto a cobblestone path leading from the Abbey. A stone wall joined the path, and together they meandered through pastures and wove through woods. He came upon a very old oak tree, somehow spared for its lumber to build ships, furniture, or floor boards. It was well poised and grand, its dense foliage creating a welcome, shady spot at the shores of a small pond. Otto plopped down next to the tree and leaned back using the trunk as his rest. He opened his musette bag and plucked from it Joseph's drawing tablet. He flipped to the first drawing of him and Joseph running together. Otto stared at the drawing for a moment and then continued flipping past many pages full of sketches and scribbles. He stopped at a page of architectural designs. He reached into his bag once more and retrieved his pencil. Seeing it dull, he flipped open a pocket knife and began sharpening it with firm thrusts, the shavings dropping to the ground at his feet. His tongue peeked from his lips and his eyes squinted as his mind focused on his craft.

Hours passed and his stomach growled, a new and now constant craving. "No matter what, I still can't grasp the idea that food is near and plenty."

Otto rested his tablet on the grass to his side. He reached into his musette bag and grabbed a sandwich Sister Rose had prepared for him. He unwrapped the sandwich and held it to his nose, retreating his head suddenly. "Yuck. It smells like horse meat. I should have never told her that story. She must be getting back at me for something."

Otto giggled to himself and took a large bite. As he leaned his head back against the trunk of the oak trunk, he watched the clouds in the sky scurry by, rolling up and over as they drifted lazily east. Suddenly, two figures in shadow parked themselves in his line of sight.

Otto swallowed hard a bit alarmed. "Auntie Rose? Rabbi David? What have I done? If it's about the mouse we put in Sister Emily's quarters, it was George's idea, not mine. I just watched."

Sister Rose raised her eyes. "That's good of you to tell, Otto. We did wonder who the jokester was, so thank you for that. However, we are not here concerning that issue."

Another figure, who had been hidden from Otto's view, came to the front. "Agent Goodwin. Is that you?"

Otto jumped to his feet and lunged at Agent Goodwin, giving him a mighty welcome.

"I haven't seen you since the Nuremberg Trials. Where have you been?"

"Hello, my dear boy."

Otto's eyes were suddenly alerted to another presence. He glanced behind Agent Goodwin and gasped. His heart began to race. He dropped his arms from Agent Goodwin's waist and stepped back. Tears fell freely and he struggled to speak. Agent Goodwin stepped aside. "I think, Otto, you may recognize this person?"

"Ekkehard?"

"It is I, Otto."

"But, but you fell. I saw it. I mean, I heard you fall."

Otto ran and jumped into Ekkehard's arms as they swung round and round and fell to the soft grass.

"You are alive!"

"Yes, Otto. I am quite alive."

Sister Rose laughed and clapped her hands. "He has something to share with you, Otto."

"Oh, what is that, Auntie Rose?"

"That's for Ekkehard to say. We shall leave you two alone. Dinner is at dusk."

"Yes, Auntie Rose. What a wonderful surprise, Agent Goodwin. I know you must have something to do with this."

"Perhaps. Now, let Ekkehard speak. I will see you back at the Abbey."
He winked at Otto, turned, and walked back towards the Abbey.

"So do tell all, Ekkehard. How did you come to me?"

"I have tricks up my sleeve as well. You assumed I fell back there inside the subway tunnel, and you were convinced the shots you heard were Russian. Except they were not. They were of my making. I pulled my pistol as they forced me to the ground. I shot two, and the other ran off. The other soldiers chased you. I wanted to pursue you, Otto, but I sprained my ankle during the struggle. I had to escape and find concealment. So I plunged myself into the deepest depths of the tunnels and hid for months living off rats and boiling murky puddle water that dripped from the walls."

"I should think we shared many of the same adventures. What of you then, Ekkehard? Certainly the Russians came upon you again as they overran the city."

"I slowly rose to the surface, acclimating my eyes to the light and my lungs to the fresh air. I lifted the cover to a sewer line and came to the surface. I was in the middle of a street unfamiliar to me. Destroyed buildings cast in rubble lay all around me. People moved slowly and mingled about like stray dogs looking for their masters. Life was in ruins. I sought someone to lend information and happened upon an old woman sitting on a park bench. She had a blanket stretched over it from the top to the ground, forming the roof of her new home. A fire burned and sputtered at its side. She told me Berlin was completely in Russian hands. She said we were prisoners, locked and held without trial. I asked her about the British, but she shook her head. She told me the Americans were near but would not have a say concerning the people. Airdrops with aid came sporadically from them but were mostly intercepted by the Russians. I thanked her for her information and crept away.

"I thought to escape to my family's mountain chalet, thinking I would find solace there. The road was difficult and crawled with danger. Beggars, thieves, and scoundrels thwarted my many efforts, stealing my equipment, pistol, and food. After a number of weeks, I came to my home in the mountains. I was surprised to find American soldiers in the village and in my home. They ransacked everything, taking my wine, cognac, and champagne for themselves. They confiscated our silver and my hunting rifle. I begged them to leave, but they did not move. A surly lieutenant told me they had every right to the spoils of war and that his men were ordered to take up residence. He pointed to the small shack in the backyard, so that's where I lived for the next few months. At least I still had a magnificent view from there."

"So what of you then, Ekkehard? How did you, why did you come to find me?"

"The lieutenant came back to me and said they were ordered to leave. He handed me a sack. I opened it and found our silver to be accounted for and intact. I thanked him graciously. He kindly apologized, hopped into his jeep, and drove off. I returned to the house and found it neat but still rearranged. It took me a month to return it to its original state, but somehow it was still not the same. I ventured down from the mountain into the village from time to time to seek provisions, but it was most depressing. People were gone. My friends all vanished to where or what ends I have not a clue. Fathers did not return, nor did their sons. The village was now left to the women and small children to run.

"I stayed in the mountains as often as I could. I hunted, fished, grew a fruitful garden, and lived a quiet life, but it wasn't for me. I yearned for voices, companionship, and life. I missed my sons' constant bickering over this or that, my wife's nagging at me to stop picking at the apple tarts cooling on the window sill. I missed the days of joy, laughing, and love. So I decided to venture west. I sold my home and land to a local farmer. I had visions of a new life elsewhere. There was a boy I remembered fondly. I supposed if he were still alive, he may wish to, well, be my son."

Otto started crying and began wiping his nose and sniffling. "You, you want me to be your son?"

"Yes, Otto, if you will have me."

Otto's cries became uncontrollable. Words escaped his mind and heart.

"Now, please don't cry, Otto, because then it will make me cry."

Otto nodded.

"So does that mean you'll agree to be my son or that you will stop crying so I won't cry?"

Otto's cries shifted to laughter as he jumped back on Ekkehard.

"My word. I think you have gotten heavier, Otto, from the first time I met and carried you to safety."

"So wait, Ekkehard. Am I to assume you have already adopted me?"

"As I was saying, I traveled west and met with an American headquarters in France. They were not so quick to hear my stories and locked me up for quite some time. They were suspicious of me and my questioning. They wondered why I was asking about the Hitler Youth, the Führerbunker, and a Jewish boy. They mistook me for a Nazi officer trying to flee. I had no identity papers, so locked up I stayed. Finally, a gentleman from the British SIS came to see me. His name was Agent Hadley Goodwin. He was very interested in my story of how you and I met. I told him about my family, my occupation as a train conductor, and what I knew about you. After a few days of relentless questioning, they saw fit to release me. As I left the interrogation room on the final day, Agent Goodwin pulled me aside. He told me not to mention a word to anyone and asked if I was interested in seeing you again. I told him I would cherish that more than he could possibly know. I looked into his eyes, held both his arms tight and told him I wanted a family again. He smiled and said I would be perfect. So we flew to London and he helped me make the arrangements. To answer your question, Otto Kaufmann, the answer is yes. It is official. You are my son."

Otto wiped his nose, his smile held wide not leaving much room for anything else on his face. He stood up and sighed, looking out over the pond, the meadows, and the mountains beyond. He turned to face Ekkehard. He walked slowly over to him and gently put his arms around him. He lay his head deep into Ekkehard's chest. "I promise to be the best son ever."

"I am sure you will, but as a good son, we mustn't keep Sister Rose waiting for dinner. It is nearly time."

Otto released his grasp. "And as a good poppa, it was smart of you to remind me. Shall we go?"

Ekkehard helped Otto gather his belongings, and together they strolled back to the Abbey. They came to the gardens and entered into the great room. There they found Agent Goodwin, Willy, Sister Rose, and Rabbi David having tea. A small fire was ablaze, and the hearth was aglow, warding off the evening chill. Otto could hardly contain himself. "Auntie Rose! I have a new poppa." He ran straight to her, giving her a warm hug.

"Well, that's the happiest we have seen you in quite some time, Otto. It will serve you well to cast off that grumpiness of yours. Any longer and your face would surely have frozen that way." The room erupted with laughter. Otto plopped down in a chair next to Agent Goodwin.

"I'm afraid there is more, my dear boy. Please, Ekkehard, it's best coming from you."

Ekkehard cleared his throat and knelt down next to Otto. "Well, my new son, I have nothing to offer but my love and guidance, but I have yet one other opportunity for you. However, it is not in this land. I have relatives in the Northeast Kingdom of Vermont. Do you know where that is, Otto?"

Otto shook his head while eyeing his friends around him.

"It is a state, Otto, in America. My relatives have land, farmland. They have asked me to join them. We can build a new life, then we can decide where to go if we so choose."

"America? We get to go to America? Where the cowboys and Indians are?"

"Yes, Otto. America."

Otto glanced over at Agent Goodwin and the rest of his friends. Anticipation held their faces, smiles hinting. Otto started nodding slowly and then faster and faster until he sprang from his chair into the air. "Whoopee! We are going to America."

Agent Goodwin began clapping, and the rest joined in happily.

"But, but how is this possible? Agent Goodwin, this smells of your doing."

"Right you are there, my boy. The Queen herself made the arrangements, phoning the President of the United States to secure your citizenship. The world has given you its thanks, Otto."

Otto sat back down in his chair, quiet took hold of him, and in a calm voice, he offered his heart. "I, I don't know what to say or feel, but I promise to repay all of you for what you've given me. I could not ask for a better family than all of you. Auntie Rose, thank you for not using the ruler on me when you could have and for being my mother when I needed one. Agent Goodwin, thank you for, well, for everything. Willy, thank you for watching over me and for your visits each month, keeping me safe. Rabbi David, thank you for giving me back my spirit, my faith, and its teachings, but I still hated the Bar Mitzvah. I, I love you all dearly."

Quiet owned the room until Otto's stomach growled. Sister Rose smiled. "Alright, Otto, I shall see to dinner. Please everyone, come to the table."

Chapter 25

Ekkehard knocked on Otto's bedroom door. "Otto, are you ready? Agent Goodwin will be here soon with the car. We should be at the port on time or we might be left to swim to America."

"You may come in, Ekkehard. I mean Poppa."

"It's quite alright, Otto. Call me whatever is comfortable."

Ekkehard entered the room and found Otto sitting on his bed, packing clothes into suitcases. "I'm hurrying as best I can. I had forgotten what a nice group of clothes Auntie Rose had gotten for me over the past two years. Such good people they are here. I shall miss them."

Ekkehard sat on the bed next to Otto. He picked up Otto's musette bag, the drawing tablet falling from the inside opening to the first page. Ekkehard studied the drawing with interest.

"This is you and your companion, Joseph, is it not?"

"It is. He drew that for me. I know I haven't told you everything of my journey since that day in the tunnels. I suppose some is buried and some leaks out, haunting me as it follows me along."

"We have all been challenged during those times, Otto. Do not trouble yourself. Talk freely about it when you wish."

"You had asked me once about the trials of the High Court. I was just thinking about that not two nights ago. I remember how angry you became in the tunnel when I told you about the High Court and their debauchery and games. I was a guest of the British SIS and attended the first day of deliberation at the Nuremburg Trials. The document I turned over to the Allies, my testimonies, along with massive accounts, events, letters, telegraphs, what seemed like pounds and pounds of information have all indicted the highest of the High Court members. Göring, Himmler, Goebbels, Bormann. All of them. They were held responsible for the mass killings and crimes against humanity. No matter if they were present, dead, or missing, they were condemned and convicted.

"While you know perhaps some of the outcome, you may not know this. When I entered the deliberation room, everyone in participation stood up and clapped. I was humbled but scared at the same time. There I was before the villains in question. They stared at me with disgust and loathing. I stared back, my eyes piercing each one of them.

"I asked Agent Goodwin to take me to the cells where they were being kept prisoner. I wanted to see Joseph's father, Rudolph Kessler. I later confessed to Agent Goodwin that I gave him a false name for Joseph. I did it to protect Joseph's legacy. I wanted Joseph's father to know how his son died. Agent Goodwin was not keen on the idea but soon relented as a result of my constant pestering. He brought me to Herr Kessler's cell. The room was dark, and all I could see was his facade in shadow, cigarette smoke rising slowly, swirling, diving, and creeping around him like a constrictor wrapping its prey. I stood square to him. I could feel his facade shift and knew he turned to face me. His stare was cold and empty. Then he turned around, looking away. 'So you are the Jew,' he said to me in a vile and foul voice. 'Is it good for you to know I am to die at your hands?'

"I did not answer. I would not play to his mind. I said one thing to him and then I left. 'No, you will die because the world has spoken, but before your last breath, please know your son

Joseph died a hero.' As I turned away, I could hear him start crying. He had already been found guilty and was condemned to death by hanging."

"That was strong of you, Otto, to speak the truth of his son. Sometimes it's more damaging and spiteful than any hateful words your mind could conjure. You did the right thing."

"I hope so. I did it for Joseph."

"Well, shall we go?"

"Yes, Ekkehard. Let us leave."

Ekkehard lifted Otto's two suitcases, full and nearly spilling out the sides. Otto secured his musette bag and leather satchel around his head, resting them upon his shoulder, and followed Ekkehard. They walked down the stairs through the great hall and out the large oak doors leading to the entrance and front gardens of the Abbey. The staff car was waiting, its engine idling and the doors open. There to greet them were Sister Rose, Willy, Rabbi David, and Agent Goodwin, his bow tie straight and proper. Otto's steps slowed as he walked to the car, his head turning back towards the Abbey. His smiles flickered, happiness flirting with fear at each step. Ekkehard reached the car and handed the bags to the driver. He turned and watched Otto hesitantly approach the vehicle.

Agent Goodwin calmly walked up to Otto, kneeling down in front of him. "It is okay to let go, Otto. The Abbey is not going anywhere, and you are welcome here anytime you wish to return. The future is now before you. It's time to go make something. I expect to see from you great tall buildings reaching into the skies all over London."

Otto nodded and wiped the tears from his eyes. He took Agent Goodwin's hand, and they walked the rest of the way to the car. Otto tossed his musette bag and satchel into the car and ran to Sister Rose, wrapping his arms around her. "I will never forget you, mother."

"Now stop this crying, Otto. I am tiring of it. If I have to get Sister Margaret's ruler, I shall. Now go. Make us proud."

Otto released his arms, again wiping his eyes. Rabbi David put his hand on Otto's shoulder and looked deep into his eyes. "Do not forget your faith, Otto. It shall be a trusted guide for you. And please send me jokes. I fear I am all out of them."

Otto laughed as he stood tall in front of his friends. Suddenly, behind them, he noticed the rest of the children, some of whom had come to the Abbey at the same time he had and some he had not ever met. They stood in a group and held up a large sign that read, 'Godspeed, Otto. We will miss you.'

Otto's tears found him again as he waved goodbye. He hopped into the car followed by Ekkehard, Agent Goodwin, and Willy. He pressed his hands to the glass of the rear windshield and smiled as the car sped off down the lane and out of sight.

Willy watched Otto turn back around and fidget in his seat. "Are you excited, Otto? A trip across the Atlantic on an ocean liner?"

"I am Willy. Where are we departing from again? I must admit I didn't quite pay attention when you spoke of it during dinner. I was so overwhelmed by the atmosphere and by my good fortune."

"Understood, my lad. Well, you shall be leaving from Liverpool, not a two hour ride from here, give or take should we run across sheep blocking the road. In five days' time, you'll cross the vast Atlantic Ocean reaching Halifax, Nova Scotia. A day later, it's on to New York City and the island of Manhattan. You know, I've quite forgotten the name of the vessel."

"It is called the Parthia, Otto."

"Yes. Thank you, Hadley. Now, from New York, you'll be taking the train to Boston." Ekkehard sat listening, his arm around Otto's shoulder. "My relatives will pick us up from there. After a few hours' drive north, we will be at our new home."

Otto gazed ahead seemingly into space. "Home."

The staff car pulled into the docks using a rear entrance just off the main gate. Willy met with a representative of Cunard, the ocean line company that owned the Parthia. As they spoke, Ekkehard retrieved the suitcases and handed them to an attendant who carted them away to the ship. Agent Goodwin and Otto walked towards the end of the dock. Otto stood amazed, for there in front of him was the vessel itself in all its magnificence.

"Wow. I could never have dreamed it would be this big."

"Quite a spectacle, is it not, Otto? It's nearly five-hundred and nineteen feet long, weighs thirteen thousand tons, and has a top speed of seventeen knots, so she'll cruise right along."

"Are you coming, Agent Goodwin?"

"I think you know the answer to that."

"I do. Sorry. I'm tiring of goodbyes."

"Goodbye? No, this is not a goodbye. Our friendship certainly does not end here. We have just only begun."

Otto offered his arms and gave Agent Goodwin one last hug. Willy walked over and confirmed the arrangements. Otto turned from the ship and noticed a glistening near Willy's eye. "Willy, are you teary? I would never have known."

"Me? No. I've something in my eye. Probably a gnat, I suspect."

The ship representative walked over to the group conferring with Agent Goodwin. "Ekkehard, Otto, this is Carlton. He will be escorting you to your cabin. If you should need anything, he will be your contact. He knows how to find me should anything arise."

Otto took Ekkehard's hand, and they followed Carlton through the gates towards the ship. Suddenly, Agent Goodwin tapped Otto's shoulder. "I had almost forgotten, Otto. This is yours." He handed Otto a torn, dirty, and crumpled envelope. On it was written 'To Otto, from Corporal Huber.'

Otto shuddered as he gasped for breath. "I, I had thought I had I lost it. Could it be?"

"I am terribly sorry, Otto. We found it when we searched all your belongings a few days after you were captured. We have kept it all this time for various reasons."

"What reasons?"

"It will make more sense when you read it, my boy."

Otto's heart pounded as fear and doubt took him. "No, I, I can't. I won't read it. Ekkehard, can you read it to me? I, I don't have the strength."

Agent Goodwin handed the letter to Ekkehard, who carefully examined the envelope. It had been opened. He pulled the letter held inside and slowly unfolded it. He cleared his throat and blinked his eyes hard.

Dear Otto,

It is with all my heart I write this letter to you, for the truth needs to be told. It will be hard to hear, but I have not time to wallow in emotion. For the past five years, you were a slave. The German High Court used you as a game. From high ranking generals to Goebbels himself, you were an object to be wagered. You were given missions to see if you would survive. It hurts me to tell you this, but I wagered on your life as well. I know I may not have your sympathy and forgiveness, but I did what I did because I loved you as my own. You see, I bet you would survive and you always did. So through the years I amassed quite a bit of money. In total, I made 7,000,000 marks (mostly from Göring, the fool!). The money is in a Swiss bank account under your name, Otto Kaufmann. The bank account number is 1778392490. This is why I insisted that I stay in the bunker until the very end. I needed to make one last deposit and secure the account. Last of all, remember what I told you. Do not let the pain of these troubled years have sway over the rest of your life.

Please forgive me, Corporal Huber

Otto stood without moving, his mind empty.

"I am sorry, Otto, but the British government had to be certain the money wasn't stolen or obtained by ill-conceived deeds, wealth made from selling property that belonged to other countries. The Nazis seized, stole, and confiscated many antiquities and art through the years, as you know from your discovery in Bormann's bunker. The funds in this account had to be clear or they would be confiscated by the British Government and given back to their rightful owners. However, during the trials, one of Hitler's ministers came forth and verified that the money was the personal wealth from each participant. He swore that the money did not come from stolen property or from civilians. Based upon this discovery, for the past three years we researched and audited every general, every court minister and official, inspecting the origin of each mark. The man who surrendered this information willingly hoped to receive a lesser sentence. He received twenty years. That person was Albert Speer, the armaments minister. He was an architect, Otto, like you will be one day. We can confirm that the money is yours. It will be more than enough to start your life with Ekkehard. Use it wisely."

Otto still stood motionless. His eyes lost and tranquil. "I have no use of the money. I shall have my own."

Agent Goodwin looked firmly at Otto and held his shoulders. "Listen to me one last time, Otto Kaufmann. I understand your sorrow, but a good man died to bring you this wealth. He sacrificed his life. You shall take the money. You shall honor his death. Do you understand me?"

Otto looked up at Agent Goodwin, his voice heartfelt. "Yes, Sir, you are right, again. It just feels..."

"What? It feels wrong?"

"Yes. I was just trying to survive, not win a game."

"You'll have to learn to accept this as truth, Otto. What is done is done. Now, get on that ship and move forward with your life. Quickly now."

Otto turned and ran to Ekkehard, grabbing his hand and pulling him to the ship. "Let's be off, Ekkehard, I have never witnessed Agent Goodwin so angry."

The whistle blew loud, announcing its presence to other ships in the harbor. The sky was bright, dawn had shown itself, and the sun welcomed a new day with energy and celebration.

Ekkehard shook Otto's arm gently. "Hurry, Otto. Please awaken. There is something you must see."

Otto shook his head and pulled the covers over his head. "Now? I must see it now? Is it morning already? Tell me we are near land. My stomach does not seem to fancy ocean travel."

"Yes, lazy head, do dress quickly and follow me. Actually, just come in your night shirt."

Otto hopped from his bunk, his curiosity hesitant but piqued. They scurried up two flights of stairs and came to the deck, their breathing labored but excited. Ekkehard pointed to the west, his head held proud and high. Otto peeked over the side of the ship, and his mind drifted. "What is that?"

"She is the Statue of Liberty. Isn't she beautiful?"

"She is, Ekkehard, but why is it there? What does it mean?"

"It means freedom and opportunity, that anything we wish to make happen, we can."

Otto stood proud, his head held high into the air. "Then let us get started."

New York City, August 25, 2014

O tto sat relaxed at the end of a large, pine farm table, bountiful with wine, meats, and deserts of all sizes, shapes, and flavors. Centered at the end of a grand dining hall in back of him was a massive, old fieldstone fireplace with hand hewn oak beams for a mantle. Upon it rested antique, wrought iron candlesticks and small historic artifacts and trinkets from his travels around the world. Centered above in a majestic gilded frame hung the drawing of Joseph and Otto, the one Joseph had made of them running together. A light shown dim yet heroic and proud upon it, capturing each stroke of the pencil. It was home. Joined around Otto at the table were his daughters and their family and friends.

A tear welled up in Alexi's eye. Her husband, Newell, held her tight, one arm around her back holding firm on her side. Otto gently placed his wine glass upon the table and noticed her sadness. "Now, why are you crying, Alexi? You have heard this story of mine many a times."

"I always cry when you tell it, Poppa. It's always hard to believe. So much suffering for such young children."

Annabelle reached over and grabbed the napkins from her children's laps, placing them on the table. "Yes, Poppa, and with all due respect, I'm not so sure the kids are old enough to understand either. Perhaps you should skip certain parts."

Otto sat slowly back in his chair and turned to Annabelle. "I applaud your concern from a mother's perspective, Annabelle, but I disagree. They need to hear it. In time, they will remember and tell it to their children. It is not a story to be forgotten. Not in this family."

Andrea sat fidgeting at the table as she repeatedly tapped the keys on her cell phone sending text messages. "Poppa, may Rory and I be excused? There's a show tonight in the park, and we're meeting friends there. I promise to be home no later than midnight."

"Yes, by all means, Andrea. You are young and need not be held here by my whims."

Andrea rose from the table and rushed over to Otto, giving him a big kiss and hug from behind. Rory gathered their plates from the table and respectfully glanced over at Otto.

"Thank you for dinner, Mr. Bauer. It was very kind of you."

"You are most welcome, and please, stop calling me Mr. Bauer. If you are to be a part of this family and court my daughter, then you better well call me Otto. Agreed?"

"Yes, Mr. Bauer."

Rory and Andrea dashed down the hall. Otto raised his head, looking past the centerpiece of late summer blooms in a crystal vase on the table. "Andrea, do not forget your door key this time. Rory, have her home by eleven. No later."

"Yes, Mr. Bauer!"

Alexi and Annabelle smiled at Otto, his face showing obvious concern. Alexi got up and started stacking empty plates on the table. "She is coming along just fine, Poppa."

"Oh, I meant to ask you, Alexi, how was your week at the beach house? I trust you put the trash out this time when you left."

"Of course, Poppa. All taken care of. As for Andrea, she is a blessing. She is precious and so very thoughtful. We had a wonderful time. The water was colder than usual, but the crisp, ocean air was very welcome."

"Good to hear. As far as Andrea is concerned, and if you all must know, she isn't any harder or easier than the three of you were to raise. Which reminds me, we need to call your sister Athalia. Her birthday is not in two days. And if you remember, all of you forgot last year, and you know how I feel about birthdays."

Annabelle rolled her eyes in a friendly manner. "Why did she not make it to dinner today? She never misses our end of summer family dinner."

"She was on call tonight at the hospital. She's filling in for a co-worker. Your sister, you know, is always caring for others."

"You taught us well, Poppa."

"Thank you, Annabelle, but perhaps not well enough. I saw you roll your eyes."

Alexi began giggling innocently, nearly dropping the stacked plates on the table.

"That goes for you too, Alexi. The both of you are guilty."

Alexi calmed, and her voice became serious. "Poppa, Newell and I have been concerned, and please don't mistake our thoughts, we love Andrea so very much, but should you have adopted her? I mean, so late in your life? It's quite a task to look after her."

Otto smiled as he sipped his wine. "Your concerns are valid, but everything has been arranged should the unforeseen arise. Besides, she spends more time in college now with all its events and schedules. No, you need not worry, Alexi. As you know, we have agreed that Annabelle will have custody should anything happen to me. I suspect I shall be around for quite a few more years, God be willing. Also, she has Ruth and Simon with her daily when I am traveling."

Alexi raised the wine bottle and reached over and poured Otto a splash. "Having your maid and personal assistant look after her when you're away hardly accounts for caretaking, Poppa."

"You are too funny, Alexi. We are all family, Ruth and Simon included. When I adopted you three girls, Ruth and Simon were very much a part of your upbringing. Who took you to soccer practice,

Alexi, when I was away? Annabelle, who attended your recitals when I could not? Let the record be known, I only missed two out of hundreds, I suspect."

The girls nodded, smiled, and laughed along with Otto. Alexi continued arranging the table for cleaning. Annabelle took her napkin and began wiping the messy faces of her two now-sleeping children sitting to her sides. "Poppa, this may be strange to ask, especially so late in our lives, and not that it matters in the least, but why did you adopt us?"

Alexi stopped clearing the table and sat back down facing Otto, waiting patiently for his voice. Newell had left the room and could be heard filling the dishwasher in the kitchen. Annabelle placed the napkin on the table, following her question with another. "Also, is it not strange we all have long dark hair and similar cute, pudgy noses?"

Alexi began laughing. "I noticed that, too, Annabelle. Interesting, now that I think about it, all our names begin with the letter 'A.'"

Otto sat quiet. He thought long and hard before answering. His voice was soft and gentle. "When Ekkehard adopted me, my world brightened and the hard years of the war washed away. I said to myself then, 'I shall follow his lead.' I shall offer others a life to be lived. No human being, my dear children, deserves to live alone without love."

Otto stood up from the table and took his leave. He walked down the great hall past the living room and its expansive windows, marble floors, and walls of art and went into the library. He unlatched the lock and swung the French doors out into the gardens and onto the veranda. He walked up to the edge and laid his arms across the top of the garden wall. Greeting him in all its grandness and resplendent beauty was the skyline of New York City. Central Park rested below, its expanse majestic in its stately eloquence. Annabelle followed him into the library not a moment behind. She slowly walked up behind him and put her arms around him, joining him in his quiet.

"I can remember when we all would play tag out here. You would chase us on the veranda. Around and around the building we'd run. Then when you were getting close, we would jump into the pool to escape you."

Otto's eyes brightened, a glow coming to his face.

"I have admired and appreciated this view all my life, Poppa. It is so peaceful up here, the heavens embracing the world below."

She could feel her father's heart and the calmness of his thoughts.

"We did not mean to question your reasoning, Poppa. You have given us all a very, very good life."

Otto turned to Annabelle, his voice gentle and understanding. "No, my dear Annabelle. No apology needed. I taught all of you to be free thinkers, to speak your mind at will. Please understand that even after all these years my story is still difficult to tell."

"We know and I promise we shall not forget it and our kids will not forget it. It shall live to the end of all this that surrounds us."

Otto reached over and gave his daughter a kiss on the forehead. Together, they stared off into the heavens, the night's first stars twinkling, announcing their presence.

Otto rose from his bed, the light of a new morning tickling his face. He entered his closet and dressed quickly, putting on worn khakis and a knitted sweater. Simon entered not a minute later, holding a large, silver serving tray.

"I have fixed your tea, Sir."

"Splendid, Simon. You are most kind. How is your morning?"

"Very well, Sir. Will you be eating?"

"No, Simon. I don't think so. I think I'll have my walk in the park."

"I have prepared your favorite, eggs with sautéed onions and minced meat and a glass of milk."

"Thank you, Simon, but no. I will be fine for now. Have you seen my walking shoes?"

"Yes Sir, but do pardon my intrusion, is everything all right?"

"Oh, all is well. Yes, all is very well."

"You told your story again at dinner, didn't you?"

"Just some of it."

"Yes, I might have known."

Simon handed Otto his shoes as they walked to the front entranceway. Otto sat down on a long wooden bench near the door and put on his socks and shoes. He opened his musette bag, and convinced his drawing tablet was inside, he smiled and shut the bag.

"Will you be gone long, Sir?"

"No, no. Just the usual."

"You mean like last time when you didn't come home until well past dark?"

"For goodness sake, Simon. You exaggerate."

Otto swung his musette bag around his shoulder, opened the door, and walked down the hall to the elevator. He pressed the elevator button, and the doors slid open to each side. He walked in, turned, and pressed the one lone button that would swiftly send him down to the ground floor to meet the rest of the world. He walked with a most chipper step, catching the doorman off guard.

"Oh, good morning, Mr. Bauer. How are we this fine day?"

"I am well, Barton, and how are you and yours?"

"The family is fine. So good of you to ask."

"Splendid then."

"Off to the Conservatory Water?"

"You know me all too well. Good day."

Otto sauntered down the sidewalk, coming to Fifth Avenue. Seeing the roadway clear, he hurried across and stepped up onto the sidewalk. Joggers, couples holding hands, and mothers walking with strollers greeted him this glorious, sun-drenched morning. The energy of life and youth filled his heart and fueled the swagger to his stride. He entered Central Park and walked down to the pond. All along its shores, fathers with their sons guided model sailboats, families racing families or perhaps new friends yet unknown to them. Otto came upon his favorite bench, one of wood painted green and set upon a concrete base. The bench rested under a grand Sugar Maple Otto had purposely chosen, as this spot reminded him of Kettlewell and the large oak by the pond. Otto sat down, opened his musette bag, and pulled out his drawing tablet. He carefully tore a piece of paper from its binding and began folding the flat piece with utmost precision. Slowly, it took shape, one fold complimenting the other as it formed into its intended use. Otto held his creation high, turning it around carefully, checking its structure for integrity and seaworthiness. He sat up and confidently walked to the edge of the pond, holding his boat at his side. The wind greeted the water lightly from the northwest, crisp yet enduring. Otto knelt down and set the sailboat free. The boat swirled and tossed in the ripples of the pond but held its own.

Suddenly, a large model sailboat intruded the water space of Otto's little paper creation and crashed into it, spinning it around and around, and it began taking on water. Otto's eyes grew large and his face became angered, looking for the captain with poor seamanship. Off to his right not more than ten yards away, he saw a group of boys laughing with their radio remote in hand. They were young, playful, and innocent but up to no good. Otto recognized the one boy and was swift to answer his intrusion. "Shame on you, Ricky Samuels. I know your father. May his hand find your backside at Synagogue when I see him."

The boys paid no mind and scurried off, proud of their unapologetic deed. Otto chuckled to himself. "Little rascals. It was rather amusing, I must admit."

Otto looked down, and the laughter wore off quickly. There floating in the water was a flat piece of paper, soaked through with nothing reminiscent of a boat except for its fold marks hinting at its shape.

"You are not folding it right."

Otto's lips trembled, and his brow twitched. The hair on the back of his neck rose and pressed against his sweater. He slowly raised his hands and dipped his head down to greet them. They shook without his consent as he turned them palm up to investigate their condition. His knees followed and grew weak as his body labored to stand still and upright. Fright and shock combined forces and overtook him. He closed his eyes and slowly turned around. When he opened them, he did not want to believe.

"Annie?"

"Yes, Otto. It is I."

Otto began crying and leaned out trying to find something to grasp. Annie came to him and grabbed hold of his arm. "Good gracious, Otto. Please do not fall and die on me now."

Annie held him tight and led him slowly to the bench. They sat down next to Otto's musette bag. Otto tried to breathe while struggling for words. He stared past Annie, uncomfortable with the thought of her next to him. This was most unfair. Why now? Then he saw him. Up on the hill on the walkway overlooking the pond, he saw an old man wearing a bow tie sitting in a wheelchair with two men dressed in black next to him. Otto smiled and thought to himself, Agent Goodwin, you old fool, you did it. You found her. You told me you would, and you did. My word, your agents are indeed everywhere. Otto then called up to him, "Thank you, my dear friend."

Agent Goodwin waved to Otto as the two men next to him turned the wheelchair around and pushed him away.

"Otto? Otto. Silly boy, where have you gone?"

Otto snapped from his trance and turned to face Annie. He took Annie's hands in his and kissed them gently.

"I'm so sorry, Annie. I wanted to run fast to you and give you a big hug, but I can't move with speed these days."

"We are not kids anymore, Otto. However, from the looks of your paper boat floundering flat in the water, you have not learned much in all these years."

"Did you not witness those terrible children spoiling my craft? I assure you, Annie, it was my best ever."

They laughed together, staring straight into each other's eyes. Otto continued holding her hands. He could not let go. He would not let go. Otto's heart calmed, and his voice became thoughtful.

"I suppose we each have many questions."

"To that effect, how come, Otto Kaufmann, you did not come and find me?"

"I did. I promise I did. I will tell you my story, but please first, tell me of my parents. There is no record of them to be found. All that exists are the papers my Poppa signed when we were first herded together in Berlin that October. What happened after that day they took me?"

"I should then share my story first since your family's story leads to mine."

Annie took a deep breath, a tear coming to her eye. Her lips trembled and her eyes were solemn. Otto pulled a handkerchief from his pocket and reached over, gently wiping the tear away.

"It's okay, Annie, we are here again by the water. None of it matters."

"No, you're wrong, Otto. It does matter. It's our story."

Annie sniffled. "I have also spent many a night researching their whereabouts, and this isn't easy to say."

"It's okay. I have come to expect the worst. Please go on."

"Otto, your family did not survive. We were taken by a truck to the train station and unloaded. Your Poppa and my Poppa resisted as we were being led away. The soldiers took them both and stood them up on the railway platform and leaned them facing against the wall. They were then shot in the back of the head and thrown like meat into the boxcar. We were then shoved in after them to be carted off to another place."

"Another place? Chelmno?"

"Yes, Otto. That is what my employer had told me."

"How did you escape that camp?"

"Well, I did not meet the same fate. We were all crying and screaming. Then I heard a commotion outside, and I recognized a voice. I slowly crept to the doorway and could see two people quarreling. It was my employer, Frau Schnabel, and a German officer. She was pleading with him. I later learned he was the man she had been having an affair with. She begged him to not let me go on the train. She said she needed me or her business would not last. You remember my job?"

"You knitted small clothing for dolls."

"Yes. Frau Schnabel pleaded for my life, crying as she pawed at the officer's tunic. He was angered but finally relented. By his orders, the soldiers entered the boxcar and grabbed me. I did not dare resist. I turned and caught one last glimpse of my Momma as she lay at my Poppa's side. She was smiling at me and blew me a kiss. I never saw either of our families again. I am so very sorry, Otto."

"It is all right, Annie. I mourned their passing many, many years ago. At least now I can rest knowing they are in the hands of God. Please go on."

"Frau Schnabel cared for and loved me as her own. I spent my days knitting for her and sewing patches on German uniforms when needed. It was not long before the Lodz Ghetto was abandoned, and we moved to the outskirts of Berlin on the east side to a town called Strausberg. We set up business and continued doing more of the same work. As the war slowly faded, we had no more orders from the German army to attend to, so we started creating our own dolls and stuffed animals instead of just knitting clothes for them. It wasn't long before the Red Army marched through our town, but they paid us no mind. I had heard stories of their treatment of women, but that was not to be what we found. A Russian officer presiding over the town rather fancied our work and sent many dolls home to his family and friends. I assume that sentiment spared us."

Otto nodded but did not speak. He was staring at Annie, eyeing her up and down and trying to picture her as a little girl.

"What, Otto? Good gracious me if you are wondering where my long dark hair has gone and what became of my pudgy round nose, need I remind you they are things of a school girl's making. You'll just have to settle for a short grey bob and a few wrinkles. Now, silly boy, may I continue?"

"I see your feistiness is still very much present."

Annie sneered at him but continued. "So, as I was saying, Frau Schnabel offered to adopt me, which meant I'd take her name. She felt that my Hebrew name may not be safe so she changed it from Ana to Ilse. I told her that your nickname for me had always been Annie, but she felt it was too close to my real name. So Ilse I became."

"So that's why I could not find you. Your name is Ilse Schnabel. It all makes sense now. I was looking for a girl that no longer existed. How did Agent Goodwin find you?"

"Sir Goodwin's investigators came upon old adoption papers held secure in archives in the town in which Frau Schnabel filed my adoption. They compared those documents to work papers found near the site of the Lodz Ghetto held by the German government. Upon these discoveries, they were convinced Ana and Ilse were the same girl."

"Goodness me, why did it take all these years?"

"Access to any of these files were nearly impossible, Otto. The Cold War and a state of political and military tension after World War II blocked any possibility of research. Neither the communists nor democratic countries were sharing anything. It wasn't until after 1991 that Sir Goodwin could even think to begin such an investigation. Despite the setbacks caused by the Cold War, our business thrived and we did remarkably well. An underground black market economy fueled our work. The Russian officer I spoke of, I have forgotten his name, well, he survived the war and was a key part of our early success. He helped distribute our dolls throughout the world and worked for very little in return. When the Berlin Wall fell, we moved quickly from the east to the small town of Potsdam just outside of Berlin to the southwest. Not much of a move really, but the differences were noticeable. It was as if a dark, cloudy veil had been lifted."

"I remember that day in 1989 well, Annie. I was there too. It was a momentous event. It was very symbolic for me because my city of birth was now free. Very interesting, Annie. Please continue."

"My adoptive mother fell ill and passed not long after our move. I was alone, young, and without a suitor and had a business to run that required my focus. I never had a formal education; nonetheless, the business flourished well beyond my dreams."

"Let me understand this correctly. Am I to assume you are the owner of the famous Fortune 500 Ilse Doll Company?"

"Yes, Otto, that would be the one."

"Which would mean you are the very Ilse Schnabel who made the exceedingly rare 'Forced Labor Dolls,' the ones made at Lodz when we were imprisoned together?"

"That would be me."

"Did you know, Annie, that there are only four of those dolls known to be in existence?"

"Oh. Really? Do tell."

"One is on display as part of the permanent collection in the Smithsonian Holocaust Museum in Washington, D.C. Another one sold through Sotheby's at auction for $1.3 million. The whereabouts of the other two is a mystery."

"That's crazy. Who'd pay all that money for an old, raggedy doll?"

"I would. I'm the crazy one who bought it."

"Silly boy. I have the other two. I would have just given you one."

They both laughed, Annie shaking her head in disbelief.

"To think, Annie, there you were right under my nose and I didn't see it. I am very fond of art and antiquities, and I read all about you and your company. I just never placed your face with the stories. It was hard growing old because, all through my life, I could only picture your long dark hair and pudgy nose. I'm so very sorry, Annie."

"It's okay, Otto. The war did many terrible things to us all. Truth is, and I hate to make matters worse, but I was right under your nose once before. This is all very funny, really. You see, my son now oversees the company. When we were selecting a site to construct a North American Headquarters here in the states, we were counseled to seek your architectural firm to work with us. My son and I came to your offices in New York. You were there that day, and your executives asked if we wanted to meet you. They said you had retired and it was a very rare event to have you in the office. I said we did not want to bother you, so we graciously passed. As we were leaving, I couldn't help but notice one specific item on a shelf overlooking the front reception area. It was a paper boat folded exactly the way my Poppa had taught me and how you and I would create them. I felt something stir inside my heart, but I did not give it much thought. So, when I was trying to find you, I couldn't because I was looking for a boy named Otto Kaufmann. I was not searching for the world renowned architect 'Ekkehard Bauer.' That name meant nothing to me. So tell me, where did the name Ekkehard Bauer come from? Sir Goodwin was not cooperative in sharing your life despite my prying."

"You should have found me sooner. I told the story of my entire journey last night. It's such a long and emotionally taxing one at best. I don't know where to start, but I do know you will come to know it all. I shall begin with your question. I too was adopted, by a wonderful man named Ekkehard Bauer.

"I stumbled upon Ekkehard during the war. There was an instant bond, I suppose, two people trying to live and make sense of the tortures of the world around us. While we were forced to part, he found me years later after the war thanks to Agent Goodwin. It was such an honor to take Ekkehard's surname for it meant a new life. However, it was advised that I change my given name for my protection, as the events of the war followed me and haunted my life. An SS officer, Martin Bormann, was perhaps still hunting me. It wasn't until 1972 that we learned his remains had been found in Berlin. It was concluded by forensics that he had committed suicide by cyanide. A fitting yet cowardly end, but I suppose better than what the Russians would have done to him. I was proud to take Ekkehard's given name, and I became Ekkehard Bauer II. I mostly used this name professionally, keeping my real name, Otto, for my closest friends and family.

"We emigrated to America and settled in Vermont. Years later, I wished to pursue architecture so we moved to New York. As fate would have it, my dear friend Agent Goodwin pulled some strings and got me admitted into Cooper Union. I loved architecture, and I wanted to create beautiful things. The war had eroded much of the world. It needed life again, art, theatre, and literature. I felt it was my duty to give something back and start a movement to elevate humanity."

"I think you've succeeded, Otto. Your work is embraced all over the globe."

"I am indeed grateful, Annie. It was a hard road. After school, I struck out on my own. There was a man I remembered from my days in France at a soldier hospital. His name was Douglas Sikora. A wonderful fellow, and we got along splendidly. He had told me that when he got back to the States, he was going to start a construction business. So, I looked him up and we joined forces. It was a fantastic union because he knew materials and I knew design. We ended up creating a world-class company for which we are most proud. Douglas and I retired together, handing over the reins to his sons and a number of trusted executives. Our career has provided a blessed life, and I feel good knowing we gave back to the world community."

Otto continued holding Annie's hand, stroking it softly, his own hand still trembling. He swallowed hard, a question coming to his mind. "You mentioned a son. You are married?"

"My goodness me, Otto. No. I was a young woman, working hard, and I had a yearning, a yearning that bore me a son. The father was a soldier, an American stationed in Germany during the Cold War. I suppose he would have married me, but sadly he was killed in a routine training accident. He was a good man, but truthfully, I was not at all interested in being married. My son has been my joy, my blessing, and my family. He has a family of his own now, and I have three darling grandchildren."

438

"Otto Schnabel? The chief executive officer of the Ilse Doll Company? You named your son after me?"

Annie nodded as Otto began to cry. Annie reached up and wrapped her arms around him.

"Shh. It's okay. So tell me, Otto, did you marry during that time? I know you have four daughters, one quite young from what Agent Goodwin had described. He said that you had once told him that your daughters all looked like me when I was a girl."

Otto wiped his eyes and blushed, his face becoming shy and his words soft. "It's that obvious, isn't it?"

"I am so very touched, Otto."

"Yes, I have four wonderful girls. Their names are Annabelle, Athalia, Alexi, and Andrea. My oldest, Annabelle, is married and has two little boys. Her husband, William, is in the shipping business. A good man and a doting father. Athalia is my second oldest and is a cardiologist. Very smart and so caring. She has not married, but we're working on it. Next in age is Alexi. She is married to a great man, Newell. They live upstate. She's an investment banker and does rather well. She has a quick wit and a big heart. My last is Andrea, and as you noted, she is the youngest. She is very precious and innocent. She is attending Juilliard and wishes to be a pianist. I can't tell you how very proud of them I am. They are all adopted, Annie. It was my way of paying back the kindness shown to me by Ekkehard. As you observed, however selfishly, my daughters were a reminder of you. Through them you were actually with me all these years."

Annie nestled up to Otto and lay her head on his shoulder, her right hand gently placed on his chest. Otto leaned his head on the top of her grey hair, and he closed his eyes.

"It's as if we had never parted."

"It feels that way, doesn't it, Otto? Yet, you did not answer my question. So then, you are not married? Surely you must have courted many girls in your time."

"Who me? Oh, sure. Many girls."

"Really?"

"Okay. No, not really."

"Oh?"

"No. I never married. I just never made time for it. Perhaps I never wanted to make time for it. My heart never had room for it. It was filled with you."

"You are as charming as ever."

The late summer breeze swirled and danced around Otto and Annie as they held each other gently. School girls walked by giggling, followed by young men not versed enough to know better. Their awkwardness was obvious. Model sailboats zoomed left to right as ducks looked on with deep suspicion. Life in the park flourished.

Otto looked up and stared at the majestic maple swaying gently above. His heart was alive, and the smells and beauty of nature around him excited his senses and alerted his mind.

"Annie?"

"Yes, Otto."

"May I ask a question of you?"

"Please."

"Do you think had our lives not been interrupted by the war, we would have been married?"

Annie sat quietly for a moment before answering. She sat up and faced Otto, still holding his hand. "It's too hard to know, Otto. Maybe we would have married and maybe not. Perhaps we would have grown up and had different lives. We might have gone off to school, moved away, or done other things as we experienced life. It's so very easy to blame the war, but I don't. Perhaps if it hadn't been for the war, I would have never been shown my gift for knitting, which led me to build such a wonderful business. I cherish knowing that my creations have put smiles on the faces of millions of boys and girls."

"It's an interesting perspective, Annie. I agree. I, too, have often wondered those very same things. Might I have achieved all that I have without the war's interruption? Then I think, what if the opposite were true? What if I would have become a better person if not for the war? What if I had positive experiences that made me greater? Would I have become the president of a country presiding over the futures of millions or a leading scientist that cures the ills of humanity?"

"I should think, Otto, life happened as it should."

"I suppose you are right. So what now? I have an ache in my tummy again."

"Well, I noticed that canvas bag next to you. Is it yours?"

"Yes. It's my musette bag."

"And that drawing tablet. It is yours as well?"

"Yes."

"Good then, hand me a piece of paper. We can start by finally teaching you how to properly fold a paper boat."

THE END